Throne of Dusäiga

THE CROWN'S

SOUL

PROPHECY

LETIZIA FIRMANI

E-Book ASIN: B0CM5JTCP3

Paperback ISBN: 979-12-210-4526-0

Cover Design: Designsbydaniellelg

Map Design: Mitchell Agema

Author's photo: Melissa Pronio

Proofreading: Chiara Pastorino, Taylor Gray

Formatting: Letizia Lorini

CONTENT WARNINGS

This book contains potentially triggering subject matter, including open door romance. For the full list of content warnings visit www.letiziafirmani.com/content-warnings

To my mom and brother:
Thank you for making sure I could dream.

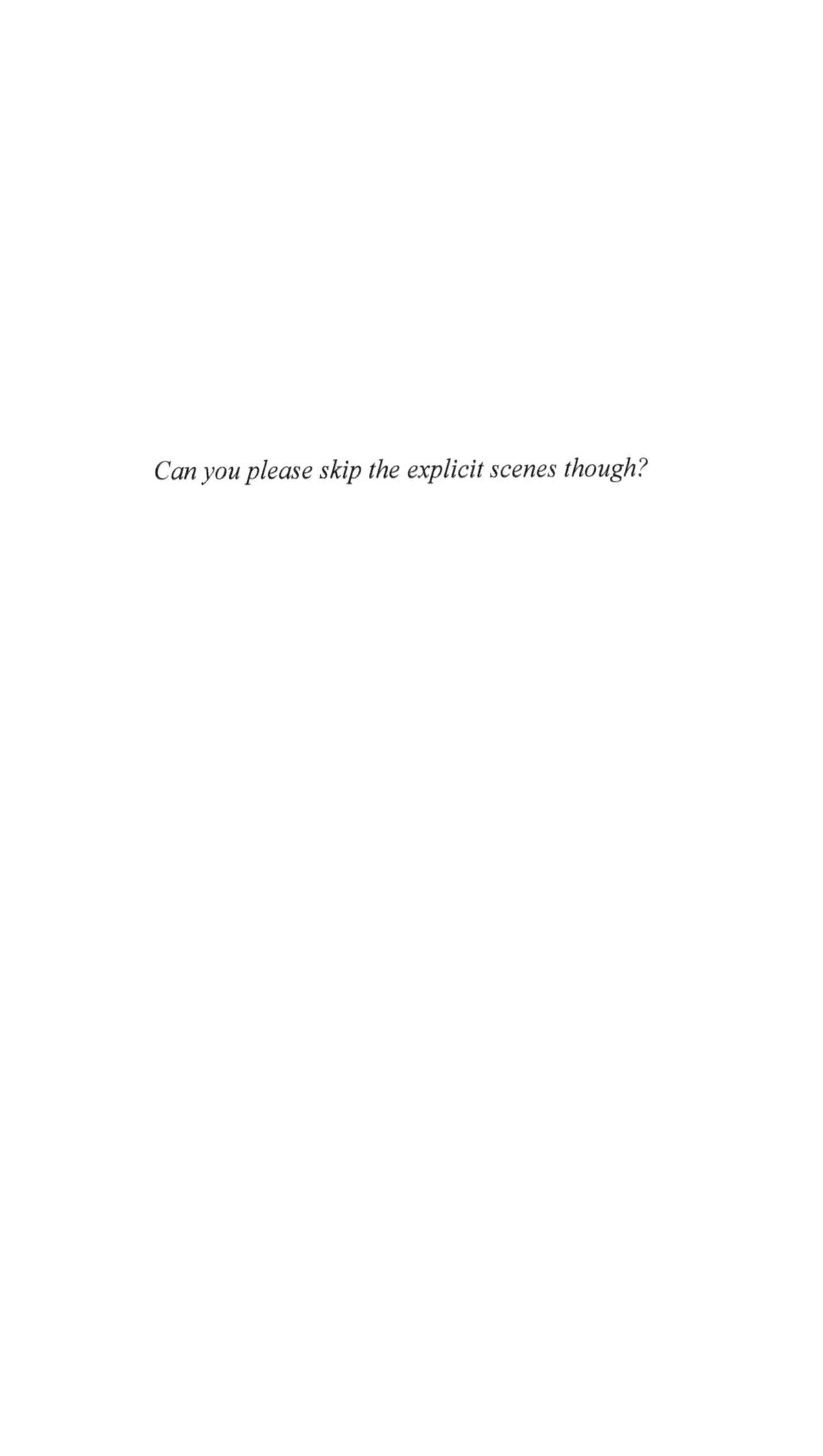

Can you please skip the explicit scenes though?

"It is a difficult matter to keep love imprisoned."

\- Apuleius, Cupid and Psyche and Other Tales from The Asinus Aureus

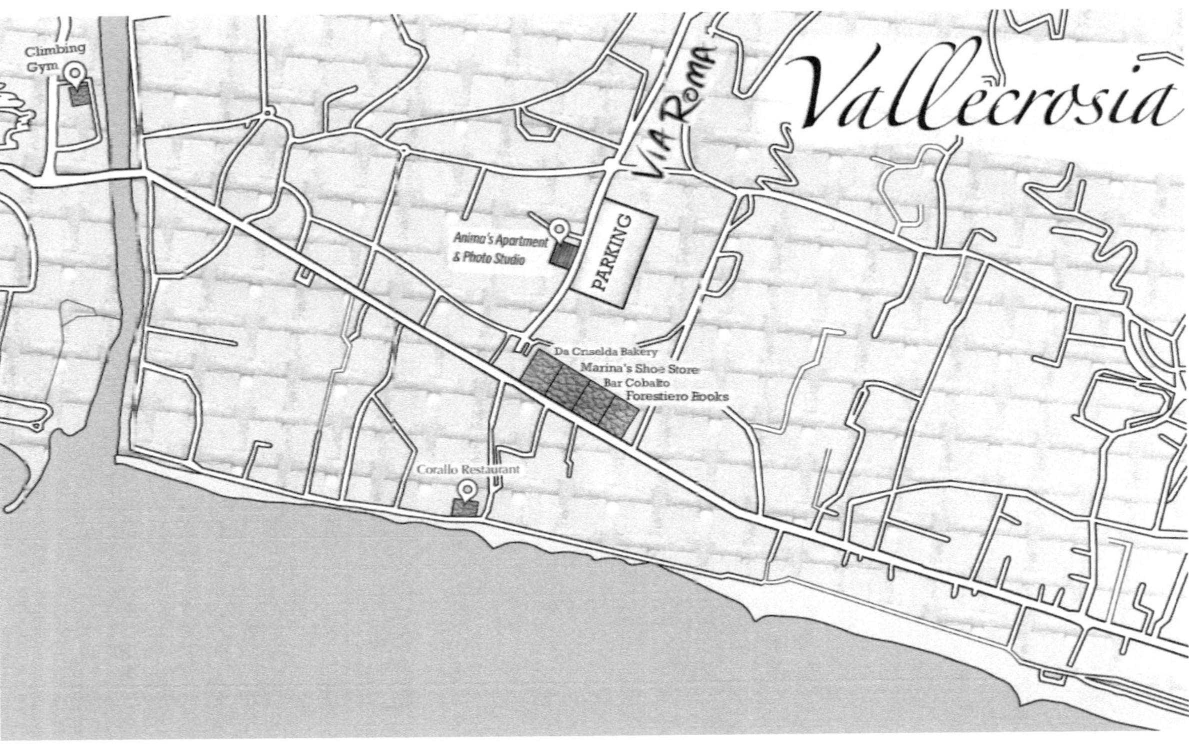

Vallecrosia
Via Roma
Climbing Gym
Anima's Apartment & Photo Studio
PARKING
Da Criselda Bakery
Marina's Shoe Store
Bar Cobalto
Forestiero Books
Corallo Restaurant

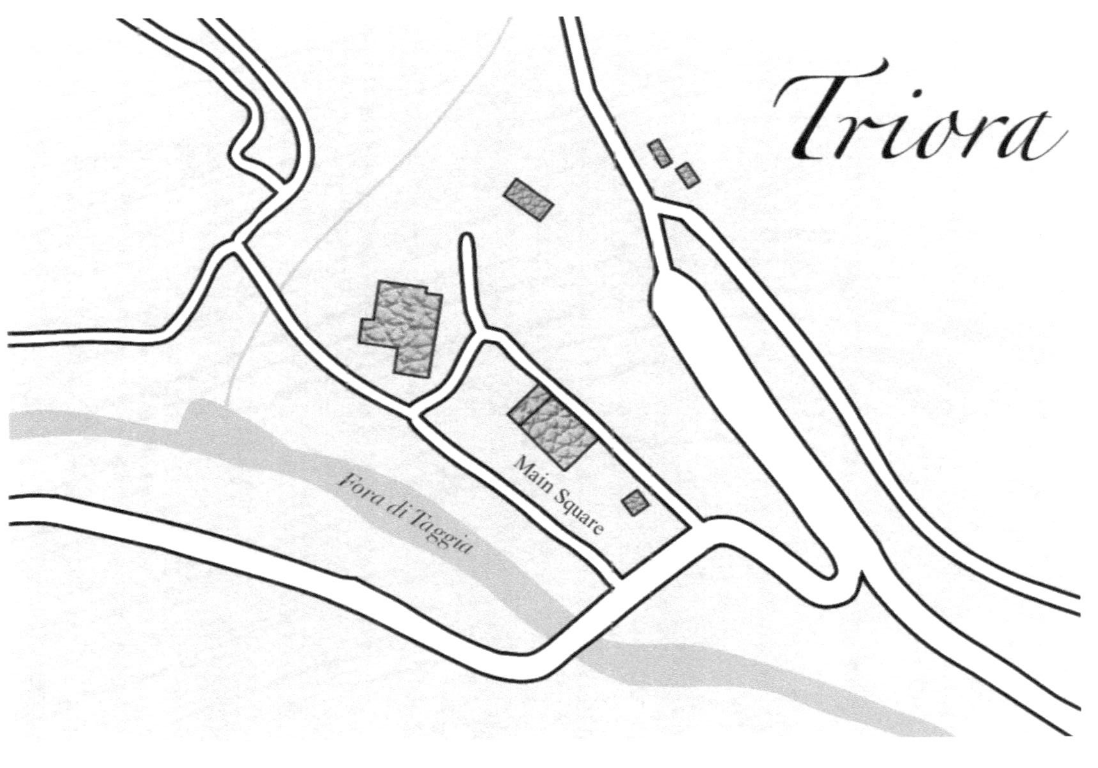

Triora
Main Square
Fiora di Taggia

Prologue

17 YEARS AGO

The two children with different eyes couldn't have looked more divergent yet so alike. One with short, sandy blonde hair, the other with auburn curls gently moved by the wind. One whose skin was amber and one whose rosy cheeks were the only color on otherwise blemish-free, fair skin. Both with souls pure and pristine, unencumbered by the future, the danger, the darkness. Both holders of the Eyes. The children were a spectacle to see, as they ran carelessly in the gardens. That's what they did most days, whenever they could, and sometimes when they weren't allowed to. They would run and play with the serenity and innocence only children are capable of, as the adults knew what was about to come their way and couldn't afford the same blissful ignorance.

Most children in Dusäiga wouldn't have played in this part of the gardens. They would have stayed in the front, where the grass was covered in blooming purple flowers and there was far more entertainment. What sort of enjoyment would someone feel by running around an old well made of uneven rocks and cement?

But the children with different eyes felt no such way. Every inch of the gardens was for them to play, because there was a third boy —a boy with green eyes. The same green of moss, forest and nature. A boy who was always ready to come to their rescue, should they ever need it. As he had done so plenty of times before. Dionisio would observe them from afar and study their every move, He did not do so out of jealousy, which was an emotion far too dark for his pure young heart, but for protection. Though he was indeed not a day older than eight years of age, there was something deep in his soul that resonated with him more than anything else.

Protect the princess.

On a sunny day, one with heat that would make most people lazy and slow, the children with different eyes were hopping on and off the stone slabs placed in a circle around a small, dying fire. To an external observer, it would have looked like a boring, insignificant day.

Until, the sky turned dark with an unforgiving gloominess. A black so all-encompassing and depleting, the whole Kingdom knew that it was no mere storm. That it was the beginning of the end.

The shivers on the princess's back made her wonder if they should go inside prior to the rain starting. Before she could say a word, a figure appeared out of thin air only meters away, and slowly walked towards the children. Petrified from fear, or perhaps hypnotized by the being pacing in their direction, they were frozen in place. The long dark curly hair was the first thing the princess and the boy noticed, followed by the smoothness on her face. No eyes. Replacing them, there was a layer of skin. The princess didn't find the woman frightening; on the contrary, she felt the need to let the woman with no eyes know she was uniquely beautiful.

"You weren't supposed to be here, princess," the figure with no face said in a very gentle voice. It felt soothing, like a light caress on her cheek. A siren's chant.

The princess didn't even notice her parents running towards them. The boy with green eyes was there too now. Hypnotized, she began to lose awareness of her surroundings.

"Dionisio, quick, get the kids, take the princess to your aunt," Aiakos, the King, yelled in despair.

The boy with green eyes ran towards the little girl, looked at his brother while tightening his hands into fists, then loosening them quickly, and proceeded to pick her up. "I'll be back. Stay here," he told the boy with tousled hair.

Dionisio ran and ran as fatigue started to set in his breath. An adrenaline rush shot through his system while holding the little girl in his embrace, as if that was the last thing he was going to do. He couldn't stop. He had to protect her. Yet the thought of leaving his brother behind was consuming him. Pain at the back of his throat started to make itself known. A sudden tightness— like his windpipe had a nodule of needles stuck in it that wouldn't go up nor down. The King and Queen had been clear though, save Princess Anima. And as much as it broke him, he'd do what they asked. He had to make sure she was safe.

"Dionisio, what is happening?" Ginevra asked her nephew, fumbling her words as she saw him running towards her. Her posture loosened as soon as she saw the princess in his embrace.

"The king asked me to bring Anima to you and said you'd know what to do. I have to go back for Eros," he said with his heart beating so fast he couldn't stop panting. Sweat was running down the side of his green eyes, his limbs were now tingling. He was ready to crash on the ground from exhaustion and fear, but he couldn't. He wouldn't let himself go—not until he knew his little brother was safe too.

"Please be careful," Ginevra called after him before taking Anima in her embrace. The young girl was shivering, her lips pale in comparison to their usual rosy pink, her eyes wide and disoriented.

Ginevra frowned. "Anima, what did you see?"

"A woman with dark hair and no face. She just wanted to talk. She said she was lonely, and she just wanted to play."

"Dark hair? No face?"

Anima nodded. "She had no face. It was a little creepy, but her voice was pretty. She said my eyes were special."

"Your eyes? Did she see your eyes and Eros's?" Ginevra questioned with her heart palpitating and tingling in her chest. A sudden dizziness stumbled upon her, as if she could pass out any moment, but she had to force herself to remain in control. This was not the time to panic.

"Yes. She said it was such a gift to have different eyes."

Ginevra's face twisted with fear, her pupils shrinking and making her deep brown eyes look even bigger in comparison. "Anima, we—we have to go. Right now."

Anima, of course, knew no better. The thought of going on an adventure filled her young, inexperienced heart with joy and excitement. "Will mom and dad come too?"

"Yes, they will meet us somewhere special."

Anima smiled, content. "Ok."

"Zia zia." Dionisio came running towards them. "I went back, but Eros is not there, and Uncle Aiakos and Aunt Bolina aren't there either."

"The king and queen are gone, huh?" Ginevra mumbled to herself. Shaking the thought away, she smiled lightly. "It's all right, my child, all will be fine. I'll just take Anima to bed." Brushing his hair off his forehead, she tried to reassure the child as he panted and looked at her in panic. His eyes were full of unshed tears. Tears he wouldn't dare to let go in front of Anima.

"Go to sleep, my child, Anima will be ok," she added, resting her hand softly on his forehead. "You are such a brave boy,

Dionisio," she whispered as he crumbled to the ground, his eyes shut and his chest peacefully rising and falling as he slept.

"Aunt Ginevra?" Anima ventured. "Eros isn't in danger, the lady said she just wanted to play hide and seek with him for a bit."

"Let's go, Anima. We can't make your parents wait."

Ginevra and Anima walked towards the door to the warehouse. Anima loved that place, full of old books, dust, and trinkets of all sorts. The bridge between two worlds. Some would call it neutral ground, but it was a connection between two realities. A place with and a place without magic. This was in between.

The two of them walked straight into the human world, hand in hand. They made their way down Via Roma. It was a sunny day, and Anima's focus was stolen by a bluebird that was chirping and hopping in the parking lot to her right. They passed a chocolate store that emanated the most amazing and tingly smell. Then they made a sudden stop in front of a little gift shop where a lady with freckles all over her cheeks and nose was working.

"Ginevra, hi, what are you doing here?" the woman asked, tucking back a strand of her gorgeous copper hair as it escaped from her messy bun.

"It's time." Ginevra simply replied.

The lady's eyes widened as she rushed to close the entrance to the store. "I'll call Giorgio right away."

"Do you still have the key?" Ginevra ran to the back of the shop.

"Of course, it's in the safe."

"Give it to her when she turns eighteen, not before, not after."

Ginevra lowered herself to Anima's height. There were tears in her eyes, which made Anima wonder what was happening and where her parents were. Ginevra was always happy around her, so why was she so gloomy all of a sudden?

"Aunt Ginevra, why are you crying?" Anima asked with a broken voice.

"This is for your own good. I'll come back to you when it's time. Just remember that your parents love you very much."

Ginevra rested her hand on the child's forehead, just like she did not too long before with Dionisio, and held her between her hands as she fell asleep.

As she set her on the small red couch by the backdoor, Mirella cleared her voice, "Is this safe? Doing that to a child? To her?"

"Mirella, she won't remember anything from Dusäiga. She will remember you, Giorgio, and living here—in Vallecrosia. It has to stay this way until it's time."

"Until she turns eighteen," the lady with copper hair simply stated.

"Yes, that's when the prophecy will commence," Ginevra mumbled after clearing her throat.

"How do we know that no one will recognize her?"

"I glamoured her eyes. Cut her hair tomorrow, and come up with a believable story. No one will look for her here. This is the only way we can make sure she stays safe."

"This close to Dusäiga?"

"Yes. If she leaves, Dusäiga will perish completely. She can't be too far away."

"Where are Aiakos and Bolina?"

"They're gone."

Mirella's eyes coated with tears, and with a tightness in her chest, she stated, "She will be safe with us. She will have the life she deserves."

"I know she will. Goodbye for now, Mirella. Come to see me as much as you can, please."

The noise of the door opening and closing silenced the two women on the spot. They waited, still, as the rushed steps grew louder and louder.

"I came as fast as I could," Giorgio broke the silence, surprised to find Ginevra holding out a knife in her unsure hands. As she set it away, he continued, "Is she ok?"

"She's just sleeping," she reassured the man while caressing the little girl's hair. "She's the most important piece to the puzzle. Keep her safe at all costs," Ginevra added before walking towards the entrance.

"We will, Ginevra. We will treat her as our own."

Lack of energy hit the body of the woman. A sudden soreness appeared in her throat and lungs. "As of right now, she is your own."

Part One

Through Different Eyes

Chapter 1

I've always loved libraries and bookstores, especially the tiny one a quick walk away from my apartment, *Forestiero*. Stranger, foreigner. Walking along Via Roma for less than a hundred meters, then turning left, past the delicious fragrances coming off the Da Criselda bakery, then the shoe store where Marina the tattler works and there it is, right beside Bar Cobalto. *Forestiero*. Definitely not a stranger to me. After spending my childhood with my face stuffed in books, *Forestiero* feels familiar, like coming home. It has intrigued me since I was a child. Maybe it's the narrow wooden entrance that disguises the paradise of books that's inside—maybe the cherry shelves that cover the walls in their entirety. Maybe it's the massive chandelier right in the center that illuminates the entire shop, one that belongs to a castle, or maybe it's the mysterious warehouse that isn't even in the vicinity of the bookstore.

Maybe it's because whenever I ask the shop owners, Ginevra and Eros, for a book that they don't have in store, I'm always given the same answer. "I'll check the warehouse."

Then they leave and disappear—I swear, they dissolve into thin air. Who has a stockroom that isn't even close to their store?

Well, they do. Just a street over. I know exactly where it is, and it's all I can think of at times—Eros finally showing me what's inside. What a strange ambition to have. He seems to be the only one I am able to freely talk to aside from Svetlana.

For years, I've heard the shop owners utter the same thing that has always stuck with me. The curiosity of what hides inside of it almost eats me alive. As I wait in the small shop for what feels like endless hours, that's the one thought that eats my brain like a fruit worm devours an apple. What's in that storage room? Why is it so far away? Do they have all the books in the world in there? Just how big is that place?

When they come back, usually covered in dust from head to toe, the book I asked for is in their hands. And every time I ask, or beg them, to let me help look for a book, the answer is, "Maybe next time." I've been waiting for that "next time" for 17 years, and still no luck.

I've got a couple of theories about that warehouse. Either the place is a secret passageway to a fantasy world with perhaps an endless athenaeum of books, or a serial killer hides their victims in there. Maybe, behind the towers of books, there are piles of heads and tongues and other small organs in green jars. You know, like the ones we have all seen in biology class. Maybe there's DNA of the victims on all the books I bought from Forestiero.

Oh god, I should disinfect them before bringing them into my apartment. I feel like I should be taking a shower right about now. And I should definitely stop offering to help every time they go to the back to look for one of my books. Surely, it would explain the long wait—you know, with all the feet and torsos laying around.

Or maybe, I'm just really bored. Whichever is true, I understand why they would avoid my assistance. They would probably have to kill me if I ever discovered their secret, and I kind of like being alive at the moment.

As I step out of Forestiero, I walk towards the city center. The unseasonably warm sun burns my fair skin as I rush to find a spot in the shade, but a group of teenagers seem to have had the same idea, and are chatting in front of Marina's shoe store.

I haven't set foot in the quirky little shop since I've been back. I haven't set foot in a lot of places since I've been back. I have been trying to avoid Marina as much as possible because I'm still not ready for the barrage of inappropriate questions about my parents she definitely wants to ask me. I can't believe tomorrow it'll be six months already. Six months since I've uprooted my whole life in Chicago and moved back into my hometown. Vallecrosia.

I quickly walk towards the bakery where Criselda waves enthusiastically from behind the shiny window, and I give her a weak nod before turning my focus to the street. If she thinks I'm ready, she'll come out and hoist me inside. I could force myself and go buy something. I miss her Triora bread so much. But I'm not ready. Not yet, at least. That was my parents' favorite bakery in the whole town—they brought me there for breakfast every Sunday, on every holiday and every birthday. And now, they're gone.

Six months. Six months since I got the call and dropped everything to be here for them. Art school, the full scholarship for the photography program—hell, my whole life.

"Anima, you have to go and explore the world. This is too great of an opportunity to turn down." My parents' words as I got my acceptance letter come back to me and I press my eyes shut. "We're so proud of you."

Breathe, Anima, breathe.

I clench my left hand around the key my father gave me years back for protection, hanging by my neck. "Always keep this with you, it will keep you safe," he used to tell me every single day. He was like that, superstitious about everything. You had to see the face he would make when a black cat would cross the road in front of him. Only thinking of it makes me giggle.

I try to refocus my pain. I find it usually helps to think of Jeremy. Yes, anger is a better emotion than pain. When there's a twinge of discomfort on the palm of my hand, I unclench my fist from around the key and see a few drops of blood. Jeremy.

Though I loved school, Jeremy Miller was the genuine mistake of my Chicago years. Or rather—falling for him was.

I almost missed my graduation day because of him. After realizing how Jeremy really was, I was so terrified of seeing him again. I got to a point where even leaving my bedroom became dreadful.

It's baffling how someone can promise you the world and then crush it so methodically by imprisoning you into your own sabotaging thoughts. He was superb at that. I bet he still is.

Now I am back to where it all started, and it's hard not to think about them. My parents. I should have been here, instead of wasting my last years with them far away. When I got the call from the hospital saying that they were involved in an awful accident, I had the feeling it was a matter of time. I rushed home, leaving everything behind. And I still didn't make it in time. I couldn't say goodbye.

What I didn't know was that my parents had thought about everything already, almost as if they expected this monumental rip in my heart to happen. They left me a place that they instructed me to turn into a photography studio, and right on top of it, an apartment to live in.

Since the accident, I've never taken off the key my father gave me. Though I've never believed in the power of crystals, luck or any of that nonsense, this rusty, golden key seems to be the only thing that still connects me to them now that they're gone.

It makes no sense. I had no idea they were planning all this for me, but they knew I was pondering coming back home after school and after everything that happened with Jeremy.

Sometimes I wonder if my parents knew they wouldn't have enough time to see me grow old.

Here I am, a 22-year-old orphan with a psychopath stalker ex boyfriend and an art degree with zero prospects in this small town. Could be worse, I guess. I could be one of those corpses probably hiding in the back of Forestiero. Or the alleged serial killer who put them there.

As I reach the big green wooden door of my building, I hear a buzz coming from my pocket. Svetlana is on her way with dinner. I quickly take a look at the shop window right beside the door 'Soleri Photography Studio', take a deep breath, and insert the key in the latch. Thank god, because my stomach is growling at the thought of a pizza margherita.

I don't think I would be able to go through all this loss without her. Svetlana, my childhood best friend, also moved back to Vallecrosia after a six months exchange to Moscow with her university and a very very bad break up with a Slavic man.

I stop and stare at the golden circular handle, take a deep breath and close the door behind me. After walking up the narrow stairway and stepping into the entrance to my apartment, I leave the keys on the side table beside the door, then look at a picture of Svetlana and me smiling under the CN Tower in Toronto that we took when we went on a spontaneous girls' trip a few years back.

It always makes me laugh seeing how I look like a toddler beside her long model material legs.

I walk towards the window in the living room, move the thick curtains and open them to air out the room. I squint my eyes to look through the dirty windowpanes. I cleaned them a couple of days back, but the sand brought by the wind is difficult to keep up with.

Still, while in Chicago, I never realized how much I missed living by the beach. The twinkle of the water hit by the sun rays, the swarms of people swimming and sunbathing like lizards, the smell of salt that pervades the air. It's crazy how important something like the sea becomes when you don't have it right there looking back at you. I wouldn't be able to imagine a life completely away from the feeling of salt on my skin, that breath of fresh sea air that makes your nose tingle. It keeps me sane, it keeps me flourishing.

Finding serenity in a town like Vallecrosia shouldn't be so hard. It's a small town in the province of Imperia and close to the French border. 6,970 inhabitants, though it often feels like it's fewer. It should be easier to be happy in a place with the sea and few people. Easier than Chicago.

Vallecrosia is calm, peaceful, and that is what my mind needs right now.

I breathe the air in, let the soft wind caress my cheeks until I hear the door opening behind me and the fragrance of water and salt gets replaced by the warm and delicious aroma of a freshly made stone oven pizza.

"Hey babe, I got a margherita for you and four cheeses for me," Svetlana says, placing the two carton boxes on the kitchen table. A chunk of her chocolate hair falls out of her messy bun as she drops in one of the chairs around the table.

Svetlana Traverso became my best friend the moment we looked at each other the first time across the old swing set in the

park beside her parents' old place. It was the summer of 2000—
we were five years old. I would spin until I'd get dizzy, then try to
walk in a straight line. It was my favorite game at the time.

She walked to me, and without a single word, started spinning
beside me. We've been inseparable since. Anima, and Svetlana,
trying to survive life together as we grew up.

It's still true today, I guess. Anima and Svetlana, trying to
remind each other we're still allowed to find happiness.

"You are my saving grace. I am so hungry I think I might
actually faint if I don't take a bite right now".

She starts giggling and I see her hazel eyes looking straight at
me as a big smile appears on her face. "I may have also stopped at
Criselda's. Got you some Triora bread, I know you're out."

Dropping myself on the chair, I turn to her with heart-shaped
eyes. "I will make you a giant monument and put it in the middle
of my living room".

'Wow, and how big would this statue be if I told you I saw
Davide earlier today, and he gave me some free samples on a new
strain he's working on?" A little tin foil wrapped cluster of weed
appears in her hands after rummaging in her purse for a couple of
seconds.

"That this random Tuesday night just turned into a party." I
move, shaking my fists in victory around the room while looking
for the lighter and the rolling papers.

"Smoke first, pizza later?"

"You bet." I open the little bag containing the green substance
and place it in Svetlana's grinder.

I've never really smoked much, but lately, weed is the only
thing that helps me sleep a couple of hours on some nights.
Besides, the euphoric feeling you get when the puff hits your
lungs is fun at times.

Sitting on the couch, we lean over the coffee table and begin
working on our joint.

AN HOUR LATER WE FIND OURSELVES LAYING DOWN ON THE FLOOR of my living room staring at the ceiling.

"Look at it, it's so pretty to look at," Svetlana says while trying to catch the mist coming out of her mouth with her hands.

"It's so thick and then thin again, it makes pretty shapes," I reply, joining her moving my hands all over the place finding it impossible to catch it. Bummer.

"Do you wanna tell me about the cut on your hand or should I pretend it isn't there even though I know it's there and I know you did that yourself?"

I look down at my palm and quickly close it. A sudden sting makes my nose twitch and reminds me why the minor wound is there in the first place. "It's nothing," I reply, giving her the fakest smile she's ever seen in her life. Who am I kidding, she knows me better than I know myself. I know this conversation isn't over at all.

"Sure." Nothing else.

"I—I was thinking about Jeremy earlier and got, well, upset."

"That's what I thought. Do I need to worry?"

"No, Svetlana, you know me, I would never—"

"I know you, I know what you're going through and this is why I am asking you. If I can do more, please, let me know, anything at all, I will be here."

"You are already doing so much. That was just me clenching my hand too hard around my necklace. Nothing else."

"Fine, sorry for being so serious about it. I just love you so much." A warm look appears on her face which makes me relax my shoulders.

I throw my arms around her and hug her tightly. "I love you

too, sis, so very much. I don't know what I'd be doing if you weren't here beside me."

"Can I ask something I've always wanted to know?"

"Shoot."

"Was he at least good in bed?"

"Meh, he was ok." I tilt my head left and right.

"So you're telling *that* guy didn't even make you come?"

I burst out in laughter, and she joins quickly. There's no filter, not with Svetlana. Not since we were kids.

"Why is it so cold in here?"

"Oh shit, I left the window open." I lazily get up and stumble to the side, my head feeling light. I then slowly drag myself to my final destination—the window.

Breathing in the tingly air that comes from outside, a figure in the middle of the road catches my attention. Weirdo. Just in the middle of the street looking up at me. Boy, am I high right now or this guy looks like he has no face?

Standing unnaturally straight and still, he looks like a statue—or is it a woman? I can't tell. I squint my eyes trying to focus on the shape. A hood covers half of the smooth, non- existent face. I glimpse a possible opening where a mouth would be. Lips but no eyes. Just a layer of skin. Shivers travel down my spine as nausea rises from my stomach. The pace of my heart quickens painfully in my chest while my vision blurs, turning everything to mist around me.

I look back at Svetlana and ask her, "Am I crazy high, or do you also see someone in the middle of the road with—no…" I swallow past the lump in my throat, drying cold sweat over my forehead with the back of my hand. "No face?"

"Yeah, it's the ghost of your past unachieved orgasms," she says, chuckling on the couch.

"Svetlana, I'm not kidding, get up here and look!"

She runs towards me with her eyebrows raised with concern

but when she looks down at the road, she recommences the laugh. The road is empty.

"No, I'm serious, there was someone there." I look at her with my eyes wide open, ready to panic at any second.

"There's no one, dude, what the hell did Davide put in this? We're done for the night."

For a moment I stare at the now empty road, my heartbeat slowing down as I look left and right. I swear there was something there.

"It's pretty good though. It feels like I'm floating." I close the window and walk back to the couch, then grab a slice of pizza and take a first bite as I drop myself onto the leather cushions. With a smile, I close my eyes in ecstasy as Svetlana talks of which show she should put on.

Yet I throw another look at the window. It's too dark for me to see anything, but I can't let the feeling of eeriness inside me go. I swear there was someone there.

Chapter 2

The following morning, I find myself walking the streets of Vallecrosia aimlessly. A sense of emptiness, like a hollow feeling in my chest, guides me to Forestiero, the only place I have been able to go to since I've been back. I take a look through the window, at the books displayed on the little tables at the entrance before going inside. I ordered something a few weeks ago—hopefully, it has arrived.

Books of all colors and dimensions are stacked floor to ceiling all over the space in such a neat and precise way that just makes sense. Walls of books and nothing else. I want my house to be like this. When I am in Forestiero, it's like I'm ready to assimilate all the knowledge that gets thrown at me.

I approach the counter and the middle-aged lady, Ginevra, recognizes me immediately. "Oh, hello, Anima, up for a new read so soon?" She asks, with a smile almost forced by fatigue that her gaze is trying to hide. But the truth is shown in the dark circles under her eyes.

"Hi, Ginevra, I was wondering if you had that book I ordered a few weeks ago."

"Let me check in the system." She fixes her gaze on the

screen while she thumbs the keyboard. "Hum, no, sorry, it's not here yet, but I do have something else in stock that I think you might find interesting."

I wonder what it could be—maybe a contemporary romance? Those always make me feel warm and fuzzy. Historical fiction? I am a sucker for a good story set in an ancient time—oh please, don't tell me it's non-fiction, I don't think I can focus on a non-story right now, I need escapism.

After considering it all for a few seconds, I nod. It's peculiar she'd suggest a different read—in the hundreds of times I've been here, it's never happened. "Sure I'll take a look. What—"

Ginevra quickly walks around the counter, bubbly as I've never seen her before. "Eros, come here for a moment, please," she interrupts before I can ask anything else. "Could you go to the warehouse to pick up the books I told you about this morning? They're for Anima."

Eros comes out of the small office and, with a stunned look on his face, he turns to Ginevra. "Are you sure, *zia*?"

With a comforting smile on her face, Ginevra gestures at him to go. "I am very sure."

Eros leaves the bookstore and says he will try to return as soon as possible. As he walks towards the door, the question I've asked countless times hangs on the tip of my tongue. I watch the door shut as Eros rounds the corner out of sight, and the question dies in my throat. I have lost all hope of ever getting into that warehouse. Plus, there's that whole potential serial killer thing.

I wait and wait, and as boredom slowly starts to sink in, I rummage through the books on display. After about twenty minutes, Eros comes back covered in dust, holding a book. As the young bookseller smiles at me and goes to the counter to his aunt, I once again notice the unusual coloring of his eyes. We've never made direct contact before, but now that we have, I want to keep looking at them as if there is a magnet pulling in my gaze.

He has heterochromia.

His right eye is every green hue of the forest in springtime, the left one is half blue like the sky reflecting over the ocean, and half brown, like sweet and delicious caramel. I have never seen eyes like his. Impossible to stop looking at—at least they are for me, now that I've looked at them. I'll find any excuse to get hypnotized by them as much as possible.

Staring at him makes my right eye twitch from a sudden itching, and with difficulty, I push against the instinct of rubbing it, blinking uncontrollably. How wonderful. Now he must think I'm communicating with him in secret eye Morse code. I'll have to go back to the apartment and put some eye drops in right after I'm done here. I hate doing it in public. Since I've been back, my eyes have been bugging me non-stop. The optometrist says nothing is wrong with them, but at the weirdest moments they just start itching, as if a thousand ants were walking over my pupils.

Crap, the burning sensation suddenly heightens and I can't wait any longer. I open my purse, grab the little container and quickly turn away from them to put a couple of drops in. There, much better. I let my head fall back with a sense of gratitude and relief. The crawling ants are immediately gone.

"Zia, the only one I could grab was this one. I was interrupted, and I wasn't able to get the rest," Eros says, his shoulders hunched and his chin tilted down as if he's been defeated.

What could have possibly interrupted him? Maybe, who? Could it be a girl? Is he seeing someone? Why am I thinking about his love life so much today? Of course he's with someone. Look at him—he certainly can't be interested in me.

"Do not dwell on it, Eros, this is the one I was most interested in anyway," Ginevra replies.

"Are you ok, Anima?" he asks. Surprised he's talking to me, my eyes go wide in surprise. I turn towards him quickly and blubber a quick, "Yes, yes, just dry eyes. I'm all good now."

With a sure nod and the gentlest of all smiles, Eros steps towards his small office. That's when I linger more on him. Why is he so compelling? His hair is a tousled shaggy mess of copper locks. He has an angular face, with a very defined squared jawline and fair, flawless skin. He must be six feet tall and slim. Almost like a giant beside my five feet. He's wearing glasses right now, which give him an intellectual vibe, and I'm certain he's plenty smart too. My stomach squeezes as I notice the way his eyes light up as they set on yet another pile of books, and what makes him look even more appealing is that I don't think he has any idea of the power he has over me right now. I am standing here in silence, in complete adoration, finally observing him as if it's my first time I've ever set my eyes on him. It isn't, I've reacted this exact way every time I've been in Forestiero for the past six months. I have no idea what to do about it and the thought scares me. It's like he has me under a spell, an incantation, a freaking curse—a beautiful one for sure. I feel like my brain is divided into two: one part is telling me to embrace it, the other one is telling me to run away from it—far far away. Jeremy really did a number on me.

He is around my age, might be a little older but I never found out for sure, and he graduated last July in modern literature. I remember Ginevra and I discussing his thesis a few months back. Well… Ginevra bragged about her nephew and his studies while I listened, not that I minded. She's also my only source of information about him, because he's as silent as a statue most of the time and it's as if he only exists confined within these walls. He asks short questions, but he never goes beyond that. He mostly listens to me. Not once have I seen him around Vallecrosia. Ever!

Ginevra looks at me with approval and says, "Eros is really a sweet young man, but perhaps a little too shy at times. You should push him a little, get him out of his comfort zone."

What does she mean by that? Should I ask him out? Do men

like it when the girl makes the first move? Do I even want to? Who am I kidding, of course I want to.

"This is a book that I'm very close to," she says as she hands me the book. "These poems, stories and descriptions are a little bit different from the usual. They talk about a place dear to my heart."

I force an expression of vague interest on my face, instead of rudely digging into the book immediately. "Really? What should I expect? How is it different?"

It definitely doesn't look like a rom com, unfortunately. It's a thick volume, and though I expect it to be heavy, it feels quite light in my hands. "Thank you," I mumble, intrigued by the thick coating of mystery around her words.

She looks at me with a radiant smile. It comforts me, how sweet and gentle this woman always is with me. I almost feel like she's my aunt too.

I pull out my wallet, but Ginevra gently cups my hand to stop me. "No, this is a gift. When you read it, you'll understand why this book is so important to me... to us."

My brows furrow at the ominous tone she's using. Important to *us*. Ginevra and I share very little aside from our hometown. "Oh, please, let me pay—"

"No, absolutely not." She pats my hand and turns around. "Happy reading, Anima."

Glancing down at the big burgundy leather-bound book, I leave the shop and walk away.

WALKING HOME, THE INTENSE FEELING OF BEING FOLLOWED consumes me. It's like having eyes on me—in the peaceful quiet, I can almost hear steps, though no one's around. And I might be going crazy, but every single pore of my skin feels on alert mode. Every instinct tells me I'm not alone.

Looking at the road ahead, I notice how dark the sky has suddenly gotten. Did I spend my entire day at the bookstore? I check the time on my phone, and it's 2:30 pm. I was out for only a couple of hours—but it appears that a storm is getting close. The air is thick and humid, my hair sticking to my face in damp locks, and the clouds are gray, ready to burst at any second.

I slow my steps and turn around, expecting to see something or someone there, but there is nothing and no one. I am alone, if you exclude a lonely squirrel climbing a pine tree to my right.

When I spot my apartment complex, I run to the front door just as the first drops of rain hit the concrete pavement, the hair on my arms are lifted with the feeling of being followed never having subsided. When I open the door in a hurry and shut it behind me, relief washes over me. I laugh at my childish reaction and enter my apartment. I might have to add this kind of paranoia to the list of things I have to tell my therapist in the next session. It's crazy what trauma can do to you. I put an ocean between me and my… *problem*, and I still feel like he could jump out of nowhere. Obviously that won't ever happen—right? Right, it won't.

After setting my bag down and making a peppermint tea, I take a seat on the couch. There's something about opening a book for the first time—a new world of possibilities to lose oneself in. It's the best form of escapism, therapy, and today, there's something even more thrilling, since I don't even know what book I'm about to dive into. I take a closer look at the manuscript Ginevra gave me and finally I read the title: *The Royal Textbook of Dusäiga.* As I open the leather cover, an inscription on the first page catches my eyes: 'Tales and Magic History of the Hidden World'.

A shiver runs down my spine as I continue to inspect the tome.

Why does Ginevra want me to read this book? And why is it so important to her—to us, even?

I can't rationally explain the perception that I have about it. Running my fingers down the spine of the book I feel a sudden reminiscence in my heart. The cold leather slowly warms up under my grip. It feels familiar. I've seen this book somewhere before—not only that—I've held it before.

CHAPTER 3

This book makes very little sense. Rather than a collection of stories, it seems to be a guide on how to get to, and survive in this hidden world, Dusäiga. I've heard this name before somewhere, but where? Why can't I seem to recall anything about it but have this sense of déjà vu? I am pretty sure I have never heard of this book before. Was it maybe a similar book to this one?

My eyes scout through the first pages, with weird poems that almost sound like spells. The rest of the book seems to be about the history of the place and how to get there.

I run my fingers over a beautiful illustration of a medieval-looking town with very narrow pathways and arcaded alleys. The slightly yellow paper feels porous to the touch. There's a river dividing the village into two parts connected by a curved stone footbridge. It's so familiar, almost nostalgic. I can nearly see this image of me walking on that bridge, feeling some of the stones under me wobbling. On top of the town, on a hill to the right, a castle rests with two towers on either side.

And it's as if a part of the book is missing, as if I could attach another volume to the back of this one. It doesn't look incomplete, but there are some references to a part of the book that doesn't seem to be in here. Maybe this is the first volume of a series. Maybe that's what Eros was referring to when he said he could only grab this book from the warehouse.

When my eyes drift to the wall clock by my right, I squirm. It's already 11:30 pm! I have been staring at the book for hours, yet it feels like I started to read it five minutes ago. I run to the bathroom to remove my make-up and get ready for bed. When I look in the mirror, I think back to Ginevra. Why did she want to give me this book? Only reading the entire thing will probably give me the answer.

I hastily remove my make-up, tie my blondish hair in a loose ponytail and start the process. When I get back in the room, I take the tome and lay on my bed.

"... ONLY THE ONE WHO BELIEVES WITH A FULL HEART,
THOSE CURIOUS ABOUT LEARNING,
AND WHO WILL BE WITHOUT FEAR OF NOT RETURNING,
WILL BE ABLE TO ENTER THE HIDDEN WORLD..."

Assuming that this world exists, to get into it you should be curious, want to learn and have to be ready not to come out of it... If the last thing was optional, I would give it a shot. Maybe I'd get over the loss of my parents faster if I went on an adventure.

Perhaps escaping for a while would give me pause from the incessant questions crowding my mind.. Should I remain in Vallecrosia? I was adopted at five years old. My early childhood has always been a bit of a dilemma to me, but I never cared much because I had Mirella and Giorgio Soleri, my parents. Sometimes I wonder if they knew anything about my biological ones. I never felt the need to research my biological parents, I never asked either, and now I couldn't even if I wanted to. Even right now, I feel like this would be a betrayal to the people that did everything they could to raise me in a loving household. But since my parents died, I've been questioning everything. Maybe it's just an attempt to replace something I lost with something else that won't ever compare. After all, those people gave me away. My nonna used to always say to me "Anima, don't ever forget that the people that you should call parents aren't the ones that make your feet, but the ones that buy you the shoes". Maybe it's better not remembering those early years. Yet, I keep wondering about it all.

My eyes pause at the sight of another type of poem. It almost reads like a prediction. A prophecy of some sort. I find myself reading it over and over again like a chant, feeling a desperate need to memorize it, until my hands tremble with the effort of squeezing the book. The Crown's Soul Prophecy. What a peculiar name. I bite my lip with a pounding heart and read it one more time.

TWO PARTS OF THE SAME ESSENCE. A FIRST AND SECOND BORN OF THE COURT. THROUGH DIFFERENT EYES, A VISION WILL BRING TRANSITION. AN UNBREAKABLE BOND. THE CONNECTION WILL SNAP INTO PLACE WHEN THEY WILL REACH MATURITY, AND WHAT WAS FORGOTTEN WILL FLOURISH ONCE AGAIN. THE GOLDEN ENERGY WILL BE THE ANSWER TO THE EQUATION. AN EYE FOR AN EYE. A SOUL FOR A SOUL. A CROWN AND A CORPSE. THE DROUGHT WILL CEASE.

As I keep scrolling through the beautiful, sepia-colored pages, I feel my eyes becoming heavier and heavier until the need to shut them is overpowering my every thought.

MY FEET SINK INTO THE GROUND AS I PACE MYSELF TOWARDS nothingness.

The floor is so cold beneath me. Where are my shoes?

I have—need to find him. Now I know. He is in danger—they all are and it's all my fault. I should have gotten here sooner.

I can't see a foot ahead, only a dark pitch around me as I keep my arms in front of me not to stumble against one of the huge bookshelves populating the space.

I take a deep breath in, and a hint of vanilla fills my nostrils.

Shivers run down my spine as a cold breeze follows me from the slightly open window on my left.

I have to be quick before they find out what I'm doing.

Wax from the candle I'm holding continuously falls on my hand making it sting so methodically.

Here's the door, the dark wood separating me from him. I open it gently and there he is, laying on his side, sleeping.

My golden light. I have to tell him everything.

Just as I reach forward with my free hand, a drop of wax falls on his shoulder.

As he starts to turn towards me, my vision unfocuses and everything disappears.

I WAKE UP THE NEXT MORNING, THE BOOK RESTING ON MY BELLY. As I look at the pages, the words seem to rearrange themselves. I'm still groggy from my restless sleep, but I blink and blink again, trying to put the black ink into focus, until I read, *You're the only one who can save us, the only one who can save him. Wake up, Anima.*

When I flinch back, my heart quick in my chest, it's gone. The words are back to normal, there's no mentioning of my name. Just some more on the history of Dusäiga. Maybe I've read too many fantasy novels.

My heavy eyes beg me to try to fall asleep again, it's still very early, but the tenseness of my body wins over. Staring at my ceiling, I wait until the sound of horns and people shouting outside of my building reach me. The world is finally awake as well.

Since I got back from Chicago, this recurring dream has been interfering with my sleep. Every night for the past six months. And every morning I wonder if the man in it is real or just a product of my imagination. I wish I could remember his face, maybe that way I could understand how to help this fictitious person, maybe it's someone I know. Every night I see him, but as soon as I wake up his face dissolves from my memory quicker than I can fathom.

In the dream, I know I need to help him with something, but every time I try to, something bad happens to me or him, then I wake up in a panic. After fetching a water bottle, putting on some light makeup, I grab my camera bag and begin walking down the stairs. The air smells like sea salt even in the building hall, and as I turn the key into the studio's lock, I can almost taste it on my lips while wetting them with my tongue. I can almost feel the sand between my toes, the warmth of the sun on my skin.

I love my job, it's like therapy for me. Taking photos distracts me, and right now I need a distraction. I need to divert my mind from these weird dreams I keep having, from the odd book Ginevra insists I have to read, and most importantly, my late parents. I need to keep myself busy so as to trick my mind not to think about them constantly. The void and absence they've left in my heart. How much I miss them.

After I moved back to Italy, I honestly thought I couldn't accept what my parents left for me. What if I disappoint them? What if I lose everything because I am not good enough? How am I supposed to just accept all this and move on with my life?

Reading helped me keep my mind safe enough, and Svetlana helped me get back on my feet by assisting me around the studio.

She's still in school, always learning a new language, and I couldn't be happier to have her around. We have a couple of shoots today so I can't wait to get my day started.

I get out of my apartment building and Svetlana is in front of the studio waiting for me, her hair scattered on her face by the wind as she fakes a tango with an imaginary person in front of her. People stare at her, probably wondering if she took her meds this morning and I just laugh at how serene she always makes me feel. Svetlana is like the sun, the person who just brightens my every day.

"Good morning sunshine! Should we go grab a coffee before we open up?" Svetlana asks me with a smile on her face as I join her outside.

"Yes, please, I am in desperate need of caffeine."

We start walking on Via Aprosio to our favourite coffee place. Bar Cobalto, right beside Forestiero. We come here in the morning at least three times a week, since they have the best croissants and focaccia of all Vallecrosia.

As we enter the brightly lit cafe, I gape at the beige walls covered in pictures of the owners throughout the years. The circular tables populating the space are mostly empty, though a couple at the far end is chatting over a slice of pie.

Svetlana leads me towards the table close to the big window that faces the sidewalk of Via Aprosio, and wiping away some leftover crumbs, I rest my back on the comfortable wooden chair.

"You know, I think it's time to change our relationship status. We've been single for far too long." Svetlana starts. I widen my eyes.

"Have we? I broke up with Jeremy not that long ago, and you're not that ahead of me. I think I'm good. You know, with being stalked out of the country," I say curtly. "But please, go for it if it's the right time for you."

Though I do think about being with someone from time to

time, I'm not ready yet. Not with all the trauma Jeremy put me through.

We get our coffees, and while Svetlana talks my ear off about dating apps versus meeting someone in real life, I see Eros walk in front of the café. As if he feels my stare on him, he turns to me, then waves before strutting away. I didn't even have time to react, and just like that, he's gone.

"You should ask the Forestiero guy out," Svetlana says as she wiggles her dark blonde brows at me. "You've been drooling all over him since you got back."

"Eros?" I can feel heat creep up my cheeks, but cross my arms and firmly shake my head. "I'm not drooling over anyone. And I'm not asking him out, Svetlana. Don't be ridiculous."

She snorts, quickly rolling her eyes. "You know you've got a book addiction when you're on a first name basis with the guy that sells you the books. And he's hot. Do you know if he has a brother?"

When she turns to look at the window of the café, trying to get another glimpse of Eros, my chest tightens with jealousy I have no right to have. Plus, Svetlana wouldn't make a move on him—not if she thinks I like him. Which I don't. Except I totally do. "Technically, his aunt sells me the books. And I think so? Haven't really seen anyone else there in a long time, though," I reply, now wondering about his family and what they do. I remember seeing another guy working with them before I left for university. He was barely there but I remember Eros mentioning him as his brother. The same guy years prior would hang around and play with Eros around the store. I can almost hear their aunt yelling to stop running around customers and causing the books to fall everywhere. I never asked the boy's name, but I remember noticing his light green eyes as a juxtaposition to his tanned skin.

"You call Ginevra by her first name, so you still have a problem," she continues.

"I might have a book problem, but, hey, at least it's not drugs!"

As she chuckles, she quickly stirs her coffee. "I am serious though, you gotta get laid. You haven't touched a naked man in almost a year!"

Thinking of the last time Jeremy and I were intimate, I tilt my head. "More like thirteen months, but who's counting? I am alright."

"Over a *year*? That's even worse! I didn't realize it had been that long."

"I am fine, Svetlana, really," I reassure her as I gently swat the top of her hand. "Anyway, we have to go. The Roberti and Martini families are coming in before noon, and I have work to catch up on."

With a sigh, she follows me out of the café.

AROUND 3:30PM I AM ALONE IN MY STUDIO IMMERSED IN PHOTO editing, music blasting in the background. I am feeling good, great even, just me, my laptop and my photos. I put some eyedrops in my eyes just to prevent the itchiness that I know will come soon, then focus on the screen. Once I'm done with work, I'll go home and read some more of that mysterious book about Dusäiga, maybe have pizza again. Life is good.

"I hope you're not trying to replace me," a voice behind me says, the hairs on my arm spiking as I jump off my chair.

Chapter 4

The Royal Textbook of Dusäiga: Tales and History of the Hidden World

"I'm sorry, I didn't mean to scare you," Eros says, almost laughing. His hand passes through his messy hair giving it a more put together look, the other is in his denim pocket. I see his heel ticking repeatedly as if he is nervous. My eyes lock on his lips as he suddenly wets them with his tongue. God, what is he doing to me?

"What are you doing here? Did you just appear out of thin air? You can't come up to people like that, I almost had a heart attack!" I say, eyes wide and flared nostrils. Not the impression I'd usually aim for, but the only one I can manage. I breathe in and the sea air mixes with his citrusy cologne.

He points behind him. "I actually opened the door, said hi and everything, but you really didn't seem to notice me. You were too busy buying books from the competition." He smirks, and it makes me feel something in my chest. As if I'm terrified, giddy, and nervous all at once. My chest is beating so fast it might break through my rib cage, and I can tell he noticed it because his eyes linger on my shaky hands. Pull yourself together, Anima. My eyes shut close as an image of Jeremy blooms in front of me. He is not Jeremy. I put an ocean between me and *him*. I open them again and focus my attention on Eros's eyes. They are not icy gray. They are green, blue and caramel. I am safe.

"I swear I was only looking at titles, I am not buying books anywhere else," I blurt out. Why am I raising my voice at him? Why am I acting like a teenager? Is it because his ginger hair looks straight out of a dream?

"Good, I would have been devastated otherwise." He walks to the wall, his eyes roaming over the pictures inelegantly taped on it. "My aunt asked me to come by. She wanted to know if you started reading the book we gave you yesterday?"

Of course, he came here because Ginevra asked him to, not because he wanted to. Trying to hide my disappointment, I lower the volume of the music. "Oh yes, the book of legends and the magical world. I fell asleep after a few pages, but I liked the description of the place. Of Dusäiga. I also found myself reading that weird prophecy over and over again."

When his eyes meet mine, he looks awfully worried. His brows are bent down and his foot taps the floor again and again.

"Is everything alright? You look a little tense." I shift in my chair. "Would a coffee help? My treat."

I don't know where this confidence comes from, but if he refuses, I'll never set foot in Forestiero again. I'll die of embarrassment.

"Just a little tired. I've been working almost non-stop." When I nod, he adds, "I'd love to get a coffee though". A grin appears on his face. That beautiful face of his. That absolutely gorgeous face of his. I close my hands into fists trying to calm the urge to trace his perfect squared jawline with my fingers. I'd spend hours counting the constellations of freckles on his cheeks and nose.

Pretending my heart rate hasn't skyrocketed through the roof,

I smile back. "Let me grab my jacket and keys, and then we can go."

"Sounds good."

I turn off the lights, close the office door behind me and begin to walk towards the bar near his shop. Stepping to my left, he places himself on the part of the sidewalk that is closest to the road, like a true gentleman would do. It's a protective gesture—something I haven't seen in a while. Even so, it's crazy how such a small thing makes my legs feel weak as I inhale his scent. He's so close to me that if I move just an inch to the left, I'll touch his arm, and boy do I want to.

"Hope I didn't interrupt important work. I wouldn't want you to get behind with anything," he says as he holds the door for me. He places his hand on the middle of my back to walk me inside the cafè, causing shivers to travel down my spine and my pulse to race. I can still feel his touch even if his hand is not on me anymore. It's there, like an imprint on my skin.

"Oh, no. Not at all. I was basically done, and I have a few days to finish up that work, anyway. So really, don't worry about it. You haven't interrupted anything important. Nothing." I roll my eyes, pressing my lips shut to force my blabbering to stop.

He holds out a chair for me, and I sit down at the table. At the perfect moment too, because as he leans closer to sit down beside me, his eyes dart to my lips for an instant, and my knees buckle under the table. My legs have been ready to give up on me for a while, with the way he's been looking at me.

Svetlana was right. I do need to get laid. One hot guy gives me two seconds of his attention and look at me, *shaking*!

We order our coffees and sit silently for a couple of minutes until the waitress brings over our order. As I take the first sip, he says, "Not that I'm complaining about your visits, but I feel like I never see you outside of Forestiero."

I stare at him for a second too long, scrambling for a relatively *normal* answer. "Yeah, same. And in such a small town. It's weird, isn't it?"

"It means we'll have to make sure to meet, from now on." He grins wide, then stirs his black coffee. "I'm happy to be here now. Tell me, how are you doing? I imagine it's been a hard time with… everything."

I know he's just being polite, but I hate when I get the newly-orphan-sympathy. With a shrug, I think of a way to quickly shift the topic. "I'm doing fine. Just working and trying to sort everything out. I'm not sleeping much, but that's because I keep having unsettling dreams." His brows furrow, and as he opens his mouth to speak, my own voice bulldozes through. "I keep dreaming about this person. A man that I don't know. Almost every night." I shake my head as I correct myself. "No, every single night. Every time I wake up, I completely forget his face or any face I see in the dream. It's weird, and I never feel rested when I wake up." Venturing a look at his expression, I don't find a derisive smirk. Instead, he looks intrigued. "What about you? Any weird dreams? Please make me feel less of a dork."

"Dreams are fascinating pieces of our subconscious," he says calmly. "I have had a recurring dream since I was a child. Mine is about a woman. We're always in the same place—I think it's a library. She always walks towards me smiling, and when I can finally see her well enough, I wake up and forget it." He hooks his arm behind the chair, meeting my gaze "See? You're not the only dork here."

I nervously chuckle. He's anything but a dork, with those gorgeous eyes and easy-going smile. "Thank you for saying that… for not making me feel too much of a weirdo," I mumble as I look away. "Isn't it so interesting though?… the fact that we are both having such peculiar recurring dreams, I mean." I like this version of Eros. The one that has no problem asking me any kind of question, even the weirdest ones. It's also weirdly unsettling. Certainly the dreams are different, I am always in a dark space and his is in a library but the thought of having something so close, so profound in common makes me tremble. I bite the inside of my cheek to the point of tasting iron as I wait for him to say anything.

He smiles at me, a wide and genuine grin that makes my toes tingle. For a second, I can't pay attention to anything else. Only his eyes. They're penetrating, and his gaze on me is almost magnetic.

"It's almost like fate, isn't it…" Eros says. It doesn't sound like a question, and I couldn't answer if I wanted to, with the way his gaze dips to my mouth.

His lips part as if he'll say more, but Ginevra's voice blasts through the cafè. "There you are! I've been looking for you two everywhere."

We both quickly turned towards her, the temperature of my body lowering as soon as Eros' deep eyes are off me. For how long had we been staring at each other? Ginevra's salt and pepper hair is tied in a messy bun and on her nose sits a pair of reading glasses. Those ones with thin rectangular lenses, the cheap ones that you get at the grocery store for five euros. Around her neck is a lanyard with little red pearls that make her look just like a bookshop owner. She's radiating, her lips curled up into a soft smile.

After clearing his throat, Eros says, "Hi *zia*! Anima and I were just drinking some coffee. Taking a little break."

"Yeah, Eros seemed a bit stressed and I could have used a coffee," I agree.

"Oh, what a wonderful girl you are, Anima. How marvelous it is to see the both of you out together!" She shares a complicit look with me, then adds, "Would you have time to come over later today?"

My brows scrunch, my eyes darting from Ginevra to Eros, then back again. "Come over?"

"Yes, to *Forestiero*."

I tentatively nod, throwing yet another look at Eros and finding his expression blank. What exactly does Ginevra want to talk to *me* about? Does it have anything to do with the book she gave me yesterday?

Probably perceiving my hesitation, she places a calming hand on my shoulder and smiles wide. "It's time you and I have a talk. And I'm sure you must have some questions for me too."

I do. For example, why did she give me that book to start with? What is Dusäiga? What's that prophecy, and why does it feel like the most meaningful thing I've ever read? Why does that book feel familiar—why does Dusäiga feel like a place I've been to before?

I guess there's only one way to find out.

"Sure, I'll come by after I'm done with work."

Ginevra nods and with a quick goodbye she steps out of the bar and continues her walk towards Forestiero.

"This was nice." I grab my bag and take out my wallet. "Thank you for not making me feel like a dork," I add. How many times have I repeated that? Now I really am starting to sound like one.

"Whenever. You can talk to me about whatever you want, Anima." His eyes lock once again with mine and once again it feels like we are the only people in the room. Nothing else around us, no one else around us.

I nod. "You too. Lately, I only have Svetlana to talk to." Blushing, I wave my hand around. "She's—she's a friend of mine."

I get up and head to the counter to pay when Eros appears by my side, quickly squeezes my hand, and says, "I already took care of it. No chance I'd let you pay."

"I thought *I* was the one offering!" I say, my lips curving in pretend-disapproval..

"Well, maybe next time, then..." he replies. Once again, his eyes dig deep into mine. Once again, it's almost as if we both stop breathing. "Ok, deal. Next time." With a final smile, I turn around, my muscles relaxing as I walk away. But I can still feel his gaze on my back, and as I reach the heavy door at the entrance, I turn to him again.

He's still smiling as he raises his hand in a wave. "I'll see you later, Anima."

"Yeah, see you later, Eros."

I FEEL OVER THE MOON AS I SKIP TOWARDS MY STUDIO, FEELING light and giggly like a child experiencing their first crush. Maybe it's finally my moment to have that big romantic story like the ones in my books. Things just feel so easy around him. I don't even know this guy… Like, I just know he likes to read. A lot. That's it. Do I even know this? I don't. I assume he does because of the job he has and the fact that I have never seen him without an open book in his hands. Except today.

Maybe I should try to be more realistic for a second. Yeah, he is very nice, but I seriously do not know anything about the guy. He does seem to want to get to know me, though. He listened to my story and didn't think I was crazy.

But I also don't want another Jeremy situation, and I can't know for sure he won't be one. And I have so many unresolved issues, I don't need to complicate my life even more.

His words come back to me, *did I just imagine it or was he going to say something about fate?* I have to admit it is intriguing to know that we both are having similar recurring dreams… I guess that is something we have in common…Or…What if this is the beginning of a thriller where I discover he read my dream journals and is using the information to lure me into the bookshop after closure so that Ginevra can finish the job? Breathe Anima, this isn't a novel, it's real life. As Svetlana says, this is probably my lack of a sex life that is making me overthink this. And sleeping with someone that makes me feel so enchanted towards them wouldn't be such a bad thing, right?

I quickly take out my phone and start writing a text to Svetlana.

ANIMA:

You have no idea who I just had coffee with.

Almost immediately I get a reply.

SVETLANA:

I hope it's a cute nerdy redhead guy that you've been drooling all over for months!

ANIMA:

I AM NOT DROOLING ALL OVER HIM

Ok maybe a little.

SVETLANA:

You so are, and I'm very proud of you, babe. Tell me everything later ;)

ANIMA:

I will! ;)

CHAPTER 5

DUSÄIGA IS A MONARCHY AND A MATRIARCHY. DAUGHTERS OF THE ROYAL FAMILY ARE THE HEIR TO THE THRONE EVEN IF THE FIRST CHILD IS MALE. IF NO DAUGHTER IS BORN, THEN THE FIRST SON SHALL TAKE THE CROWN.

My eyes keep drifting to the big wall clock, counting the minutes until I'm done with work and at Forestiero, so I can see Eros again. My knee jiggles under the desk, causing a mini-earthquake that has my coffee shaking, and my heart seems to beat faster, stronger, louder than usual. My mind travels around Ginevra and the book. What's this big secret she keeps hinting at? What in the world does she need to talk to me about, of all people?

Around 6:00 pm, I clean up and walk to Forestiero. While strolling, a thought pops up. A thought so ridiculous and far-fetched, I'd never actually say it out loud. What if Eros is the guy I see in my dreams? Maybe my subconscious is playing a trick on me, I should talk to my therapist about it. I'm sure she would give me a legitimate answer, but she would also tell me to try to get to that answer on my own. Dreams are just dreams, but something tells me there's more to it. Maybe this need to latch onto something, onto someone, is just a way to cope with the death of my parents. This could also be a way my mind elaborates the trauma that Jeremy created, making me imagine that Eros is in trouble. Me having to save him could just be a representation of me trying to save myself. Or maybe I want to be happy, to smile again so badly that I'm picturing that Eros will be the one who helps me get there. This is so stupid. He's just a guy, and dreams are just dreams. Fate isn't a real thing. But even as the depressing thought comes to me, a shiver down my spine makes me doubt it. Perhaps there *is* something more to this.

When I get to the bookstore, Ginevra is talking to a customer, but Eros sees me right away and waves at me to follow him to the back office. "Hey! I'm glad you passed by," he says, staring at me with an amused look on his face. The scent of markers and highlighters mixes with the one of paper and his citrus cologne. Even in this small room books cover every inch of the surrounding walls, they're piled up on top of another. On the small metal desk in the middle of the space, an open book rests lit up by a small desk lamp. I notice the written notes on the side of the pages and the underlined sentences. He's an annotator. The corners of my lips lift at the thought of reading his thoughts on his favorite books.

"With how much I love this place, you're most likely to find me here than anywhere else."

"May I ask you why? I know you love books, obviously, but you've been coming here basically every day since you've been back. Ever heard of Amazon?"

"I thought you didn't like competition," I reply, chuckling, quickly joined by him. Have I really been coming here that often? He must be thinking I am an obsessive freak. Or even worse, a stalker.

Swallowing down the rising panic, I fidget with the hem of

my shirt. "Have I really?" As he nods, smiling wide, it doesn't look as if it bothers him, so I continue, "This is the only place where I don't feel judged, where nobody asks any unwanted questions. I am still trying to process all the changes in my life, and I guess I knew you and Ginevra would give me the time I need."

A sudden warm wave travels up my neck and cheeks. I've never really thought about this, and why it's so important for me. It's true though, Eros and Ginevra have been a constant in my life even before I left for university. I never realized it until I left and came back, but they've always been here, even if just as booksellers, they have always been part of my everyday life.

Eros tilts his head, leaning closer to me, and as the side of his eyes crinkle he says, "I would never push you, but if you ever want to talk, I will be here to listen."

His soothing voice suddenly makes all the muscles in my body relax. I didn't even notice I was as stiff as a statue, but I'm not anymore. His eyes sparkle as they look into mine. He has me under a spell. A beautiful spell that I hope will never break.

"Thank you Eros, I—that means a lot. Same goes to you if you ever want to talk about anything," I say with heat on my cheeks. This is how a crush feels like, and I missed it. It feels so unfamiliar, and at the same time, I can only see him in this room right now. I can't notice anything else. He tentatively moves his hand forward, and when he realizes I don't recoil, his fingers land on my cheek, brushing it delicately. I unawarely close my eyes to his touch on my skin. Shivers travel down my spine, my hands tingle. I almost can't feel my own body anymore.

"Okay, sorry to keep you wait—" Ginevra barges into the room, Eros' fingers quickly abandoning my skin just as she claps excitedly. "Oh, I am so happy to see you two together!"

"Zia…" Eros warns her. It does nothing to stop her, and instead, Ginevra begins hopping on one foot, then the other. "Please, zia, stop," he insists.

"Alright, alright." Settling on the chair beside me, she grabs my hand in hers. "So, I guess you're curious to know why I asked you to come here, Anima. Frankly, there's no easy way to say it, but I think you already know that our warehouse is a bit... peculiar."

"Peculiar?" I ask, my eyes shifting from her to Eros and back again. I've always thought it's weird how it's not attached to the bookshop, yes, but beside that? "Peculiar how?"

"Don't you feel drawn to it?"

I immediately open my mouth to say that no, I'm not. But then, I think of all the times I've asked to see it, of how much time I spend fantasizing about it. Svetlana always said it wasn't normal, but I figured... I don't know... that it was my weird obsession. Is Ginevra saying it isn't? "I guess I've..." I roll my eyes. "Thought about it a lot."

My theory of the serial killer comes back to me, my eyes darting to Eros. Is *he* the serial killer hiding his victims' bodies in there? Shit. Did I fall for a psychopath again? Maybe this is how they do it. The attractive guy shows some interest, deceives me, and then—*bang*—, his aunt goes in for the kill.

Eros' eyes narrow with amusement, as if he's reading my very thoughts, then he walks to the door and locks it. Oh no, this is bad. Very bad. Is there something around here that I can defend myself with? Maybe that paper cutter?

"Anima, there is a reason why you're so drawn towards that place and to us..." Eros starts saying, but he gets cut off by Ginevra right away.

"And that is because you're a *striga*, a witch, and the warehouse is a portal to the Hidden World, to Dusäiga. Remember the book I gave you? It's not a book of legends. It's a guide."

My entire face scrunches up as I study their expressions. Maybe they won't kill me, but they look serious, which means they certainly must be lunatics.

Before I can stop myself, laughter bubbles out of my lips, my voice reaching a pitch so high, I wouldn't be surprised if glass started shattering around me. What are they talking about? This is the stupidest joke I've ever heard.

Needles begin prickling at my eyes. Again, that awful sensation comes back at the worst time possible. "Fuck," I whisper under my breath as the last chuckles subside and I look for the eye drops in my bag. My hands shake with adrenaline from the weirdest encounter I've ever had in my life, and as the purse falls from my hands and all my belongings scatter over the floor. Eros picks up the little container, rushes to me and places it in my hand. I can sense his gaze on me as he rests his hand on my shoulder. Once again, the contact makes me dizzy.

"Let me help you, please," he says, his voice low and trembling as if he is the one in pain. "It seems worse this time."

It *does* feel worse, the sensation almost unbearable. I can't even keep my eyes open as it feels like fire is bursting through my corneas. "This is so embarrassing," I finally utter.

"Remember what I told you earlier? You don't ever need to worry about anything with me, ok? Now lay your head back—I got you." He gently lowers us until we're on the floor, and my hand brushes over his chest. His hard, flat, gorgeous chest. What would it feel like if fabric wasn't between me and his skin?

He holds the back of my head with one hand while he puts the drops in with the other. His eyes focused on the task. Thankfully, I am already laying on the floor because his orange cologne mixed with the scent of soap is making me lightheaded. "Better?"

Instant relief flows through my entire body.

"Much better, thank you." I reply with my eyes closed.

Eros brushes my hair off of my face, still keeping his other hand to the back of my head. "Anima, my aunt is not joking. You're a *striga*, Ginevra is one, I'm a *veneficus*. We're witches.

Do you remember that dream I talked to you about? It's you, saving Dusäiga."

Way to ruin it. I thought we were having a moment—that he really liked me. But nope, just going about the same nonsense his aunt put him up to.

Quickly, I get up and start collecting all the stuff that fell out of my purse. I don't understand the purpose of messing with me. They've always cared about me, so why try to hoax me? "Is this an early April's fools joke? It's still the middle of March, not funny." I begin walking toward the entrance. "Eros, do you understand that what you're saying is completely nuts? I don't know any spell. I don't fly on a broom, and I certainly don't have a cauldron in my house. Oh, as for the warehouse? It's just a place full of books. That's why I always wanted to see it."

"Do you remember the prophecy you read in the Royal textbook? It's about you," Eros says as he quickly steps behind me.

With a deep sigh, I turn around. "How can it be about me, Eros? I am not a striga, witch—witches aren't real."

As he bursts into a deep, belly laugh, I scowl. This guy is supposed to have a degree in literature, and he believes in fucking magic. More than that, he thinks *I'm* ridiculous because I don't.

"Are dragons and vampires real too?" I mock. "Have you ridden any unicorns lately?"

He smirks. "Vampires are fiction. Sorry, I know you love those. Dragons…" He tilts his head. "They were real, once upon a time. We haven't seen one in centuries though. That would be a cool encounter for sure."

"Right. That makes total sense. What about zombies? Mummies? Uh, how about fairies? Do fairies exist?" I go for the door, but his hand reaches it first and keeps it closed. When I turn to him, ready to unleash the full extent of my fury, he smiles candidly, lightly. He almost looks genuine.

"Think about it, Anima. Think about something you want, and

see it happen. Forget about flying brooms and cauldrons. You are a witch. Do you remember what people say about the town of Triora? This isn't any different."

This is so crazy, I can't handle it anymore. I don't know what would lead Eros and Ginevra to believe I would appreciate these jokes, but I don't. When instead I pull the door to me, Eros lets it go. I turn to him, his lips bent into a sad frown. "Triora is just a little town that uses the excuse of witches for business and tourism. Now, if you don't mind, I'm gonna go."

"Why do you think you like Triora bread so much then?" Eros asks as I step outside. How does he even know?

"Because it's bread. I fucking love bread. How do you even know I like it? Have you been following me?" How does he know that's the only bread I am able to put in my mouth without gagging?

"The bread they make in Triora is the kind of bread they make in Dusäiga, same recipe. You like it because it's familiar to you. Criselda is from Dusäiga. You just don't remember it. You will though. I promise I will help you remember, Anima. "

"Maybe we should have waited for Di—" Ginevra says as she pops up behind Eros.

Before she can finish her sentence, Eros waves her off. "No, this is about her and where she belongs."

Studying their pained face, it almost looks as if they mean every word. Which is a whole different kind of unsettling. Are they crazy, and I just never just noticed? Or are they such good liars? Sure, there's a remote possibility they aren't lying, and all of this is true. The thought is so ridiculous, I quickly brush it off. "I—I need to go."

Ginevra approaches me, her hand wrapping around my arm and lightly squeezing. "I understand, sweetheart. Go home, and rest, you need it."

"Just think about your parents and everything that happened, it will start making sense. Think about the key you wear around your neck."

Eros' voice reaches me as I take a few steps, then all of a sudden, there's a depleting silence around us. It feels as if every inch of my skin is electric, as if every pore is awake. When a series of loud bursts come from behind me, I turn around and see several light bulbs from the chandelier explode in a thousand pieces. They turn into dust, which deposits all over the books inside the shop.

Wait—did I… did I do that?

"Well, I think that might have been a little much, Eros." Ginevra scolds him.

"And it's gonna be a bitch to clean up," Eros whispers under his breath. Meeting my gaze, he smiles, proud. As if the explosion of light bulbs somehow proves I am whatever they say I am, a stri–something. A witch. Which it does not. If anything, it proves glass shatters, and the shop needs maintenance.

"Don't you dare mention my parents." I cross my arms and flatten my lip, my icy stare directed towards him. I finally turn around and walk away, hearing my name echoing as Eros calls me.

The sky is dark and gloomy. I grab my phone from my pocket to check the time and read 8:30pm. I quickly put it back, my mind in a haze. For some reason, I clench my jaw and start to sweat. I am terrified. My eyes start getting cloudy again, pain resurfaces. Here we go again. Pins and needles.

Why do I always fall for the weird guys that turn out to be stalkers—maybe even killers? No wait, *witches*. Hysterical. And I probably have to find a new bookstore now. I can't show my face there anymore and risk hearing all that nonsense every time I walk in, because those two want to play mind games with me.

A witch. No wait, what did they call me? A striga. Svetlana is going to have the time of her life when I tell her what happened.

We always pretended to be witches when we were kids. We used to make fake potions, use sticks as our wands..

I can't believe he mentioned my parents. First, he says he won't push me, and then he says stuff like that? Unbelievable.

I close my hand around the key that suddenly starts to feel heavy around my neck. What did he mean by thinking about it? What is there that I need to remember?

While walking towards my apartment, I feel the usual sense of danger. That someone is following me. I know it's my brain tricking me into thinking I am being watched, but the awareness of it doesn't help. Could it be Eros?

I start taking out my phone to text Svetlana to see if she wants to come over and talk when quick steps echo behind me. Maybe this time, it's not all in my head.

I pick up my pace until my walk turns into a march, then it quickly grows into a run. It's useless though, because in just a matter of seconds pain increases on the back of my head and I feel liquid coming down my face. I raise my hand to touch the sensitive spot and feel wetness dripping off my fingertips. Pulling my hand away I see red. Blood. Someone hit me.

I swiftly turn with a racing heartbeat. I am trembling, blinking rapidly trying to stay focused. It's like I can't stop moving, like I am spinning. Black dots appear in front of me, obscuring my vision, and the only thing I notice before closing my heavy eyelids, is a figure with no eyes and a hood on. It looks somewhat familiar. Unsettling, dark, but known.

Then, everything goes black.

CHAPTER 6

I wake up to the sound of Eros' struggling voice telling me to stay down. From where I'm lying on the sidewalk, I can only see his back, his lean muscles flexing with effort as he's fighting someone or something, but though I blink again and again, I can't see clearly—fog fills my vision.

I might be going blind, because it looks as if the person in front of Eros has no face. My mind slowly pieces it all back together. How I passed out, and the person I saw right before. That's them—same hood and everything. Or is it?

My tongue darts alongside my bottom lip, the taste of iron taking over my mouth. The soil under me vibrates and as I look around everything starts spinning, a low ringing in my ears prevents me from hearing any noise coming from Eros and his attacker. My head continues to thump with pain, as I bring my hand up I can still feel the warm liquid trickling from where I was struck.

When Eros's assailant corners him at the wall, a knife dangerously close to the skin of his throat, I know I need to gain control of my body again and try to get up. This is all so surreal, I am pretty sure I am hallucinating.

I shield my eyes when a strong, white light violently erupts in front of me. Squinting, I look for the source and notice it's coming out of his hands hitting the figure with no eyes. Then another appears right where the last one was. A sphere of light and electrical charges is sitting on his palm, no, it's floating on top of it. Are those—energy balls?

As Eros frees himself from the chokehold he's kept in, he delivers a punch into the other person's stomach, then twists into a crouched position and stabs the side of his thigh, the knife jabbing into their flesh with a loud, wet noise. It breaks into little grains of gray dust, which float above our heads as if there's been a breach between time and space and we're frozen. Dust that reminds me of the pieces of lightbulbs from earlier back at Forestiero.

A voice whispers in the back of mind, saying words that fuel my deepest desire. Before I know it, my arm is stretched forward, my fingers straining to reach the nearest cluster of silver dust. Once it does, it mixes with the viscous burgundy liquid on my hands, little sparkles of electricity moving through me. My surroundings spin again, and stumbling back, I fall to the floor with a muted thump. Everything's turning dark again. Maybe I'm just sleeping. Maybe it's all just a dream.

"Anima? Anima, please wake up," I hear a panicked voice call me. It sounds like a command, like whoever's calling me *needs* me to open my eyes and show him I am here, real, awake, alive. I blink the world into focus, the ground hard rock against my back. But my head rests on the most comfortable of all places.

A smile blossoms on my lips as I see his worried gaze on mine, the multi-colored irises of his eyes shimmering with unshed tears. There's a horrible smell of iron, and blood is dripping from an angry slash on his forehead and right onto my chin. Someone should probably do something about that.

I don't have the strength to react, to freak out, to do anything. I just reach for his face and gently caress his cheek.

"Thank god you're awake," he breathes out. His voice is still muffled in my ears, but it's much better than before. Maybe whoever hit me gave me a concussion. "How are you feeling? That Opacum hit you hard."

Not moving away from his embrace, I manage to ask, "Opa—what? What are you talking about?" My throat is in knots, every word that tries to come out feels like it's being grated like cheese.

"Opacum, a dark veneficus. He was following you." He brushes some hair off my forehead as he examines the spot over my ear that hurts so badly. "I saw him going in the same direction as you when you left the shop, so I followed it and saw what happened. I shouldn't have left you." I feel my body being pulled up, one of his arms tight around the back of my knees and the other one against my back. My heavy head goes to rest on his shoulder, my arms flopping down from exhaustion.

Heaviness hits my vision again.

Darkness envelops everything around me, the beats of my heart slow down until they feel like the ticking of an old clock. Tick Tock.

LIGHT STRIKES ON MY FACE, BLINDING AND SUDDEN. I SLOWLY open my eyes and as I look around, I see a wooden bookshelf filled with neatly placed books, a desk covered in papers placed beside a sliding glass door. A light scent of oranges impregnates my nose and skin. The walls are light blue and don't look familiar. At all. The couch where I'm laying is dark gray and the fabric under my skin feels textured.

My eyes burn. It's not my usual itchiness, the pain quickly bringing me to tears that make my corneas sting even more. It's the large spotlight placed beside the couch—the harsh light directly pointed toward my face. The door opens with a loud screech, and I shut my eyes, letting my muscles relax against the soft cushion. "Is she ok?" A voice asks. It's low and sweet —comforting like a hug. My body freezes as I realize it's Ginevra. She's panting like she's been running a marathon. "They almost got her, *zia*," someone answers. I'm pretty sure it's Eros. "You should have let me go with her." There's a low thump, as if he's hit his hand somewhere. With a frustrated grunt, he continues, "God, why are we wasting time, did you —"

"I did. The Court knows, and guards are already searching Vallecrosia. You should call him." I squint, observing them as they talk at the edge of the couch. Eros looks better—he changed into a pair of gray sweats and a white t-shirt and his injuries are all clean and almost fully healed. They looked much worse earlier. Ginevra's hand moves to his shoulders, which lightly slump. Who was she talking about? Who should Eros call? As I rub my fingertips with my thumb, the sensation of the dust I touched earlier re-flourishes. I can still feel the tiny grains. Like sand. Eros turned someone—something, into dust. Were they going to call someone about that? Like the police? Maybe I should be the one doing that.

"As soon as Anima wakes up again."

"She's going to be ok, Eros. She has you now."

He clicks his tongue. "And she got hurt the one second I turned away to give her space."

"This won't happen again. I know you will make sure it won't." With a loud kiss to his cheek, she leaves the room.

For a while, I lie there, waiting for Eros to leave or say more —maybe to call whoever they were talking about—but when nothing happens, I stretch my arms up, the injury to the side of my head stinging with the movement Eros is by my side in an instant, his gentle hand on my face. With his gaze on my eyes as I open them, his lips raise into a beam.

"Hi," he says, "never scare me like that again." A sigh leaves his mouth and his forehead touches mine. Electricity sparks as the connection is made. The sudden soft pressure of his skin on mine gives me a sense of relief. As if I needed proof to know I am still alive, that I am indeed awake.

"Sorry."

"It's so nice to hear your voice again. You shouldn't apologize. I shouldn't have let you go home alone."

"You have to tell me what's happening," I say as I slowly sit up with my back against the wooden headboard. "What was that thing, following me? Why was it following me?" Thinking of the faceless figure, I scoff. "Am I going crazy?"

"You are not going crazy, Anima." His hand rests on my cheek. "That was an Opacum, a dark wizard, and it was following you because you are very powerful." His voice is low, soft, a caress in my ear. "You just found out what you are, and you can still decide which side you want to take: good or evil, and they— the Opacums know that."

My eyes widen, "I don't think I am following—"

"Opacums are evil, they're wizards that hide their identities by masking their faces… or better, making it look like they have no eyes, just a layer of skin." An image of the entity that Eros faced comes back to mind. "They don't just appear out of nowhere, there has to be a veneficus or a striga that has been planning your capture."

"Why would you think that?"

"Because we haven't seen an Opacum in a long time, seventeen years to be exact." Seventeen years. It can't be. My parents adopted me seventeen years ago. My muscles feel rigid and my head can't stop pounding. This has to be just like the worst hangover in history. I'm still not sure if this is really happening or if it's still an illusion.

"Where are we right now?" I take a peek behind him and notice a dark wooden kitchen with stainless steel appliances. As I turn to my right, I see a wooden coffee table with a couple of books on top of it. My vision is a little blurry because even if I was at arm's reach, I couldn't make out the titles.

"We are in my apartment, my living room to be exact. I took you here so that I could clean and heal your wound."

Bringing a hand to my frizzy hair, I turn away from Eros. My face must be a mess. I remember the blood dripping down and instinctively touch the point that was hurting, a sting hitting every single bone in my body.

"Careful, it's still fresh." He rushes by my side again. "I needed to make sure you were safe before healing you completely."

"What do you mean?"

"Let me just show you. Do you trust me?" He stretches his hand towards me.

"That is a question I don't know the answer to yet."

"I would never hurt you, Anima. It literally goes against everything in me. You are too important."

His hand gently cups the back of my head. Sudden warmth fills my skull and then travels down my spine and rest of my body. It feels as if every little part of my existence is being filled with shock waves. And it is—pleasurable. Comfort replaces the stiffness of my nerves. Relief replaces the pain.

"That—that feels amazing."

"Good. Now you can probably try to get up, slowly though. You'll still feel weird for a while. You can sleep in my bed. You need to rest as much as you can. I'll explain more tomorrow, I promise." A hand gently goes behind my neck as the other one ends up on the small of my back. He touches me as if I was made of the most fragile material, and maybe I am made of the softest porcelain. Thinnest glass. Something that could break at any moment.

"And if all this is true, how do I know I can trust you?" I ask while holding onto his shoulder, letting him help me get up. The words come out before I realize I am saying them out loud. It was meant to stay in my head but now it's out in the open—and it feels like a rhetorical question after everything he has done to help me.

Eros's eyes meet mine, he rests his hand on top of mine. All this skin to skin, his soft voice, the sweet and fresh fragrance that surrounds him, everything about Eros right in this moment is making me feel lightheaded as if my bones were now liquid.

"Trust your instinct. Your gut." His thumb gently rubs the back of my hand. "I will make sure to prove to you that you can rely on me." His finger stops moving as he takes a deep breath in. "And I will show you how much you mean to me." He squeezes my hand before adding, "If you feel unsafe, I'll take you to your house, but just so you know, I will spend the night at your doorstep and make sure no one will pay any visits."

"I'm sorry, this—this is kind of scary." I sigh. "And confusing."

"What did I tell you earlier? You don't ever have to apologize, not to me. You have every right to be scared and confused."

"Have you seen my phone?" I ask, and I see Eros turning towards the coffee table.

"Here. Just…" he brings a hand over his head and looks away, "I have to ask you to keep this a secret." When he notices the way my brows arch, he quickly adds "Just, for the moment. Until I can explain it all."

Pinching my lips together I stare at the screen, Svetlana's messages open, ready to reply. My throat closes up at the thought of not calling her right away and telling her what is happening but it is late and this is not a conversation to have on the phone. What would I say anyway? I sigh heavily before tapping my fingers on the keyboard.

Svetlana:

A, why did you send me your location? What's up?

ANIMA:

I'm spending the night at Eros' place. Don't ask, I'll tell you everything tomorrow. I swear it's not what you think.

SVETLANA:

YOU ARE WHAT? ALREADY? DIDN'T YOU MISS LIKE 100 STEPS? Wow, that coffee date was that great, huh?

ANIMA:

It's not that... It's just complicated.

SVETLANA:

Complicated? If you need me to pick you up, let me know. You're freaking me out.

ANIMA:

I will, thank you. Everything is good right now, I promise.

With that, I put the phone back in my pocket. Eros analyzes me, his eyes focused on mine. His fingers reach my hands as he moves closer to ask me if I'm doing ok.

"I think I am. I just have a headache from all this," I say.

I feel my phone buzzing in my pocket, but I honestly don't

think I can pick it up and have a conversation about any of this right now, so I let it go to voicemail.

"You need to rest. You hit your head pretty hard and lost a lot of blood. If you need it, the bathroom is just down the hall. I'll get you an aspirin in the meantime."

I nod and walk towards the bathroom and stop in front of the sink. My hands clenching on either side of the cabinet, I can't bring myself to look at my reflection. I turn the warm water on and wash my hands and then splash some water on my face, still not paying attention to the mirror right in front of me. After a few minutes I turn the water off, sigh and look straight up. The person I see looks like me, yet she is so different. I instinctively touch my eyes but I'm not feeling any pain. My eyes are completely fine, but the right one looks different. My left eye is the usual hue of green, my mother used to say it was the same colour as moss, but my right eye is now split into two. One half blue like the sky reflecting over the ocean, and the other half caramel brown. Like Eros' left eye. Exactly like his. Eros's voice echoes from the hallway. "All good in there?"

"My—my eyes," I stutter as I open the door. The perennial itchiness is gone.

"They're beautiful, aren't they?" He walks behind me and nudges his chin toward the mirror. Looking at the reflection is almost like seeing the piece that was missing, as if my face now is complete. Yet it seems like two strangers are looking back at us. A faint stain of crimson covers the top of my scalp making my sandy blonde hair look almost—pink. The blood that was on my face is now all gone and I wish I could say the same about my gray t-shirt that now looked like the worst crime scene I've seen in any tv shows. A bruise was forming on my left biceps, the skin is tender and reddish. That's probably the arm I fell on when I fainted. I brush it with my fingers and I flinch at the sudden sting of pain.

"What did you do?" I ask with tremors in my voice. My eyes widen as I stare back at what is supposed to be my reflection.

"I didn't do anything, that was all you."

I follow him back into the living room where he hands me a tall glass of water. "What do you mean it was me? Why would I do this? How would I do this?" He drops a pill into the palm of my hand. "To stop the pain, you let the glamour fall. A glamour that was put in place years ago," he says casually.

A glamour? Is he high? Why would anyone do this? Why would someone go out of their way and change my eye colour and cause me such discomfort? No, not just that, actual pain. The kind of pain that makes me stop doing whatever it is I am doing to make it go away for just a moment. A glamour. A spell. It just sounds—absurd.

"I—what? What does this mean?" I ask, swallowing air, blinking rapidly, almost hoping to make them change again. Make them go back to what they looked before.

"I'll explain more tomorrow."

I finally shove the pill in my mouth and let it go down with the water.

Eros then takes my hand and walks me towards the hallway to a bedroom. His contact remains soft on my skin, almost as a continuous caress. It makes my entire body shiver, craving for a tighter grip. He has never touched me this much. I haven't experienced so much affection from someone of the opposite sex in a while and I—like it.

"Are you sure I should stay here?" My body tenses up. That question is more to myself than to him. Should I stay here after everything that has happened tonight?

"Yes, absolutely. I'll be in the living room making some calls, I won't disturb you," He replies.

The queen size bed placed under the window is neatly made with a dark blue comforter covering it. Only one nightstand on the left side with a small lamp, a couple of books and a pair of glasses. This is Eros's room."Is this—never mind. Do you have anything I could borrow to wear to bed?"

"Yes, of course." He walks towards a closet, opens it and grabs a t-shirt and sweatpants. They'll be huge on me, but they're his, and the thought of wearing his clothes clouds every other rational thought I have in my mind at this moment.

I sit on the bed glancing at the window and he sits right beside me as he hands me the clothes.

"I know they're not really your size, but at least you'll be comfortable"

"Thank you." I take the clothes and rest them on my lap.

His hand reaches a chunk of hair in front of my face. He gently tucks it behind my ear and sighs. "You scared me to death earlier. Seeing you hurt like that…" He seems to choke onto his next words. "I thought I'd lost you."

"I'm sorry." I tilt my head. "And I am sorry I just apologized."

A short laugh escapes from his lips, then turns into a light smile.

"I won't ever make you go through that again," he states, like a promise to reassure himself, more than to me.

"I know." His face is to mine, our lips basically brushing. Heat feels my chest. If he doesn't kiss me now, I might just die right here.

As if he heard my thoughts, he rests his lips on mine. They feel warm, soft. I part mine slightly, allowing his tongue to slip inside. My body leans forward and I rest my hands on his chest, feeling his heartbeat quickening right under them. His hands cup my cheeks keeping me in place, never breaking the kiss. A rush of blood goes to my head, my cheeks feel so much warmer than his cold hands. The room was suddenly 100 degrees hotter, this is the only explanation I can come up with because my entire body is on fire.

"Fuck," he whispers under his breath, breaking the connection to catch a breath. I haven't had much practice lately, but the kiss, his lips on mine, it was—fucking good.

"Was it... bad?"

"No, it was perfect." His hands squeeze mine tightly.

"Ok, good." A weight lifts from my chest.

"You should sleep now. Goodnight, princess." My body stiffens at the sound of the pet name. Jeremy's words come back to mind. *You're mine, princess.* The thought of it makes me shiver as if it was yesterday. Don't love that, but it's a conversation for another day. Still incredulous and doubtful of everything I witnessed tonight.. Maybe if someone pinches me I'll wake up from this strange dream.

"Goodnight, Eros."

With that he walks towards the door, turns to me one last time and then closes the door behind him. I quickly change into his clothes. They smell like him. Oranges. As I stare at the ceiling, I brush my eyelashes thinking about earlier. How am I going to explain what happened to my eyes to Svetlana? To everyone that knows me?

CHAPTER 7

My feet sink into the ground as I pace myself towards nothingness.

The floor is so cold beneath me. Where are my shoes?

I have—need to find him. Now I know. He is in danger—they all are and it's all my fault. I should have gotten here sooner.

I can't see a foot ahead, only a dark pitch around me as I keep my arms in front of me not to stumble against one of the huge bookshelves populating the space.

I take a deep breath in, and a hint of vanilla fills my nostrils.

Shivers run down my spine as a cold breeze follows me from the slightly open window on my left.

I have to be quick before they find out what I'm doing.

Wax from the candle I'm holding falls on my hand making it sting so methodically.

Here's the door, the dark wood separating me from him. I open it gently and there he is, laying on his side, sleeping.

My golden light. I have to tell him everything.

Just as I reach forward with my free hand, a drop of wax falls on his shoulder.

As he starts to turn towards me, my vision unfocuses and everything disappears.

The sun rays caress my face, and I start stretching in bed. Heat radiates through my chest as the rest of my body feels light, weightless. I haven't slept this well in a long time. The blanket around me is thick and heavy, and with a smile, I tug it closer, tucking it under my chin. I could wear Eros' clothes forever. The smell of orange is now mixed with something else. Cedarwood and mint, the fresh fragrance making me dizzy as I rub the side of my head and take a deep breath.

As soon as my eyes focus around my surroundings, I realize my head isn't resting on a pillow, but something that rhythmically rises and falls. Hard but soft at the same time. Just so comfortable.

Am I dreaming? If I am, I don't ever want to wake up. This is much better than my recurring vision. Finally, something that doesn't make me dread falling asleep.

"Good morning, sweetheart," a voice says. The voice that comes from the muscles under me. The rock solid chest where I am still resting my head on. The absolutely most comfortable pecs I have ever laid on. Oh my god, I am resting my head on a body and the said body spoke to me. Eros? No, it's not his voice. The tone is similar yet so much huskier. I blink my eyes quickly a few times and finally raise my head. Piercing green eyes stare back at me. A grin that the devil would be jealous of. This is definitely not a dream. I gasp and out of instinct, kick him out of bed. News flash, I did not want to kick him out of bed.

"Calm down, little ninja." He laughs while getting up. "Didn't mean to scare you. I was waiting for you to wake up." He adds.

"And you thought hugging me without my consent was the way to do it?" Now that I take a closer look at his face, he seems familiar. Do I know this guy from somewhere?

"Hold up, you're the one that decided to nestle in, I literally just came into the room, layed a moment to whisper your name and wake you up gently, and then you just—attacked me."

"Attack you? I was sleeping!"

"Your words against mine."

I prop myself up. "Who are you?" When he clears his voice, I jerk back, startled at the noise coming a few inches from my mouth.

"I am the man of your dreams."

My eyes go wide. Did he really just say what I think he just said?

"Settle down, it was a joke. I'm Dionisio, Eros' older brother," he adds in a fruity voice. An image of a younger Eros running around Forestiero with another kid plays in my head. It's him. I wonder why I haven't seen him for so long, haven't met him until now, yet, it feels so familiar being in front of him.

Standing at the edge of the bed, I look down at the floor, rubbing my eyes. I don't even know why I am still here. Where's my phone? I need to call Svetlana, maybe she can pick me up. I have to get to work.

"Dionisio? Like the pope?" I raise one eyebrow as I focus back on the man, trying to tease him. Did I just do that? He stops scratching his short dark beard and my eyes fall on his defined jawline. I feel like I am fighting the urge to trace it with my fingers. What is wrong with me?

His broad shoulders start jiggling up and down as he quirks

his eyebrows bursting out laughing. "Definitely not like the pope, sweetheart."

My legs wobble and I instinctively reach for the headboard to keep myself up. I bring my eyes down and stare at the bed. Eros' bed. Then, I look back up. I almost forget where I am because of these spring coloured eyes—concentrated on mine. The way he's looking at me—it's like I'm being seen for the first time. And his smell—a woody musky scent mixed with the balsamic, delicate, cool aroma of mint.

"Sure," I say as I roll my eyes, letting go of the headboard of the bed. Eros' bed.

"I'll let you change. I'll go see what my brother is doing," he says while he strolls toward the door.

He really is dangerously handsome with dark hair nicely collected into a bun and deep green eyes, a lighter shade than Eros and I share. Dionisio's eyes are the colour of the forest. A green so bright someone could think he was wearing contacts. It reminds me of the vivid hue of absinthe. I feel like I could get drunk from looking at his eyes. His tanned arms look even bigger than they are with the tight black t-shirt he is wearing.

His intoxicating smell is still all I can focus my attention on. He stops at the door and turns to look at me. His hand grips the frame, making a vein appear on his forearm.

"I'm Anima by the way, but I guess you already knew that," I say to Dionisio. He smirks at me. Again.

"I do, but it is still a pleasure," he replies before leaving the room.

I turn to the chair by the corner of the room and grab my clothes that have been neatly folded on it. I fit into my skinny blue jeans and gray t-shirt that was now magically clean and steal a glance at the mirror on top of Eros' dresser, then mess with my hair until it looks acceptable. Walking to the door, I hear a whispered conversation. It must be Eros and his brother. I smile to myself, remembering last night.

He kissed me.

He fought a creature that I didn't think could exist, told me I am a *striga* and then kissed me.

I can't wait to tell Svetlana. About the kiss at least. For now.

"D, thank you for coming, but it's—unnecessary." I hear Eros whisper to his brother from the living room. I shouldn't eavesdrop, but I feel I shouldn't interrupt them, mostly because I have no idea how to approach Eros especially after waking up with his brother in my personal space.

"Brother, you know I would do anything for you. For her," Dionisio replies to him with a pat on the shoulder.

"And I'm telling you we're fine." Eros's voice is low, firm, and tight.

"I'm not going anywhere. You need me. I am here to help."

"Dad sent you, didn't he?" I hear him sigh. "Unbelievable."

"Did you tell her yet?"

Tell me what? I guess this is the moment where I get out of this bedroom and see what they're talking about. *Come on Anima, grow a pair of balls and get out of here.* I pace up and down the bedroom, rubbing my palms on my thighs, I take a deep breath in and finally grab the door handle.

"She was already freaked out enough from finding out she's a striga and being attacked by an Opacum. I didn't think it was the right time to tell her she's my soulmate and that we have to get married too, you know."

"Fair enough."

His *what*? Marriage? Ok, now it really is time to leave.

My heart tingles in my chest followed by an arising sense of nausea. Can I get out of here without having to face them? I wonder if I can jump from the window—if I can make it down without breaking every single bone in my body. I open the window and look down. Definitely not ideal. We are on the third floor, I would probably not make it in one piece. I desperately rest my back on the wall trying to stay up as if I'm not able to get enough oxygen in my system to remain awake, vigilant.

Would it be that terrible to find out Eros is my soulmate? I have been crushing over him since I got back, and maybe that's why I always feel the need to go to Forestiero. Maybe this is the answer. The thought isn't too comforting at the moment, my heart is still racing, my fingers tremble on the door handle. I have to leave, right now.

I finally step out of the bedroom and drag myself into the living room, unsure of what awaits me. Pull yourself together, Anima, maybe they were just speaking in code, take your phone and leave.

"Good morning, Anima," Eros utters as soon as he sees me approach them. He gently brushes his hands through his auburn hair, which looks fiery in the morning light. His eyes lock with mine and for a moment I forget how to speak. I turn towards the figure beside him and see a smirking Dionisio leaned against the kitchen counter with his arms crossed on his chest. If Eros is handsome, Dionisio is godlike. He is—a mountain. Wide shoulders, flat chest, I could literally envision the six-pack through his skin tight shirt, the fabric doing very little to conceal the rigid lines of muscle. And those arms—he definitely doesn't skip arm day. Or leg day. Or cardio. This guy lives at the gym. Artists would pay big money to draw his features and try to paint his perfect tanned skin. The juxtaposition between his skin and his eyes is absolutely jaw dropping.

"Good Morning Eros." I turn to Dionisio, "Nice to see you're still here." Dionisio chuckles as his brother narrows his eyes at him.

"I'm so sorry about him," Eros says to me, before adding, "Dionisio is a complete idiot and it won't ever happen again. He snuck into the bedroom without me noticing, and that absolutely won't happen again." He brushes his hand on my arm. I instinctively flinch. Not good.

"Sorry guys, I need to run to the studio like now," I say quickly as I look away. "I forgot I had two shoots this morning. I will see you when I see you." I walk towards the door but Dionisio walks between the door and me.

"You can't leave," he says. His voice is firm, low, monotone.

"Yes, I can. I have to, I have a job, bills to pay," I reply, my voice stiff.

I need to leave because I don't know if I am ok with finding out that your brother is my soulmate.

Dionisio's cold stare suddenly softens, and his crossed arms relax. "I realize what you found out yesterday is a lot to wrap your head around, but we need to talk about this."

"Who, me and you?" I ask. "Or me and my soulmate?" I glare at Eros, who rubs a hand over his face.

"Shit. You heard us."

"Yeah, well, you aren't the spies you believe you are."

"Anima, you weren't supposed to find out this way." Eros curses under his breath.

I turn towards him, my posture rigid, my jaw locked. How can I even believe something like this? I can barely grasp onto the idea of the existence of magical creatures. "I don't know what I heard, but I don't have time for explanations. I need to get out of here."

"Anima, you just found out you're a striga and got attacked. We need to talk about this," Eros says, scratching the back of his neck.

"Sure, later. Now I am going to walk out that door. It's the middle of the day, and I need to process all this and go do my job," I reply, raising my tone, voice cracking. His eyes go wide.

"Let me at least walk you to the studio."

"No, please, no."

"You can't be alone right now."

My chest grows tighter and tighter, his concerned look a reminder of the kiss we shared last night.

"I definitely can. Svetlana is waiting for me at the studio," I utter in a cold voice.

Eros takes a step closer. "You can't tell her about any of this, please, let us explain first."

I take a step back, scared by the angry sneer on his face. Then, feeling the prickle of anger moving up my spine, I spit back, "You know what? If what you say is true, then let me fucking process it. Let me process everything that happened in the last 24 hours."

"How about we take a deep breath and find a compromise," Dionisio says in a ringing kind of way. I forgot he was still in the room.

"What do you mean?" I raise an eyebrow at him.

"I mean that I have to go to Forestiero to talk to my *zia*, I'll just walk behind you, far enough that you won't even know I'm there. It's on the way, right?" He smiles. "Then I'll continue walking once you've entered your building. Easy." Dionisio offers, giving me the biggest smile I've ever seen.

"I guess that can be arranged." I crinkle my nose.

"I don't like this," Eros whispers under his breath.

"Great, let's accidentally walk together." Dionisio starts pacing towards the front entrance. I turn back at Eros. He's now leaning his back against the side of his enormous bookshelf. "You process it however you need to process it, but please don't shut me out. We're in this together. You're not alone," he says with a heavy sigh.

My heart twists as I notice his distraught expression. His eyes locked on mine. I kill the desire to run to him that suddenly fills every pore of my skin.

"I'll see you later, Eros," I quickly reply. Am I really going to see him later? How about a one-way ticket to Tibet? That sounds way more inviting right now.

With an understanding nod from him, I leave the apartment with his brother. His godlike brother with an addicting smell. My supposed soulmate's brother. How ironic life is. Is it too early for a joint?

PART TWO

A Vision Will bring Transition

CHAPTER 8

"I swear I don't bite," Dionisio says, "Unless you want me to, of course."

I look up at him, on the other side of the street. Every time he walks closer, I switch to the other side, maintaining the same safe distance between us. My fists clench at the thought of Eros and the discussion we had, or better, that I heard him have with Dionisio.

"I'm sorry, I just feel—I don't even know what I feel." And it's true, I don't know what I am supposed to feel and I don't know what is really happening. Maybe I am going crazy, or I might have surrounded myself with nutcases. As we both stop walking, we stare at each other. Dionisio tilts his head, his eyes are on me as if he could sense the frustration in my rigid posture, my tight jaw, my clenched fists. Surrounding us are people walking up and down, minding their own business. People going about their day, probably rushing to work, dropping off their kids to school, some are gesticulating while arguing on the phone, some are speed walking while eating a slice of focaccia. Now that would be good right now.

I breathe in and breathe out, trying to calm my fast beating heart while Dionisio stands there, his arms crossed over his chest and a weird look on his face, like he's trying to read me.

"You aren't supposed to feel a certain emotion, Anima, you can feel whatever you want. Anger, confusion, pain, all of it, or nothing." He stops and sighs. "No one but yourself knows what you're going through, but just know that you're not alone in any of this."

Dionisio's words make my shoulders relax. As weirdly as it sounds, I believe him. Not making me feel anything I don't want to feel, no pressure, just being there for me. Not many people in my life knew how oppressed I can feel when being pushed into feeling something. Without even knowing it, Dionisio gave me the one reason to believe his words, to trust him.

He's being sincere, with me, basically a stranger. Maybe Eros is as well, they're brothers after all, and Dionisio obviously trusts his own brother. How can I believe that what he said is true? That we're soulmates?

We arrive in front of my studio and the question just bursts out of me, "How can Eros be so sure he's my soulmate?"

Dionisio stiffens up. "The prophecy says he is."

"What prophecy? The one from the book?"

"Anima, you wanted a free morning from this, from us. I suggest you take it because you will be seeing us a lot from now on."

I look around while threading my fingers through my wavy frizzy hair. "What if I don't want any of this?"

"It's in your blood. You want this, you just don't know what this is yet. You will."

"You're not going to tell me more, are you?"

"And deprive myself from seeing you learn it all little by little? I could never."

I roll my eyes at him, even if the silky sound of his voice plays in my head over and over again like a chant, like a catchy tune that you hear on the radio. I shake my head and turn towards the studio door, ready to unlock it.

Dionisio gently grasps my arm before I go inside. "Before I let you go, Eros asked me to give you this." He hands me a ring. "Keep it on at all times, and we will be able to track you down if you're in danger."

I have never believed in anything remotely close to soulmates. The ring is probably bogus as well because how can it be magical? How can any of this be real?

"What else does this ring allow you to track?" I ask before quickly adding, "Will you be able to know where I am at all times?"

"No, that's not how it works, it only works when the person wearing it is in danger." He lifts his hand up showing me the same exact band on his index finger.

"You're wearing it too."

"I am. Eros as well."

"And how would you know if I am in danger?"

"Trust me, we'll know." He walks away from me, then stops all of a sudden. As a light wind caresses my cheeks and brings his cedarwood scent right to my nose, I breathe in and let it fill my nostrils.

"Anima," he calls. His husky voice seems to be stuck in my head. *Don't get into trouble.* He gives me a quick wink and then resumes his walk towards the bookstore. Did I just imagine him telling me not to get into trouble? I am going insane.

I open my firmly closed palm and look down at the thin gold band. Well, at least it's not an ugly, huge gothic ring with an enormous fake gem. I take the band in my right hand and start trying to slip it until I find the right finger for it. My left index one. Looks cute. I know it won't save my life, but at least it's stylish.

I start my day as I usually do. The lights are on, the computer is on, but my brain is off. I can't focus. All I can think of is Eros—what I heard him say to Dionisio. Could he really be what he thinks he is—to me? Does this mean that my dream actually has a bigger meaning? I hate this feeling of the unknown. It feels as if I am swimming in the middle of the ocean and the current of the water pulls me into the deep end. I try to swim towards the shore but I just end up farther and farther away from it. I'm just there trying to keep breathing, keep my head above water, begging for someone to come and save me. I am here waiting for a ghost to show up at my doorstep.

Through different Eyes, a vision will bring transition. An unbreakable bond. Was that what that prophecy said? Maybe the prophecy refers to Eros and my eyes, since they became the same. An unbreakable bond. I guess that would be the 'soulmates' part. I need to read the prophecy again.

I text Svetlana not to come in today and tell her we will hangout later so I can go to my apartment and grab the book without worrying about explaining anything to anyone. I don't even know what I would be explaining. I quickly close the studio and go up the stairs towards my house.

I get to my front door, get inside and quickly look for the book; I find it where I left it, on my bed. A big old red leather book full of rubbish.

Mom would have laughed at all this. Just like me, she was skeptical about, well, everything. She needed visual proof, or in her eyes, it wasn't real. My dad, though, was a dreamer. Gosh, I miss them. I guess I should be upset in finding out that the only true thing about my life is that I was adopted. A heavy sigh escapes my mouth. I bite my lips subconsciously to the point of feeling iron on my tongue until the pain overtakes my anger. It's what I seem to be doing a little too often lately to calm myself down.

I close the door behind me, and start walking down the stairs towards my studio again but my feet don't stop moving. I feel as if a force is pulling me towards something. My body proceeds on autopilot. I continue walking. Towards what? I don't know. I walk and walk. I turn to a small crossroad of Via Aprosio, it's a narrow pathway, not much sun comes through here, the sea is behind me. The temperature here seems a few degrees lower than the open busier street I just left. Then, I suddenly stop in front of a door. A big dark wooden door. My guts pulled me in front of a big dark wooden door. It's in a smaller street in the insides of town. Not much light seems to be passing through here. Cars also can't possibly drive by, the street is so narrow only pedestrians can walk through it. A cold breeze makes me shiver. I suddenly turn towards my right, feeling a presence close by. Nothing. Then I turn to my left. Nothing again.

"You are going crazy, Anima," I say to myself out loud. No one is here. It's just me.

I turn towards the door again. Why am I so interested in a closed door? Could this be the entry to *Forestiero*'s warehouse? I turn the nob, and with a click, it opens. The door is unlocked. Would it really be that bad if I were to sneak in and look around? Probably. I still cross the entrance and close the door behind me.

I turn towards the dark room, blindly looking for a light switch beside the door I just entered. As soon as the space is lit, I notice a corridor made of bookshelves that points to another door at the other side of the room. Big metal bookshelves completely filled by tomes. I could spend hours here looking at the inventory.

The door at the end is big, the top is arched. The colour reminds me of blood, a deep red just like the leather book that Ginevra gave me. I pace towards it, determined to turn the knob and see what's behind it. I grab the golden ball that is the door handle and try to twist it. Nothing. It is obviously locked.

"This was way easier than I expected it to be." A low voice whispers in my right ear. This is not good. A sudden sting fills the back of my head as my vision unfocuses. Really? Here we are less than 24 hours later.

Yup, I am going to pass out again.

CHAPTER 9

I have to stop waking up like this. Where the hell am I? Am I still at the warehouse? I can't recognize anything around me. Nothing is around me. No windows. No shelves. I had to be brought in here from somewhere, where's the door? Probably behind me. As I try to lift my arms up and move my legs, I realize I am tied up to a chair.

Ok, that's it, this is the day I die. Holy fuck, I'm not even wearing cute underwear. Where's Eros? As I try to speak out loud, my throat closes on me, making it harder to breathe. I close my fists and as I do so, my thumb rubs against the ring on my index finger. Why would I believe a ring on my finger would magically make them know where I am? Of course they have no clue. Maybe they are even behind all this. It would be quite ironic, wouldn't it?

"Trying to talk won't do you any good."

The low guttural voice sends shivers down my spine. A figure with no eyes appears in front of me. A layer of skin covered their eye sockets just like—just like the one Eros fought last night. This is—an Opacum. The creature gets down on one knee and then tilts his head down, is he—bowing to me? With the sleeves of his black shirt rolled up, he rests his forearm on his bent knee, that's when I notice the scars covering his skin. They are of every length. Some are cuts, some are burns. Some older, some fresher.

I attempt to get words out again, but the same needle reappears in my throat and makes it impossible to vocalize anything. I'm completely mute. Voiceless. Silent.

"Your highness, the master will be so pleased to have you back," the Opacum whispers in my ear. My posture goes rigid as I try to lean away from his cold breath and a chuckle escapes from its thin lips. Then, a flash blinds me for a moment. The motherfucker just took a picture—of me. Is this some sort of a sick joke? If I had any sort of sympathy towards this man after seeing his scars, it now was completely gone. Forgotten. Never existed.

As I start to think of an escape plan, the door barges open and two silhouettes emerge on the other side of it. It takes me a second to focus on them. The light coming from the opening is so strong compared to the darkness of this room. Eros and Dionisio are right here, in front of me. Their heavy breathing makes me think they ran here. They came to me as they told me they would. The Opacum disappears as soon as he sees and locks eyes with them and realizes who's in front of us.

Eros's fists clench as a growl comes out of him. He's ready to follow the Opacum, the only thing bringing him back to the room —to me, is his brother's hand on his shoulder. His body relaxes as Dionisio's grip tightens. Eros's eyes now search for mine.

"Anima, can you stop putting yourself in danger? I have other things to do, you know," Dionisio's musky voice echoes in my ears.

You're going to make me worry non stop, aren't you?

I turn towards Dionisio with a sudden fluttering in my stomach, and he exchanges my look with a raised eyebrow. Did he say that? Or did I imagine it?

I try to open my mouth, but the words seem to still be trapped. Eros falls on his knees in front of me, his eyes analyzing my physical state, his eyebrows drawing together as he brushes chunks of hair out of my face. He rests his hands on my cheeks and his body tenses while he tries to focus on what's happening to me.

"Anima, can you talk?" I lower my head, a tear escapes my eye, then shake my head lightly with defeat.

"A silencing spell. Classic," Dionisio utters as he walks towards the door behind me and turns on the light. This room—it looks like an interrogation room from a horror movie. Dark gray walls, no windows. Just me in the middle of it still tied to a chair.

Eros looks at me, then he places his left index finger on my mouth. "Loquere!" "You're—you're here," I am finally able to say. My eyes go wide with the realization that the knot in my throat is finally gone. I can't take my eyes off of Eros. He tries to stabilize his breathing as his nostrils continue to flare. His eyes are still looking around me to make sure I am ok until they finally stop and lock on mine. His shoulders drop and his look softens for just a moment.

"Everything is clear. The warehouse seems empty. No magic trace left either. Glad to hear your voice again, little ninja," Dionisio says, breaking the moment of tension as he….

"I'm here—we're here." Eros whispers in a low voice. Is he worried? Angry? His stare is cold and his posture stiff once again. He's trying to suppress his anger. An ocean is preparing for a storm to explode out of him. His breathing picks up again as he clenches and unclenches his hands, moving up and down the room.

"Eros, look at her." Dionisio's voice, making Eros turn to me. "She's fine. Everything is fine."

Eros turns to his brother, his eyes cold on him. "Everything is not fine, D. Whoever is trying to hurt her will pay for it."

"Yes, they will, we will make sure of it."

"I will make sure of it." Eros' words were final. Then he was on his knees again, avoiding my stare.

"Thank you," I just say while he unties me and helps me get up. He gives me a quick nod before he says that we have to leave right away.

As soon as we get out of the building, I feel the sun caress my face. I inhale deeply, then exhale. Finally able to breathe fully again. The sun is strong, the little side road now doesn't seem so cold and moldy. I hug myself finally able to move freely. My wrists still show the red sign of the ropes that kept me immobilized. As I brush a hand on it, I feel the indent of the skin under my fingertips. A light sting followed my immediate pleasure. I turn my body towards the direction I just came out from. The same big dark wooden door as earlier is staring back at me. "So this is the warehouse?"

A small grin appears on Eros' face. "This is the warehouse." His hand lies on the middle of my back, and he keeps it there, never leaving me untouched. I swallow some air at the gentle gesture. His posture is looser and his breathing is normal again. I feel his fingers moving up and down, caressing my body. I wish I could feel his hands on my skin, no clothes in between. Feel that this is real, that I am real, that what I just experienced was real because if I let myself believe so, then I have to accept the fact that what Eros and Ginevra told me is also the truth.

"It seemed so much darker before—the street I mean" I say, touching my head. A way too familiar sting rises as I put a small pressure on the back of it. Great, I did hit it again.

"You might see it as sunnier now because you're readjusting

to natural lighting. Anima, are you ok?" Dionisio asks as he stops walking.

"Yeah no I'm good, just dizzy I guess."

His lips form a tight line., but he doesn't ask anymore questions. That doesn't mean I won't ask any though.

"It was the same thing that attacked me last night, wasn't it?"

"Yes, it was an Opacum," Dionisio replies, looking shortly at me, then back to the road in front of us.

I shiver at the confirmation.

"We're gonna get to your building and I'll take a look at your head, ok? We're almost there," Eros says, tightening his hold on me, my stiff shoulders relaxing in his embrace.

We arrive at my apartment, and we don't dare to say a word to each other until we get inside and I shut the door. Dionisio quickly closes the distance between us and turns the lock without taking his eyes off of mine. I almost feel violated by the way he's looking at me. His absinthe eyes hypnotize mine until he harshly turns to Eros and walks towards him, leaving me there, my back against the door.

"What the hell were you thinking? You could have died, Anima!" Dionisio's breathing is heavy. His raised voice feels rough, thick. A knife through the stomach. He's clearly upset.

I'm livid.

I stay on my spot, petrified, because I honestly don't know how to respond. I have no idea what's happening around me anymore. First, they tell me I'm a striga and that I come from another world, a magical one and give me this big red book to prove it. Then I get followed and hit on the head. Then I wake up in Eros' arms after he fights off who knows what. Then I faint again because of course I faint again. Then I wake up in his apartment and fall asleep in his bed after we kiss. Then I wake up with his fucking brother beside me and then guess what? I get hit on the head again when I decide to go for a walk.. What the hell is going on in my life?

Eros glares at his brother. "Ok, no need to yell at her."

"Really?" Dionisio continues with the same tone. "You're worried about me raising my voice?" Eros shakes his head in defeat and turns his attention back to me. "Why were you at the warehouse, Anima?"

"I—I didn't even know that was the warehouse."

"Fuck," Dionisio swears under his breath.

"Besides—I kinda felt dragged there," I add to my previous statement.

"Dragged?" They both ask at the same time as their eyes widen.

"Yes, dragged, like my body moved on its own."

"Did you—try to open the red door?" Eros' question surprises me.

"I did."

"Did it open?" Dionisio asks.

"It was locked."

They shortly look at each other and then Eros walks towards me and takes my hand, pulling me off the door. "You have to be careful where you walk, Anima. You don't know how to defend yourself—yet."

"Guys, I walk around town every day, and all this weird stuff started happening after Ginevra gave me that stupid book, so I am sorry if I don't know where the hell I can go anymore." I say with my chin high.

"You're right. We should have told you to be more careful, but you will be free to walk as usual very soon. After your training," Dionisio replies.

"My training? What? I do not train, I stay inside and read books. I don't want to train, I can't, and I don't need to." Now I gotta fight people too? No, thanks.

"I have specific orders, Anima." Dionisio crosses his arms on his chest.

"What is that supposed to mean?"

"Don't you want to find out what you're capable of with your magic?" Eros asks.

Curiosity takes the best of me even if I know what they're saying is impossible, but I also don't want to end up facing another faceless being—ever.

"Oh right, magic… Because I should have some sort of powers… Right… Forgot about that part…" I say with a chuckle. "So what type of powers would I have?" Raising an eyebrow at them.

The words of the Opacum come back to me.

Your highness, the master will be so pleased to have you back.

Dionisio tilts his head slightly on the side. "Well, you specifically should have an attitude of mind control and telekinesis as active powers. I wonder if you can read minds. Now that would be a discovery. Did anyone say anything to you while you were there?" He asks me with a grin on his face. His look is penetrating, it feels as if he knows what was said to me.

"How did you—never mind. Yeah, the Opacum said something about someone being pleased to have me back… and I think he took a picture of me. He called me your highness," I tell them.

"Did he, now…" Dionisio says under his breath.

"Can we go back to the reading mind part again for a second? Is it really possible?" Is that what I heard earlier? Dionisio's thoughts?

"For you, it could be a possibility, one that I've never heard of before. Usually mind reading is done with a spell, I've never heard of a striga or veneficus being able to do it on their own," Eros tells me brushing his hand up and down my biceps.

"I don't know, Anima seems pretty unique to me," Dionisio adds with a wink.

Eros shakes his head at his brother. "What we're pretty sure about is that you can move objects and manipulate thoughts." He says to me.

"I—I can manipulate thoughts? Like compulsion?" My eyes go wide. "That's insane. I don't want to do that. That's so—evil."

"It can be, if used by the wrong person, but you Anima, you are good." Eros tells me.

"Opacums, dark wizards, know your powers and want you." Dionisio starts.

"There's someone that clearly doesn't want the prophecy to be fulfilled." Eros continues. "Someone that doesn't want our dream to become reality."

Our dream. Not just mine, ours.

"So the person the Opacum was talking about, do we know who it is? He called them his master."

"Unfortunately no, we don't" Eros takes a seat on my couch and I follow him. My legs feel weak, numb as I rest my back on the soft cushion.

"We will find out soon though, we have people searching everywhere." Dionisio lays his back on the wall across from us, keeping his distance—his eyes always on me.

"So the man in my dreams is a real person that needs real help —you." My eyes meet Eros's.

Dionisio begins walking toward the door. "I guess this is my que to leave you two alone."

"Maybe I should come with," Eros says as he turns to look at his brother.

"No, it's cool. Make sure she's good, I'll go update the guards on what happened tonight." Dionisio gives me a quick nod and leaves the studio.

Only once he's gone do I realize my heart was beating much too quickly, and it's now back to a regular rhythm.

Eros brushes a chunk of hair out of my face as he moves

closer. He studies my head, making sure there are no new wounds.

"I think I'm fine." I look up to his eyes, they seem wet, lucid. His stare checking around me. I rest my hand on his cheek and the sudden skin contact makes him close his eyes for a moment and sigh. With that he finally stops worrying about my head as his eyes land on mine. He's obviously concerned, and I don't know what to do about it. I don't know what to do about any of this.

"Are you really?" He finally asks.

I replay what we just talked about in my head and get back to it. "The prophecy I read in the book—"

"We don't have to talk about it now, Anima." He stops me.

"If we don't start talking about it, I might actually implode."

He sighs. *"Through different Eyes, a vision will bring transition. An unbreakable bond,"* He recites.

"Through different eyes. Our eyes."

"Yes."

"A vision—the dream?"

"Yes, yet again."

"An unbreakable bond. We are the unbreakable bond."

"Yes."

"Are you going to stop replying with a monosyllabic answer?"

"Anima, this morning was already eventful enough, I don't want to bring more of this to you before you're ready for it."

"Are you going to tell me why my eyes were different until now?"

"The glamour was put on you a long time ago to protect you."

"That's all you're going to say, really?"

"No, of course I will tell you everythi—" Eros stops at the sound of my phone ringing on the coffee table.

I sigh, looking at the screen lighting up. "That's probably Svetlana wondering why I'm not at the studio."

"Remember, don't tell Svetlana anything, yet."

I don't like keeping things from Svetlana. I don't like when people ask me to specifically keep things from Svetlana. I don't protest though. I understand his concerns and just nod.

"Thank you for the ring, by the way, I guess it really does work," I say, trying to change the subject. His eyes are narrowed as he stares at me. He looks down and takes my hand into his. I can see his lips rising into a smile.

"I would have preferred to be the one giving it to you, but I am glad he didn't wait—considering the circumstances," he says as he plays with the thin band on my finger making it rotate around it.

"I'm sorry."

"What did I tell you about apologizing?" He is only a couple of inches away from me now, and I can smell his citrusy cologne and feel his breath on my skin. I can't tell if I am getting high from being this close to him or if I'm still feeling lightheaded from the encounter with the Opacum. My legs wobble and I instinctively wrap my arms around his neck and he takes no time to wrap his around my waist and pulls me closer.

"This—this might take me a while to accept." Words come out of my mouth without me even realizing it.

"Wasn't planning to go anywhere, anytime soon." A grin appears on his face, and I can't stop staring at his mouth. Staring at his perfect lips and remembering how they felt on mine the other night. As if he could hear my thoughts, he crushes his lips on mine and our mouths finally connect again. My heart beats so fast in my chest as his tongue wettens my lips before sliding in. Tears come streaming down my face as I bring him closer and closer to me. My embrace tightens as if I am worried he could slip away at any second. As if this is all a dream and I am going to wake up at any moment and not find him there.

"Everything will be ok, Anima. I am right here." His thumb

catches the tear trailing down my cheek. We close the distance between us once more, like a promise being sealed.

"I'll let you get back to what you were doing. No more wandering around for the day, please. I need to see if Dionisio and the guards have found any leads on who is behind these attacks."

"I'll keep the excitement down. Got it."

"Thank you." He kisses my forehead before walking towards the door.

"Will I see you later?"

"I have a lot more to explain, if you'll let me."

"I'd like that."

"Then I'll knock at your door as soon as I am back." With that, he gives me a last good look before heading out the studio.

Maybe he is right. Maybe everything will be ok. He's right here and I'll be ok.

CHAPTER 10

Svetlana got to the studio about an hour ago, and I barely talked to her since she stepped a foot inside. I've been too nervous to say even a word because I know she will know I'm hiding something right away. She knows I'm keeping stuff from her. She can tell—I know she can.

"Are we going to pretend you weren't at Eros's place last night?"

"No…"

"Ok, good, because being the supportive friend that doesn't ask questions is getting old and I need to know everything."

"We—we kissed." My eyes don't leave the screen of the computer while my stomach does a double backflip.

"Go on."

"That's all."

"You spent the entire night at this drop dead gorgeous guy's place after he's been drooling all over you for months and you just—kissed?"

"Just kissed."

"Was it a good kiss, at least?"

"It—it was. The one earlier today was much better, though."

"Ok, now we're talking!" She wiggles in her seat, clapping her hands in approval. The corners of her lips lift up forming one of the biggest smiles she's given me in a long time. Crazy what my possible sex life can do to my best friend.

"Also, I probably should mention that we just kissed because his brother showed up."

"This is the beginning of a smut romance."

"Svetlana!"

"What! You clearly thought the same thing." She giggled, clapping her hands rapidly.

"No, I did not. Dionisio is—well... I can't really say much about the guy."

"So, he's even hotter, interesting."

"He's definitely easy on the eye." I look at her quickly before going back to my computer.

"So he's a god, got it."

I mean, she's not wrong.

"You're absolutely unbelievable." A chuckle leaves my mouth.

"I know, and you love me for it. Now, how do you feel about the kiss—es?"

"I—I don't know Svet..."

"No, don't start with the self sabotage talk. You have been eye fucking for so long. Don't give up on something that could make you happy."

"He is very caring." Caring? Is that all I can come up with? Really?

"I bet he is."

"I just—" I'm absolutely terrified about the entire situation, but I can't tell you about it because I don't even understand it and it kills me to keep secrets from you. That's what's up.

"What?"

"I have to be careful."

"Of course you have to be careful. And you will be careful—you'll make him wear a condom." Waving me off, she continues, "You'll be fine."

"You know what I mean."

"Yes, I do. I'm right here, babe. If he hurts you, I will melt him in acid."

We get back to our editing. She's right, I deserve this. I deserve someone that cares about me and is there for me. Even if this someone told me I am a witch and he is a wizard trying to make me remember my forgotten past so that I can go back to the place I belong to and save my people.

"Your eyes look different. Are you wearing contacts?"

I hate it when she's observant.

"Do they?" I tilt my head, trying to hide away. "No contacts."

"Yes." She leans forward, only inches from my face, taking a closer look. "How is it possible that in seventeen years of knowing you, I've never noticed you have heterochromia? Something is up, Anima."

"My eyes have been bothering me much less, actually. Maybe it's a good thing that they look different. As long as the itch and burn are gone, I am ok with anything."

"Sure." She can tell I'm hiding something. I can tell by the way her shoulders are stiff, her lips stretched in a thin line. She's trying with every fiber of her body not to ask more questions. It's killing her, and she's obviously worried about me, but she knows that pushing me to talk won't get her anywhere.

"He's coming over later," I say, trying to change the subject.

"Who—Eros?" A light sparks in her eyes.

"Yes."

"Can't get enough of you, I like that. I'm gonna have to talk to him about visitation rights."

"You will always come first," I try to reassure her.

"Of course, I always come first! I wouldn't want it any other way." She winks at me.

"You're unbelievable." I jokingly slap her on the shoulder, making her giggle.

She goes back looking at the screen, and I do the same, noticing her glances from time to time, her finger tapping nervously on the desk.

"Is everything ok, Svet?" I ask her. Her teeth biting her bottom lip ready to say something, but then she doesn't.

She smiles lightly, then shakes her head. "Everything is good, I just want you to be happy."

I GOT TO MY APARTMENT ABOUT TWO HOURS AGO, HAD SOME dinner and now I am sitting on my couch with my legs crossed and my heart racing at 100 beats a second while waiting for Eros to knock on my damn door. Frustrated, I get up and grab the book Ginevra gave me, The Royal textbook of Dusäiga and continue reading. I turn the pages until I get to a part that talks about a power that hasn't been witnessed in a while.

SUSPIRIUM IS ONE OF THE RAREST POWERS THAT IS SAID TO BE PRESENT IN THE PSICHE FAMILY, THE ROYAL BLOODLINE, AND PASSED DOWN FROM GENERATION TO GENERATION. IT APPEARS WHEN THE STRIGA OR VENEFICUS HAVE A UNIQUE AFFINITY WITH COMPULSION. SUSPIRIUM OR THE WHISPER IS THE CAPACITY OF MIND TALKING. A STRIGA OR VENEFICUS WITH THIS POWER CAN

SEND MESSAGES THROUGH THEIR MIND WITHOUT SPEAKING A WORD.

I check the time—almost 10pm. Maybe he's not coming over. Perhaps something happened when he went to do who knows what after he left the studio, and he can't even let me know because he doesn't have my number.

As I mumble a curse word, a buzz comes from the coffee table. I just got a text from an unknown number.

UNKNOWN:

On our way, little ninja. - D

D? Who's D? Dionisio? How the hell did he get my number when not even his brother has it?

ANIMA:

Drop the pet name. How the hell did you get my number?

DIONISIO:

I have my ways, little ninja. Being angry suits you.

Here I thought the night was going to be pleasant. Looks like I was wrong.

ANIMA:

Just get here.

DIONISIO:

As you wish.

At that moment, I hear a knock on my door. No wait, on my window? There they are, waiting for me to open the screen door of my balcony.

How did they come up from there? Did they fly?

Eros wanted to make a theatrical entrance, Dionisio says to me, making me smile. But he didn't say it. He's not even looking at me while I walk towards the screen door. He's talking to his brother. Did I just imagine that?

Dionisio turns towards mine. His eyes widen. Shock fills his stare. We fixate on each other for a couple of seconds before we break the stare and go back to what we were doing. I definitely imagined that, there's no way I heard him say something with his mind.

"First of all, I have a front door." I gesture at them to get inside. "Second of all, when do I get to do that?"

"Good evening to you too, Anima," Eros says, dropping his head towards mine. His lips quickly touch mine and I forget everything surrounding us. His sudden embrace tightens around my waist and my hands rest on his chest. I can feel his heartbeat through my palm. It's so calming.

Of course, Dionisio's voice echoes in my head. His jaw is tense and clenched as my head snaps towards him.

Get out of my head. He's clearly playing games with me and I don't like it. I don't like it at all.

Get out of mine! His voice again fills my head, no words come out of his mouth. He rubs the back of his neck with a scowl on his face.

"Hi," I somehow manage to say to Eros. "What is *he* doing here?"

"He insisted on tagging along. Don't worry he'll be on his way very soon." Eros reassures me with a grin on his face.

"Don't sound too ecstatic to have me around," Dionisio utters.

"Maybe you should take the hint." I don't even know how the words come out of my mouth. I clearly didn't want to be that harsh. I am not this harsh. Not when—nevermind.

I would prefer to be anywhere else, trust me. Dionisio's words appear in my head again.

How are you doing this? I ask.

I have no idea, and I don't enjoy having you in my head either.

His reply is cold and I can tell he's wildly frustrated. He's doing everything in his power not to look at me. Earlier when we were walking alone, he seemed like such a different person. Calm, serene, protective. Now he's completely avoiding my stare and his posture is so rigid I feel he could compete at a statue contest.

We should—

Do not say anything yet. No need to worry him with this. Let me ask around first. He doesn't even let me finish my thought. Maybe he's right. Maybe I should learn more about this world before saying anything to anyone out loud.

One thing is certain—knowing that Dionisio can hear me without me having to say anything is something that doesn't affect me the way it should be. I feel relieved at the connection between us. Like I have a cushion to rely on if everything else should fail. Like I won't be judged about anything ever again.

You're safe now, Anima.

"Are you ok?" Eros asks as he cups my shoulder.

"Yes—sorry." I shake my head. "I just went somewhere for a moment."

"As long as you're ok." His lips brush my forehead.

With that, I let them sit down in my living room. Eros and I are beside each other on the couch facing my tv, while Dionisio is spread over the loveseat close to the wall of books.

I wonder if the power I read about earlier has something to do with this.

What power? Dionisio's eyes widen.

"Do you know anything about suspirium?" I suddenly ask Eros.

"I see you were doing some reading." His lips turn into a grin.

"I was reading that it's a power that is passed down to the royal family."

"It is. It has also not been seen in almost a century though. It's more like a legend," Eros adds.

"No one else could have it?" My eyes lock with his.

Eros grabs my hands in his. "Anima, you are royal."

"Wait, what?"

"That's why the Opacum called you your Highness," Dionisio adds to his brother's statement.

"How is that possible? I—I am not royal."

"This is what I was trying to tell you earlier, about the glamour as well. It was put on you to protect you until it was time. You are the last of your bloodline."

Maybe that's what's happening with Dionisio, maybe it's the suspirium power. Maybe that's what happened with Svetlana earlier.

You could have it, but I wouldn't be able to reply to you.

"This is insane." I'm going insane.

No, you're not.

Stop that. My head snaps towards Dionisio. My eyes are wide.

Hey, it's hard! He simply replies. A soft grin appears on his face. He doesn't appear so irritated anymore.

It is. I'm sorry.

Why are you apologizing, now? Dionisio's head is slightly tilted.

I don't know. A sigh leaves my lips and I turn back to Eros.

"Should we talk about the book and the—prophecy? The part we didn't talk about earlier."

"Do you feel ready for it?" Eros's words play back into my head a couple of times. Am I really ready to listen to a semi-stranger telling me we are destined to be together. Again.

"Ready? I never will be, but I need to know."

"All right." Dionisio and Eros say in unison.

I grab the book that is on the coffee table—The Royal Textbook of Dusäiga. My hands caress the spine, I bring the book to my nose and smell it. I love the smell of old books, but this one? This one smelled like a drug. Old parchment paper mixed with burns and ink. The more I hold it in my hands, the more I can't stop looking at it.

"Why do I feel so drawn to it?."

Eros starts. "You feel drawn to it because it is part of you."

"You're doing it again."

"What am I doing?" Eros asks as his brows bend over his eyes..

"Being cryptic," I say. I close my eyes and bring my index fingers to my temple to massage them.

Dionisio laughs. "Forgive him, he does that a lot."

"The Royal Textbook was—is yours. It belongs to the royal family. It's one of the most important volumes. That, and the Book of Souls, but that was lost a while back."

"Ah yes, I almost forgot about that part... what are you then?"

"We are part of the family that works—worked with yours for centuries."

"Your family and ours lived at Court for a long time. Your family ruled while ours advised your parents. Our father was your father's right hand."

"Where are they now?"

"Your biological parents went missing seventeen years ago," Eros starts explaining.

"That is when my parents—adopted me."

"Mirella and Giorgio were close friends of your biological parents."

"This is a lot." Nausea hits me. I get up and walk towards the sink to grab a glass of water. How could they do this to me? Lie to me about all this? Did they even care about me or was I just—an assignment to them?

"It is. We can stop." Dionisio's voice rises out of the blue. I look in his direction and I notice his hands closed into fists resting on his lap, his head tilted down trying very hard not to catch my gaze.

"No. Tell me more about the prophecy."

Dionisio grabs the book and opens it to the page I've read over and over a hundred times now.

"*Two parts of the same essence. A first and second born of the court. Through different Eyes, a vision will bring transition,*" He starts to recite.

"A first and second born of the court. That is you and me, Anima," Eros says.

"I was my parents' first child, you are your parents' second."

"Yes. Well, I am my father's second child. Dionisio and I have different mothers but that's besides the point." I fight the urge to ask more about that and go back to the prophecy.

"*Through different Eyes, a vision will bring transition.*" I repeat. "The heterochromia," I mumble. "And the dream. We have the same dream. This is what I know already."

"Yes, and the two parts of the same essence——-" Eros starts saying.

"Our soul. It's the same." I mumble.

Dionisio is as stiff as a sculpture. He looks uncomfortable as his left foot taps the floor again and again.

"*An unbreakable bond.*" Eros adds.

I take the book from Dionisio's hands and continue reading the rest out loud. *The connection will snap into place when they will reach Maturity, and what was forgotten will flourish once again. The golden energy will be the answer to the equation. An eye for an eye. A soul for a soul. A crown and a corpse. The drought will cease.*" I take a deep breath before asking, "What maturity are they talking about and what drought?"

"Based on what the prophet Astro told your great grandparents, it means when we turned eighteen."

"But I'm twenty-two."

"So am I."

"I don't think I am following."

"What Eros is trying to say is that Mirella and Giorgio did everything in their power to get you out of here before you turned eighteen. They knew you were supposed to fulfill your destiny at that point and they did all they could to keep you safe and away."

"Fulfill my destiny?"

"Stop the drought. The horrible curse that was put upon Dusäiga. A child hasn't been born since you were born, Anima." Eros sighs before adding, "A very powerful striga hundreds and hundreds of years ago thought she got betrayed by the entirety of Dusäiga and cursed the entire Kingdom. She wanted the place to perish slowly."

"How is that possible?"

"The drought started a long time ago. Then, you two were born, and no other child did and when you left—the heart of Dusäiga left with you."

"Well now, I am definitely not following."

"Without you, Dusäiga is nothing. Your essence is what keeps our home alive. You belong to Dusäiga and Dusäiga belongs to you."

Dionisio's words cut me like knives on my back. How can I be the answer to the future of an entire world, a magical one? Why would my parents send me away if that was the case, why was I sent away as a child in the first place? Not remembering anything is so frustrating.

I sigh. "Why don't I remember my first few years of life?"

"Dionisio and I had the time to recoup our memories. You didn't, not yet at least."

"You also didn't remember?"

"They took away our memories to protect us, to protect you."

"This—this is a lot." Suddenly a tear starts traveling down my cheek. Eros notices it right away and catches it with his thumb.

Dionisio's eyes are on mine. His jaw is locked. "I will leave you two alone. I think this is enough for one night."

"I agree." Eros nods.

"I'll go update the guards on our progress." Dionisio turns towards the balcony and then changes direction completely and goes for the front door.

Goodnight, little ninja. I hear him say in my head.

Goodnight.

Eros smiles at me before taking me in his embrace. "How are you feeling?"

"Overwhelmed."

"Very understandable. Let's talk about something that isn't magic related."

"I thought I was supposed to start learning how to control my powers right away."

"We can start tomorrow."

"Thank you." I stuff my face on his chest. His orange aroma filling my nostrils calming me down.

"Anything for you, Anima."

I tilt my face up, resting my chin on his chest. "How about you kiss me right now because I feel I am going to faint from the amount of information that has been thrown at me tonight?" The words burst out of my lips.

Eros chuckles and leans closer.

It feels like I can breathe again.

"As you wish, princess." His eyes stare into mine, a mirror of gorgeous colors. Then his stare falls onto my lips.

"No pet name, please," I beg, not getting into details, this is a story for another day.

"Anima. No pet name." He nods, resting his forehead on mine.

Hunger grows inside of me. A sudden heat radiates between my legs, and I can't stop myself any longer. I pull him to me while I lay down on the couch, and he follows with no hesitation as his lips finally crash onto mine. My hands wrap around his neck and I open my legs so that he can fit between them. One hand settles on my cheek while the other one travels on my arm, down my side and hips and ends up grabbing my thigh, pushing me to wrap my legs around his waist. His hard length pushes onto my bundle of nerves. My eyes close and suddenly a path surrounded with lavender flashes in front of my vision. I can almost smell the wonderful sweet and tingly perfume of the pretty purple flowers filling my nostrils. If this is how I feel just by kissing him, what the hell am I going to feel when I sleep with him?

"You are a dream, Anima. My dream. I can't believe we're here together again after all this time."

Together again. After all this time.

For some reason, I'm speechless as my stomach protests and chills crawl up my spine. Needles start pinching the inside of my throat, as my heart stops for a moment and I forget how to breathe.

I'd like to think this is normal, just nerves. But I know it's something else entirely.

I don't think fear is what I should feel when my soulmate tells me he's happy to be together.

CHAPTER 11

W e didn't start magical training the day after, in fact, we haven't started any sort of training at all. Svetlana and I have been working non-stop at the studio for days, which also means that I have barely seen Eros in the last week. I have been given homework though, read the damn Royal textbook on my own. He has been busy—he and Dionisio have been working on finding out who is behind the Opacum attacks in Vallecrosia. This is the justification he keeps giving, but I have a feeling he's been avoiding me, which makes no sense at all given the inexplicable attraction between the two of us. It's there, and you can't possibly miss it.

"Have you guys done the deed yet or what?" Svetlana wonders from her laptop.

"We haven't even gone on a proper date. We've both been so busy."

"He hasn't asked you out? Really?" Her eyes go wide.

"Nope."

"You are joking, right?"

"I wish I was."

"Look, why don't you—"

"Hello lovely ladies." Dionisio's voice overtakes Svetlana's.

Both Eros and his brother walk into the studio, Eros fidgeting nervously while Dionisio rests his back against my desk, his spring forest eyes locked with mine.

"Hey guys," I say, trying to keep my heartbeat in check. "This is Svetlana," I say pointing at her. "Svetlana, you already know Eros."

"It's nice to finally properly meet you," Svetlana says to Eros. He awkwardly extends his hand to shake hers.

"And this is his brother—Dionisio." I point at the mountain beside me.

Mountain, you say. Dionisio smirks.

Shut up.

This is the second time you call me a—-.

Please.

"Pleasure to meet you, Dioniso."

"Dionisio." Both him and I say in unison.

"I know, I just feel the name of a pope is not really appropriate for him." Her eyes move up and down analyzing him, no not analyzing, she's totally checking him out! My jaw locks as my chest tightens. I feel as if someone stuck a pin right in the middle of my chest. My entire rib cage stings as my breath gets heavier. Am I—jealous?

"Svet!"

"What?"

"I can't believe you said that out loud."

"You know I have no filter."

This is going to turn out extremely badly, my God. My temples begin to feel heavy, and the pressure soon turns into agony. Great, a headache is exactly what I need at this time. With his eyebrows arched and his body as tight as a guitar string, Dionisio's head whips in my direction. Eros has his lips in a thin line and is tapping his finger on his left thigh. I feel as though everyone in the room stopped breathing simultaneously and that the air isn't moving because there is so much tension and silence. Could I halt time? I feel like absolutely no one has moved.

Now, that would be a cool power to have. Dionisio says in my head.

It really would be cool. Scary, but cool.

"Svetlana, how about we leave these two alone for a moment and we go grab a coffee?" It's Dionisio's voice that breaks the quietness in the room.

A protest starts in my head. *No wait—*

You two need to talk. His firm voice shakes me into place.

Fine.

"Yes, great idea." She gets up, winks at me and with a wiggle, she hops out of the studio arm in arm with Dionisio. Another sting in my chest.

You know when you're in school and you haven't studied the night before and you have that gut feeling you're going to be called out by your teacher? That is how I feel right now, being alone with Eros. This is ridiculous, I can't be so nervous to be alone with my soulmate.

"Hi," I say in a soft voice.

Eros lips turn into a smile as he walks towards me. His arms wrap around my waist and his lips crash onto mine. His citrusy fragrance makes my nose tingle with pleasure and as I try to fixate on his cologne, a light moan escapes my mouth.

"Hi," He replies after the sudden kiss. My eyes are still closed, and I'm hoping to get more of his mouth on mine. The knot in my stomach is suddenly gone and I feel I can finally take a breath.

"Hi." My voice echoes his and he laughs. I have never realized how sweet and sour his laugh sounds. A single kiss and I have completely forgotten where I am and what I was doing before he entered the studio.

"I am sorry for being so distant the last couple of days, I guess I was a little nervous about coming on a little too strong."

"Says the guy that told me I am the heir to a throne and his soulmate."

He chuckles at my words. "Touché."

"It's ok, I get it. It's a lot for you as well."

"It's hard being responsible when all I want to do is to be around you." Eros's eyes are on me. The feel of his stare making my cheeks burn.

"I—I think I understand what you mean." I look down trying to cover the colour of my face.

"We haven't found out much about the attacks yet."

"Things seem to have been calm the last couple of days— haven't ended up with a concussion, so that's progress."

"I know you are being sarcastic, but I really don't want to see you hurt again—ever."

"I'd also like to remain with an intact skull."

He chuckles. "Have you been reading the Royal Textbook?"

"I read a bit more about Suspirium, and I actually have questions."

"Have you felt like you used it? That would be—huge."

"What do you mean?"

"Your father and grandfather did not have it, you'd be the first in a very long time." His lips lift into a smile. "But you are special, I wouldn't even be that surprised."

"I know that the power works both ways only if two people have the power, right?"

"That would be correct."

"Are you sure it's only passed in the royal bloodline?"

"That's how it has always been, I can ask my father though, why?"

"I feel I have it but I'm not sure."

"That—that is amazing, Anima, your compulsion powers must be strong. I can't wait to see what you'll do with your magic!"

"I think I might have used it on Dionisio, accidentally, obviously." My face staring down at my shoes.

"It might have been triggered by your emotions, maybe you felt frustrated or angry and you said something." He sighs. "Why are you avoiding my stare?"

"Because I used it on Dionisio and not you."

"Anima, princess, look at me." I lift my head searching for his eyes. "You didn't do it on purpose, I am not mad if that's what you're worried about."

"You're not?"

"Why would I be mad, you're discovering your magic, any progress is good progress and I am happy we're talking about it."

"Thank you for saying that."

"Anything else you'd like to talk about?"

"The princess pet name—"

"I'm so sorry you told me already, I just—it's your title, and it's hard not to use it."

"I understand." My voice is low, almost a whisper. One day I'll be able to talk about Jeremy and what that word does to me.

He caresses my arm. "No pet name. Anything else?"

"How—" I clear my throat. "How about we try to do something normal?"

"What do you have in mind?"

"Like maybe go out for—dinner?" I manage to say. "Is that silly? It is, isn't…"

His hand tilts my chin up, forcing me to look at his eyes, the perfect copy of mine. "I think that's a wonderful idea."

"We can go—"

"No no no, you already asked me out. Let me please plan the date so that I feel less dumb about not asking you earlier."

"I guess I can let you do that."

"Thank you."

As soon as those words escape his mouth, loud chatters and laughs come from the entrance of the studio. Dionisio and Svetlana are back from their coffee run. Any other day, I might have jumped out of Eros's embrace, but I feel at the right place where I am. In his arms.

"I guess the lovebirds did some kind of talking," Svetlana says to Dionisio. His tenseness comes right back as soon as his eyes lock with mine.

"Sorry to be a party pooper, but we have to go." Dionisio says before adding, "I got a call from Markus."

They seem to have a lead. I hear his husky voice so clear that my eyes widen in response just to realize that he didn't state that out loud. If I have suspirium, how does he do that? Can I allow him to do so?

Suspirium? Are you sure? Dionisio looks at me for a second.

Eros's hand lands on the small of my back and his thumb rubs my skin slowly. "We'll talk later, ok?" His lips brush my forehead leaving the softest kiss I have ever received. My toes curl at the sudden absence of his warmth around me.

"Be safe," I reply. "Both of you."

"We will." Eros nods in my direction.

Always. Dionisio's voice echoes through my mind.

The brothers walk towards the exit, and as soon as they disappear behind the door, Svetlana runs towards me with a grin on her face.

"You seem quite cheery. Had a good time?" I ask her, raising an eyebrow at her.

"You did not tell me that Dionisio was well—that." She

gestures towards the door where only moments ago the two brothers walked out from.

"What do you mean by *that*?"

"He's a god, Anima, a god." That he is. I certainly try anything I can not to think about that while he's around though. This weird communication we have created is, well, quite intrusive.

"He's Eros's brother." I have to try to bring her back to planet Earth. I have to come back to planet Earth. We both need to stop thinking about how he looks. Besides, Eros is truly more my kind of person. Isn't he? He is. I feel good when I'm between his arms.

"A fucking god." She repeats. "A god that is absolutely crushing on you."

"What did you say?" She did not really say that, did she?

"Nevermind. How are things with your boy? You two seemed very cozy."

"We talked a little bit—I might have asked him out."

"Ok, that's progress! Where are you taking him?"

"He insisted on wanting to plan the date."

"Hhmm ok. Good, this is good." Her stare is low, avoiding mine. She's nodding as if she approves but the fact that she can't even look at me makes me think that she might not. Svetlana can't lie, she just can't, I love that about her but it's also frustrating knowing she's trying to keep something to herself with the worry of hurting me. How the tables have turned. We are both doing the same thing.

"It is. I like being around him.".

Svetlana looks in my direction and gives me a quick nod. "Good. He does seem really into you. I'm happy if you're happy."

"Did Dionisio say anything in particular?"

"He hyped his brother up quite a bit, but I still told him I will end Eros's life if he hurts you."

"Oh yeah? And what did Dionisio say to that?" I tilt my head to the side and my lips slightly part waiting for her answer.

"He said that he would help me hide the body if that ever happened," Svetlana replies, nodding with approval.

Of course he said that.

Pressure weighs down on my chest. My eyes are heavy too now. I already know he's a protective guy. They both are. How is it possible that even in such a small amount of time I know for a fact that no matter what happens, Eros and Dionisio will always be there, for me, like family would? Thinking about them makes me somewhat nostalgic.

I take a deep breath in. A delicate sweet floral smell fills my nostrils, evergreen but woodsy at the same time. A powdery, tingly fragrance. Lavender. This is the second time that this has happened. I guess it's not really a coincidence, is it?

I SPEND THE NEXT COUPLE OF DAYS WITH SVETLANA AT WORK, and texting Eros non-stop.

My palms start to perspire just thinking about him finally taking me out to dinner tonight. I think he's trying to give me a couple of 'no magic, no threats' days. I'm relieved that everything appears to be rather quiet and that I haven't just passed out in someone's arms.

Keeping all of this a secret from Svetlana is becoming harder and harder, but if nothing happens, then at least she won't ask more questions. I also feel she's keeping a smile on her face for me—but I can tell she has some doubts about Eros. I wonder if these concerns are the result of something Dionisio said to her, or if she is the source of all of them. I could simply ask her, but the potential responses make my throat tighten. I'll tell her everything and then we'll talk about it—perhaps then she'll view things differently and change her mind.

As of right now, all I can think of is trying to remember anything from my past. The Royal Textbook is helping with sensations, but I still don't remember anything. I feel that spending more time with Eros and Dionisio will help with that— and Ginevra, who apparently was very important to me. I still haven't seen her since the day she and Eros told me who I was. My head ends up between my hands. Even thinking of spending more time with someone like Ginevra brings dryness in my mouth. Pain in my throat rises followed by the taste of iron coming from my left cheek. I haven't even noticed I was biting it down. Why do I feel this sense of betrayal towards my adoptive parents when they are the ones that made the decision to take me away from this world? Dusäiga is where I belong and I hate not remembering walking those streets. I clench my teeth and exhale.

"Are you ready to close? We gotta get you all cleaned up and looking smoking hot for the read head!" Svetlana tells me, snapping me back into reality.

"Yes, please, I have no idea what to wear," I snort in response.

We close the studio and walk upstairs to my apartment when my phone vibrates in my pocket.

I pull it out and see a new text from Eros, and I can't help but smile like an idiot.

EROS:

Can't wait to see you. I'll be there at 7pm. Wear flats, I know you love the sea at night :)

ANIMA:

Will do. Can't wait to see you as well :)

"Ok stop giggling at your phone or you'll never be ready for prince charming when he shows up!" Svetlana orders as she takes my phone from my hands.

"Ok that's cute, you do love to walk on the beach at night. Now let's get down to business," She adds while walking towards my closet.

"I was thinking, tight jeans and a tight turtleneck."

"Oh, so basically what you're already wearing."

"No—ok yes but I was going to put on a different turtleneck."

I see her pull out a dress and I start shaking my head before she even shows me which one she picked. Dresses are for club nights and special occasions only. I hate being uncomfortable.

"Before you even say what you're thinking, you're going on a date. This is *the* special occasion."

I guess she got me with that one.

It's still technically winter, but this side of Liguria never gets too cold. I could definitely wear a dress and a light coat, and I'd be ok even though I think Svetlana is hoping for me to freeze my ass off so that Eros has to be very close to me to warm me up. A Machiavellian plan, if you ask me. I love her for it.

"Svet, I don't know if wearing a dress is really necessary," I protest.

"Yes it is, a tight one too! This is comfy to wear and shows that great ass you have." She adds.

"No wait, that's the one with the incredibly deep v neckline," I reply, starting to worry about the entire situation.

"Yes, it looks so good on you cause you have small boobs. It was made for your body type. Wear it and stop complaining, you know you look good in it." She is right, I know I look good in it and I think that's what I'm more afraid of. Getting ready for someone again makes me shiver.

"Ok fine, but I will complain the entire time about it."

"Eros won't complain about it at all. I am ready to bet big bucks on it," she says with a giggle.

I put on the short stretchy black dress, loosely curl my already half wavy hair and put on some makeup. I opt for a pair of black flats to go with the dress just because Svetlana made me do it. I was ready to put on my trusted pair of converse. At least the dress has long sleeves, I feel less exposed knowing that at least my arms are covered.

Svetlana leaves my apartment a couple of minutes before I hear a knock on my door. I look at my phone, and it's 7 o'clock on the dot.

I open the door and am welcomed by Eros' soft look and piercing smile. He's wearing a nice pair of black jeans and a tight light blue-button-up shirt, currently half covered by a knee-length black coat.

"Hi." I smile at him. His eyes go wide for a second while he checks me out.

"Hi, wow, Anima. You look gorgeous." He finally starts breathing again and quickly leaves a soft kiss on my cheek.

I smile at the gesture. "Thank you. You don't look so bad yourself."

He clears his throat. "Ready to go?"

"Yes, let me just grab my bag and coat and we can go," I say while gathering my things.

"I got us a table at Ristorante Corallo. Wanna walk there?"

"Yes, sounds good!" I've missed being able to walk around town because everything is within walking distance, and I missed the smell of the sea. It always gets into my skin and makes my nose tingle. "Actually, it sounds perfect," I add with a smile.

We start walking, hand in hand, and we chit-chat about our day. We get to the restaurant, and we sit down at a table. The waiter brings us the menus, and we order red wine and pizzas. I'm probably too nervous to eat anyway.

I look to my right, at the perfect backdrop created by the reef and the sea. "I missed the sound of the waves." My eyes close as I try to focus on the water crashing on the rocks—I take a deep breath in and the sparkling fragrance of salt and seaweed fills my surroundings.

"Your devotion to the sea is quite poetic," He says while gently caressing the hand I had rested on the table.

I like this. A lot.

The sudden buzz of my phone on the table snaps me out of the trance I was in. Thinking that it's Svetlana already questioning me about everything, I quickly take a peek at it only to find out that it's someone else checking in on me.

DIONISIO:

> How are my favorite brother and my favorite Chicagoan doing? I didn't want to bother, but my brother needs to look at his phone right now.

"One day I'll find out how your brother got my number." I tell Eros as I show him my phone. "He says to check your phone for something."

"My brother needs to learn about personal space, I am sorry, I was trying to avoid him, but I guess he found a way to reach out to me through you." With that, he picks up his phone, and with a sigh, reads whatever it is that Dionisio sent him, types something back, and puts the phone away.

"Is everything ok?" I ask. Is he jealous? I mean, it could be anything. Maybe he got a new lead on the attacks and just wanted to update us.

"All good, nothing to worry about, it's just D being D."

The pizzas arrive, and we start chatting, forgetting all about those texts and just trying to learn things about each other.

"So, how was living alone in Chicago?" he asks.

"Scary, but fun. I loved school, and almost all the people I met, but I feel it wasn't really my place, you know? It's a nice city, for a while, but it's too chaotic and there is so much happening all the time. It can be very overwhelming."

"Yeah, I completely get what you mean. I lived in Milano for my undergrad and it's wonderful for a while, but it really isn't the place I want to be."

"Exactly, and don't get me wrong, I love to travel. But I don't feel at home in a big city. I like the quiet." I feel the words just slip out of my mouth with no effort, like I have been dying to share my thoughts to the other side of my soul for a long time.

"Just like Vallecrosia," He adds with a sweet smile on his face.

"Yes, just like Vallecrosia," I confirm. "The seaview is a plus too".

"Oh yes, the view is definitely quite something."

I feel his eyes on me, his hand still interlocked with mine on the table. I pretend not to notice him watching me while I stare at the water once again.

My cheeks grow warm and the heat doesn't stop there, rising between my legs as well.

I find myself shifting my position by crossing my legs under the table, trying to give myself some sort of temporary relief.

"After my parents passed, I just felt that was the only possible solution for me, the only thing I needed to do. Being here just seemed right," I say, trying to regain some sort of control.

"I'm sorry, I didn't want to make you think about all that, we don't have to talk about it"

"Thank you for not pressuring me into talking about it—or anything else."

We continue talking for hours, and the glass of wine turns into an entire bottle. I haven't felt so free and comfortable with someone in a long time. It's baffling to see how Eros opens up when he's outside Forestiero and not hiding in his little office. It's nice, refreshing. I guess the amount of wine helped as well.

He pays the bill, then we walk toward the beach, sit on the small rocks and watch the view. The sky connects with the water like a gradient of pastel blues and pinks. The waves are soft when they come in contact with the rocks. They're gentle. It's a calm night for the sea, just as it seems for me. I feel quiet and serene on the outside but on the verge of a storm on the inside.

I take in the breezy saltiness with a deep breath and exhale out loud.

He wraps his arm around my shoulder and brings me closer. The sudden warmth makes me realize how cold I was before he embraced me. I look up at him and bring his head closer to mine by resting my hand on his cheek. I press my lips on his and the heat from before comes back with the force of a tempest. The way we are kissing is way too much for a public setting, and I almost rip his clothes off. Am I ready for that yet? I need to pump the breaks. We both had a lot to drink.

"Oh, wow, it's getting late!" I say with wide eyes, looking at the time while trying to regulate my heartbeat.

"I'll walk you home, let's go," Eros says. He offers me his hand to help me get up.

We start walking towards my apartment in complete silence with our hands interlocked, as if we are worried to lose each other. I haven't been with anyone since Jeremy, and that thought brings restlessness. Svetlana was worried about me getting hurt, but she was right about something—if I don't try to give me and Eros a chance now, I will never be able to.

We get to my building, and I know he will be the gentleman he is and only kiss me goodnight before going home, but my heart races again and I am not ready for our night to end just yet.

I find the courage to get my words out. "Want to come up? We can have a coffee and... I don't know, continue talking maybe?" Lame, Anima, lame.

He smiles, gives me a quick peck and replies with "I'd love to".

We walk up the stairs. I open the door, and as soon as we get inside, he quickly locks it, keeping his eyes on me. He holds a hand on the door, lowers his head and touches my forehead with his, then he starts kissing me. It starts soft, gentle, and it quickly deepens and becomes rough and hungry for more. Finally, now we're talking.

Eros starts wandering around my body with his other hand, and I lock my arms around his neck and just let him explore. Without breaking the kiss, we start moving and he pushes me against the wall in my living room. There, pinned on the wall, he squeezes my left thigh and I wrap it around him, locking him in place just like he did with me. I can feel him against my most sensitive part. The friction of his movements between my legs is unbearable. My entire body is throbbing, craving for more.

"Did I tell you how much I like this dress? Cause I like it very much," Eros says, breaking the kiss to catch some air.

"I am glad you do." I push my lips back on his, like it's the last thing I was going to do on this planet.

"Well, this is definitely something I didn't want to witness." Dionisio's voice startles us, and we quickly turn to him. He's sitting in the loveseat, an elbow on the armrest and his hand holding his head. His lips are in a thin line and one of his eyebrows is raised. "I am afraid I'll have to ask you both to put your legs and tongues back to their places, please and thank you." Why is he always there whenever something is about to happen?

"D, this better be good or I will actually kill you this time," Eros utters, folding his arms across his chest in annoyance.

"How did you get in?" I ask, narrowing my eyes at him.

Trust me, I wouldn't be here if it wasn't important.

"I am here for a pretty damn good reason. Some guards were able to take some pictures of the man that seems to be behind the

Opacum attacks in Vallecrosia. They are getting more organized and ready to attack us, Eros. She needs to be ready and we need to keep her guarded at all times."

Eros looks quite shocked, but not as shocked as I am hearing Dionisio's statement. He gives his brother a quick nod.

"Did you say you have pictures?" I ask, ignoring everything else Dionisio just said. I nervously start fidgeting with the ring they gave me until Dionisio grabs his phone and starts looking for the images.

"Here, take a look, maybe it's someone you've seen around."

As soon as I peek at the photograph, I feel the room starting to spin. My heart pounds in my chest, my feet start tingling as the surroundings blur in front of me. I have to leave. My voice is blocked by pins and needles in my throat.

It can't be him.

"Anima, what is it?" Eros leans closer, and wraps an arm around my waist making sure I don't fall.

"It can't be him. How did he find me?" The tightness in my chest is too much. I'm sure my ribs will crack and nausea rises from my belly.

"Who are we talking about?" Dionisio asks, right when I pick up my phone and look for an old picture of me and Jeremy.

I show it to him and after a few seconds of silence he just says, "Well, look at that, it seems to be the same guy…"

How can he be sarcastic when I am having trouble breathing right now? I don't understand how this happened. I thought all this started when I got back, when Ginevra gave me the book and told me who I really was.

Anima, we're gonna fix this, he's not going to get to you, Dionisio tells me through this weird bond we have. I try to take a deep breath before saying anything.

"I—I don't understand. You are telling me that my psychopath ex boyfriend is a fucking dark lord?" I yell at them. "I can't take this. I had a restraining order on Jeremy. I can't—I am going to be sick." And with that, I run in the bathroom, quickly close the door, and vomit.

"I am sorry Anima, I didn't mean to upset you like this. I had no idea. We both had no idea." Dionisio sighs loudly from the other side of the door. "We are going to get through this, and we will protect you at all costs." This is the first time that Dionisio says something like this, out loud, in front of his brother. His voice cracks while talking to me. He's making a promise, like his life depends on it.

It does.

"Nothing will happen to you, trust me princess, I mean, Anima. I will do anything to keep you safe," Eros adds.

We stay like that for what seems like forever. Me sitting on the floor hugging the toilet, and the two of them outside of the bathroom, in silence, waiting for me to feel calm enough to come out.

"Were you seriously going to sleep with her in this state? I could smell the alcohol on her breath as soon as you walked in. I can smell it on you right now," I hear Dionisio whisper through the bathroom door.

"I'm not drunk and she is not drunk. She's upset—I'd be as well if I found out my ex was trying to find and kill me to drain my powers and who knows what the fuck else that asshole wants to do," Eros yells back at his brother, trying to shut him off.

"I can hear you both," I start with before adding, "And I preferred the silence". I quickly rinse my mouth and splash cold water on my face before walking out of the bathroom.

"The princess is back!" Dionisio says with a breathy voice.

"I preferred the other pet name by the way, it feels weird saying *princess*, especially when I specifically said I don't like it," I say, opening the door of the bathroom.

"Time to get used to it—" Dionisio starts saying, but gets cut off by his brother right away.

"D, shut up. She doesn't like it. You gave us the news, now you can leave," Eros barks. I can't tell if he's annoyed because we got interrupted, or if this is just stress from learning about Jeremy.

No P word here. I'm sorry. Dionisio's voice fills my head.

"Can we please not scream at each other? It's not really helping my stomach," I say, sitting down on the couch resting my head between my hands.

"I am sorry, you're right, no more yelling," Eros replies, his voice back being soft.

I nod in response. "So if this is true, all the time I spent with Jeremy was a lie. All of it, a lie. Why would he even go out of his way to be with me when he just wants to—"

"He won't get to you," Dionisio's husky voice plays in my ears over and over again even after he's stopped speaking. *I won't let that happen.*

"I won't let that happen," They say at the same time, but only one of them is out loud.

I start nervously picking at my nails before asking, "So what are we going to do? I need to learn how to protect myself. I don't want to feel defenseless anymore."

"My father sent me here for that reason. I'll teach you every-thing I know," Dionisio says right away, giving me a quick nod.

"I'll show you how to use spells and potions," Eros adds. Then continues, "And if you hurt her, brother, I will end you."

He thinks he's the alpha. Oh boy, here we go.

"I think Eros is a little overprotective of you," Dionisio replies, making me chuckle.

That he is, I answer.

"You say overprotective, I say caring," Eros utters before adding, "I just don't see why I can't teach her how to fight, your presence is—unnecessary."

Dionisio's nostrils flare at his brother's use of words. "Because I'm the best at what I do and you know it."

I look at the both of them doing a staring contest. Tension fills the room. Their bodies are stiff, immobile. "Well, this has been lovely. Now if you please excuse me, I am going to get ready for bed."

"Sorry I ruined your kiss goodnight," Dionisio says with a devilish look on his face.

As if you're really sorry about that, I tell him back, making him grin from under his breath. Asshole.

"With you, brother, news can't wait even a night to be told. Your timing is impeccable." Eros's soft voice fills the room and brings me back to him.

"This couldn't wait."

"We are going to put some guarding spells around the apartment, and we are going to stay here tonight if it's ok with you. We can talk more in the morning. Tonight was already eventful enough," Eros says, and I just nod and walk to the bathroom. I quickly turn and see them moving their hands up and down, left and right, and I see a faded light coming out of their hands and moving all around my apartment almost creating a seal that then disappears as soon as it goes into place. I notice they're whispering something while they trace the frame of the windows and screen door and then on the front door. It's hypnotizing looking at them using magic.

"What are you chanting?"

"*Clypeo protego te.* It literally translates to "I protect you with a shield."

Latin, ok, makes sense. I nod and then close the bathroom door, and change into sweats and a t-shirt, I wash my face, then go into my room and grab extra pillows and blankets for the guys.

"Here are blankets and pillows. I don't really have space for guests out here"

"These will do perfectly, thank you." Dionisio grabs them from my hands.

"Let me walk you to your room, we are going to be right out, I'm just gonna put a guarding spell on the window and I'll leave you to sleep," Eros tells me, grabbing my hand and starting to walk towards my door.

"Thank you."

He starts chanting the Latin phrase again, tracing the frame of my bedroom window, and when he's done, he turns to me, and slowly walks towards me. His eyes staring at mine.

"We clearly didn't want this evening to end this way, but I did have a nice time with you tonight."

"I did too," I manage to say before his forehead gently rests on mine.

"God, I really wish my brother didn't show up."

"I know. You'll make it up to me."

And before he can do anything, I rest my lips on his. As soon as my eyes close, an image of me running in a garden full of lavender fills my every thought. A moan escapes from his mouth that brings me back to my apartment.

"I definitely will make it up to you," he says while wrapping his arms around me, deepening the kiss for a few instants.

"Does lavender mean anything to you?"

"What?"

"It's the third time that I smell or see lavender when we kiss."

His lips lift into a smile. "The gardens. You're starting to remember Court."

"Dusäiga has lots of lavender?" I ask.

"The gardens at Court are filled with it."

"That—that sounds so lovely." Lavender is my favourite flower. Maybe I subconsciously picked it as my favourite because my brain wanted me to remember where I come from.

"It is." He simply replies before adding, "I can't wait to take you there."

"I can't wait to go."

"Goodnight prin—Anima," he says, and with that he leaves and closes the door behind him.

CHAPTER 12

My feet sink into the ground as I pace myself towards nothingness.

The floor is so cold beneath me. Where are my shoes?

I have—need to find him. Now I know. He is in danger—they all are and it's all my fault. I should have gotten here sooner.

I can't see a foot ahead, only a dark pitch around me as I keep my arms in front of me not to stumble against one of the huge bookshelves populating the space.

I take a deep breath in, and a hint of vanilla fills my nostrils.

Shivers run down my spine as a cold breeze follows me from the slightly open window on my left.

I have to be quick before he finds out what I'm doing.

Wax from the candle I'm holding falls on my hand, making it sting so methodically.

Here's the door, the dark wood separating me from him. I open it gently and there he is, Dionisio, laying on his side, sleeping.

My golden light. I have to tell him everything.

Just as I reach forward with my free hand, a drop of wax falls on his shoulder.

He quickly turns and as I start to speak, his eyes widen from something he sees behind me.

I turn my head towards the entrance and as I focus on the image in front of me, Jeremy stares back into my eyes with a grin on his face.

MY EYES SHOOT OPEN AS I SIT UP IN BED—MY CHEST TIGHT AS I try to catch my breath. Looking around, I see it's still very dark out, and I don't realize I am screaming until Eros shakes my body, trying to bring me back to the living world.

"Anima, it's ok. You're awake now." Eros wraps his arms around me, the soft cotton of his shirt and his body warmth keeping me grounded. "What happened?" Dionisio is leaning against the door frame, looking at me with a straight face and his arms crossed over his chest.

"I had a dream—the dream." Did I really see what I think I did? Was Dionisio really the guy sleeping? It's—impossible. The vision is part of the prophecy, isn't it? What did my therapist say about dreams? Sometimes people appear in them, but it doesn't necessarily mean they portray who they are in real life. Jeremy though—he was there. He was waiting for me. "I think—I saw Jeremy."

Dionisio's sigh makes me turn in his direction. He knows. He knows he was in the dream—vision, as well. And I don't know what that means. I don't know what any of this means.

We can talk about it tomorrow, I hear Dionisio say in my head, and I give him the most subtle nod.

"I'll let you deal with this, brother. You should try to go back to sleep, Anima. We're starting training tomorrow." He leaves the door frame and disappears from my line of sight. A jump in an icy lake would seem warmer than Dionisio's statement.

"Excuse him. He doesn't do late night talks… Are you ok?"

"Yes. I'm sorry, I don't usually wake up screaming in a panic like this from a nightmare. It was just… I had this really bad feeling… I don't know, it's ok, I'm ok, go back to sleep."

"I mean, I would probably panic as well if I saw my psycho ex in a dream. Would you feel better if I stayed here?"

"That would be great," I reply.

I don't realize I'm shaking until he cups my cheeks. "Hey. It's ok. You're ok. I'm right here."

I nod, and as we lay down, I automatically rest my head on his chest. Closing my eyes, I listen to his heartbeat trying to match his pace. My body relaxes as he starts brushing my hair. I fall back asleep with the aroma of oranges impregnating my every pore.

I WAKE UP IN THE MORNING, IN THE SAME POSITION AS THE NIGHT before. I try to shift out of Eros's embrace cautiously but end up waking him up in the process.

"Good morning, prin—Anima."

"Good morning, thank you for stopping yourself with the pet name."

"I'm trying even if I like the sound of it, don't you?" He says, smiling at me and softly kissing my forehead.

Not really.

"Stop flirting and get up," Dionisio shouts from the kitchen. "We have work to do, coffee is ready, Anima needs to be on her best behavior."

And with that I mean, leave the sass at home because you're going to hate me after your first training.

"Am I that sour before coffee?" I ask Eros, making him chuckle.

"D is in your kitchen, you have every right to be sour about it."

I grunt as we unlock the embrace we were in, get out of bed and make our walk towards the living room.

"Ok so I had a lot of time to think last night while you two were—bonding."

"I think we have different views on the meaning of—bonding," I say sarcastically, trying to reassure him. I grab a cup of coffee and start drinking, trying to brush off the subject.

"D, you worry about our personal life a little too much. Now, what did you think about for so long?"

"I am taking Anima to the gym today. She needs to be ready to fight back as soon as possible," Dionisio says before turning his attention to me. "We're going to warm up by climbing. You need to get some stamina quickly and then we'll start with self-defense. We're going to alternate the two things. One day climbing, one day self defense and cardio. You're going to be in pain. A lot of pain."

"Perfect. I'm ready. Hopefully, I won't be as hopeless as I think I am."

You're definitely not hopeless, he says.

"Get ready. We're leaving in fifteen." He turns towards his brother. "Eros, are you coming?" He asks his brother, a shadow of annoyance on his face that dissipates when his brother shakes his head. Only then, Dionisio smirks.

"I am going to the bookstore. I'll fill in *zia* Ginevra on Anima's memories when I get there. Maybe she has some advice on how to speed up the process. I'll touch base with Markus as well. Then I'll find you," Eros replies before adding, "Actually before you leave for the gym, let Anima come say hi to *zia*. She doesn't stop asking about her."

"I haven't seen her in a while. I hope she doesn't feel like I am avoiding her."

"She knows you need your time." He gets up and walks to my chair, never taking his eyes off of Dionisio. He then lowers down to give me a quick kiss and walks out the door.

Still trying to mark his territory. I don't know how I feel about that.

"He was always like that. He'll stop—eventually," He says, staring down at his mug.

"Can we please talk about what happened last night—what has been happening since I met you?"

He looks up at me, silent. *Not now. Later.*

I get dressed, grab a bag and then we're out the door and walking to *Forestiero.*

"Ok, we say a quick hello to *zia*, and then off we go."

"I'm actually pretty excited about it. I tried climbing in Chicago a couple of times. It was fun."

"Good. Try to remember that when you're shouting at me, begging me to stop."

Well, now I am a little worried.

As we walk towards the bookstore, I notice Dionisio's firm shoulders and closed fists. I gently brush his arm. "You ok?"

"Hhmm? Yeah, all good, let's go." He gives me the most forced smile in history and then walks into the shop.

"My dear, there you are! So nice to see you, and to see you,

Anima. Eros was just telling me the latest news. Are you ok?" Ginevra's look shifts to me. Her eyes on mine.

"I'm… Taking it as it comes. Gonna start training today," I quickly say, before she rushes towards me and locks me into the tightest hug I've received in a while.

"You're so strong, Anima. I swore to protect you, and I will. Always," she whispers in my ear.

I close my eyes and an image of Ginevra walking into my parents' old shop appears in front of me. She was holding my hand. Then her palm gently rests on my forehead and I fall asleep.

"You took me to my parents—to my adoptive parents."

"I—I did." Her eyes widen, then she adds, "You're starting to remember."

"I guess I am."

You ok? Dionisio's voice makes that image disappear like smoke in the wind.

Yeah, I just feel a little out of it.

"Hi *zia*, sorry I haven't been around much, I will make it up to you. I gotta break up the lovebirds for a bit." He gives me a wink. "We best head off. We have a lot of work to do."

I roll my eyes at his use of 'lovebirds', say a quick bye and follow him outside.

"Ok Mr. Sarcasm, that was unnecessary."

"Was it? I don't think so," He says smirking at me. "Besides, I like it when you roll your eyes at me."

He's infuriating. Has to have the last word every time.

"Are you really ok? I know how it feels when memories just come crashing back at you."

"How did it happen for you?"

"My aunt was able to reverse the spell in time."

"I guess she can't do that with me. It's too late."

"Unfortunately, it wouldn't work."

"I'll be ok, it's just—a lot."

"It is."

We start walking towards the parking lot in Via Roma, and as I check the cars parked, I notice a black Mitsubishi Lancer. What a beauty. The compact sedan looks sleek, and the spoiler adds the perfect edgy touch to the entire design. As my eyes analyze the car, I notice the golden rims. Now, that's a nice touch. Douchy, but nice. What I wasn't expecting was Dionisio stopping in front of said car and unlocking it. Of course he drives the Fast and Furious car.

He opens the passenger seat. "When you're done drooling all over my car, you can continue doing so in it."

I roll my eyes and get inside.

He starts the engine, then hands me his phone. "You can pick the music, I am curious to see what you listen to."

"I don't think my music is a good idea."

"Try me."

"No, like… I like heavy stuff."

"Do me a favor and open my music library."

I do as he says, and can't believe what I am seeing. This could be *my* music library.

"I can't believe you know Slaughter to Prevail." Eastern European death metal is certainly not for everyone. Svetlana complains about my music taste any chance she gets.

"I can't believe you know them!"

I just hit shuffle and let the phone pick the tune for us, then I put down the phone and look out the window. It's a gloomy day, the sky ready to burst out in anger and the clouds a pretty shade of steel.

"Huh."

"What?"

He keeps his eyes on the steering wheel. "Oh nothing. Just interesting."

"What is?"

"You completely respecting my privacy and not snooping around my phone—at all."

"Oh no, I saw you have Taylor Swift on your playlist, I just didn't want to embarrass you."

"Hey, Red is a great album. Her voice is angelic, pure poetry." He shifts his position so that he can look at me.

"Sure it is. Swifty," I say grinning at him. "I am not the kind of person that checks phones usually, don't want to repeat what happened to me."

"Well, thank you." No, thank you for not asking questions.

"Besides, I really don't want to see all the naked girls you probably have saved in your camera roll."

"Those are clearly saved in a very hidden place." He replies, making me go stiff on my seat. I know he's being sarcastic, but the thought of him with someone makes me feel uneasy for some reason.

"Of course." I choke out in response. How did we even get to this subject?

Heat rises to my cheeks. I rest my cold palm on my forehead, trying to cool down the warmness that was created.

You know I am not like that, right?

Do I? I barely know him.

"Can we talk now?" I clear my throat, trying to change the subject.

"One second, let me at least leave the parking lot."

Dionisio starts driving, and we remain in silence for a good five minutes. His car smells like him. I breathe in the cedarwood and minty scent and exhale out loud.

"Why didn't you tell my brother I was in the dream with you?" His hand clenching over the gearshift.

"Why haven't you told Eros that you have suspirium too?"

"I don't think I have it. I just seem to have this—connection with you," he starts saying before adding, "It has to be something related to your use of suspirium. I need to research more about it."

"Eros says it's a pretty big thing."

"It is. The Gods—they don't gift such power to anyone. It connects to your power of compulsion."

"The Gods?" I turn to look at him.

"Yeah, did you get to that part of the book?" A grin appears on his face.

"I guess I haven't."

"It's said that the four Gods used to walk the Earth in ancient times. Their names are Ignis, Ventus, Humus and Fluvius. The four elements. They lived in harmony with humans. They lived in harmony with humans and even fell in love so they tried to keep their loved ones' souls alive through the ages, granting them immortality through power."

"That's how we were created."

He nods. "Our powers are what remains of our ancestors. Dusäiga is what remains of those gifted people."

"Why aren't these Gods on Earth anymore?"

"If I remember correctly, they got tired of mortality. I'm sure you'll tell me why as soon as you get to that part of the book."

"I should have brought it with me. I have so many questions."

He chuckles. "Does Eros know you used suspirium on me?"

"He does. I was worried about telling him—but he was very understanding." I sigh. "The dream—there's more to it, I don't know why yet but there is."

"I wish I could give you more answers, but truly, I have no idea why I'm in it as well."

"How am I going to tell Eros that the guy in my dreams might be you?"

"It doesn't change what you two are for each other, Anima."

"Right..." I can't tell him that I am supposed to help that person in my dream because I care for him.

"This isn't Cupid and Psyche. You won't have to pass some trials to be with Eros. You already have him, so don't worry too much about the vision. We'll figure it out."

"Look at you, reading Greek myths about love, didn't think you were the romantic type," I quickly say.

With a chuckle, he answers, "Eros isn't the only one that likes to read in the family. We do own a bookstore after all, and come on, I was just being observant. I noticed the Cupid and Psyche photograph of the Canova statue you have in your living room, which I suppose you took?"

"I—yes, I did take that in Paris a few years ago. Are you going to tell me now you care about art as well?"

"Just because I may sound like an ass doesn't mean I have no interests. You should focus on your black and white and stop with the family shoots. You clearly have a talent for fine art."

"Ok mister Art Critic, you have me all figured out, I see," I say, chuckling in the passenger seat.

"I have a couple of things down."

I tap my finger on my thigh nervously. "So—"

"Yes?"

"Did Eros tell you what I also remembered last night?"

"No."

"Lavender."

I see his lips curl into a smile. "Your mother loved lavender."

"Eros says that the gardens at Court are filled with it."

"You two used to run around those gardens and create trouble every second of the day."

"I always loved lavender. I guess my body has been trying to tell me where I come from all along."

His hand squeezes my thigh gently, before going back on the gearshift. "I can't wait to see your face as soon as you step foot into those gardens."

I turn to him with serenity coming out of my pores. "Me

either."

We remain silent for the remainder of the drive, and my mind travels and rethinks the comment he made on my photography. I do love fine art, a lot. I definitely wasn't expecting such a critique from—him.

"I have a degree in classical literature and a minor in art history."

"Excuse me, what? Why didn't you tell me before?"

"Thought Svetlana told you. We talked about it the other day."

"No, she didn't! Dionisio, what the hell!"

"I like pretty things." His eyes are on mine for just a moment. His lips turn into a grin as my cheeks start to burn up. I know he means he just likes things in general, but the way his eyes feel on mine make me wonder if I could be one of those pretty things.

We arrive at the gym, and before I can even open the door, Dionisio does it for me. This is all so unnecessary but I feel he's being so nice because I will insult him after the workout he has planned for me.

We get inside, the guy at the counter says hi to Dionisio and lets us in. I guess he comes here a lot. He shows me where the changing rooms are and I go get ready.

As soon as I get out, we get down to business.

"Before we start anything, warm up. I don't want you dead after five minutes"

"You really have no faith in me. I am not that bad!"

"Quite the opposite, actually."

We start with some stretching, and I notice D looking around at all times, checking the place. I look around as well and it hits me. It's a gym and lots of girls are in here, all sweaty with minimal clothing on.

What is it with you today? I am checking to see if anyone is giving you too much attention. You're my priority, Anima. No one else is.

I look at him quickly, then I turn and see what or who he's staring at, and of course there's the typical creepy guy checking every girl out.

"Focus on me, Anima. Focus on the wall. See this route right here? You're going to flash it. Look at the holds. I'll make sure you're safe."

I start climbing, and I quickly remember how tight these shoes are. I haven't worn them in so long, I don't know how much I'll be able to do.

"Just like that Anima. Heel hook with your right foot right there. Yeah, come on, girl! You're so close, yessss! There you go!"

I finish the route without falling even once and totally enjoy the high five Dionisio gives me. It's his turn now. He quickly gets up on the wall, and he makes my performance look terrible compared to his. He's light, and quick, his moves make no sound at all. He finishes, gets down, where I wait for him with my arms crossed on my chest.

"Well, there's no need to show off."

"Show off? You literally just flashed a V3. A route that isn't easy for basically a first timer and you did it with barcly any beta. Stop comparing yourself to me. You'll get to my level very quickly and probably surpass me."

"Thought I was going to hate you, but you're being so supportive."

"You will soon. Get your hands and feet back on the wall. You're trying this V3 now."

"Yes, sir." He grins at my choice of words.

The second route takes me a bit longer than I expected to get through. I don't finish it on the first try. Sloper holds are my weakness. My hands are small and I find it hard to find a grip on such big holds. I prefer the smallest hold possible to any sloper. I fall. More than a couple of times, but I get back up and finally get it.

"Good girl. Perseverance works for you."

I take a sip from my water bottle and then get back on the wall for the next route. We continue like this for a good hour and a half. My forearms are tense and my hands start feeling a bit numb.

"So—how are things with my brother going? Is he treating you well?"

"Things are ok." Svetlana's uncertain look comes back to mind. "I guess—I mean, we're getting to know each other, you know…" The fear I felt the other night reflourishes. Are things really ok?

You know you can talk to me, right?

"I know." I sigh. "We're gonna have to tell him that you can respond to my—power."

"We will. Let me see if I can find out more about it first though. I know there has to be an explanation."

"There has to be more about suspirium in the book. I haven't used it with anyone else."

"It's probably tied to your emotions. I freaked you out the first time we met."

"That—is true. I didn't take that into consideration."

Suddenly my heart fastens, and a tickling sensation reaches my abdomen. My eyes close and as I breathe in, shivers travel down my spine.

I turn towards the entrance door, almost knowing that Eros is going to walk through it at any second.

"I think Eros is here," I say, keeping my eyes on the entry of the gym.

"What do you mean by—" Dionisio doesn't even have the time to finish the sentence when Eros walks through the door, and a smile grows on my face.

"Well, that was definitely something," D says as soon as Eros approaches us.

"What is?" Eros says without taking his eyes off of me.

"She sensed you." Dionisio's arms cross on his chest.

"I just had a feeling he arrived. It's a coincidence. It could happen to anyone," I say, trying to brush it off.

Eros gives me a quick kiss, and says, "Your powers are growing."

"Could be a soulmate thing," Dionisio's voice is low.

"That or it's another power we didn't know she had, like suspirium."

"So I can sense people now?"

"Possibly. We're going to test it later. What did I miss here?" Eros rubs his hands, getting ready for the chalk.

"Anima is actually in decent shape."

"Wow, such a compliment." He just finished saying how good I was doing, then his brother arrives, and I suddenly am only decent.

"Coming from D, that is actually a compliment. Want to show me something? I have to distract myself from the fucking guy over there with his eyes glued on you," Eros says, obviously irritated, looking right past me.

"See that V4? That route on your left," D asks close to my ear. "Make it your bitch."

"I don't think I—" A V4 is for a climber that has been training for a while. He can't seriously think I can get this done on my first time back into a gym.

"You're not getting out of here until you get that V4 done." Dionisio's voice is firm, someone would think he's pushing me, but the grin on his face tells otherwise. He truly thinks I can make it right to the top.

"Now I see where the insults might come in handy." I stick my tongue out at him.

"Get a move on it."

"Do you really have to talk to her like that, brother?" Eros jumps into our conversation.

"Yes."

I start walking towards the wall and as I turn to look at them, I notice Eros is not paying attention to me at all. He's still looking at the stranger that seems to be pretty interested in what I am doing.

I rub my hand in chalk, take a look at the wall, and start climbing.

First try. Fail. As I try to get a grip on the second hold on my left, I slip as I put all of my weight on my left foot.

"You have to heel hook at the hold on the right, try to shift the weight of your body on your left foot right after that move. Not before."

I get back on the wall, do as Dionisio said to do. Fail again.

"You're not shifting your weight enough. Try to do it static, slow moves, don't rush yourself or you're going to tire yourself out too quickly."

"News flash, I am already tired," I yell at him as I fall down again.

"Ok this is it. She did enough. I think we can call it a day," Eros shouts at his brother.

"Don't baby her," Dionisio gets back at him.

"Don't pressure her," he says back.

"Anima, am I pressuring you?"

I think about it before replying. Dionisio has been cheering for me the entire time. He's been testing my limits but always making sure I am ok. His cold voice softens every time I fall. He gets close to me and gives me advice. He sees me as his equal. He wants me to succeed, and this is why he's pushing me to get this route done. I haven't felt this way in a long time. People pity me for what I've lost. He doesn't. He shows me what I can accomplish.

"No, not really." Eros's nostrils flare as my words come out. His jaw locks as his eyes stare at Dionisio. His hands clench into fists. He's mad, not with me, never mad at me, but mad with his brother.

"Good, now try again. You almost got it."

I need to get this route done. I want to prove to them that I can do it.

And you can.

I start climbing again, slowly. I take my time, hold after hold, and then I see it. The last hold. Finally, both my hands grab it.

I climb down with euphoria coming out of all my pores. I've never felt stronger than I do right at this moment. I, Anima Soleri, am capable of climbing mountains. Nothing can take the grin off of my face after this.

"See? Told you she could do it." Dionisio says, grabbing his brother's shoulder and squeezing it for a moment.

"I did it!" I hop towards them, then high five Dionisio.

"Proud of you." Eros's lips end up on mine. "Now can we leave, before I end up killing some stranger?"

"Please don't make a scene. He's harmless," I beg Eros, trying to pull him in the opposite direction.

The guy that was looking at me though, has the bright idea to start walking towards us. This is the day I start digging a hole and bury myself in it. Eros was ready to leave and now he's ready to rip his head off.

Why are some men just so oblivious? Does he have a death wish? I am here with two guys. I don't get how someone can be that stupid.

"Is there space for another man in your heart? I know you are busy with two, but three is the perfect number." I have never been shoved away from someone this quickly in my entire life.

"Dude, you better walk away right now or I swear on anyone you care about that your head will not stay attached to your body for long," Eros says, putting himself between me and the guy. Dionisio positions himself beside his brother, creating a wall in front of me.

"Calm down prince charming. I don't care about her. She's nice to look at, but she isn't yours. Never was. Jeremy will come for her."

"He's gonna have to go through me to get to her, and I won't make it easy," Eros spits back.

"Through you? Ha, you're hilarious. This is a battle you won't win. He will take her as his queen. The prophecy won't be fulfilled."

I reach for Dionisio's arm and push him on the side so that I can put myself in the middle. I look at the guy in front of me. The person that was here to scare me, to make me panic. He wants to see my eyes grow wide, my palms sweat. He's waiting for me to start trembling. Well, I am not shaking right now—not anymore.

"Tell Jeremy that I am not afraid of him—not today, not ever." My voice is firm, no sign of panic. "I am not the gazelle nowadays."

No, you're not. You're the lion.

Yes. I am the lion.

The guy salutes me with a bow and leaves the gym. Eros is ready to follow him but my tight grip on his arm stops him.

"What was that?" I say, my eyes wide.

Eros sighs. "Jeremy's way of letting us know he has minions everywhere."

"This is not good, Eros," D says.

Eros's stare is deadly. His jaw is so tight that if he doesn't stop biting down so hard, he might break his teeth. "You shouldn't have brought her here, I told you."

"You're the one that thinks Anima needs to be put under a

glass container."

"I want her alive," Eros yells back at him.

"She's not that fragile, Eros. She's stronger than both of us put together, and you know it."

"Why are you even still here?"

"I am following my orders," Dionisio replies, crossing his arms on his chest.

"Orders of a false king."

"Our father will remain king until she's ready to take his place. You know this as well as I do."

Eros shakes his head and laughs. "This is so unnecessary. I don't need a babysitter. I am capable of doing my part."

"I am not here for you. I am here for her."

"Why are you playing the bodyguard, the trainer, the friend, when we both know what you have to do?" Eros's words make Dionisio flinch. I see him breathe heavily, trying to calm himself down.

"You both clearly need to talk and figure your shit out. I don't need to be in the middle of this. I'm gonna go get some fresh air," I say walking away from both of them.

They both catch up to me outside and stay silent for a while until Dionisio breaks the silence.

"You are the heir to the throne, and you and Eros are destined to fulfill the prophecy. We're going to make sure of that."

The words of the stranger come back to me. "Could Jeremy even do that? Take the throne, I mean."

"Dusäiga belongs to you, the throne belongs to you and— well, the person you decide to spend your life with," Eros says.

I nod at him with my mouth in a thin line. "Can we go somewhere else? I'm feeling a little—overwhelmed."

"Yes absolutely, we can leave. I'll take you to get something to eat."

"I'll leave you two alone. Got someone inside who's waiting

for some beta."

"How the hell did you pick up someone? You were with me the entire time! Actually, don't tell me. I don't want to know," I manage to say shocked, crossing my arms in front of my chest.

D winks at me before walking back inside, and Eros and I get into his car and drive away. No, Eros doesn't drive a fast and furious car. He drives a toyota yaris. A reliable car. For some reason I find it very fitting. Am I really analyzing people based on what they drive? No, because I know nothing about cars.

"How are you feeling?" Eros says after a few minutes of silence.

"I don't know. Until two weeks ago I was a photographer obsessed with books, and now I find out I am the heir to a magical throne, and that my psychopath ex is still stalking me because he wants to rule with me and probably kill me or I don't know what, because he has been involved in all this since day one, and that my boyfriend and his brother are... drum rolls please... also two fucking magical beings that tell me I have powers, so you tell me—how do you think I'm feeling?" I spew out, raising my voice with each word. My breaths are quick and heavy as I lay my palm on my chest trying to control my heartbeat.

"Boyfriend, you say." Eros looks at me, smiling before adding, "I like the sound of that."

I did say that, didn't I? Do I like the sound of that? I think I do too.

"I never really asked about Jeremy before… Did he hurt you? You said you had to get a restraining order… Did he physically hurt you?" He asks.

I shake my head no.

"We met in school, he was a teaching assistant for one of my Art History classes, even though I guess he wasn't really an assistant and he just played the part to get close to me," I start saying before adding, "He would wait for me to leave the classroom and just chat for a few minutes, then he started being around a lot more. We started going out. We got close, and he got really possessive right away, but I liked the guy. I didn't take it too seriously—at first." I sigh before the next part. "One night, after a couple of months of us going out, we were at a club and he didn't take very well anyone that would look in my direction. He got into a fight, and really hurt a guy without any reason at all. That poor guy really didn't do anything! Anyway, after that I broke things off, but he didn't take it well." My hand clenches around the key around my neck, the ridges digging into my skin. "He started following me around, leaving gifts at my apartment. Every time I would be talking to someone, even a stranger on the street to give directions, he would just show up and pick fights saying that I would always be only his and stuff like that. So I went to the police and got the restraining order, but it really didn't do much. I was finishing school. I didn't have much time left there, anyway. Then my parents passed away, so I came back home and left everything behind me." My eyes stare at my shoes. "Or so I thought."

For a minute he doesn't say anything and takes in all the information I just gave him.

"He's not going to hurt you, I won't let that happen. That explains why you don't like it too much when I am being protective of you, even though I wouldn't pick a fight unless someone else started it."

"No, I know you wouldn't." Do I? Reality is, I won't know until I give him a chance, a real one.

"Whatever you need me to do to make you feel better, I will."

I rest my head on his shoulder. "Just being around you is enough."

As soon as I say that I realize we are parking close to a bar, and I feel my phone buzz in my pocket.

DIONISIO:

All good there?

ANIMA:

Thought you were too busy giving beta to someone

DIONISIO:

Jealousy doesn't suit you, little ninja

ANIMA:

I am not jealous.

DIONISIO:

Whatever you say.

ANIMA:

Go back to your beta, we are just grabbing some food. We are fine. I am fine, really.

"Is my brother bugging you?" Eros asks, smiling at me while he opens up the passenger door for me.

"He just wanted to see how I was doing." I say, quickly putting away my phone.

"He's getting close to you. I haven't seen him so protective over someone in a long time."

"He cares about you, so he cares about me."

"Sure, let's say that," he says, rubbing the back of his neck.

I tiptoe and leave a quick peck on his lips. His stiff shoulders relax at the sudden touch of our mouths.

"It's us Eros. You and me."

"You're right. It's us."

It's us. Soulmates. Probably getting married to get this throne that apparently is mine. Why is it so hard for me to see it as a good thing?

On the contrary, my stomach closes at the thought of it. This is not good. Not good at all.

CHAPTER 13

My feet sink into the ground as I pace myself towards nothingness.

The floor is so cold beneath me. Where are my shoes?

I have—need to find him. Now I know. He is in danger—they all are and it's all my fault. I should have gotten here sooner.

I can't see a foot ahead, only a dark pitch around me as I keep my arms in front of me not to stumble against one of the huge bookshelves populating the space.

I take a deep breath in, and a hint of vanilla fills my nostrils.

Shivers run down my spine as a chilly breeze follows me from the slightly open window on my left.

I have to be quick before he finds out what I'm doing.

Wax from the candle I'm holding falls on my hand making it sting so methodically.

Here's the door, the dark wood separating me from him. I

open it gently and there he is, Dionisio, laying on his side, sleeping.

My golden light. I have to tell him everything.

Just as I reach forward with my free hand, a drop of wax falls on his shoulder.

He quickly turns and as I start to speak, his eyes widen from something he sees behind me.

I turn my head towards the entrance and as I focus on the image in front of me, Jeremy stares back into my eyes with a grin on his face.

As I sprint for the door, I bump into something. Someone. My eyes stare at the perfect copy of them.

I WAKE UP WITH CHILLS. NO, NOT JUST CHILLS, BUT FULL BODY tremors. I can't breathe and my heart is racing so fast I feel it will break my rib cage and race out of my body.

The pain in my chest is so unbearable I know I have to do something, get a grip, but my body is paralyzed.

A panic attack.

How wonderful. I try to focus on my thoughts and what could have triggered my brain, but the thing with panic attacks is that rational thinking becomes really really difficult. My vision blurs, and with that, my brain shuts down. I look down at my numb hands. They're so white, pallid. This is it. This is how I am going to go. Scared to death by—life.

Was it the dream I had? Was it the fact that I had no time to process the loss of my parents? Probably the second one. Probably both. The eyes. The dream. That was—Eros. It had to be him. I squeeze my eyes shut, crumbling to the ground.

Knowing that I will have to marry someone because some

silly prophecy said that we're destined to be together also might be a reason to panic.

I try to force myself to pick up the phone and dial the last number that called me. I don't know how I manage to press the call button, but I am so glad I do.

"It's the middle of the night. Is everything ok?" A dark, groggy voice says.

"I... I can't... breathe" I say between a rapid inhale and exhale.

As I hear the line drop, my mouth dries up and a knot of barbed wire closes my throat.

I am alone again, and I don't know what to do. I might have felt like a lion the other day, but here I am, back being the scared gazelle.

What did my therapist tell me to do in these situations? Start looking around, try to name things I see in front of me. Maybe I can try to count the books on my shelves.

I hear a knock on the window. I turn but I can't seem to be able to get up from the floor. How did I end up here? I can't remember.

A pair of green eyes stare at me. Tilting his head, drawing his eyebrows together, Dionisio opens up the sliding door on my balcony.

"I'm right here," He says before he takes a few quick steps towards me. When he's beside me, he falls down on his knees. "Why aren't you wearing the ring?"

"I—I feel trapped when I wear—" Breathe in, breathe out. "When I wear jewelry at night."

His hands grab mine, and while I try to control my breathing I stare into his eyes. Suddenly, the noise of a single car driving by reaches me. Then my quick breathing, then his, until I can hear even my own heartbeat. His touch. So gentle. The black spots that were filling my vision are slowly disappearing, and the room that was spinning just a few moments ago ceases to move.

"Good girl, look at me, focus on me," He starts saying. "Deep breaths in, deep breaths out."

He rests my right hand on his heart. I close my eyes and concentrate on the sound exploding from his chest.

"Close your eyes. Focus on my heartbeat. Follow my breathing."

I concentrate on his words, and we remain still until my heartbeat goes back to normal.

"You should always wear the ring. I would have been here faster." He picks up the thin band from my nightstand and positions it back on my index finger.

I notice he is wearing the same exact golden ring on his finger, but my lips remain shut.

"I'm sorry," I whisper under my breath.

Don't. Apologize. Echoes in my head. "I'm just glad you're ok." Dionisio's low voice sends shivers down my back.

"I think I am." My hands aren't tingling much now. My legs aren't wobbly anymore either, and the cold sweats have calmed as well.

"Wanna talk about what happened?"

"Not really."

"Why did you call me?" His voice cracks. Low. Soft. Almost a whisper.

My cheeks flush as I stare down at the floor. A lump in my throat makes it impossible to reply to his question. My chest tightens when I look back up and he's right there, staring at me, waiting.

"Let me call E—"

"Because I knew you'd come." I blurt out, looking down at my pale numb hands, thousands of pins and needles stabbing every inch of them.

"What?" He asks after a couple of seconds.

"Because I knew you'd come," I repeat, now gazing at him. My eyes turn watery, ready to explode.

Always, his voice echoes in my mind. His thumb catches a tear falling down my cheek. *I will always make sure you're safe.*

"No matter what?" I ask.

His eyes widen for a brief moment. *No matter what,* he promises.

"I don't want him to see me like this—so weak."

"Weak? Anima, you've been dealing with so many horrible things all at the same time. You're not weak, quite the opposite, really."

"I don't feel particularly strong today."

"That's ok. You don't have to be strong all the time. You deal with your pain like you want to. He's not going to judge you for it. You know that, right?"

"I think he's the reason why I cracked."

"Want to elaborate?"

"It's one thing to find out you're the heir to a throne, and this person is your soulmate. It's another to know that I am supposed to marry this stranger to get what is mine by birthright."

"Your biological parents wanted to change that law, you know? They couldn't before everything went down. The low birth rate caused by the curse also didn't make it easy for the citizens of Dusäiga to accept such a big change, but they were trying to find a solution to make that change."

"I should feel ecstatic to know who my soulmate is, but look, here I am panicking and calling his brother to vent."

And I am so glad you did.

The sudden need to get up and get some fresh air abruptly makes me whisper something I would probably regret later. "I need to go for a drive."

"Like now?" Dionisio asks, raising an eyebrow at me.

"Yeah, it helps me calm down."

He nods. "Ok, let's go. My car isn't too far from here."

"I mean I need to drive."

"Oh." His face and shoulder drop. "Yeah, I'll let you be. You do whatever you need to feel better."

A soft chuckle escapes my mouth. "No, I meant we can take my car cause I would like to be the one driving."

"Well then, little ninja." His silky voice makes me shiver as he calls me by my pet name. "Drive me around."

Without even bothering to change, I grab an oversized sweater and my car keys and head for the door. Dionisio follows me in silence. We go down the stairs and as I step outside, I breathe in the night brisk air. Even with my eyes closed I can sense Dionisio's stare on me. I ignore it and start walking towards the parking lot. When I get to the farthest corner lot, I turn to him.

A sudden sense of uncertainty makes my stomach feel uneasy. I bite my lower lip before asking, "Are you sure you're ok with this?"

The corners of his mouth lift up as his green eyes stare at mine. The moonlight makes his irises look even lighter than usual. "Never been this sure about something in my entire life."

I roll my eyes and unlock my car. He rushes into the passenger side, moves the seat back to fit in comfortably, and puts on his seatbelt right away.

"I've never seen someone put on a seatbelt that fast in my entire life. I promise, I am capable of driving."

"I always put on a seat belt. I am a saint that follows the rules like a good boy."

I shake my head before starting the engine. "Sure you are."

You wound me with your sarcasm.

No I don't, I reply, smirking at him.

As a random playlist starts, I get out of the parking lot and drive away. We remain in silence as I take the first left turn and then a right. He doesn't question where I am going and I am glad because in all honesty, I don't know where I am going either. Driving around Vallecrosia this late at night during the week is calming. The entire town is asleep. The odd car drives past us and no sound comes from the outside world. I take another turn and park the car in front of the seashore. The death metal gets replaced by the sound of the water crushing on the big rocks.

I should have known we would end up here, eventually. Dionisio's velvety voice fills my head.

Then, I finally ask something that I've been wanting to say for a while now. "There has to be more to this—to why the law was written in the first place."

"What?"

"The marriage law," I clarify.

He sighs. "The marriage law was put into place when the drought started. Unfortunately, this also meant that people in your family married for convenience in the past instead of love. Your parents though, they loved each other very much."

"Do you remember them?"

He smiles under his breath before replying, "Very little but my dad tells me all the time how lucky someone would be to have what your parents had."

"That's—beautiful."

"It is. It's hopeful."

"What about before the curse? Was there another way to become queen?"

"There was another way to show yourself worthy of the crown and its powers. The Royal candidate would have to face four deathly tests. These tasks were related to the elements. Remember the story of the four gods I told you the other day? *The Ancient Trials* were decided by them. No one has dared to call on them in hundreds of years—for obvious reasons."

The thought of going through a test, four of them to prove I was worthy of something that was going to be mine somehow makes more sense than just marrying a random person. Ruling a kingdom can't be easy. A wedding wouldn't magically teach me what has to be done. Unease comes back to me. My shoulders loosen and my arms fall down my sides.

"Can we keep this between us? Just this time, and if it happens again, I'll call Eros."

Dionisio leans over the center console and brushes a chunk of hair out of my face. "Yes, of course." I feel butterflies in my stomach being in the enclosed space, breathing the same air he's breathing. Then, suddenly, the butterflies turn into guilt because of Eros.

Silence comes rushing back after I thank him. I start the engine and drive us back to the same parking spot I always drive my car. We reach my apartment once again and as I lay my back against the wall in my bedroom, I slowly slide down and end up sitting on the floor again. Dionisio always on my side, waiting for me to open up, never pushing me.

"He is in the dream too now. As I leave the room with you and Jeremy, he's right there," I say remembering the dream that started the panic attack in the first place.

"Yes. He is."

"Took me a bit to realize it, but I guess things are starting to slowly make sense."

"They are. How are you feeling, aside from all this?"

I take a moment to think to find the right words. Discovering so many things about my biological parents makes me think about the two people that helped me grow. Mirella and Giorgio. My adoptive parents. My hand instinctively closes around the gold key around my neck, and I sigh.

"I miss them, you know?"

"Who?"

"My adoptive parents," I manage to say before adding, "Even

if they kept so many secrets from me. I didn't have the chance to say goodbye and I—I think it's starting to hit me for real."

"Keeping those secrets was their way to protect you, and it worked for a long time."

"Until it didn't."

I feel him picking me up from the floor as if I weigh less than a feather and I feel that light too—in his arms. He lowers me down to bed and covers my body with my blanket, the warmth encompassing me further making me feel back at ease.

"We're going to figure it out. You're not alone, Anima, not anymore."

More silence follows us. I close my eyes and focus on the absence of noise around us. With that, I finally have the power to get out the words I couldn't before.

"*You* gave me the ring."

"Yes, I did," he says as he slightly tilts his head.

"No, I mean—Eros didn't ask you to. You gave me the ring because you wanted to."

He looks into the distance, swallows nervously and then turns back to me with a smile. "Close your eyes, little ninja, I'll stay until you fall back asleep." I feel his gentle touch one last time tucking some hair behind my ear.

And just like that, I drift back to unconsciousness knowing that I'm finally safe and that in one way or another, I'm going to figure things out.

Chapter 14

HEALING POTIONS ARE AT THE BASICS OF POTION MAKING. IT'S VERY IMPORTANT FOR EVERY STRIGA AND VENEFICUS TO KNOW HOW TO PREPARE ONE. NOTE: A HEALING POTION CAN'T CHEAT DEATH.

The soreness of my body after the last few weeks of training with Dionisio seems to be perennial.

As I yawn and stretch, a ray of sunshine peeks from my bedroom window getting right into my eyes. Wonderful. I thought I was supposed to feel invincible by now, instead I feel absolutely broken. I should get up. Dionisio will text me soon to tell me to get my ass out of the house for our morning workout, but I am really hoping he will suddenly forget I exist so that I can sleep in a little longer before heading into the studio.

Eros and I have been working on my magic very cautiously. We're trying to understand what I can do based on what my parents appear to have been able to do. The suspirium seems to be working only with Dionisio, and I'm only able to sense Eros, which could be a soulmate thing and not really something I can do with everyone. Sensing him is quite peculiar, my heart skips a beat, my jaw drops and all of a sudden I know exactly where Eros will appear. The shiver on the back of my neck almost makes me jolt every time I experience or use this power unintentionally.

I am supposed to be able to manipulate minds and move objects with my own mind, but still nothing. Ginevra says that there could still be traces of the glamour she put on, and unfortunately the only way to wear it off is by continuing to practice the magic I am actually able to do.

My heels ache when my feet hit the floor as I get out of bed. My Achilles tendons beg me to stop attempting to stand. The tightness on every limb of my body makes moving a little more difficult. Walking burns and I feel every little muscle spasm as I try to move my shoulders to loosen them up.

I reach the kitchen and leisurely start preparing coffee and a slice of Triora bread with jam.

Missed me, gazelle? Oh wait, I was told you're the lion now. Cute.

A voice inside my head makes my ears pop. It feels like an incessant buzzing.

It's not the same as when I hear a thought or when Dionisio talks to me, no, this is intrusive—trespassing.

It burns down my spine as if someone is pouring hot sauce all over my vertebrae.

That soft dark raspy tone. I know exactly who it belongs to.

Jeremy.

How—how is it possible? This has to be just a horrible joke of my imagination.

Thought you'd know by now that many things are possible.

Get out of my head, psychopath.

You know, I really don't like that ginger guy around you, and let's not even start with the other one. But that's just how you are. Does the redhead know about the bond you have with his brother?

Suspirium doesn't work that way, I'd love to see his face when he finds out.

Show yourself if you really think you can get to me. I am not scared of you, Jeremy.

You'll see me soon enough, princess, and you'll join me, I know you will. We will take our throne.

The buzzing ceases, and the burning sensation disappears completely as my ears pop once again. *Princess.* The old pet name makes me gag at the memories of him in my bed. His hungry eyes on my body. His rough fingers caressing my skin. I shut my eyes, trying to get those images out of my head, and then run to my kitchen sink letting everything come out. As I dial Eros's number, he picks up before the first ring.

"We're outside."

I falter to my front door, and as soon as I unlock it, I throw myself to Eros in shock. He waits no time to wrap me in his arms.

"Hey, it's ok. I'm right here, nothing is going to hurt you, my love."

My love. The words hit me. Or better… They don't, and they should. I thought I would feel more hearing such a strong sentiment. My heart doesn't skip a beat. My cheeks don't flush. My hands don't tremble. Nothing. The image of Jeremy is a permanent tattoo in my brain.

"What happened?" Dionisio's voice snaps me back into reality. His eyes fixated on me.

"Jeremy talked to me," I say as I free myself of Eros' hold and pace back and forth between the two brothers. "In my head!" Frantically waving my hands around, I shake my head. "The creep was in my *mind.* I could hear his voice as if he was right beside me whispering in my ear. How is that even possible?"

Eros sighs and reaches for my arm trying to make me stay still. "Well, what did he say?"

"That I'll see him soon and that I will join him and together we will take the throne."

"The guy can't take a hint, huh?" D says, shaking his head.

"You're not going to like what I am about to say," Eros starts, looking straight into my eyes.

"Then don't say it." I know where this is going, I can feel it.

"Actually, you'll probably hate it," D adds, his smirk growing.

"Then you should definitely not say it," I repeat. I raise my hands and place them on my ears trying to muffle the words that will be coming out of Eros's mouth in three…two…one.

"We can't leave you out of our sight now."

There you go. What did I say?

Crossing my arms on my chest, I say, "Yeah as a matter of fact, I do hate this."

"He's going to make a move soon, and we have to be ready, Anima."

I know Eros is right, and I know he is saying this because he just wants to protect me, but I will be a prisoner in my own house. A prisoner in a jail where the guards are two sexy brothers. I mean… it *could* be worse.

Sexy, huh? Dionisio says through the bond. Of course he was listening, he always is.

I'm not in the mood to play.

As I take the deepest breath in history, the muscles of my chest burn. Ouch. Working out sucks.

"I thought only I could talk with my mind," I say. "So how's it possible *he* can talk to *me*?" I turn to look at Dionisio, his eyes searching mine. He can talk to me as well, Jeremy knows he can. What if there's a connection between us three that we don't know of? As my thoughts come flourishing, Dionisio's lips are in a thin line. He's listening to everything I am thinking. Every single word.

"You are the only one that we know of. We're still not sure how he would be able to do it," Eros starts, before questioning, "How did it feel?"

"Imposed. It felt like he was forcing himself into my head."

Dionisio swears under his breath. "It could have been a spell, which means—"

"He was close to her. Too close. Probably in the building." Eros concludes. That would strike out the possibility of Jeremy sharing suspirium with me, unless by accident I opened some sort of connection like the one I have with Dionisio. Jeremy's words come back to me. *Suspirium doesn't work that way, I'd love to see his face when he finds out.*

The brothers nod at each other. My eyes go back and forth between the two. I sink into the couch feeling completely powerless.

"I'm gonna go update dad," Dionisio says, getting up from the loveseat he sat on right in front of me. Keeping his distance from me.

"Good idea." Eros nods, wrapping his arm around my shoulder, staring at his brother.

"What are we going to do?"

"We are going to take the day to learn some magic and relax, how does that sound?" Eros replies should make me feel—happy, instead my throat closes at the thought of staying in this apartment a minute longer.

"No training today?" I ask, looking in Dionisio's direction.

Trust me, I'd love to get you into a gym, but you need this.

"I managed to convince Dionisio to give you a rest day."

"I can train. I don't need a rest day" I jump on my feet regretting the decision right away as my body starts stinging once again.

"You can barely walk." Dionisio laughs. The sound of it causes the corners of my lips to lift. My eyes focus on his white teeth, then his cheeks, and the dimple that appears on the left side of his mouth. It's such a beautiful melody, one that I could listen to on repeat every day. My face feels warm as my heartbeat fastens. "You're doing great. One day off will get your muscles to heal. You're going to be fine." My eyes go wide and I quickly turn to look at Eros.

"Ok but I want to try to do something with my magic, then."

"That's a promise." Eros's lips touch my forehead softly.

"Before I go, here, take this." Dionisio hands me a little flask.

"What is it?"

"Low dosage healing potion. Since Eros can't heal sore muscles."

"And you waited this long to tell me this existed?"

"I would have waited even longer if your psycho ex hadn't done his creepy thing this morning."

You like seeing me suffer, don't you?

Actually, it's my least favorite thing to witness. You should feel your body loosen up pretty quickly after you drink it.

"Well, thank you for your pity. You can leave now."

"As you wish." He gives me a wink and then heads for the door.

While my butt crashes on the couch, I sigh, knowing that I won't be able to solve all this mess today. It would be nice to just get it over with, but I am not ready, not yet. I open up the little bottle with the green liquid and down it like a shot. Relief fills my body within seconds. God how much I love this shit.

Eros sits down beside me. "Feeling better?"

I smile at the ease my body feels. "Much."

"Good."

My eyes search for his. He was already looking at me when I turned in his direction. "Can we go out for a bit? Being in this apartment is making me feel—trapped." I sigh. "Especially after finding out Jeremy knows where I live."

"Yes, of course, let's go. Let me buy you a coffee and something to eat." He stands up and extends his hand reaching for mine. "We can go to my place afterwards to practice some magic."

Relaxing at his words, I nod and take his hand. Knowing I will be out of here with Eros, someone that wants to protect me, makes me feel somewhat—safe.

Reaching for my phone I send a quick text to Svetlana, telling her I won't be opening the studio today because of some errands I have to run.

SVETLANA:

Anima, please don't push me away. I know something is up.

I sigh at the words.

Eros's eyebrow lifts. "Is everything ok?"

"Yeah, just Svetlana being worried about me," I reply, putting my phone in my pocket.

AS WE STEP INTO *BAR COBALTO* I THINK OF THE LAST TIME WE were here—together. We talked about our dreams. I didn't know I was a striga yet. I didn't know the person in front of me would be my soulmate and future husband. I didn't know we were destined to fulfill a prophecy and save a magical world by becoming queen and king.

"Here." Eros places a Cappuccino and a plate with a slice of focaccia in front of me. I smile at the food in front of me.

"Why don't we just go to Dusäiga and ask your father for help?"

Eros shakes his head. "Trust me, he's already doing a lot."

"I just feel like I am left out of everything."

"You still are trying to remember your first few years of life, and it would be dangerous to attempt to go through the warehouse again before you're ready—before you can protect yourself—before you truly accept who you are and are able to open the red door."

"I do believe you." Do I? "That Opacum encounter was a one-time thing. I didn't even know what I was doing, and you would be with me this time!"

"That was the second time, after I specifically told you not to do what you did."

"Ok, but that's on you."

An amused grin appears on his face. "How's that on me?"

"It's like when you see a sign that says wet paint—you want to touch it to make sure it's indeed wet."

"You are going to give me so many headaches," Eros says, shaking his head.

"Not my fault the gods decided I was the right pick for you."

"I am very glad that they picked you as my match, Anima."

I disregard his words and nervously bite my lower lip, trying to keep the eye contact to a minimum as heat blossoms on my cheeks. As his match. The gods picked us. My match.

"How are we going to test if I'm ready if I can't even try to open the red door?"

"You will be able to open the door, Anima, and you'll go to Dusäiga. I know you believe in who you are."

"It's good that at least one of us does."

"Anima—"

I rethink about the dream, Dionisio's wide eyes as he takes in Jeremy behind me. The cold shiver that runs down my spine when I'm met with his cruel smirk and ice-cold gray eyes.

"I have to tell you something about the dream we share—the vision."

"Go on."

"I saw you in it. Vividly."

"You did?" Eros's eyes widen.

"That's not all, though."

"There's someone else in it." He states.

Panic fills my lungs. He knows. Having this confrontation makes my palms sweat. I rub them on my jeans. "Yes, there's a third person." My eyes stare at the cup of coffee in front of me. "The vision isn't just about us."

"I got the same feeling. Since Jeremy showed up, I had—I also had this new version of the vision"

"You did?"

"Yeah, but I can't figure out who it could be, do you?"

"No," I lie for a moment, before adding, "I mean, I have a feeling but I am not sure."

"Anima, why won't you look at me? We are in this together, don't forget that."

We're in a public setting, no better way to break the news. "I think—it's Dionisio."

Eros's jaw locks. His eyes lock on mine. I reach for his hand and squeeze it. "There has to be a reason why we are all in it."

"Dionisio could symbolize us saving Dusäiga. It could be him." Eros nods at his own words.

"That—that kind of makes sense." My head tilts on the side.

"I will take you to Dusäiga and do everything I can to make sure you get your throne back, Anima, that's a promise."

"I know."

"Now let's work on getting you there a little faster." He rubs his hands and quickly rises to his feet. "Let's see if you can compel me to do something."

"Ok maybe don't yell it in public," I whisper at him.

"I got a little carried away, come on, let's go." I take his hand once again and we walk out of the bar.

As we reach his front door, I stop right before crossing the entrance.

"What is it?" Eros asks. His eyes are studying me, making sure I'm ok.

I shake my head and smile under my breath. "Nothing." I look up at him, the corners of my lips still lifted up. "This is the first time I will enter your apartment without a concussion."

He chuckles at my statement. It's a full high-pitched laugh. It warms me up. "Let's keep it that way, please."

I nod, and follow him inside.

"Make yourself comfortable, I'm just going to grab us some water before we start."

Walking towards his big L shaped couch I stare at the bookshelves behind it. A wall of books. My arms cross on my chest as I examine the titles.

"You can take anything you'd like to read." His words are like music to my ears.

"I don't think that's a good idea."

"And why is that?"

"Because I'd borrow everything."

"I said take, not borrow. Anything you want. It's yours."

My legs wobble at his words. *Anything you want. It's yours.* I sink into his couch, and as I do so, he does the same after putting two glasses of water on the coffee table.

"If you continue saying stuff like that I might actually believe you," I say jokingly, slapping his arm.

"You get everything, Anima. Everything." His lips brush my temples.

Clearing my throat, I get back to the reason why we're in here in the first place. "Ok, how do I compel you to give me all the books in the world?"

"That's gonna be expensive." His lips lift into a smile. "Come on, let's get up. It's easier to concentrate while standing."

I do as he says and stand in front of him. The sun is hitting his face so perfectly. The few freckles on his nose are more visible. I stare at his eyes and wonder if even mine have those flakes of amber in them mixed with everything else. "What do I have to do?"

"Close your eyes. Take my hands and follow my breaths."

I start following the pace of his chest rising up and then going down. Then I close my eyes and continue to do so.

"Nothing else is around us. Just silence. Concentrate on the silence."

"Ok?"

"Now think of an action that you want me to do."

An action? What is this, Charades? I close my eyes once again, but knowing he's staring at me makes me chuckle. I open one eye and here he is, looking at me, his head tilts on the side. "You're not taking this seriously."

"Yes, I am!"

"Then close both eyes."

I do as he says. What should I make him do? Run around the apartment? Strip naked? Now that would be nice. Would that count as harassment? Compelling someone to strip naked. Yeah probably. I open my eyes once again.

"Anima." Eros's tone is bossy.

"Sorry, sorry, I swear I'm trying."

I groan with defeat because nothing is clearly happening. Maybe I can't compel, maybe this power skipped a generation just like suspirium did.

"Focus, Anima." He gets closer to me. "Take my hands and try again."

Our fingers touch, and a little spark makes me jump in surprise. I close my eyes once again and think of something to make him do.

Suddenly, the urge to ridicule him takes over me. After all,

I've been the one in the child-like position in this ordeal. It's time for Eros to look like the silly one. Opening my eyes, I lock them with his and let that feeling come out. Vocalizing it.

Slap yourself.

Eros brings his hand close to his face and hits himself with it. His jaw drops open in surprise.

Rubbing his cheek, he asks, "Did you just make me slap myself?"

"I—" Laughter fills my lungs to the point of hyperventilation. "I did, I am so sorry"

"That was—"

"Stupid, reckless, pointless, I know." I am still trying to catch a breath.

"Hot. I was going to say hot." His eyes darken as he grins at me.

"You are sick."

"Maybe."

"I can't believe that worked." My mouth slightly opens while I cup my cheeks with my hands.

"Wanna try again?"

"Yes."

"Go on then, be gentle this time, please."

I look at his eyes once again, give him a soft smile, and think of something else. Something I've been dying to do since we walked into his apartment. Something that after what we just shared just seemed so right.

Kiss me, Eros.

And as soon as the voice inside of me comes out, his lips are on mine. I push my body against his. A moan of approval escapes his mouth as soon as my breasts press on his chest. One of his hands is steady on the small of my back while the other one is entangled with my hair.

I forget everything, all of the bad that was planning to take us down and every rational thought I had.

The only important thing is his shirt, and how I would love to rip it into shreds—his citrusy smell that always makes my nose tingle with pleasure—how my lips fell open at the touch of his to let his tongue move with mine.

He breaks the kiss for a moment, keeping his forehead on mine. "That was unnecessary."

"What do you mean?"

"You don't ever have to compel me to do that."

"You asked me to be gentle."

"That was all but gentle."

I reconnect our lips and slowly move us towards the couch. It's now or never. I need to embrace what my body is asking before my intrusive thoughts make me change my mind.

"Anima, you have no idea how much I want this, but I want you to be sure."

"Stop talking." I lay down on the couch and grab him by his shirt, forcing him to lower down on top of me.

"Anima."

"Eros."

"How about we drink a glass of wine first and see if you still want this after you've rationalized the entire situation?"

"I thought you wanted this—me?"

He helps me sit down and rests a hand on my thigh. "I do want this, but I want to be sure you want it too."

"Ok fine go get that wine." I sigh. He just wants to make sure I'm not overly emotional, there's nothing wrong with that. On the contrary, he wants me to be comfortable. It's a very good thing. This is how it's supposed to be. Isn't it?

He gets up and walks towards the kitchen to pour us some burgundy liquid luck in a glass.

"Here." He hands me a glass while he sits down beside me.

"You know, no guy has ever stopped me before."

"No other guy is your soulmate."

Touchè.

"It scares me," I whisper.

He takes my hands in his and chuckles. "It scares me too, Anima. I've had more time to get used to it than you have, but it doesn't mean it's not terrifying. I don't know you just as you don't know me, and though I have strong feelings for you, it's all so... unreal. Sometimes it feels like a dream."

"I think—I think I'll need to hear you say that from time to time. The thought of having to take a throne with basically a stranger, or well, someone that my brain doesn't remember yet, terrifies me."

"Anima, you're not alone. Not in this."

I take a sip, and right away the sweet dark flavour fills my throat. The pungent herbal aftertaste hits me with surprise, which quickly turns into pleasure.

"It's just..." My shoulders slump as I bite my bottom lip. "I don't know how... How can I marry you when I don't know anything about you and your world? How can I trust someone who a billion years ago decided you and I are soulmates and that the faith of our whole world depends on us?"

His hands rest on my cheeks. He wets his lips, growing unusually quiet. Did I just seriously ask him how could I marry him? God, no tact at all.

"We were supposed to have all of our lives to learn about each other, to be friends, to fall in love, to have everything before the moment." He pauses for a moment. "I promise you, Anima, that I will do anything in my power to show you that I am worthy of that love, that I am worthy of being yours. Seeing you grow up without me was the hardest thing I had to do. Seeing you smile kept me alive, knowing you were safe kept me put, but I promise you, I won't leave now that I am back in your life."

"I know you won't. I am sorry that I even said that."

"Don't apologize, not when it's about your feelings." His hand slowly moves down to my chin, lifting it up slightly.

I clear my throat as my eyes find his once again. "I just wish I didn't waste my last years on another continent. I hate that my parents did anything in their power to keep me away."

"They wanted to protect you. I would have done the same thing."

"No, you would have told me who I was much earlier if you could have."

Our lips connect again. My eyes close and I am back running in a garden full of lavender. A peaceful laughter fills my mind. I turn to look at who's following me and it's a boy with strawberry hair laughing with me. Eros. Then I look a little further in front of me and another boy, a little older than me is there waiting for us with his arms crossed on his chest. Dionisio is shaking his head at us in disapproval. My eyes open up and the realization hits me. I might feel like they're strangers right now, but I know deep down they are my only family. That thought comforts me.

I take another sip of wine, gently put down the glass, and grin at Eros.

"You're planning some trouble with that devilish look on your face," He says, jokingly poking my nose.

"Show me, Eros."

"What?"

"Show me how much you want—need my love."

His eyes darken and never leave mine while he puts down his glass beside mine. I lay on the couch once again and he quickly positions his body on top of me, his thighs resting between my legs.

"Are you sure?" He asks as soon as his hands land on my body.

"Oh my god, if you ask me one more time I swear I'll make you slap yourself again. Harder."

"Kinky," He replies, making me laugh against his mouth.

He takes that opportunity to bite my lower lip, sending shivers of pleasure down my spine. I giggle in response and open my mouth for him to give him access to my tongue once again. I didn't know I loved oranges so much until my entire house started to smell like Eros. He leaves a trail of kisses down my neck and I moan in response as soon as he nibbles one of my ears.

"God that feels good," I whisper as he continues the gentle biting.

At that praise, he groans. He picks me up and I automatically lock my legs around his hips as he walks us towards his bedroom.

My body is still entangled with his as we hit the mattress, the zipper of his jeans rubs right on the perfect spot. I feel the heat grow between my legs, my thighs shifting uncomfortably with the wet feeling increasing.

"What do you want me to do, Anima?"

"I want you, all of you."

"You already have me. What do you want me to do?"

"Everything."

"Fuck." He groans, taking his shirt off in one simple gesture.

I feel drunk from what I am witnessing. Dionisio might look like a god, but Eros definitely is quite the competition. A competition he was currently winning. His lean body is firm on top of mine. My hands trace his wide shoulders while my eyes study his flush face, and his messy strawberry hair. I try to reach the hem of my shirt, but he gets there first, helping me take it off. I have no bra on, so as soon as the shirt is out of the way, his eyes shoot to my breasts as he heaves out a breath of lust. "God, you're so beautiful."

One of his forearms rests on the mattress, keeping him propped up, and his lips clasp my left nipple while he pinches the other one with his fingers. This position has him pushed against my bundle of nerves that if he doesn't do anything about it soon, I might just die.

"Please, Eros."

"You can have everything, Anima, everything."

His lips slowly trail down my abdomen and reach my belly button. He reaches the button of my jeans, opens it effortlessly, and slowly moves them down my legs, leaving me only in my now drenched black thong. He takes no time to rest his lips on the soft fabric that separates my flesh from his mouth. He takes a nice breath in and smiles.

"So wet for me, baby."

I moan as he gently pulls aside the fabric and leaves a soft kiss on that sweet sweet spot. He grabs the sides of the panties and takes them off, throwing them on the floor with the rest of our clothes.

"Your scent is intoxicating."

"Eros, please, I want you—"

"Say it. Tell me what you want me to do."

"Kiss me, eat me, fuck me."

"As you wish, my love."

He crouches down between my legs and starts touching me up and up. As he opens my legs, he leaves a trail of kisses on my inner thighs. Kisses evolve into bites. A cry of pleasure leaves my mouth as soon as his tongue reaches my folds and parts me in one flick. My legs become the consistency of jello quickly as he continues to play with my folds and circles my clit with his fingers with slow precise movements. Eros's breath is hot against me and the anticipation is killing me in the most delicious way. I need him inside of me. I need him inside of me *right now*.

"Your sweet taste is addicting. I don't know if I can stop."

"Please—I need you.'

"Soon. Let me play a little longer first."

While he says that, he pushes a finger inside of me while his thumb and tongue are racing as if to see which will make me come first. My legs tighten around his head and he moves his free hand on the back of my thigh, squeezing it. He adds a finger, and as he starts pumping, I clench around them.

Being able to do this, to be vulnerable with someone again feels nice, being so open about what I want—what we both want feels right.

As that thought takes my mind, a heat of pleasure consumes me. His tongue rests on my clit once again, and then his entire mouth does. He sucks at it gently while continuing the movement of his fingers. In and out. In and out.

"Eros, oh my god."

"Yes, my love, say my name as you come on my lips."

With those words—his possessive tone—his low voice, pleasure hits me like a wave, no, more like an entire ocean. I grip his hair as I come harder than I have in a while.

"I could do this all day." His breath on my bundle of nerves makes me throb.

"I might just let you."

"We're not done," He adds, giving me one last lick making me moan once more.

"No, we're not," is all I am able to say while I try to catch my breath.

He leans on top of me and kisses me like it's the last thing he is going to do on this planet. I can still taste myself on his lips. The sweet and sour flavour mixed with his orange fragrance makes me feel lightheaded. I reach for his jeans and he smiles before helping me take them off.

"You can have everything, princess, everything."

His gray boxer briefs outline his shaft perfectly, his size apparent through the thin fabric. He's hard as a rock.

He reaches for his pants to look for something in his pockets and as soon as the little packet is in his hands, he turns back to me.

"Ready for more?"

I pull him closer and grab him where he jolts in surprise, I say, "Yes, I am."

He slips his boxers off and I don't even have the time to admire his shaft as he slides the condom on. No time to waste. He slowly pushes himself inside, making sure not to hurt me while his cock stretches me to accommodate his size. I gasp at the sudden fullness, and the friction makes me sob in pleasure as he starts to move in and out.

"Fuck," He groans.

"What?" I ask, my voice laced with concern.

"You feel so fucking good. I want to last forever but holy shit, Anima, you're perfect."

He leaves a trail of kisses on my collarbone, and as I feel his breath on my skin, shivers travel down my spine. This is good, right? This is really good.

"You're my perfect princess."

A deep thrust makes me jolt. The pet name that surely escaped his mouth unintentionally makes my eyes widen.

"A perfect queen."

A second one makes me grip at his shoulder, leaving marks on his skin.

"My perfect match."

Another one.

"Mine."

He moans deeply, and I wish I could enjoy it, but my body goes stiff. *Mine.* There's something about it that feels...just plain wrong.

Princess. What Jeremy used to call me.

He orgasms with his cock so deep inside of me I think for a

second he might snap me in half, and his lips latch to mine possessively.

He collapses beside me and we stay entangled for a while longer, in silence, him kissing my forehead from time to time to let me know he's still here—with me.

I should feel complete, full, serene at the thought of sharing my body with my soulmate, yet, as soon as the word *mine* escaped his lips, something inside of me did a triple backflip. Something is terribly off and I don't know if it's just me anymore.

Chapter 15

Suspirium is a rare power given only to the members of the Psiche family. It is donated by the Gods when they feel there's a need of redefining balance. It is not given by accident. It is gifted by fate.

The early morning lights peek from the curtains and the yelling on the street forces me to open up my eyes. Did we seriously spend the entire day in this apartment and sleep until now? That is—absurd.

"Good morning, princess." Eros's voice is warm and raspy in my ears.

His arm tightens around my body, and my eyes widen. His chest is pressed against my back and the warmth of his body feels nice at the contact with mine.

Princess. Yesterday I thought it was unintentional. Today I am starting to think it isn't anymore.

"Oh god, I am so sorry. I used the P word, didn't I?" He whispers in my ear.

"It's ok," I start saying. He apologized, it should be ok. It doesn't feel ok. "Good morning," I add, trying to focus on my surroundings and trying to remember what happened the night prior—after we—finished. Everything's a blur.

"What do you want to do today?"

"I should catch up on work after training." I wiggle in his embrace, making him tighten his arms even more. His lips fall on my shoulder, pressing an invisible mark on my skin.

"How about we take another day for ourselves?"

"I have to pay bills or I can say goodbye to my apartment."

"You have a castle waiting for you, an entire court of people that will do anything for you. We should start getting used to it."

"I don't think I could ever do that." I don't even know how anyone could even think to do such a thing.

He releases my body. "No. You could never." His arms end up at the back of his head. "You're you."

"Is that a bad thing?"

"No, it isn't. It's refreshing."

As I grab my clothes from the floor and head to the bathroom, my mind is racing, searching for answers. Did I really drink that much to forget half of the night? No—we barely had a glass. Is the old memory spell playing tricks on me? We had a good night, didn't we? I had a moment of doubt during—but that was just a moment. The words he said about seeing me grow up without him, those were real, I know they were.

And then his words from the night before come back to me. *My princess. Mine.* My stomach feels uneasy at the thought of them.

"What did we do last night after—well, you know what?" I ask, heading into the kitchen where Eros is currently making coffee.

I look at the bottle from last night that is still sitting on the counter beside the sink, and it's almost full, so that definitely isn't the reason why I feel so out of it.

"After I showed you how much I care about you?"

His arms pick me up and put me on the kitchen counter, making me squeak in surprise.

"Yes, after—that." A rush of blood goes to my cheeks.

His citrusy smell fills my nostrils and I can't contain the soft moan my mouth makes while breathing him in.

His hard shaft is pressed against my arousal, and I am losing myself once again in his movements.

Mine. Nausea hits me again, and I try to push him away softly.

"We put on a movie and you passed out during the opening credits."

Flashbacks of him turning on the tv in his bedroom come back to me.

"I didn't realize how tired I was, wow." I rub both hands under my eyes, and make my way down to my cheeks.

"I wish I could say it's because I tired you up that well, but it was also probably the mix of that and the healing potion you drank earlier."

The healing potion. Right. The one Dionisio gave me.

I turn to look at the wine bottle beside me.

"Right, I guess that makes sense."

"Here, drink some coffee. I'm gonna head to the bathroom."

I take the mug he's offering me and get off the counter to walk towards the coffee table in the middle of the living room.

The urge to talk to Svetlana about everything makes me pick up my phone and send her a quick SOS text. She's the only one that knows how much Jeremy affected me. I need to find a way to accept that not every man is going to turn into *him.*

My phone buzzes right back at me. Dionisio sent me a text, and as soon as I open it, I realize I sent him the text that was meant for Svetlana.

DIONISIO:

Be right there.

DEFINITELY DIDN'T WANT HIM ASKING ANY QUESTIONS.

ANIMA:

That was for Svet. I'm sorry.

DIONISIO:

Well, you get me anyway.

While I stare at Dionisio's text, Eros appears from the bathroom in only his jeans, freshly showered.

"Dionisio should be here soon," I tell him while sipping my coffee from the couch pretending to check on my socials.

"Of course." The sigh that comes out of his mouth. His jaw is so tight it could probably break a rock if someone threw it at his face.

"Eros, is everything ok?" I ask, tilting my head slightly.

"What? Yeah no, it's all good."

"I understand you don't—love the situation, but your brother is just following orders."

"I know. It's just that I should be the one training you. Not him."

"You decided on this arrangement. You help me with magic. He helps me with self defense. I am getting better. Good even."

"It just seems a little unnecessary at this point. Especially after last night."

As I am about to respond, Dionisio's voice does it for me. "What is unnecessary is having you whine about it."

I turn and see the older brother leaning on the doorframe of Eros's front door with his arms crossed on his chest. He's in his gym attire, black joggers that are hanging so low that it makes it impossible not to wonder if I could see his v by moving the shirt he's wearing just up a bit. A black t-shirt so tight I could easily memorize every single muscle on his body.

He looks indecent, that's what he looks like. An indecent god that knows exactly how good he looks.

You're drooling, His voice echoes in my head.

Am not!

"Forgot how to knock, brother?" Eros asks with a sarcastic sneer.

"Let's go, Anima. We're wasting precious time."

"Be gentle with her. She might be a little sore today." Eros's words feel like a dagger in my heart.

"Excuse me?" I turn towards Eros, my eyes wide open and my jaw so tight I might just break a couple of teeth if I don't soften the grip.

"You know what I mean." He tries to reach for my arm and I dodge him.

"No, I don't think I do." I walk to the bedroom to grab my bag and head towards the front door, where Dionisio is still standing.

"Jesus Christ, Eros. Are you jealous or something?" His brother asks, shaking his head.

Eros turns towards Dionisio. "Should I be?"

"Where is this coming from?" I ask him. My jaw is still as stiff as a rock.

"Every time something between us happens. He shows up." Eros replies, pointing at his brother.

"She's your soulmate, Eros. I am doing what I have to do to make sure you two get to fulfill your destiny."

"Dad could have sent Markus, but nope. He sent you. As per usual, he likes to mess with me."

"Don't bring your daddy issues into this. He sent me because I am the best option, and you know it."

"He sent you because he wishes you were in my place," Eros shouts at his brother.

"Ready to go?" Dionisio looks down at me, resting his hand on my shoulder.

The sudden touch feels warm on my stiff body and I loosen as soon as his palm touches my skin.

"Yes," I reply, looking back up at him.

"Anima, please." Eros tries to reach for me once again. "Princess—"

Now that was definitely intentional.

"Think about what you told me yesterday. You're supposed to be my soulmate, Eros. If you want to see me happy—safe, don't act like a total asshole, and then try to keep me trapped in four walls," I shout at him before adding, "And for the millionth time. Do not call me princess."

Eros's cold stare is on his brother. His body is stiff and full of tension as he tries to hold himself back.

Dionisio and I walk in silence towards his car. I ignore the buzz of my phone as soon as I see that it's a text from Eros saying that he will wait for our return at my apartment. Dionisio's body is stiff. His hands closed into fists. His stare is on the road, trying not to look at me.

I brush his arm. "Are you ok?"

"No. Anima." He sighs before looking back at me. "I'm not ok because you're not ok."

THE DRIVE TO THE GYM IS SILENT. WE DON'T SAY A WORD TO each other, but he gives me his phone so that I can pick a playlist, just like he does every morning.

His jaw remains clenched for the entire drive. His hands grip the steering wheel so hard I can see his raised veins on his hands and forearms. His words play back into my head over and over again. *I'm not ok because you're not ok.* I swipe a tear that tries to escape down my cheek with the sleeve of my hoodie, hoping that Dionisio doesn't notice it. He doesn't say anything if he does.

The wall facing the door is all mirrors, the others are a dark grey, the same shade as the wooden floor. He drops his bag on a corner and takes out a pair of boxing gloves. They're red. Small. With that, he goes towards a gray closet placed close to the door. He puts the gloves under his armpit while he takes out some rubber pads. He marches towards me. His green eyes piercing mine.

"Here, put the gloves on."

I grab them. Put one on and strap it. The second one is on, and before I try to strap it, he gently grabs my wrist and does it for me.

"Something happened last night, didn't it?"

"I don't want to talk about—that. Not with you."

He nods. "I am your punching bag today, you do whatever you need to take all the anger, all the frustration out. Here. With me."

"Di—"

"No Anima, you make this work because if you don't, I will lose that last cell of self control I still have and kill my brother, and end Dusäiga's future because he's an idiot."

"No, you won't—"

The crack of his knuckles makes me jump. "Don't test me."

"I'm fine, it's all good."

"Hit me." He puts the pads on his hands and gets into position.

"This is so unnecessary." I let out a loud breath.

"Do not fucking say that word to me, not now, not after what I had to witness and accept."

"Ok fine we can talk about—"

"No, you need this. We can talk later. Now hit me."

Dionisio, please.

Hit. Me.

And so I start punching him. Hard. And he takes every single hit without defending himself, he lets me get it all out.

Tears are ready to burst, but I don't let them. I just continue to fight.

"Harder, Anima. You can do better than this."

I kick him, punch him, and he just stands there, taking it all in. The pads he's holding barely move. He's implanted like a tree. Firm like a statue.

"I said harder," He commands. His voice is low, rough.

My chest rises fast, the room spins around me as my quick heartbeat makes me feel lightheaded. "I think I need a minute," I say, trying to catch my breath.

A drop of sweat trails down my face as I hit his chest with all the force I have left in me.

Nothing. He still stands. I'm still not hitting him hard enough.

"You're small, agile, precise, and very smart. You can be David," Dionisio says, nodding in my direction. "Make me your Goliath." He gets closer to me, and then whispers, "Make me fall, little ninja."

A voice from inside of me wants to come out as I continue to punch him.

On your knees.

He finally drops. And with him, I fall as well.

Now in front of each other as I try to catch my breath, he looks at me with amusement in his eyes. Proud.

"Talk to me, say something," I yell with tears now marking my entire face.

No response.

And then I break.

"How am I supposed to accept all of this? First my adoptive parents die, then I find out who my real parents are, and guess what? They're also dead, but that's not it. I find out I am the future queen of a cursed magical kingdom that my psycho ex also wants to take away from me, and I can only save all of us by being with my supposed soulmate, a person I barely know, that is suddenly acting like a dick, and I am here, yelling at his brother because I still don't understand why all of this is happening to me."

His thumb catches a tear on my cheek. "There you go." The only words that escape his mouth.

"There you go? Really? This is all you have to say to me?"

"You needed this, Anima. You needed to get it all out."

"No, what I need is you telling me why Eros is my soulmate when I——" I stop before saying what I really wanted to say. I don't feel the same way he does. "When he acts that way after what we—shared."

"He's very protective of you. I'm sure he's currently trying to find every possible way to apologize to the both of us for how childish he acted."

"Why are you pushing me to him—" I start asking. A knot in my throat makes my already exasperated voice barely come out. *When you're—you.*

His eyes darken. "Do not ask me that. You can ask me anything, but that."

"Why?"

"I can't let you see what I feel for you. I can't let myself have those feelings for you, Anima, not when I know I won't ever compare to him."

"You're the one here, with me, making sure I am ok."

"He was literally made for you, Anima. Your souls are the same. How can I deny that? Look at your fucking eyes."

"Well, guess what, I don't believe that for a second right now."

"You're angry, and I am too, but I won't ever be able to compare to that bond you two have. Especially when I know I will have to leave when you get your crown back."

"What is that supposed to mean?"

"Don't ever, not even for one second, think that *this* is unnecessary. What we do here is for your protection. I will always do whatever it takes to make sure you are safe."

Eros's words play back in my head over and over again. Just like Jeremy's do. I feel like an object in their eyes. "I feel so powerless—useless. No, used, that is how I feel. I feel used."

"I know, and I wish there was another way. If I could take all the pain, all of it, I would. I would add it to mine and carry it with me, for you."

"Take me home."

"Anima—" His voice shutters.

I'm tired, I wanna go home.

"We're going to get through this, Anima. He's scared too, you know."

"Oh, fuck that. He took what he wanted and displayed it like a trophy. How can you even defend him?"

"Anima, did he hurt you?"

I exhale. "This is why I needed Svetlana. You wouldn't understand. You're a man."

"It's a simple yes or no question. Did he hurt you?"

"Not in the way you think he did. Don't push it, please," I beg him.

His eyes are lucid while he stares at me. My jaw locks. He can read my thoughts, he knows exactly what I experienced. Is it what Jeremy did to me? Possibly. Could what I've felt be my fault? Eros's? All possible. He wraps his arms around me, his hand caresses my hair.

It's not your fault. Never. His words feel like the softest whisper in my head.

"Now please take me home. I'm tired of yelling."

He nods. "For what it's worth, I really do wish I could stop you—stop the inevitable."

A sigh leaves my mouth. "I know."

Do you remember what I told you the other night after the panic attack? He asks through the bond as we get our bags ready.

You will always make sure I'm safe, I state.

Always. Don't ever forget that.

No matter what? I ask knowing exactly what he will say back.

No matter what. He repeats.

"It's funny how you talk so much about the bond I should have with Eros, when we have *this*."

CHAPTER 16

We get back into Dionisio's car and as soon as he takes off, his thoughts fill my brain.

I should have known something was up last night. I felt you.

"You felt me?" I ask out loud.

"This mind power thing is nerve-wracking."

"Why didn't you come to check on me?"

His fingers tighten around the steering wheel and I see him starting to fidget with the knob at the top of the gearshift.

"Trust me, that is a mistake I won't ever make again."

Says the guy that cryptically tells me he won't be around after I get the crown. Maybe I don't want it then.

Why didn't he come to check on me if he felt something was up? Maybe because he was with a g—

"Stop. Anima, please stop," he says as his voice breaks.

"Yeah this suspirium thing is really nerve-wracking."

"I came over to see what was happening. Eros was in the

living room, and you weren't. I freaked out. I called him on his cell, he let me come in and showed me you were in his bedroom."

I saw you in his bed, peacefully asleep.

A chunk of hair falls in front of my face, and I quickly move it behind my ear. I feel my cheeks heat up. The slight gesture makes Dionisio's lips lift into a smile. The dimple appearing always in the same spot. I have to fight the urge to trace it with my fingers.

"Everything seemed—normal. I trust my brother, Anima. I know he would never purposely do anything to hurt you." He takes a few moments before saying, "You had to see his face every time you would walk around town after we started remembering everything, it would light up and he would be in a good mood all day… but—"

"But what?"

"But you weren't ok, not mentally at least. I thought it was just me overreacting—overstepping my boundaries. I made you a promise, Anima, and I broke it. I will never make that mistake again."

"You couldn't have done anything. My internal pain, and trauma are mine to work on."

"Talking about it with someone you trust could have helped though."

"It's complicated, D. This is why I texted Svetlana."

"I know."

"And you didn't break your promise. You came last night, and today when I accidentally texted you. You made sure I was safe."

He turns to look at me and gives him a quick nod in response. His hands are still clenched on the steering wheel. Silence returns to surround us as a song ends and another one prepares to begin. I focus my attention on his movements while he scrolls down on his music library without even looking at his phone, his attention only on the road in front of us. His thumb moves so methodically and I fixate on the way his hands move, the way the veins on the back of them appear more visible with certain motions.

As we continue the drive, Jeremy's words come back to me. *Suspirium doesn't work that way.* If this isn't what Eros and Dionisio think it is. What is it then?

"You can clearly compel people. You might just have an advanced form of suspirium that we don't know about."

"How he said it… He either was trying to confuse me or he actually knows why we have this connection."

"What did Eros say about it?"

"I didn't tell him about what Jeremy said."

"Anima."

"I just—Jeremy is very good at making people feel as small as ants. I feel he's intentionally trying to freak me out."

"You guys need to talk about these things."

"I know… I will."

Silence comes back to us as I pick at my cuticles nervously, trying to avoid eye contact with Dionisio.

"I wasn't with anyone, by the way, not in the way you're thinking about."

"So you were with someone," I state.

"I—yeah, just having a drink with a friend. Your future Royal Guard."

My eyes snap in his direction wide open. "My what?"

His low laugh makes my heart skip a beat. "Yeah, you get one of those. The best of the best, I am making sure of it."

"That sounds incredibly unne—"

"Please, you know I am not too fond of that word today." His right hand ends up on my leg to squeeze my knee.

"Sorry."

You'll like Markus, Dionisio says through the bond.

As long as he's not going to be a replacement. I haven't questioned what he told me earlier, but I also haven't forgotten it.

A buzz in my pocket makes me flinch. I look at the screen and see Eros's message. My lips close in a thin line.

EROS:

Please let me apologize properly. I'm going to wait for you by the front door for as long as you need.

I sigh at the words. *I'm going to wait for you for as long as you need.* That should make me feel better, but the worry of seeing another unpleasant version of Eros makes my stomach feel uneasy.

Told you he would crawl back with puppy eyes, Dionisio says through the bond.

ANIMA:

Keys are under the doormat.

I quickly reply back, without saying a word to the guy in the driver's seat.

We pull into the parking lot in Via Roma and after grabbing our bags, Dionisio starts walking in the opposite direction of my apartment.

"You're not even going to say bye?" I ask, staying put beside his car.

His feet abruptly pause. The hand that was holding his bag behind his back comes down while the other one ends up in one of the pockets of his loose fitting joggers.

"I am not going anywhere, you're the one that decided not to follow me."

"D, where are you going? My house is the other way."

"We have to make a stop first. Let'g go, I'm getting hungry, and when I'm hungry, I get cranky."

"Wow, didn't think it was possible for you to be even crankier."

"If you don't stop with the sarcasm, I'll make you come with me by force, little ninja," he replies with a mischievous grin.

"I'd like to see you try, Pope Dionisio."

He comes to a full stop once again and with a laugh, he says, "No one, and I mean, no one knows who the hell that guy was, and I am so lucky to get the pain in the ass that knows about a fucking forgotten Pope in history."

"You are indeed, very lucky."

"Do I really have to tell you that my name is still related to the Greek God even though I know you know it and you're doing all this on purpose?"

His reaction makes me chuckle. "So where are we going?"

"I gotta get something, and you are coming with me."

"Ok fine, Pope D."

He grins at me, and his eyes roll dramatically.

As we start roaming around town, I realize we are going towards Forestiero. We pass a few stores, we go by Marina's shoe store and then Dionisio stops right in front of Criselda's bakery. The bakery. The one where I used to go to with my parents every Sunday. My heart skips a beat as my mouth dries up instantly.

"I'll wait here, I don't need anything," I say before he can protest.

"You're gonna come inside—with me."

"I—can't."

"Anima, *sweetheart*, did you forget what you did today? You are strong. You can do anything, and I am not going anywhere. I am right here."

"Does she know who I am?"

"She hasn't seen you since the glamour fell. She had no idea before, she will wonder now after seeing your eyes."

"Is that wise?"

"Well, if you don't go buy yourself some Triora bread from

her, you're gonna have to wait to meet her wife in Dusäiga and have her deliver it to you at Court."

"Her wife bakes in Dusaiga?"

"Yup, they have a bakery here, and one in Dusäiga. These two women really know how to be boss babes."

"I haven't been in since—"

"I know, Anima, I know. I am right here, it will be quick I promise."

A loud sigh escapes my mouth."Ok, let's do it."

"Good girl," He says in a soft husky voice.

The praise makes my cheeks heat up.

As Dionisio opens the door to the bakery, a familiar fragrance impregnates my entire body. I never understood why the yeasty aroma of bread freshly out of the oven tastes warm, but somehow it does. Clean, slightly sweet. It reminds me of a cold day inhaling a heavy blanket.

We get in line and as I take in the space, I start eyeing the pastries behind the window of the cabinets. Those *maritozzi* look so mouthwatering. The whipped cream inside looks so fluffy I would love to sleep in it.

Now that is an interesting image. Dionisio's voice chants into my brain and feels like a whisper in my ears.

It's how I wanna die. Bathing in whipped cream. Write it down.

I mean if you gotta go, that is definitely the way. A smirk appears on his face.

It's our turn in line and Criselda's face lights up as soon as she sees me in front of her.

"Now this is a pleasant surprise. Welcome back, Anima, it's so nice to see you here." Her stare fixates on my eyes and I know she's pondering about who I could really be.

"It's nice to be back," I quickly reply.

"And hello Dionisio, it's nice to see you back here as well." She slightly turns towards the man standing right beside me.

"Always a pleasure to see you, Criselda."

Her attention turns back to me as she studies my face a little longer.

An immediate beam appears on my face as soon as her eyes lock with mine. My shoulders relax and my stiff body normalizes itself. Maybe I can do this, maybe I can really embrace this old new self and accept who I really am. I am a striga, the daughter of the King and Queen of a magical town, Dusäiga.

You can do anything, little ninja.

"May I have a loaf of Triora bread?"

Dionisio's hand brushes against mine, the sudden touch making my toes curl as electric pulses travel down my spine.

"Of course you can, love!" Criselda's face gleams and she turns to grab a paper bag and the thin loaf of beige bread. "Here it is, my dear, your favorite."

I grab the brown paper bag she's holding, and as my fingers close around it, the palm of her hand rests on the back of mine. Heat travels up my arm straight to my chest, and I immediately feel lighter, stronger. Like I could drop everything and climb Mount Everest.

Turning to Dionisio with a confused look, I see him smiling back at me.

She's an empath. She takes away the pain of others and lets them feel better for a while. Dionisio's words whisper in my mind like a sweet soft wind.

That's why I always felt better when I came here growing up. Every single time I did, Criselda would pat me on the shoulder and touch my hands. She'd make sure to get that little moment of contact so that she could take any possible pain away.

"Thank you so much," I mumble, equally surprised and grateful. Once I take out my wallet, she holds her hand up.

"This is on the house, my dear. I don't want you to run away again. I love seeing your friend here, but I prefer to see your face and know that you're ok.'

"I will—I *am* ok. I really am."

I can feel Dionisio's eyes on me. He's standing there, right beside me with a big grin on his face, his chin held up high.

After we say our goodbyes, I turn towards the door and before I can grab the handle, Dionisio does it for me. "After you."

As we make our way towards my apartment, my phone starts ringing in my pocket. I pick it up, knowing it's Svetlana calling me for the fortieth time. Keeping her in the dark on this is like keeping a part of me in the dark, and I can't stand it anymore. I let the phone fall back into my pocket right after I read her name on the screen, and notice Dionisio's jaw tighten while he jolts his neck to the side, and a loud crack follows.

"Would it be so bad if she knew?" The question is more directed at myself, but he looks at me seeing the guilt I feel in my stomach—in my heart.

"No. It wouldn't."

"Then why can't I tell her anything?"

"I never said you couldn't. My brother implied it." That is true. He never said anything about it. Eros was the one telling me to be careful who I trust.

"I understand why Eros would say that, but she's my best friend, she's—"

"More than a friend. She's like a sister." Dionisio finishes my sentence.

"Yes, exactly that." My voice cracks. Basically a whisper to myself.

"My brother will understand. And if he doesn't, I'll help you make him understand."

"I'll call her back later. I need to deal with him now. Hopefully, he's in a better mood."

"I won't leave unless you tell me to leave, ok?"

"Thank you."

We reach my apartment building. My hand trembles as soon as we get to my front door. I'm worried about which version of Eros is right behind the door. The hair on my back rises letting me know I am in his vicinity. I wonder if he can sense me as well.

As soon as the door opens, my eyes are on Eros. He's sitting on the couch with his elbows on his thighs and his head in his hands. And my living room is filled with—carnations.

"You're back." His voice cracks. His eyes still staring at the floor.

I soften at his expression, his eyes are ready to explode, and make my way to him. Slowly. "I'm back. What are all these?" My eyes travel around the room, looking at all the colorful flowers, the subtle balmy and spicy fragrance filling the air.

His arms wrap around my back pulling me in closer to him. There it is, the citrusy sweet smell. "I am so sorry, Anima, what I said—"

"Well, this is definitely a statement. I am going to steal your shower for a minute so you two can have a moment." Dionisio interrupts him walking towards the bathroom avoiding eye contact with me.

"That jealousy stunt can't happen again, Eros. Not when we're supposed to be a team."

His hand rests on my cheek so softly that I can barely feel his fingers touching my skin. "I will make it up to you."

"It will take me a bit to get over it—to forgive you," I reply, my voice still firm.

"All the time that you need. Just please don't shut me out."

A quick nod comes automatically. "I can tell you're on a mission here." I gesticulate, pointing at the absurd amount of flowers surrounding us.

"I was hoping to find lavender, but apparently it's too early for
——."

I crash my lips on his, and a sense of familiarity starts to ease
my body. His hands end up in my hair and the sudden soft touch
makes me tingle and I end up giggling in his mouth.

"What are you snickering about?"

"You're tickling me."

"Where? Here?" His fingers end up at the back of my head
again and the laughs start again.

"Stop, stop oh my god."

"Now, that is very good information."

This version of Eros is nice, comforting and playful, but a part
of me still feels like he's like a ticking bomb. The way he moves,
the words he uses, everything reminds me a bit too much of—
Jeremy. The possessiveness. The way he needs to remind
everyone I am *his*. I am my own. I don't want to be property. Not
again—not anymore.

As my brain travels, we hear the front door unlock and open.
A singing Svetlana steps into the living room with a small tray of
pastries and headphones on.

"You bought bread!" She squeaks with a smile.

"Hey—what—what are you doing here?" I mumble, uncomfortable because she must know I purposefully ignored her call.

"Dionisio texted me asking if I wanted to join for lunch.
You've been avoiding me for days, Anima." He texted her.
Dionisio texted her because he listened to me and understood how
much I needed to see my best friend. Svetlana frowns, then chews
on her bottom lip. "I went to buy you some Triora bread just like I
normally do and Criselda told me you already got some!"

If speed talking was an Olympic sport, Svetlana would be the
best athlete in the world winning gold medals every day.

"I wasn't avoiding you—"

"Yes you were, but it's ok because you went and bought

bread!" Her attention then turns to the person that is holding me in his arms, then around the room, noticing the flowers. "That is a lot of carnations."

I hate carnations. She knows I do, but let's not say that out loud. A few, nice, but these many? The smell is making me feel a little nauseous.

"I might have gone a little overboard." Eros scratches the back of his head as he sheepishly looks down at the floor.

"Just a little. But better overboard than not enough, because if you hurt her, I *will* kill you," she says, pointing her index finger at him with squinty eyes. Turning back to me, she throws herself at me, locking her arms around me in a tight hold. "You bought bread."

"Technically, I was given the bread for free."

"I am so proud of you."

Her energy is absolutely mindblowing. Dionisio's voice says in my head.

I turn to face him, and his hair is out of his usual bun, the soft damp waves frame his face perfectly. His hand reaches his beard for a slow scratch, and all I can think of is burying my fingers in his locks. This is bad, this is very bad.

It is. Thank you. For everything, I tell him.

Always.

"I am *also* very proud of you," Eros whispers in my ear while caressing the small of my back. A small gesture that makes my knees wobble. What's up with my hormones? I'm still mad, but hearing those words from Eros is—nice.

"You know what? I am also proud of myself," I say, quickly changing the topic. "This is good. I can finally buy my own carbs."

I enter the kitchen to prepare something to eat, Eros joins me while Dionisio and Svetlana set the table. It's nice seeing us all together, almost like a family.

I get some deli meat out of the fridge and prepare a quick *tavoletta* with different cheeses, salami and *prosciutto*.

Eros gets the pot ready with water and while we wait for it to boil we sit down at the table, chatting and drinking wine. The tension I was feeling earlier is almost gone now that I have Svetlana here and everyone is getting along.

I get the pasta ready and Dionisio helps with the plates.

We sit down once again after I take care of the pasta, and Svetlana entertains us with stories of our childhood. How we met in a park and all the trouble we got in while being in school.

After lunch Eros stops me from cleaning up, and together with Dionisio, he grabs the plates and puts them in the dishwasher.

"Ok well, this was lovely, we should do it again sometime, but I think Eros and I should leave you two alone now." Dionisio's hand squeezes his brother's shoulder.

"I think we could sta—"

"Eros." Dionisio's voice is low.

"I just think we coul—" Eros tries to continue, but gets stopped once again.

"You need to start looking at the signs when two women want to be alone. These two right here?" He points at me and Svetlana. "Need to have some girl talk probably about you. Get your ass up and let's go."

Eros's sigh is loud. "Yeah. You're right, brother."

I nod, and after a quick kiss on his cheek that makes the corners of his lips lift into a grin, he walks to the door.

"I'll see you tomorrow bright and early," Dionisio says, pointing at me before joining Eros.

"Yes, sensei." I say, bringing my hands together in front of my chest, bowing slightly at Dionisio. The low chuckle he replies with brightens up the entire room.

He waves and then the two of them step out of sight, closing the door behind them.

My phone buzzes in my pocket a few seconds later.

EROS:

Didn't know she had a key to your place.

ANIMA:

Eros, this isn't helping your case. I just need some time with my friend.

EROS:

I know, and I am sorry. Just be prudent on who you share our secret with.

My eyes go to Svetlana. She's sipping on some red wine, waiting for me to be done with the phone.

She raises an eyebrow before asking, "Is everything ok?" Her words of concern remind me exactly who is on my side, and who has faith in me.

"Yes. Everything is ok," I reply, before sending my last text of the night to Eros.

ANIMA:

Someone told me to trust no one.

EROS:

Good girl.

My fist closes into a tight lock. Nails almost breaking my skin. Those two words don't have the same effect as they did earlier with his brother.

SVETLANA AND I HAVE BEEN TALKING ON THE COUCH FOR A FEW minutes while drinking wine, just as if nothing happened. "Are we going to talk about Eros and Dionisio racing to see who gives you more attention?" She asks as she takes off her shoes and crosses her legs on the couch. The wine glass never leaving her left hand.

"There's no race," I reply as I also get in the same position as hers. My fingers tapping nervously on my knees.

"Sure there isn't."

"I'm—I've been spending time with the both of them because of how close I am getting to Eros."

"Sure. And why have you been such a fugitive lately? You're hiding something and it's killing me not being able to ask you what's happening."

"I know, and I want to tell you everything, but you have to keep an open mind about this."

"Oh my god, you're dating both of them."

"No I am not, I'm with Eros—I think I am, at least."

"Wow, you seem so confident about it." Her lips press into a white slash. Her tone is sharp, sarcastic.

"You don't like him."

"I—it's not that I don't like him, I just feel he's—"

"A little clingy?" I suggest raising my pitch.

"Yeah. Have you seen your apartment? It's filled with freaking carnations, which by the way is literally the worst flower to show you care about someone."

"It's because he couldn't find lav—never mind."

"No, stop keeping everything inside when you clearly want to say something. It's me, not a stranger."

"We—need to talk."

"No shit."

"There is something that I found out about myself and Eros is the reason I know all of it, and that's also the reason both him and Dionisio have been around so much."

"Ok, go on."

"It'll make you think I'm a mental patient."

"You've told me incredulous things before. I survived. Shoot."

"There's a reason why I don't remember my first few years of my childhood. This is also connected to why my eyes look different right now."

"For a second I thought you weren't going to bring that up. They are different. They have been for a while and it was killing me staying in my place seeing you almost run away from me because of it."

"I wasn't running away." My eyebrows draw together. "My eyes—they match Eros's eyes."

"Oh my god. They do!"

"Yeah."

"Ok, why is that?"

"Because I am a striga, the heir to the throne of a magical town and Eros is supposed to be my soulmate, and we know all this because of a magical book him and Ginevra gave me that has a prophecy that talks about us and how we are supposed to fulfill said prophecy." I utter so fast I have no time to think at the words that come out of my mouth.

"You're high," Svetlana says with a tentative smile as she shakes her head.

"No, I'm not," I insist. My voice remains stable as I remind myself this might take a while. She'll probably think it's a prank. I know at the beginning I did. "I'm a striga."

She rolls her eyes with a loud snort. "You are high." Narrowing her eyes, she smirks. "And I need whatever you took."

"I am a striga and Eros is a veneficus, Dionisio as well. Witches. I think that would be the normal term? Basically a bunch of gods who knows how long ago decided to give some powers to some people and here we are."

"What the hell did this guy do to you?"

"Told me the truth."

So I tell her everything. I tell her about my dreams, about Eros and Dionisio, and that Jeremy is here. I tell her about the book Ginevra gave me, then about my powers. I tell her about my self defense training with Dionisio, and how Eros and I started something because we are soulmates, and that I have a special connection with his brother as well that is connected to my power of suspirium, and she doesn't freak out at all. She listens to me, to everything I have to say, just like she has always done for the past seventeen years.

"Ok, this is a lot, and you know it sounds crazy, but show me what you can do."

"Well, I can apparently compel people to do things."

"That's creepy, show me."

So I focus on her. I focus on her chocolate brown eyes and how attentive they are right now, on me. I focus on the voice inside of me wanting to come out. I focus on my fingertips and how they tingle whenever I try to use compulsion—magic in general.

Take out your phone, and text me the phrase 'Anima is the most badass friend I have, and also the only friend I have.'

Svetlana takes out her phone and texts me just that without even blinking once. As soon as she hits send, her eyes widen, and she stares at me in shock. Her jaw drops open. "Oh my God. I don't know why I did that! Wait—was it—was that you, making me do it?"

"I know, it's a lot. I don't even know how to take it, but I am so glad you know everything now."

"Hey, I have other friends, I just prefer to spend my time with you!" She says with a grin.

"So, the last thing you need to know is that I found out Eros is my soulmate. The prophecy I mentioned... It says we should be together to save Dusäiga."

"Oh." She shifts uncomfortably. "So that's why…"

"Why what?"

"Never mind."

"Why what, Svetlana?" I insist, gently pinching her arm.

Reluctantly, she looks up at me, then turns her focus to the floor. "Well, why… why you're with him despite how he…*is*."

When my lips purse, she whines an apology. "I'm sorry, Anima, but there's something about Eros that doesn't convince me. He's supposed to be your one true love, your soulmate, but it seems to me like he's playing a part. Dionisio on the other hand, I see how he looks at you. Don't tell me you haven't noticed."

"It's complicated. I can see his affection, but based on the prophecy, Eros and I are destined, and Dionisio told me straight up he could never compare to that," I say, avoiding eye contact.

"I think a couple of words on paper aren't the answer to what really is in your heart. Besides, based on what you told me, the real connection is with Dionisio. "

"What do you mean?"

"You can talk to him with your mind when you are close to each other, no?"

"Yeah it's something that we can do."

"Does Eros know?"

"Yes—well kind of. He doesn't know Dionisio can do that too… He says it's probably the suspirium coming out." I admit as I turn my gaze away.

"Mm-hmm. Dionisio didn't say anything either, I suppose." She takes a sip of wine, then points her finger at me. "Because he knows this is quite the bond you two have."

"Ok, but that doesn't change the fact that Eros and I share the *eyes*. And the attraction I felt."

"Felt. You said felt."

"Feel, I meant to say feel."

"What about the dream then? The vision you have?" She questions.

"Both Dionisio and Eros are in it. Actually, Jeremy as well."

"All the men in your life are in it because your mind decides who you want to be with, not a stupid prophecy!"

"I wish it was that simple."

"Maybe it is that simple. Can I read it?"

I get up from the couch and pace towards my bedroom. I feel so much better now that I can talk freely to her about all this. A weight that has been finally lifted now that my friend knows everything. I grab the large red tome and go back to the living room.

"Here." I open the book to the right page and put it on the coffee table.

"*Two parts of the same essence. A first and second born of the court. Through different Eyes, a vision will bring transition. An unbreakable bond. The connection will snap into place when they will reach Maturity, and what was forgotten will flourish once again. The golden energy will be the answer to the equation. An eye for an eye. A soul for a soul. A crown and a corpse. The drought will cease.*"

"See? It can't be Dionisio, it's Eros."

"And why is that?"

"I am a firstborn, he is second born. We share the same eyes and the same dream. And we do have a connection. I've felt drawn to him since I moved back from Chicago."

"This was written a bigillion of years ago, come on! And the connection kinda mutated when you realized his brother was around. What does this part mean, though? The one about the connection that will snap into place when you reach Maturity and what was forgotten will flourish once again?"

"I was supposed to have this glamour fall when I turned eighteen, but as you already know, I moved away a couple of weeks before my birthday."

"Ginevra couldn't take the glamour off." She acknowledges. Her hand rests under her chin, trying to think about other possible solutions. "So now what?"

"Now that it is off, I am slowly starting to remember pieces of my childhood, but apparently it will take longer that it should be because I had it on for too many years"

"This is a lot."

"No shit."

"I can't believe you were able to keep all this hidden from me for this long."

"Trust me, I didn't want to keep you in the dark, I kinda was told to do that."

"Can they read my mind?"

Tilting my head slightly, I reply, "No they can't."

"Then they will never know. I will keep your secret and everything will be ok."

"Dionisio will know."

"I don't think Dionisio is the problem here."

"No—he isn't."

After a nod, she starts to browse through the pages. "What does this mean?" She asks.

"What?"

"There's something here about a second born sacrifice law."

"A what? Where?" My body is in alert mode.

Svetlana places the book in my lap and points at a page. "Here."

As soon as my eyes get to where she's pointing, she starts to read out loud. "With the worsening of the drought, the Elemental Gods came down to Earth and asked for a sacrifice in exchange for future help."

"What the—" Only a whisper comes out of me.

"From that moment on, the second born male child of every family in Dusäiga has been sent to the temple at the top of Mount Nemo to devote their life to the Gods."

"Ok but the drought is still in place. A child hasn't been born since I was born."

"Yeah, this seems to me like the Gods are just playing with the citizens."

"This is the dumbest thing I've ever read," I state with my eyes wide open in shock.

"At a moment in time, the Gods come to Earth and request the sacrifice of the second born. It could be as newborns. It could be in their adult life."

"This is fucked up."

"Does this mean Eros might leave at any time?"

That thought hadn't crossed my mind until she spoke those words. "But we have to fulfill the prophecy to save Dusäiga—"

"What if that's why the Gods put the law into place?"

My jaw drops. "So that they could continue to get their sacrifices until the absolute end of Dusäiga."

"It's better to have some meat than no meat at all..."

Is this what Dionisio was talking about? Is this why he says he has to leave? Closing the book quickly, I almost throw it to the coffee table, not wanting to read a word more.

"There has to be a way to fix this."

"I'm going to have to talk to Eros and Dionisio about it. They talk of these Gods as if they're good... This makes me think they're the real villains."

"You mentioned that Jeremy is also involved and that there are crazy dark wizards that work for him?"

"Yes, those are called Opacum, they mask themselves with a spell and they look like they have no face. Quite creepy really."

"Oh my god." She claps her hands once as if she remembered something.

"What?"

"We saw one of those. Actually you saw one, and then when I looked, it was gone"

"When was this?"

"That night a few weeks ago, we were crazy high, and you said something about a man with no face in the middle of the street looking up at us."

"Holy shit! Yes!"

"So I wasn't that far off, it really could have been the ghost of your past unachieved orgasms."

"Svet!" This is how she is. Trying to lighten up the mood and make me laugh.

"What? It's true. Jeremy is super slimy and based on what you told me, he's the reason a lot of bad things happened around here. Maybe he's the one that made this prophecy up. Maybe he made up the entire book!"

"The drought has been a problem for centuries. Jeremy just wants to get to me so that he can get to the crown, which apparently would mean he would get a lot of power and do who knows what—end the world, probably."

"He won't get to you. He will have to go through me first," She says with her chin up high.

"I can't believe my adoptive parents knew about all this."

"It explains why they had so much prepared for you in case, well, something happened."

"And something did happen."

"Are you ok?"

"Not really, but weirdly enough, I kind of feel relieved knowing that this part of me is slowly coming back to the surface."

"It suits you."

"What does?"

"You being this badass witch or striga or whatever that is

destined to rule a magical place," Her voice is surprisingly calm. "You always were a leader, Anima. You are the rational one of us two. The one that tries to find a solution to every problem. You will find a solution to all this."

"I mean, I am kind of freaking out on the inside."

"It's understandable, but you also haven't run away like I would have done by now."

As I nervously pick at my cuticles, I reply, "I just feel like I can't leave."

"Is that a bad feeling or are you ok with it?"

"I feel drawn to this place, Svet. I feel like my heart is in this town and I haven't even been there yet."

"Well, you've been there, you just don't remember it—yet."

"You know what's funny?" The corners of my lips lift up into a smile at the thought I just had.

She raises a brow and tilts her head a little to the side. "What is?"

"The bread."

"What about bread?"

"The Triora bread recipe comes from Dusäiga. There are some people that decided to live out of Dusäiga, people that decided to start a family with regular humans so they settled in Triora."

"That is mind-blowing. We've been around them our entire lives and we had no idea."

"I know, it's wild."

"Also explains why the culture of witches in Triora is so out in the open. We just didn't know they were being serious about it."

We remain in silence for a couple of minutes, and I take this opportunity to check my phone for possible unwanted messages.

DIONISIO:

Whatever you decide to do, I am on your side,
always. This is your choice, not his.

ANIMA:

Thank you, pope D.

It takes him a few seconds to reply to my text.

DIONISIO:

Little ninja.

I smile at those words and rethink what Svetlana said about me. I am this badass striga. I am the future queen of Dusäiga, and I am going to save my people from this stupid curse that we were put under. Jeremy won't get to me. The Gods won't get to me or anyone I care about.

"Anima, are you listening to me?"

"Huh, what did you say?"

"I was asking if you know anything about your real parents?"

"Not much, just that they disappeared when I appeared here in Vallecrosia."

"Did Eros text you a love poem or something? You have heart-shaped eyes."

"What? No, it's nothing. I was just thinking about what you said earlier about me."

"So the text was from Dionisio…"

"Svet!"

"Oh shit. I said that out loud, didn't I?"

"Yup, you did, and not helping!"

"So, did you like, sleep with Eros yes or no?"

"Svetlana!"

"So that's a yes? No? How's his d—"

"We are not talking about this right now."

"Ok so it's not great, got it."

"You're unbelievable."

"I just think your veneficus hot soulmate should have a nice, you know, member."

"It's not small, it's—average I guess. I just need to loosen up a little I think." Because apparently I am incapable of having sexual intercourse without thinking about Jeremy and how he treated me.

"You know who I think isn't average? Dio—"

"Oh my god."

"He definitely would help you loosen up real good."

"We are done talking about this. How about a movie?"

"How about we do a Charmed rewatch, seems way more appropriate."

CHAPTER 17

My eyes open wide as a fluttering in my stomach alerts me that someone is in the apartment. The hairs on the back of my neck stand up. My pulse races as I turn towards my nightstand, checking the time. My phone reads 7 am.

EROS:

Don't freak out. It's just us in the living room.

Eros and Dionisio are here.

I slowly get out of bed, making the smallest movements to not wake Svetlana up.

As I close the door to my bedroom behind me, I see the two brothers laying on the couch and loveseat, on their phones, in silence. Both of their scents now mixing with the spicy one of the carnations that have taken over my living room. I should bottle this fragrance and smell it every time I feel down.

While walking towards the curtains of my balcony, I hear them both shift their bodies.

"Good morning, pr—Anima." Eros's arms wrap around my waist from behind, his voice a subtle whisper in my ear that makes me shiver in response.

I lean into the embrace and let my body relax under his touch as my knees feel weak. "Good morning. Gotta be careful with the words you use. Svet is in the other room," I whisper back at him.

"Noted. I'm glad you haven't said anything to her. It's too dangerous."

"For now. I can't keep her in the dark forever though," I reply to his condescending words.

Eros gives me a quick nod before turning and pacing towards the kitchen.

She knows, doesn't she?

I turn to Dionisio, who hasn't moved. His legs are crossed at his ankles and his arms behind his head, his t-shirt is slightly up, showing his belly button and a hint of his abs. I swear he does it on purpose, to just look like—that.

Yup, I reply, trying to not look suspicious in front of Eros.

We aren't telling Eros aren't we?

Nope, we are not. My internal voice is firm, just like it would be if I was speaking out loud.

Cool, cool, cool.

"Good morning everyone, didn't know we were having a family meeting," Svetlana's cheery voice comes crushing in.

"Family meeting?" Eros asks, raising an eyebrow at her.

"Yeah. You're part of Anima's life now, so you're a part of mine. It was a joke Eros, look at the definition of it in a dictionary if you need to," She replies all in one breath, and my jaw drops before I start laughing.

"So you're just as sweet as Anima is at the crack of dawn, I see," Eros says with a wink.

"No beef so early in the morning. Coffee first," I say while grabbing some mugs.

Eros pours some coffee into one of them and hands it to me "Can we talk for a moment? In private?" Eros asks, and I nod.

You sure? D asks.

Yeah it's ok.

He follows me into the bedroom, and closing the door behind me, I turn to him. "So here we are, alone,"

Eros slowly paces towards me, getting close. "Here we are." His voice penetrates my every pore.

"You wanted to—" I find myself swallowing air. "Talk." I take a sip of my coffee and never stop looking at his eyes. His look fixated on me.

He looks radiant and mischievous at the same time, here, when it's just the two of us, alone. My mind is divided, that at one moment my legs melt at his looks, his touch and words. Within a second, though, I want to run away and be sure to not ever be in his presence ever again.

"I just feel I should apologize for my behavior. We had an unforgettable night and then I ruined it by getting jealous of my brother as if he was trying to steal a toy. My reaction was absolutely childish and controlling. Then I try to fix everything by filling your house up with flowers when really, I should've just spoken with you to let you know that's not me. That's not who I am."

His words sound like a chant reaching my ears. They fill me up. His apologetic look on me feels like hypnosis. I almost feel dizzy at the sound of his voice whispering so close to my skin. Then, that lightheaded feeling gets replaced with calmness. "Thank you for apologizing—again, and I did appreciate the flowers, just maybe next time, a couple will be good enough."

"Yes, I absolutely got that."

"Maybe we just went too fast. I feel a little overwhelmed."

"You're right, I pushed you when you clearly needed more time," he says, wrapping his arms around my waist and looking down at me.

"No Eros, you didn't push me, don't think that, I wanted—it." I did want it, right? I wanted it and then my brain told me I didn't feel it anymore. Right now though—right now I want everything.

There's something going on but I do want to believe his words. I get on the tips of my toes, put my hands on his chest and rest my lips on his. A quick soft peck to show him I am ok.

He smiles against my mouth and reciprocates the kiss.

My fingers interlock with his as we get back into the living room hand in hand.

Dionisio throws a look our way and says nothing. Instead, he looks up at Svetlana, who in the meantime turned and winked at me. In that moment it is like the trance breaks and I get back into reality. The sense of dizziness comes back like a rush of blood to the head.

"All is good in paradise," she says before starting to pour herself some coffee. I suddenly feel a shiver of fear and drop Eros's hand, but he seems not to notice because he sits down and grabs a cup.

Are you ok? Dionisio asks me.

I don't know. I thought I was, and now I don't know, I say.

I am not going anywhere, he adds.

Though that's somewhat comforting, the sudden jolt of unease doesn't fully leave my body. Svetlana's questioning look makes me think she also noticed my sudden change of mood.

"Ok so are we all hitting the gym?" She asks after a minute of complete silence.

"We are." Dionisio's firm voice fills the room, as he gestures at me and him. His eyes narrow on Eros with a look that has me wondering if lasers are about to shoot out from them.

"Am I seeing you later, Eros?" I ask, hoping he won't suggest tagging along.

"Yes. I'll be at Forestiero. Let me know when you're back, and be safe, ok?" Eros says, looking at me. I just nod in response.

He kisses my cheek, then ambles towards my front door.

As soon as he is out of sight, I feel my phone buzz on the kitchen table.

EROS:

I'm going to teach you how to make a healing potion later, please, don't get hurt.

ANIMA:

Wouldn't it be the perfect opportunity to get a new concussion?

EROS:

My poor sanity.

"Why is he so confusing?" I shout, putting away my phone.

"He's a veneficus with a lot on his plate. What's bothering you?" Dionisio asks me as soon as we are sure that Eros is not in the building anymore.

"I don't know, one moment it seems like I am totally fine with him, the other I just want to run as far away as possible."

"Well, that's not good. I told you I am on Dionisio's team," Svetlana states, her voice breathy. I don't need Dionisio thinking anything about this. Eros is my soulmate and I will save Dusäiga before the Gods decide to show up.

"Svet." A sigh leaves my mouth.

"I'm just saying, your gut is usually right, I would listen to it."

"Svet." My eyes narrow at her and I fight the urge to sigh a second time.

"Just stating facts, babe," Svetlana says while sipping on her coffee.

"There's no Dionisio's team here." Dionisio chuckles, before adding, "But thank you for finding me this hot. It does wonders to my self esteem." He winks at her.

"Oh god, here we go," I whisper under my breath, bringing my fingers to my temple to massage them.

"So, how much did you tell her?" Dionisio asks, trying to change the subject.

"Everything," I say, putting the empty mug in my dishwasher.

His eyes light up as he smiles at her. "Welcome to the family drama Svetlana. Buckle up, because it's going to be a crazy ride."

"When do I get to see this Court and hidden world you all talk about?" Svetlana asks.

"When it will be safe for you to get there," Dionisio says.

"So I can let her come with me to Dusäiga?"

"She's your best friend, and you're the heir to the throne. You can do whatever the hell you want. I am certainly not going to be the one to stop you."

"Now I feel better," I say, releasing a sigh. The thought of being in this mysterious, strange place where people expect so much of me is terrifying, but knowing Svetlana will be by my side surely helps.

Good.

"We should get going. I want to kick someone's ass today, and by someone I mean you, Dionisio," I state out loud with a smile.

"We're going to see about that, little ninja." A smirk appears on his face. Our eyes lock and for a moment, I forget we are not alone in the room.

"I can literally cut the tension between you two with scissors," Svetlana states under her breath bringing me back to reality.

"I don't know what you're talking about," I say, pacing towards my bedroom to change into my gym clothes letting her know we both heard her.

"Sure you don't," I hear her reply back to me from the living room.

I close the bedroom door to get five minutes of privacy. I think back to my conversation with Svetlana last night, and the thought of the prophecy being interpreted wrong right now seems the only thing keeping me somewhat sane. The second born law comes back to mind and all of this seems to be a horrible joke. How am I going to figure this out? I wish my parents left some sort of a clue on what to do.

My hand latches on the key around my neck, and the image of Mirella and Giorgio, my adoptive parents, revives once again. What would they say if they knew that their plan to keep me safe out of this world just didn't work at the end? They knew, and they still preferred to keep me in the dark. I should be furious. I should be livid, but the thought of never being able to hug them again makes my eyes water.

A knock on my door brings me back.

"Are you ok in there, babe?" Svetlana asks as she enters and closes the door behind her.

A sigh escapes my mouth. "I don't know. I am frustrated. I am trying to keep it together and sometimes I wonder why," I reply back to her. I haven't cried in a long time, but I can feel tears burning in the back of my eyes. The salt that I usually feel on my lips from the sea air gets replaced with the one coming down from my eyes.

Svetlana walks forward, sits down beside me on the bed, embracing me in a tight hug as I let it all out. And I do. I let the tears come out. I let the sorrow fill my lungs, and make a knot in my throat. My cries crack my voice. They are filled with desperation and uncertainty of the future.

And then something hits me—something not good for my sanity.

"I am the reason why they aren't here anymore. Both my biological parents and my—parents."

Oh Anima. Dionisio's voice infuses my mind. He's behind the door, hearing everything. Knowing I need to be vulnerable right now. I wish I could keep this side of me hidden, but with them—I can't.

"Come in, D." My voice is soft, basically a whisper.

He comes in and closes the door behind him, remaining in silence with his arms folded across his chest and his jaw firmly clenched. Immediately, his cedarwood minty scent makes my nose tingle in pleasure.

"Now that is cool," Svetlana says, and I almost laugh between the tears.

"It's not your fault, Anima. It was handled—poorly by our parents, but this is not your fault." He slowly paces towards me. "Blame me. Blame Eros. Blame the entire situation, but never yourself." Dionisio kneels down in front of me, resting his hands on my thighs. The sudden touch makes my heart skip a beat. "We will take care of Jeremy and then go back to Dusäiga, where you belong, and the prophecy will be fulfilled. No one will hurt you again. I will make sure of it."

My arms end up around his neck as the tears keep streaming down my face. The sudden affection makes him stiffen up in my embrace, but he stays there, with my head on his shoulder, accepting the situation as it is. Messy. Just like everything around here. His arms close around my waist as he brings me down to him.

No matter what, remember? Dionisio says through the bond.

No matter what, I say back.

"Ready to kick my ass?" Dionisio whispers in my ear.

"Absolutely."

We get out of my apartment in silence and as we head towards Dionisio's car, Svetlana finally breaks the silence.

"And you have a hot car? Dude, you're making it very difficult for your brother to be her soulmate."

"Hey, it's not my fault. I have good taste."

AS WE ENTER THE GYM AND SAY OUR HELLOS, DIONISIO WALKS US to our usual private room. The savory and musty smell immediately penetrates my nostrils.

He lets his bag fall to the ground. "Svetlana, welcome to my favorite part of the day," he says with a devilish grin staring back at us.

"You like getting hurt?" She asks, tilting her head to the side.

"I like seeing your friend over here persevere until she gets what she wants."

Crossing her arms over her chest, Svetlana asks, "And what does my friend here want?"

"To kick my ass, obviously."

"There is something seriously wrong with you," I reply with a chuckle.

"See? This is what I meant when I said the prophecy is wrong."

Svetlana's words make my eyes go wide. She's always so direct, never worried about the consequences. A trait that I always envy her for. A trait that comes out only in specific circumstances. She knows she can talk freely around him. There's already a sense of trust being established.

"You think the prophecy is wrong." Dionisio repeats, raising an eyebrow.

I sigh. "Svet, you literally barely read it once—"

"Why do you think it's wrong?" Dionisio interjects. My mouth snaps shut as his hand reaches his chin.

"I think it was interpreted wrong." She shifts her weight from one foot to the other before adding, "Can I be brutally honest?"

"Were you stopping yourself before?" His question makes Svetlana snort.

"Eros is suspicious. I don't like your brother. There's something that just doesn't feel right and with all the ups and down, how he treats Anima, he just reminds me of—"

"Jeremy. He reminds you of Jeremy." I mumble.

Svetlana's hand cups my arm. "Anima, I know I am the one that basically pushed you towards him, but you are on the edge, all the time. If this is how you're supposed to be around your soulmate, then I am sorry, but I think you're better off alone."

"My brother cares for her. I know he does."

"And you don't?"

"I am not in the picture, Svetlana. I can't be." His fists clench as his body stiffens. "Their souls—they're the same. What could be is nothing compared to what they are to each other. My brother devoted his life to her. They literally revolve around each other. She felt the attraction even before she knew who she was." His voice is rough, cracking.

"Then stop being you. Stop flirting the way you do, because Anima is not a freaking toy. She can't get her heart broken again, and you won't be there to pick up the pieces, I will."

"Svet, please," I whisper.

"No, I am sick and tired of this. Not after all you've been through. I won't allow anyone to be around and then disappear because they are cowards who can't accept their feelings." Svetlana's hands are on her hips, her lips forming a thin line, and I stand there in silence, my body petrified like a rock.

He marches towards her with a certain tightness in his eyes. "Do you think I like this? Do you think this is easy for me? It isn't. Every day I wake up, put a smile on my face for *her*, and pretend I'm fine. I show up and make sure Anima and my fucking brother work out their issues, because this is what their destiny is. A life without me on their side. And every day I go back home livid, because I am not Eros. Her soulmate. Something that was told to us—to *me*, every single day of our lives."

Tears are about to spill once again, but my clenched jaw keeps me somewhat together. I wasn't expecting this reaction from Dionisio.

A life without *him*. Well, this makes his promise quite futile, doesn't?

I will always make sure you're safe, Anima. I won't ever break that promise. Ever. His words don't stick as they usually do. I feel like my body is floating. Weightless. Powerless once again.

I wasn't expecting today to go this way at all. My hands close into fists, and my entire body is firm, paralyzed. Moving seems impossible right now. My head feels light, just like my muscles. I start opening and closing my hands trying to regain control of my body. But I am so numb.

"Anima, are you ok? You're—pale, very pale." Svetlana's voice feels so far away.

As I try to stay upright on my feet, Dionisio rushes to catch me as I am about to fall .

Stay with me, little ninja.

"Do I need to call an ambulance?"

"No—it's ok, I just—I'm ok. I just need a bit of water."

"Of course, little ninja." Dionisio rummages in his bag. "Here, have some water with electrolytes."

"See? This is what I am talking about. How can Eros be her soulmate when you have—*this*."

"Svet, please, change the subject," I beg her between sips.

"Fine. You both keep being oblivious." Her words feel like knives on my numb body.

"You're not going to change your mind, are you?" Dionisio asks, while helping me up.

"Very unlikely. Especially when he can't even make her c—" I stop Svetlana before she can finish her sentence.

"Ok, no need to talk about *that* like this in the open, please and thank you." I get out of Dionisio's embrace feeling much more alive than a few moments ago. My cheeks feel hot thinking about the embarrassing conversation I would have had to have if I hadn't stopped Svetlana.

"Now, can I please kick someone? I am tired of this conversation."

"Then kick me, *princess*." His stare is cold. I know it's hard for him to be around me this much. I feel it as if I am the one having to leave him at the end of all this. Using the pet name is just his way to provoke me to actually do something about it.

You're an asshole, I state before throwing a punch. "I told you —" Then another. "That I don't like that term."

He stops both hands with his strong grip and keeps me there in place.

"You're not wearing gloves. You're going to hurt yourself." His hands keep putting pressure on my fists. His hold getting tighter and tighter. "Besides," he adds, somehow still making sure he doesn't actually hurt me. "I told you to kick me, not punch me."

Our eyes stare back at each other, my jaw is so tight trying to keep the tears from streaming down for the third time today. I do the only thing he won't ever expect, not even with the power of our bond. I knee him right between his legs. And as he drops I can almost see a proud smile appearing on his face followed by his laments of agony.

That was quite the low blow.

"Good, next time you'll think twice about the words you use." My hands are still closed into fists. My nails almost puncturing the skin.

"Jesus Christ that hurts like a bitch."

I raise an eyebrow. "That was the point."

"The P word after everything was a little too much, wasn't it?" He manages to ask between chokes.

"Yes, it was."

"Anima—"

"I kicked you enough today. I think we can go home."

"Anima, please—"

"This is all my fault, isn't it? I talk too much." Svetlana's voice reminds me that she is still here, and she saw and heard everything.

"No, it's not. It's the entire situation, you just gave Anima the opportunity to get some anger out—on my balls—and my poor pee pee," he says, gasping for air from the pain. "Which apparently she enjoyed a lot."

"I've got another brother to deal with now." My voice is monotone.

"Speaking of my brother—"

I pinch the bridge of my nose. "What now, Dionisio?"

"I just wanted to ask if you're ok being alone with him."

"He cares for me, does he not? I have to be ok with it. Do I like it? Not much at the moment, but I have to spend time with him to understand what's happening."

"He does care for you. Be angry. Take the time that you need but know that he would give up his own life for you." His hand scratches the back of his head. "We all would."

"Don't you have the rings?" Svetlana asks us.

My eyes look down at my hands as my thumb starts to play with the thin band that has been permanent on my index finger since the night of the panic attack. "We do have the rings." My voice softens as the corners of my lips curl into a smile.

"Just stay close to her apartment and if something happens, you can be right there to help with the situation. I'll keep you company so you can use me as an alibi if he sees you at the bar across the street."

"That—that would make me feel—better. We'd be alone, but I'd know you're close in case we need you. And we all have the rings on, you made sure of that,' I add to Svetlana's thoughts.

"I never said the rings were my idea."

"D, do you really think I'm that oblivious?"

His lips form a thin line. "He did agree though, it wasn't all me. Rings were a group effort." Still gasping at the pain while readjusting his crotch.

Why don't I believe you, not even one bit?

I can't answer consciously to anything right now, my balls are still throbbing from the pain of that perfect knee that decided to get a close encounter with them.

So dramatic, you'll survive. I snort.

Have you ever stubbed your toe? It's like that, but on your balls it is a thousand times stronger. I might have to stop and throw up on the way home.

Are you done?

I might have to get a balls replacement.

You're unbelievable.

"When you guys are done being rude for having your own conversation right in front of me, I am ready to go. That was enough excitement for one morning. I need a joint to chill out. You are exhausting."

"I think Svetla and I are about to become BFFs," Dionisio says as he gives a friendly squeeze to her shoulder.

"Get in line, she's my best friend first."

"Sharing is caring Anima, didn't anyone teach you that?"

"I don't like sharing. At all."

Svetlana chuckles at my statement. "This is true. Have you already noticed how territorial she gets when she has food in front of her? Cause there is no way she will be giving you anything."

Dionisio nods. "It's the only child syndrome."

"And her eyes go into a thin line ready to burst lasers out of them."

My hands end up on my hips, forming an amphora. "I do not do that!"

You look so cute when you get all prickly.

"I am not prickly!"

Dionisio's mouth turns into a grin as his finger gently pokes my pointy nose. *Sure you aren't.*

"Let's go. I have a veneficus to interrogate!"

"Anima—"

"I'll be fine. He's gonna show me how to make a healing potion tonight so I'm sure he won't find any of my questions troubling. Besides—I thought we were gonna give him the benefit of the doubt."

"I know he won't hurt you. I still would like you to be careful though."

"You said it. My *soulmate* would never hurt me."

His eyes darken. "Right. Let's go."

CHAPTER 18

Ok Anima, now you get into your apartment, put a smile on your face and remind yourself that Eros is your soulmate, that he is just trying to help you and that all will be ok.

My heart stops beating as I turn the key into the lock of my front entrance. I spring the door open and realize that the lights are all off. As I step into darkness, I register that no one is in here. I sense nothing. My house is completely empty. I exhale, finding it ridiculous how nervous I was to just get back into my own living space. I turn on the lights and sit on my couch while I send a quick text to Eros to see where he's at.

ANIMA:

Hey, I'm back home, thought you'd be here, is everything ok?

No immediate response.

I let my phone drop onto the coffee table with a sigh and walk to my bathroom to take a quick shower while I wait for him.

Pacing back to the living room with my laptop and my hair still a little damp, I grab the phone to check if he replied.

No messages. Weird. He's very quick to answer. Usually.

I'm sure everything is fine and that he will get back to me as soon as he can. I can use this free time to catch up on editing and everything will be ok. I will call him in a bit if he doesn't give any sign of being alive. What if the Gods got to him? What if Jeremy got to him?

Almost two hours pass and I am basically caught up with all the editing I have to do for my clients. This is enough time between a text and a call, right? Right. I pick up my phone, and with shaky hands, I dial his number.

One ring. "I know, I know I am so sorry I was just going to call you, I was with Markus doing some patrolling and forgot my phone in the car."

I hear fatigue in his voice, as if he was running. "Is everything ok?"

"Yes, everything is fine. I was trying to give you some space, didn't want to upset you by seeing me in your own apartment, it is your house after all."

"Tha—thank you, that is actually very considerate."

"Good, trying to learn some boundaries, not overfilling your house with flowers and stuff like that."

A giggle escapes my mouth."That is much appreciated."

"But I'm on my way to your place if that is ok with you."

"Yes absolutely, I was just doing some work while waiting for you."

"I'll be there in ten minutes."

And right on the dot, I hear a knock on my door. I rush to open it and I find Eros standing there, smirking at me with both his hands full of bags.

"That is a lot of stuff." I point back and forth at the things he's holding.

His lips find mine. "I missed you too, Anima."

"Yes—also that." I manage to say under my breath while I close the door and follow him into my kitchen.

He drops a bag on my table. "Got you some bread, Criselda says hi." Then the second one. "Here are all the supplies that we'll need for some basic potion making."

"Buying me bread—are you trying to romance me?"

"Perhaps. Is it working?" Eros's voice is fruity, his eyebrows raised, waiting for my response.

"Maybe." I smile at him, focusing on the freckles on his nose. The sun lately is making them more visible. They're—cute.

"How was training?"

"Good. I kicked Dionisio in the balls, and he plopped like a bag of potatoes. It was great." I think it's better if the reason why I did what I did stays between me and well, me.

"Remind me to never upset you."

"He kinda asked for it." Not a lie. He did ask to be kicked. Didn't elaborate on where he wanted to be kicked.

"I am sure he deserved it."

Silence infuses the room for a few minutes. His fingers tick nervously on his leg, waiting for me to say something. Anything really. So I try to get back to the subject. "Ok so where's my calderon?"

A chuckle followed by a shake of the head comes from Eros. "How about you get any kind of container that isn't made of plastic. Glass would be perfect actually."

"So, no cauldron?"

"Not this time, I'm afraid."

"In the future, though—"

"I'll get you the prettiest cauldron and engrave your name on it."

My lips lift up in a smile. "Yay." I bring my hands together and clap them a couple of times in excitement.

I head towards one of the top cabinets, where I keep my baking supplies and reach on my tiptoes to grab a glass container. While I struggle to get the bowl down, a hand cups the small of my back and shivers travel down my spine.

"Let me get that for you." Eros's voice tickles my ear.

I see his hand reaching for the dish, and as it comes down, I turn to face him. His eyes are on mine, and now we are only a couple of inches apart. I can smell his fresh breath and the citrus of his cologne and I forget how to breathe for a second. Being this close to Eros right now when I have no idea what his intentions are making me nervous. I can feel my hands sweat. He closes the space dividing us and his lips rest on mine, pulling me closer to him. My hands end up on his chest as I reciprocate the kiss for a few seconds before breaking it.

"Ok potion master, teach me your secrets!" I manage to mumble while getting out of his embrace.

He scratched the back of his head. "You might want to write this down while I tell you all the steps."

"Right, let me grab a notepad."

I run to my bedroom to find some paper and a pen, and quickly check my phone for possible messages.

SVETLANA:

Trying really hard not to barge in there.

I look outside the window and see Dionisio's car in the parking lot on the other side of the road. Two shadows are in it.

ANIMA:

Everything is good, Svet. Don't have too much fun without me down there.

SVETLANA:

Hardly any fun, the boy over here is being annoying.

ANIMA:

How so?

SVETLANA:

He clearly cheats at briscola.

ANIMA:

Svet, I've been telling you for years, you are terrible at playing cards.

SVETLANA:

I AM NOT!

I get back into the other room chuckling.

"What's up?"

I look up at Eros holding lemons. "Nothing, Svetlana being Svetlana."

"Ah." He puts down the lemons. "Ok, come over here."

"I suppose I am going to squeeze a lemon?"

"You're supposing right. First ingredient in the potion is lemon juice."

I grab my pen and write down what he just said before proceeding to cut the lemon in half and adding it to the clear container on the table.

"Good. Now you're gonna cut about an inch of this ginger root into thin slices and add it to the lemon."

I get my cutting board out while Eros gets me a knife, and I start cutting.

"Like this?" I show him the first slice, and he gives me a nod and follows it with a smile. I cut about ten thin slices and eyeball it before adding them to the juice.

"Yeah that should be good enough. Ok, perfect, now you're

going to add about a tablespoon of water before doing the next step."

"What's the next step?"

"Add the water and I'll tell you."

I get a glass of water and tilt a bit into the mixture.

"This is a very important step." He looks in the bag for the next ingredient. Dried lavender. "You're going to light the lavender up, and while you drop it in the container, you're going to recite two words."

"Ok, light the lavender then drop it."

"You recite the words *virtus medendi* while you drop it in. If you do it after, the potion will have the opposite effect."

"Got it. We clearly don't want that."

"No, we don't. Ok, ready?"

I nod.

Eros hands me the lavender, and I automatically bring it to my nose to smell it. That gesture makes him light up. His eyes sparkle as they fixate on me enjoying the fragrance penetrating my nostrils.

"The nice thing about this is that my apartment will smell amazing afterward."

I grab a box of matches that's on my coffee table and go back to the kitchen to finish the potion. I light the lavender on fire, and as I drop the flower into the mixture, I recite, "Virtus medendi."

The container starts to smoke and then Eros moves me away from it before it makes a small contained explosion.

"There you go, you just made your first healing potion."

"How can we test it to see if I did it right?" I ask while Eros starts pouring the mixture into a vial.

"Like this." He puts the vial down and proceeds to grab a knife.

"Eros what are you—"

He cuts his palm open. No sign of pain in his expression. His face is completely blank. "What are you doing? Are you nuts?"

"Proving to you that you made the potion correctly." Eros grabs the vial that he just put down a moment ago, downs it as a shot and lets me look at his cut slowly disappearing from his hand.

"And you had to cut yourself to prove that?"

"I'm fine, Anima, see?" He moves his hand in front of my face. I grab it to examine it. No cut. Completely gone. Just blood that is quickly drying up.

"That—that was insane."

"I knew it would work."

"Please don't ever do that again."

He kisses my forehead. "You're cute when you're freaking out."

I narrow my eyes at him for a moment before I go back to his healed hand. "I made a potion." My smile filled with glee.

"You did."

"And you almost gave me a heart attack." My smile dropping at the reminder of his bloody palm.

"Again, it was a little cut, I would have survived either way."

"Don't you have healing powers? Why would I need to learn this?"

"Because those healing powers don't work on myself, they also don't work well on big wounds and what if something happens and I am not right there ready to heal you? You need to be prepared."

"Good point. What is it with magic and Latin, anyway?"

"I think our ancestors just thought it sounded cooler."

"Fair enough." I yawn.

"You're exhausted. Let me clean up here, you go to bed, I'll come say bye before I leave."

"Or—"

"Or?"

"You could stay." Why do I do this to myself? He has been perfect today. Made me learn something vital. He clearly wants me to know how to protect myself in case he isn't around. Is he doing this because of the second born law? Making sure I can protect myself because he knows at some point he will also have to leave?

"I can if you want me to."

"Yes, I'd like that."

"Ok, then go get into bed. I'll clean up, put the rest of the potion into vials so you have some in the house and I'll join you soon."

I give him a quick nod and a small kiss on his cheek before I start making my way to the bedroom.

I take my phone out and send a quick update to Dionisio and Svetlana.

ANIMA:

Made a healing potion that actually works. All good here.

DIONISIO:

Proud of you. I'll stay around, I just sent Svet home. She is terrible at cards, like really bad. I had no idea someone could play that badly at briscola.

ANIMA:

He seems totally normal. I'm fine, you should get some sleep too. And yeah…. Believe me, I have been trying to teach her how to play for 17 years.

DIONISIO:

I'm not tired.

As I lay down in my own bed, the softness of the pillow makes me realize how worn down I actually am. It wraps around my head and neck like a crown on a cushion. Eros takes another ten minutes before he joins me in the room. He smoothly takes off his shirt, exposing his bare chest. He might not be as built as Dionisio is, but he still is very nice to look at. His pale skin and lean body make him almost look like a Renaissance sculpture. The need to pay attention to every detail is stronger than me, especially on someone who is so pretty to look at.

I blame my fixation with beauty on my love for art, but who am I kidding, everyone could see how attractive a body can be.

"If you continue giving me that look, I might lose the bit of self control that is making me remain a gentleman."

"What kind of look am I giving you?"

"Like you're admiring a piece of artwork."

"Maybe I am."

He locks his eyes with mine and sighs. "You really should get some sleep."

"Can I ask you something?"

"Of course."

"Your brother mentioned something a couple of times now without going into detail."

He raises an eyebrow. "What?"

"He said that he won't be around after—"

"After we fulfill our destiny?"

"Yes."

"That—is something I can't answer, it's his place not mine. Dionisio likes being a martyr, he likes to self destruct. He never sticks around too much, he's afraid of getting too attached, he's been like this since we were—kids."

"That behavior has to come from something though, no?"

"It definitely comes from his mother passing away while giving birth to him, and then, well, my mother also leaving when I was born definitely didn't help make him feel that motherly love that people usually have."

"That is—terrible."

"It is what it is. We both survived."

"You did. And it's nice to see."

"Why is that?" He tilts his head slightly to the side, waiting for my response.

"Because it gives me hope that I will also survive."

"You're much stronger than me and him, Anima. You can survive anything."

"Thank you. For today and—this."

"Anytime. Now sleep."

"I read about the second born child law in the Royal Textbook —is that why you wanted me to know how to make a healing potion?" I ask, my hands brought together on my belly, the thumbs nervously circling around one another. "They're not going to take you—the Gods, right?"

Eros's arm ends up behind my neck bringing me closer to him. My head on his chest. His lips resting on my forehead. "No one will take me away from you, sweetheart. The Gods won't take me. Jeremy won't take me. Nothing will separate us." He brings my chin up so that he can look at me. "Our eyes, just like our souls, are the same." His lips press on mine. "Now sleep."

The thought of never being separated should make me feel better, and it does—kind of. Do you feel nauseous when you're assured your soulmate won't be taken away from some evil veneficus or evil Gods? No? Just me?

"Good night," I say with a quick peck on his lips. His hand lands on my cheek and lingers for a moment. I feel his thumb moving up and down, caressing my skin.

"Good night, Anima."

I turn to face my nightstand and pick up my phone to check my emails, then I decide to send one last text to the person staying in his car on the other side of the road.

ANIMA:

Good night, pope.

The person that seems to be there for me when I need him to be, never judging, always listening.

DIONISIO:

Good night, lion.

The person I wouldn't mind never being separated from.

CHAPTER 19

A voice makes my eyes open wide. My arm stretches on the side trying to find the person who was beside me the last time my eyes were open. My body is fully alert as I realize I am laying in bed alone. No Eros.

"I need more time." Eros's barely recognizable voice comes from the living room.

I get up and carefully make my way to my bedroom door. A sigh comes out of me as I rest my ear on the door to see if I can hear what is happening on the other side of it.

"She's already on the edge, let me do my job."

A moment of silence follows his words.

"No, stay put. I decide when it's time." The sound of the phone call ending makes my eyes widen.

I rush back to bed, and a couple of seconds later, the door slowly opens and Eros walks in cautiously.

As he lays back into bed, I pretend to stretch and open my eyes.

"Hey, all good?" My sleepy tone makes the corners of his lips lift into a smile.

"Yes, I just needed some water."

"Oh, I thought I heard something, must have been a dream," I reply, yawning and rubbing an eye. I need to find a way to contact Dionisio and tell him what I heard.

His eyes widen for half a second. "Go back to sleep, Anima." He leaves a kiss on my forehead and suddenly replaces it with his palm. My eyes shut close and I slip into unconsciousness once again.

My feet sink into the ground as I pace myself towards nothingness.

The floor is so cold beneath me. Where are my shoes?

I have—need to find him. No, I can't be here, I need—-

Suddenly my eyes stare down at a river that flows right under me.

A little stone bridge is the only thing preventing me from falling down into the loud water. There's a light wind caressing my face, my nostrils fill with the smell of pine trees that I see in the distance.

The birds chirp as I hear the water running under me. While I close my eyes to concentrate on the sounds surrounding me, I get a sense of déjà vu.

"This place seems so familiar," I say out loud. My hands land on the cold stone of the bridge.

A whisper caresses my ear. "We're in Dusäiga." A low husky voice that I would recognize anytime anywhere.

"I think I am starting to remember my childhood," I tell him as I turn his way. Am I dreaming? How did we get here?

"That, or maybe you just memorized Monet's paintings really well," Dionisio says to me with an amused grin on his face. I can tell he's happy to be here. His shoulders are relaxed, he has a sort of glow on him, his eyes look even lighter in this light. His tanned skin was made to be hit by the sun.

"How did we get here? I don't remember anything. I was trying to—" What was I trying to do?

"You did it. You made this happen. I was sleeping just like you were."

"Is this even real?"

"It is in our heads. This is Dusäiga when your parents were ruling. The best magical place to be. Thank you for taking me here."

"Yes, but how did I do it?"

"I guess your subconscious wanted to show you what you will be bringing when you get your crown back. Peace. Don't you feel peace right now?" He's facing up, eyes closed letting the sun caress his face. "You can walk into dreams. You can even make dreams."

A smirk appears on his face. "I wonder—". My t-shirt and sweats that I was wearing to bed suddenly switch to the little black dress I wore the first time Eros took me out.

"What the—" My eyes widen as I touch my body trying to understand what happened.

Dionisio chuckles at my reaction. "Now this is interesting."

"I didn't do this, why would I?"

"Oh, no." He walks in front of me before saying, "That was all me."

"Do we have the same power?"

"No, I don't think so at least. You are making me a participant of this dream, which I guess means I can have some fun as well."

"And you wanted me in a dress?"

He grins as his eyes travel up and down my body. "I wanted you in that specific dress."

"Are you happy now?"

A low groan escapes from him. "Can't complain."

"What did you mean by Monet's paintings? Did Monet visit Dusäiga?" I ask, trying to move the subject to something that doesn't make my cheeks turn into a shade the same as tomatoes.

"Monet was very close to your great grandfather. They had this bond... very similar to yours and Svetlana's"

My jaw drops open. "I can't believe my great grandfather was my favorite painter's bestie."

"Maybe that's why you feel so connected to his art."

"Thank you for showing me all this."

"You did this. You made this dream. I should be thanking you for making me part of it"

"It was all so sudden—"

"What was?"

"I heard Eros in the other room talking on the phone, then when he came back he pretended he just went to grab some water and—"

"And then what, Anima?" The serene glow around him is replaced with concern.

"I think he made me fall asleep."

"Did he touch your forehead?"

I nod as the image of Eros placing his palm against me resurfaces from my memories. "He did. And then I think I started having my regular dream but then it shifted—to this."

He swears under his breath before starting to speak again. "You were trying to reach me, and you did. Proud of you, little ninja."

"He was talking to someone on the phone, saying that he needs more time to do his job, that I am already on the edge."

"What the—"

"He told me he was with Markus earlier today, maybe I am just overreacting."

"Maybe he was patrolling for my father."

"That's what he said." I reply, nodding my head.

"But you're still not sure of it."

"Not really."

"That call did something to you."

"Yeah—why would he hide a call from Markus?"

"I don't know, Anima, but I am going to find out."

Could he have done the same thing the night we slept together? I felt so weird in the morning not remembering how I fell asleep. "I think—"

"What, Anima?"

"I think he did it already. Once before at least."

Dionisio's eyes widen before he asks, "When?"

"The other night when we—you know." I turn towards the water. "I don't remember falling asleep."

His head snaps in my direction. "But I came around. You were ok and asleep."

"Maybe that's why he did it." Realization hits me. My jaw drops open at the thought of Eros purposely making me fall asleep to show everything is fine.

"He knew you weren't feeling ok that night. He knew something was up with you and how you were hurting internally. Maybe he wanted to find a way to help you get over that feeling of angst—or"

"Or what, D?"

"Or he knew I would show up because of the rings."

The uncertainty of what has been happening around us makes my heartbeat speed up and a lump in my throat makes swallowing painful and nearly impossible. I chew on my lower lip before continuing the conversation. "You said that you trust this Markus —"

"With my life. With yours." His hand rests on his heart, like he's promising.

"Ok." I state before adding, "What if Jeremy got to him or something?"

"What if Jeremy got to Markus?"

"Yeah..." My eyes look at my feet. At the little irregular stones under us creating the bridge. They all look neatly placed. Bigger and smaller ones. Nice and shiny as if someone polished them before we got here.

"Anima—"

My eyes lock with his as my eyebrows draw together. "He can be extremely manipulative, D, he can—"

His hand lands on my arm and squeezes it gently. "He's not going to get to you."

"How can you say that?"

The hand moves from my arm to my cheek. He cups it gently. "I won't let him get to you, or Markus, or Eros, or my father, damn, I am pretty sure Svetlana would jump in before he can even remotely get in the same vicinity as you."

"And that terrifies me," I reply before turning my face towards the pine trees once again. I reach the edge of the bridge and look down. The water crushing on the rocks, raging fast.

"Her coming to your rescue?"

"All of you coming to my rescue when I am supposed to be this badass striga."

"And you are. You are incredible, Anima."

His words make my cheeks heat up. I brush my dress with my hands, trying to avoid looking at him. I know he's looking at me. "Why isn't your father showing himself? Is he—ok?"

A soft apprehensive chuckle comes out of his mouth. "He's totally fine."

"I feel there's something you aren't telling me." My eyes snap back up to look at him. His green irises almost match the leaves from the trees in the background.

"My father made a promise to yours."

"To keep the throne for me, I know. But why doesn't he care to see me?"

He exhales before formulating the next sentence. "Anima, you have no idea how much he would want to do that. It's— complicated."

"Elaborate please, I'm tired of not knowing."

A sigh escapes his mouth. "He made a blood promise with your father a long time ago. He literally can't leave Dusäiga, Court, until you are back in Dusäiga fulfilling the prophecy."

"What happens if he tries to leave?"

He clears his throat. "He dies."

"Holy shit, my father was a psychopath."

"No, he really wasn't. My father willingly accepted the terms, we just didn't think it would take this long to have you back."

"This is all my fault, I have the brilliant idea of moving abroad and look how well that turned out." Both my hands cup my cheeks. My jaw drops open from the realization.

"How is this your fault? You didn't know and even if you did, my father would have begged you to leave and go abroad as well."

"Eros told me about your mother." I regret saying those words as soon as they leave my mouth.

"He shouldn't have done that."

"He actually said it wasn't his place to tell, if that is of any comfort."

His hand touches the stone, as he leans on the edge, resting his forearms and elbows on the cold surface. His eyes avoiding mine. "It's something I don't like to talk about."

"Understandable, but I just wanted to let you know that if you

ever want to talk about it, you can with me." My hand lands on his back. "Just like I know you'd be there to listen if I needed to talk about my parents."

"I know."

"I'm going to deal with Jeremy and then go back to Dusäiga and liberate your father."

"I like this determined side of you. My father doesn't need liberation but I'm sure he'd appreciate being able to step out and see Vallecrosia once again after so many years. You will turn the gold handle. You will open that red door. You will get back here, where you belong."

"Who am I kidding, I can't kill him. D, how do I kill someone I thought I loved?"

"I know you would if you had to, but good thing you have me. You won't get to that point. I will kill him first, for everything he did to you. To us."

"Would you stay—after if I asked you to?"

His eyes, just like mine, are pooling with moisture ready to burst into tears. We don't let them though. We look at each other and stand here, in Dusäiga together. "I am trying to find any possible way to stay, believe me, Anima."

"Your future queen is asking you to?" My pitch raises while I talk.

"My queen. Mine. What a beautiful thing to call you. No one owns you though, Anima. You on the other hand... You own me. I've been yours for a long time."

My heartbeat races as he says those words. It beats so fast I think it might actually explode. "Just—don't go? It's an order."

"I wish it was that simple." He smiles before adding, "I will try anything in my power to follow that order, your majesty."

"Yeah no, I will never get used to that."

A chuckle escapes his lips while he shakes his head. "Wanna walk around a bit? I wonder how good your memory is."

"Are the Court Gardens far from here?"

"Not at all, we just have to walk through town first, which I am sure you won't be mad about."

My lips lift up on the side. "Definitely not mad about that."

Dionisio starts marching towards the group of houses on the right of the little stone bridge we are on. "I'm afraid I can't take the gardens to you, little ninja, you're gonna have to walk a little."

I shake my head and stick my tongue out to make a face to him before I start following his lead.

As I look straight ahead, Dionisio gives me a look and then points at something. Following his finger with my eyes, my jaw drops as soon as I see what he wants me to notice. Right at the top of all the houses in front of us, on a hill, sits the castle. Court, the place where I come from.

I start pacing fast, letting the little roads go past me. There's no time to admire how perfectly stacked the buildings that surround the castle are. Dionisio is now following me in silence. I can feel the smirk now, permanent on his face. I don't need him to tell me where to go because my legs just know. I know these streets better than anyone else even if I look around with my mouth open in admiration. I feel like I am reliving every little stone, every little path, every little corner like it is the first time. As we start making our way up the hill through the path of stairs that passes through the town I start smelling a very familiar fragrance.

"Lavender." I say under my breath.

"We're almost there." I hear him say from behind me.

I pause for a quick second, turning my head back. A smirk appears on my face as my eyes find his green ones. "I know."

As we reach the top of the hill, the gates of the Court gardens appear in front of me, and the scent of lavender takes over every other smell around us.

"I wish I could take a picture of your reaction, you look like a child in a candy store, it's adorable."

I turn to where the voice is coming from. Dionisio moves beside me. "I can't believe I am here whatever this here is."

"It's our dream, we can do whatever we want here." Our dream. This is just ours.

I cautiously move towards the open golden gates and walk past them. I feel like my heart stops beating for a second as if crossing the line was going to make me turn into dust. My eyes travel around me, the green grass below my feet looks unreal for how perfectly cut it is. I notice how the lavender plants are so meticulously placed, forming little paths that bring to the entrance of the castle. Almost like a maze.

I know I used to run around these little paths. I can see a well in the distance covered in ivy.

"I kinda feel the need to run around."

"Then run around, no one is stopping you. We are the only ones here. Run around, play, laugh, let me watch you like I did when we were kids."

I turn to where he's standing behind me, so close I can almost feel his breath on my skin. "Will you follow me?"

"Of course." A soft smile appears on his face.

I hesitate for a second. "What if I fall? I wonder if I would get hurt just in the dr—"

"You'll never fall with me." A finger reaches my skin and moves a strand of hair out of my face.

That's all the reassurance I need to hear. As the words escape his lips, my feet dig into the ground as I turn and run.

Wind caresses my face as my legs continue to carry me around the green. I stop at the edge of the well. Drawings of people doing chores cover the entire surface. No, not doing chores. These are images of the Gods and the elements. A picture of Ignis, the God of

Fire lighting wood is right beside who I believe is Fluvius, the God of Rivers standing in front of a stream of water. Then, not too far from the two, Humus and Ventus the Gods of Soil and Wind stand. Humus with a flower in his hands and Ventus with his arms up in the air.

Putting my hands on the cold stone I try to catch my breath while Dionisio catches up to me and laughs. It feels so good on my overheated skin. I feel my body moving in auto pilot as I turn and run towards him. In his arms. I run and I see his green eyes locked on me waiting to feel my body engulfed by his. As I reach him and throw my arms around his neck, the surprise in his stare gets replaced quickly with softness. He towers over me closing the little distance between us, bringing me in closer by locking his arms around my waist.

My body fits perfectly into his. And the realization scares me. What am I supposed to do with what I am feeling and what I am supposed to accomplish with Eros? I wonder why Dionisio isn't saying anything about my thoughts right now. Can he hear me? I can't hear him. "Have you noticed we can't hear each other's thoughts right now?"

"Uh, you're right. Refreshing, isn't it?" He grins.

A chuckle comes out of me. "Didn't know my mind was that annoying."

"It isn't. Not even a little bit." One of his hands moves a chunk of my hair behind my ear, I feel his fingertips caress my cheeks, as he leaves behind a lavender flower. We stay like this in silence for a moment that feels like an eternity. If only it were eternal. Our eyes connected, never leaving each other and our lips slightly ajar waiting for more. We both make a move at the same time, not being able to resist any longer. His face comes down to mine as I get on my toes and reach up to get closer. There is no space between us as I feel my breasts compress against his pecks.

Dionisio's smile intoxicates my thoughts as my hand lands on the side of his face, our lips almost brush on one another.

"You are quite a dangerous lion, Anima."

"Is this the moment where I say that you are my gazelle? Because it feels a little stu—"

"I've always felt like the gazelle around you."

I can feel his breath penetrating into my mouth, mixing with mine.

As our lips are finally ready to connect, a sudden push makes my eyes widen.

"You're waking up." Dionisio's words cut me like a knife.

"No, not yet. Please" I beg, trying to force myself to stay in the vision. My hands strongly wrap around his as if by holding him will keep me, keep us here forever.

"You'll be back here in no time, little—"

Dionisio's words fade into nothingness as my eyes shut close.

Then, they open again. But this time there's no Dionisio waiting, and no lavender surrounding me—us.

CHAPTER 20

THE ABILITY OF DREAM WALKING AND DREAM MAKING IS GIVEN TO SOULS THAT HAVE AN INCREDIBLE AFFINITY WITH MIND CONTROL.

Eros's voice brings me back to my room. My head is resting on his chest and my arm wrapped around him, keeping him as close to my body as possible. His skin feels soft under my fingers and warm on my cheek. For a moment, I really feel like I have nothing to worry about and I can just stay here, on my bed cuddled up with my supposed soulmate, no panic, no disturbances, just peace. My eyes close as I reimagine being in those gardens smelling lavender while Dionisio watches me amused with a smirk on his face. The light hitting his eyes reveals specks of yellow in his deep green irises.

Guilt fills every fiber of my body. This kind of touch and closeness with Eros feels wrong after the dream I just came out of. Or maybe it's the dream making me feel guilty of something that should be here, in this room, between Eros and I that I am definitely not feeling at the moment.

"Anima, I hate to do this, but you might want to wake up."

An unrecognizable sound that resembles a groan is all that

comes out of my mouth before I stuff my face into the pillow. It smells like fresh laundry. Maybe if I pretend I'm not here, he will stop trying to wake me up and I can return to Dusäiga.

As I think about the drawings on the well and how the cold stone felt under my fingertips, Eros's fingers start poking my shoulder.

"Baby girl, don't you want to wake up?"

Is he for real? My eyes narrow as I look into his. "No, I don't."

"Anima." A soft whisper in my ear sends shivers down my spine. "Babe, come on." My eyes open once again. Baby girl? Babe? Really? I swear he looks for the worst pet names to piss me off.

"You're such a party pooper," I rumble against his chest. Eros chuckles as a hand ends up in my hair, caressing and moving it away from my face. I take a deep breath in and his well known citrusy smell infuses with the air in my room.

"Do you really have to call me—*that?* Before coffee?"

"And deprive myself of this little interaction where you list all the reasons why you hate basically all pet names? Never."

False. I don't hate all pet names. I despise all those he used though very much so.

"You're evil."

"Absolutely I am." He grins, holding me there in his arms. The hair at the back of my neck stands up to those words. A shiver travels down my spine. "You were smiling, having a good dream?"

Silence follows his question. "I was. Don't remember much but it's the first time since I got back that I dreamt something that isn't—our dream."

"Glad you were able to get a little break from that."

A few more seconds pass, and I come to terms with the fact that I'm indeed back in my bedroom resting my head on Eros's body and not walking the streets of Dusäiga with Dionisio. My eyes widen as a realization slams into me. I know I have a photo-shoot at 9:30 a.m., and it's too light out to be early in the morning.

"Oh my god, what time is it?" I shout as my head snaps.

"That's what I was trying to get to. Svetlana just called worried, it's already ni—"

"Oh my god." I rush out of the bed, gathering the clothes that are neatly folded on the chair beside the dresser and run to the bathroom.

"Hey, hey you have time." I hear Eros say from behind the door. I know he's trying to calm me down, but anything that comes out of his mouth right now seems to have no meaning after —Dusäiga. Actually seeing where I belong. I don't think I've dressed this fast in my entire life. When I have a morning shoot, I like to prepare everything for it the night before. Being stuck in front of my closet getting behind with my set schedule is one of my biggest fears. I physically can't be late especially when I am trying to get good publicity for my new business.

"I hate being late. I am always at least fifteen minutes early," I explain as I quickly get out of the bathroom now dressed.

"You are panicking and you are not late, your place of employment is literally a floor beneath you. You can take a minute to breathe."

"I know you're trying to be comforting, but I really really hate —this. And now I don't even have time for a coffee." I throw my hands up in the air as I sigh in defeat.

"Svetlana is already downstairs getting stuff—"

"I know and she shouldn't be. I am supposed to be there." I storm out of the bathroom, almost making Eros tumble.

"Yes, and sometimes life happens and look, you have someone that is there ready to help."

"I am *never* late."

"You're being a little ridiculous now, Anima."

"It physically pains me not being in control of my set schedule, don't you see that?"

"I do, and I am sorry for saying I find it ridiculous, I can tell you are freaking out, but you really should take a moment to—why are you looking outside the window?" I don't even realize that I am staring at a parking lot. My heart skips a beat at the thought of Eros possibly figuring out the real reason for my touchiness this morning. I do hate tardiness but this? This is something else. The unsureness of his intentions is still present, I haven't forgotten the fact that he made me fall asleep when he realized I was awake after that mysterious call from last night.

"Nothing, I thought I saw something." I wish I did.

"Can you sit down for a moment before you storm out of here? You are clearly on edge."

"Eros, what part of I hate being late don't you get?" My fingers press on each side of my temples. Pressure builds, slowly becoming pure agony.

"You know what? That's ok, it's morning, you woke up later than you wanted to and I won't keep you any longer."

"Thank you, gotta run and I am sorry. Lock the door on your way out, please?"

"How about you ask for forgiveness over dinner—tonight maybe?"

I have no time to protest or process what he just asked me. "Yes, absolutely."

"Do you have any spare light bulbs by the way?" He asks, scratching the back of his head before pointing at my completely blown out chandelier. All eight bulbs are now dust on the floor. "Gonna have to change the ones that exploded."

"How—I didn't even..." My eyes widen in shock. My jaw drops open. I didn't even hear the bulbs going off. Shards of glass are sprinkled all around the living room and I heard nothing.

"It's ok Anima, your powers are entangled with your

emotions." His hand brushes my hair making sure I have no shattered glass in it. "You go, I'll clean up here."

"I—" No words come out.

Eros's hand lifts my chin up. "Everything is fine, go." His lips leave a soft peck on my forehead. I nod and pace out. I feel like I'm running from my own apartment.

I close the front door behind me and sigh. Will I be able to survive a normal dinner with him? I have to, just like I have to stop pining over someone who will always be unavailable, no matter what he or I are feeling right now. I've been trying to find a way out of this since they told me what the prophecy meant for me—for us. I have a duty to fulfill, nothing will come between me and my people—Dusäiga. I have to do this for myself, learn about my family, and understand why they did what they did to protect me. My heart belongs in that place. My soul is in those lavender gardens.

As I walk downstairs and out of the building, I stop when my hand reaches the door handle of my studio. My head impulsively turns towards the parking lot and my heart starts to race in my throat. An ascending rhythm.

I swallow some air to try to calm my heartbeat as my eyes scan the area and stop where *his car* was parked last night. My right hand playing with the gold band that never leaves my left index finger.

"Anima, are you coming in?" Svetlana's voice echoes in my head.

A sigh escapes my mouth while I look at my phone once more. No calls. No texts. And the black Lancer is gone. The parking space is empty as if he was never there. Empty is how my body feels looking at something that isn't present—real.

My hand now closes around the gold key dangling around my neck. "Yes, sorry I'm late."

CHAPTER 21

"Are you ok? The Grimaldis will be here any minute."

"Had trouble waking up I guess, sorry, let me just grab a camera and get it set up quickly."

"Anima are you—" Svetlana is unable to finish her question as the family walks in, screaming baby and all.

"Good morning, girls. Sorry, we got here a couple of minutes early, can we come in?"

"Of course you can, Giovanna. We were just finishing setting up," I quickly reply with the fakest smile on my face. The pressure on my temples gets more intense every damn time the child screams a higher octave.

"Sorry about Simone, he is really cranky this morning."

"That's alright, we're going to find a way to calm him and get a couple of shots, right Svetlana?" She turns to me with thin eyes and mouths the words, "you owe me big time" before walking towards the small 2-year-old trying to make him laugh. She's really good at that, kids adore her.

"A magician. Have you ever thought of babysitting?" Giovanna asks as Svetlana finds a way to make Simone stop crying in less than five minutes.

"She is amazing with children, but you can't steal her. She's my only good assistant."

Svetlana turns to me with an evil grin on her face before she starts talking again, "Depends, how's the pay? Cause this one sucks."

I wish I could pay her more, she *does* deserve it. "Hey!"

"Love you babe! You know I'd be doing this for free." It's true, she would. I would never let her though.

"Wow Anima, now that I see your eyes hit by the sunrays, they're beautiful, how didn't I notice them before!? You gotta show them off!"

"She always finds a way to mask and hide them, I've been telling her since forever how pretty they are!" Big lie but I am telepathically thanking Svetlana for coming to my rescue as soon as Giovanna starts talking about my new set of irises.

"Be proud of your uniqueness."

"Thank you Giovanna, I needed to hear that this morning." A smile appears on my face. I am proud of where I stand.

I take one last look at my phone before turning on my camera. "Ok, let's capture some magic."

Svetlana's wide eyes make me chuckle.

WE'VE BEEN EDITING FOR A COUPLE OF HOURS, TRYING TO CATCH up with galleries to send out and starting to work on the family shoot we shot earlier. No sign of Dionisio. Nothing. Picking up my phone I release a breath filled with disappointment as the blank screen stares back at me, I place it back down noting nothing has changed.

"Ok I heard you sigh enough for a lifetime. Are you going to tell me what's going on?" Svetlana finally breaks the silence.

"I just… I feel that something is wrong."

"Well, that isn't cryptic at all."

"Eros came over yesterday as you already know and—well, he taught me how to make a healing potion and it was nice even though he scared the shit out of me when he took out a knife and cut his hand open to show—"

"He did what?" Svetlana's eyes are so wide open right now if someone patted her on the back of the head they would fall out.

"Yeah, he wanted to make a point."

"That isn't psychotic at all…"

"No, it was just to show that the potion I made worked… Anyway after that it was—nice. He stayed the night."

"…Ok then why are you so moody and checking your phone every two seconds? Did he tell you he was going to call you and he didn't? Cause the guy is probably outside waiting for an excuse to come in here."

"What? No, he isn't the problem, or at least he isn't what is worrying me."

"What is worrying you is how Dionisio left this morning."

"Yes."

"He didn't tell you he was leaving?"

"He did not and after last night—"

"I thought he stayed in the car."

"He did but—" I take a deep breath. "There was this dream where we were in…"

"You had a sex dream about him—the god?"

"Stop calling him that, and no it wasn't a sex dream, but it was—real, like we both knew we were there. Another one of my tricks, apparently."

"That is so sick, holy shit!"

"I woke up in the middle of the night and thought I heard Eros on the phone. There was something off, it scared me a little, and I think he may have forced me to fall back asleep with the use of a spell or something... So I guess my subconscious went to the one person I thought could help."

"So you dreamed of Dionisio and he happened to be asleep as well, in his car, in the parking lot right in front of your apartment building."

"Yes," I say before adding, "And we were in Dusãiga. It was —It was a beautiful dream."

"How's that even possible?"

"I guess my memory is coming back in full force. I knew exactly where I was supposed to go and—we had a bit of a moment."

"Go on."

"I can't have a moment like the one we had, Svet, it was— intense, the dream was so profound. Every emotion was enhanced."

"You can't force yourself to do something you don't want to, Anima, not you, not ever, not after what you went through."

"Turns out Eros was probably just talking to my future security guard, and now I feel terrible because the moment I had in that dream—" A sob escapes my mouth.

"Ok maybe Eros was talking to this guard person, so what? He's sketchy, we all see it, and I am the first one that doesn't fully trust him."

"He's my soulmate, Svet. And I had a beautiful moment with his brother."

"We're still going with that then..."

"What do you mean?"

"You know this whole thing is bullshit and you don't want to let yourself accept the fact that you have real feelings for Dionisio"

"I was hoping to talk to him this morning after—never mind."

"What happened Anima, you literally look like someone that just lost a piece of their heart."

"We were in the gardens of the Court and there was so much lavender around… I started running around and laughing. He was looking at me with so much admiration, almost adoration and I took the moment and ran towards him. In his arms. And he let me do it. We stayed in each other's arms for a moment that felt endless. He said some things that—that's not important now, but we almost kissed before I woke up and realized I was back in my apartment."

"The guy is madly in love with you and he can't even hide it anymore."

"I think he's avoiding me."

"Maybe he just had to go check on something."

"He isn't replying to my text, or calls, nothing. He is avoiding me because he knows what happened can't happen again and I am worried I've ruined everything."

"Because of Eros."

"Because I am supposed to be with Eros."

"Are you?"

"Am I? I don't even know."

"Just cause you sleep with the guy doesn't mean he owns you."

"I mean sleeping is a big word."

"Ok no, Anima, I might not like Eros but I still thought the guy knew what he was doing, please tell me he did the job."

"I mean… I truly think I am the problem lately."

"You didn't come. Yesterday at the gym I was saying it as a joke. Oh my god, Anima!"

"It was like a very small one at the beginning I guess? I was having a great time. Everything was absolutely wonderful and great, he knew what he was doing, until—"

"Until the fireworks didn't go off. Oh my god Anima what the fuck is wrong with men?"

"I think I just got worried. He said something in a certain tone that I didn't really like much and after that thought. That night is a total blur, I remember very little of it."

"Did you drink or something?"

"Just a glass of wine—"

"I bet Dionisio would make sure he gets the job done. I'm sure you wouldn't forget the night either."

"Svet."

"What? Look at him, that man knows exactly what to do."

"Not helping."

"I know, I'm sorry." Her hand scratches the back of her head.

"I feel like I am missing something. I guess the idea of a soulmate is not like the one we see in movies… This almost feels like an arranged marriage that was destined to happen to save a kingdom. I thought we'd have that kind of connection that would make us feel like we can't breathe when we aren't around each other."

"You do have that connection. With his brother."

"What if my brain is just trying to cope with this huge change with my life and it's making me think I am attracted to this unattainable man? What if I want this because he told me he can't let me see what he feels for me—that he can't let himself have feelings for me?"

"Wait, hold the fuck up, what?"

"He slipped the other day at the gym, I was angry so he let me spar with him. I got upset with him too because I see the affection he has for me and I just—lost it."

"And he basically told you he can't let himself love you… and then he said all the other shit yesterday at the gym… and then you almost kissed in your dream."

"Oh my god I am awful. Eros should be the one not trusting me."

"Eros is being sketchy as shit."

"He was so nice to me this morning, and I was a total bitch."

"I don't trust him, at all."

"Dionisio does, and that's all the reassurance we need to also stop questioning his methods."

"I hate seeing you like this and not being able to do anything to help you."

"You could help me pick something to wear for tonight?"

She sighs, shaking her head. "Anima—"

"Eros asked me out this morning, and I had to say yes. I am supposed to want to say yes and spend time with him. For fuck sakes, I woke up in his arms this morning and I actually didn't hate it, at all."

"Oh wow, that's exactly what we all aspire to have. Not hating the person sleeping beside us."

"Svet, please st—"

"Hey ladies." A voice comes from the entrance. Svetlana and I both turn towards the door, clearly not having heard it open. A very distinguished smell penetrates my nostrils. Eros was holding a big bouquet of fresh lavender.

"Eros, what are you doing here?"

"I had to make sure of something before tonight."

"Ok," I say, tilting my head on the side with curiosity.

"Svetlana, would it be possible to have a moment alone with your friend?"

"Not a chance."

He sighs. "I thought you might say that." He takes out a smaller bouquet under the big lavender one. Mimosas, Svetlana's favourite flower. How did he know? "These are for you." He hands her the flowers.

Her eyes widen as her hands close around the yellow bunch of joy. "Tha—thank you."

"My pleasure."

"Eros, what are you doing?" I ask while I watch him nervously walk towards me.

He hands me the flowers. "No carnations, not anymore. I'm not making that rookie mistake again."

"It was a cute gest—" I try to protest but in vain.

"You're sweet, but it really wasn't."

Svetlana's nose comes up for air from her flowers. "It was pretty over the top."

"Svet!" I turn towards her with thin eyes.

"No, she's right. It was crazy. I am sorry, I am sorry I seem distant at times, I am sorry if I ever made you feel pressured to do anything, I am sorry for worrying you when you already have so much to worry about, I am sorry for being insensitive this morning—"

"You were nice, I was the insensitive one."

"The point is, I know this entire situation is absolutely unbelievable and that you are dealing with so much and that I have no right in being here asking you to be part of your life when you almost don't know me even if—well you know what I mean."

"Eros, what are you trying to say?"

"I will be patient with you, I will be here ready to listen and to remind you how smart, funny and beautiful you are. What I ask in return is to be patient with me as well, as I try to learn all the ways to make you see how much I care about you."

"Eros, this is unnec—"

"Don't say it's unnecessary, this is the bare minimum."

"Of course I'll be patient with you as well, but can I also make a request?"

His head tilts with curiosity. "Please."

"Communication."

"What do you mean?"

"We need to be honest with each other and talk about anything that might be concerning us."

"Yes, absolutely, I can do that."

"Then you can pick me up at 7 p.m."

A soft grin appears on his face. His eyes are sparkling with joy. This is good, isn't it? This is what I am supposed to be doing, learning about Eros and bonding with him, not trying to kiss his brother.

"I came here for another reason as well."

"Which is?"

"My zia Ginevra would like to see you this afternoon if you're not too busy." Eros gets closer to my ear and whispers, "She might be of better help with magic today—after the accident this morning. Don't want to upset you."

"I—I'm sorry about that," I say out loud. "Yes, I'd love to see her."

"Great! See you later, prin—Anima." He whispers in my ear before leaving a peck on my temple. I grab his cheek with my free hand and turn my face towards his. My lips crush on his, catching him by surprise. They are soft and he tastes minty. It takes him a couple of seconds before he reciprocates the kiss. When he does, he deepens it, resting a hand on the small of my back moving me closer to him. With that, he salutes us and rushes out of the studio.

"Well, how did that feel? As good as his brother's breath on yours?"

Not even close.

I pretend not to hear what she just asked. "Can you help me pick what to wear tonight?"

She sighs. "Of course. I'll be at your house at 6 p.m."

"Thank you."

"What was the Ginevra thing about?"

"Oh nothing, I just pulverized my chandelier this morning because I was upset… He thinks Ginevra might be able to help with that."

Her eyes widen and her jaw drops. "You did what?"

WHEN EROS TOLD ME GINEVRA WANTED ME TO WORK WITH HER, I wasn't expecting her to close Forestiero for me so that we could work in the bookshop.

"Ginevra, are you sure you want to do this here? It might get messy."

"You won't. This is why you're here."

"I don't want to ruin the boo—"

"We're going to meditate a little and see if you can learn how your breathing works."

My mouth shuts at those words. No magic? I raise my brow. "How is that going to help me?"

"If you can control your breathing, then you can control your reactions to your emotions."

"Ok," I mumble while checking the time on my phone.

"Don't worry, I'll have you out of here in time for you to get ready for your date."

"Sorry." My lips close into a thin line.

"Don't apologize for being in love." She smiles at me. "Now put the phone away. No distractions here."

"Yes, *zia*," I say while dropping the phone in my bag. "I used to call you that, right? As a child I mean." I add.

"You did." Ginevra's sweet eyes soften. "Ah, now that's a sweet memory," She says while pacing towards the back office. I see her come out a few moments later with her hands full. She's holding three big white candles.

"Candles?"

"Yes, candles always make the environment more relaxing, don't they?"

"Is that why you wanted me to do this here? Because I find this place relaxing?"

"It's where you come to seek refuge. Isn't it?" Her smile is like a sudden beam of sunlight illuminating my every dark thought.

"It is." Forestiero has always been my refuge. The place where I could always be myself. The smell of paper, and vanilla filling my nostrils and making every bad thought go away.

"Sit down and cross your legs."

I do as she says and end up sitting in the middle of the bookstore in silence. Ginevra sits in front of me and places the three candles in a triangle in between our legs.

Her index finger taps on the top of the three wicks, and I hear her whisper a word. The three candles magically light up.

"You—can create fire?"

"I can use a spell to do so. *Igneus*."

"Igneus," I repeat as a way to memorize it.

"You will learn how certain spells can be used to help you with small tasks. They won't help you to win the lottery though. That is something that the Gods won't let us do."

"Party poopers."

Her chuckles fill the room. "Close your eyes and rest your hands on your knees." I do as she says and remain silent. "Yes, perfect. Now drop your shoulders. You're tense."

"I'm not tense," I protest.

"Anima. Drop your shoulders."

My shoulders come down as she starts humming a slow repetitive melody. Two low notes followed by a semitone higher one, then the same low note again.

"What are you humming?"

"Just a little chant. Follow my voice. Close your eyes and continue focusing on my voice."

My eyes close once again, and I go back to listening to the repetitive melody. My breathing stabilizes and slows down. It goes with the song. Breath in. Breath out. Two low notes. A semitone higher one. Low note.

"Meditation helps us understand our bodies reactions, and it helps us control them. If you learn how to control your breathing in every circumstance, then your powers can be mutated in whatever you want them to be."

"Mutate?"

"Yes. You decide how you use your powers. Not your surroundings. Not your emotions. You. Your brain. Your soul."

"How can I just stop being upset or sad or angry?"

"I never said you have to stop. I am just giving you a tool to help you deal with your own emotions. I would never tell you to stop feeling, Anima. You have to feel."

"Sometimes I wonder if not feeling might be better."

"No, my child. Not feeling might look like a simple solution, but it's just a temporary fix. You need to walk into your pain with your chin up high. You need to feel it, understand it and accept it."

"Can you tell me something about my parents?"

"I remember the moment your father found out your mom was expecting you. I've never seen two people so devoted to each other as your parents."

"I wish I could have known them."

"You know—your dad called all the gardeners that day."

"Gardeners?"

"He was going ballistic. He couldn't stop talking and he

decided that was the right moment to plant hundreds and hundreds of lavender plants in the gardens."

"Because my mother's favorite flower was Lavender."

"Yes."

"I can't wait to see them."

"Your heart is the mirror of theirs. It's pure and loyal and curious. You Anima are destined to do so much good."

"I really hope you're right," I whisper under my breath.

"I am right," She says before adding, "Move the candle, Anima."

My hand moves by itself. It waves a candle away. A slow movement of my arm. The candle moves away from me following my hand.

"I—" My eyes widen in shock. "I did it."

"You did." Her eyes expressing tenderness, practically sparkling as they look at me. The corner of her lips lift into a soft smile as she watches my reaction.

"Thank you."

"You just needed a little reminder."

PART THREE

An Unbreakable Bond

CHAPTER 22

"You've been staring at the same pile of clothes for twenty minutes."

"Well, I don't know what the hell you're supposed to wear when your soulmate you've been treating poorly organizes a surprise date."

"I am still wondering how he knew about the mimosa."

"He probably asked around. He is a veneficus after all, he has his ways I'm sure." I shrug.

"I don't like it."

That makes two of us.

A beep surprises her. She picks up the phone quickly trying very hard to cover who sent her the message.

"Why are you being so flinchy about who's texting you?"

"It's no one, really."

"Do I have to remind you that I can compel people?"

Svetlana flips the screen to let me see who she's talking with and I sigh as soon as my eyes lock on the contact name. Dionisio.

"I—I thought I would keep him in the loop even if he won't talk to any of us."

"Well," I say, noticing the blue text box appearing. "He clearly replies to you…"

"Anima—"

"No, it's ok, being angry makes it harder for me to think about him right now."

"He is with his dad if you were wondering…"

"I wasn't."

"Ok." She sighs. "Let's completely repress your feelings and prepare you for this absurd date you're going to go on."

I can't even control how much my eyes roll back. "It is not absurd, he is clearly trying, and I appreciate that very much."

"Too bad he doesn't try enough in the bedr—"

"Svet!"

"Ok fine, we're not going to have the sex talk, got it."

"Thank you."

"Is this date going to be fancy or casual?"

"No idea." I shrug my shoulders.

"It's getting warmer, but you can never go wrong with high-waisted jeans and a nice blouse… maybe the burgundy one."

"You always say I should wear more burgundy…"

"Because it looks so good against your amber skin and blonde hair." She pauses for a second. "Oh, and the black high waisted pants, not jeans, I changed my mind, it's more put together but still casual enough."

"My fashion genius."

"And layer a couple of necklaces, yellow gold, cause I know you'll never take off the key your dad gave you."

"Never," I whisper, fixating on it while I check myself in the mirror in my bedroom. I can't help but shift my eyes towards my phone that sits on my nightstand.

"I know I joke a lot about the situation, but I am right here

Anima, and you know I hate seeing you like this. I just wish I could take your pain away."

"Maybe I imagined everything… Maybe it really was only a dream, and he doesn't know what happened."

"He probably needs some time to think. Try to put yourself in his shoes. I know you're doubting yourself and you might have the right reason to do so, but you should see how you two look at each other..."

"I…" A sigh escapes from my mouth. "I just wish he would talk to me," I say, holding my face in my hands.

"And he will, maybe a little time apart will do you some good, both of you…. now you are going to enjoy your time out with Eros."

"Yes, I'll try."

"But please be careful."

"We're just going out for dinner, which is good, because that means public space. Not much can happen in a public space, right?"

"Fair. Keep your location on though."

"I will," I say almost as a whisper while my attention immediately falls on my left index finger and I incessantly twist the thin gold band around.

"And if anything happens, you have your ring."

"I have my ring."

"He will show up." She tries to reassure me. Her hand rests on my shoulder, giving it a gentle squeeze to let me know she is still here, beside me, as always.

"No matter what." The words come out without even thinking about them and a smile appears on my face. That was Dionisio's promise. Always. No matter what. He will always make sure I am safe.

A sudden shiver sends goosebumps down my spine. My heart rate speeds up and as I turn to look at my front door, the sound of the intercom makes Svetlana jump. Eros is here.

"Well, at least he showed up on time."

My fingers type a quick message before I start moving towards the door.

ANIMA:

Always?

Three dots appear fast as soon as the message has been delivered but they disappear just as quickly. My heart aches at the empty screen. He is not going to reply.

Svetlana opens the door, letting my alleged soulmate in, the rays of the setting sun making his hair appear even more red.

"I'm gonna go. Have fun, kids." Her voice echoes from the set of stairs she's running down on.

"She seems to be a woman on a mission." Eros's voice breaks the silence that fills my living room.

"She is, always."

"You look beautiful, Anima." His eyes travel up and down my body, checking me out. His eyes on me make me feel uneasy, almost—violated at how hungry they look.

"Thank you."

"Ready to go?"

"Yes."

A buzz on the back pocket of my pants catches my attention while we're walking out of my apartment building.

DIONISIO:

No matter what, dangerous lion.

That is all the confirmation I need, to know the dream we shared was more real than anything we've ever experienced when awake.

Eros's hand reaches for mine and as our fingers interlock, a sense of nausea comes creeping in. It's one dinner, that is all this is. And he's been trying to be better after that one night. My chest tightens and my jaw aches from how hard I am grinding my teeth.

"Is everything ok?" His words snap me out of the trance I was in. I didn't even realize we were standing in front of his car.

"All good!" I force the corners of my mouth to lift into a smile. "Sorry, I zoned out for a second there."

As my back touches the edge of the passenger seat, I realize I've been in Eros's car only a couple of times and the thought worries me so much that my heart rate picks up. We should be in public, not in a car just the two of us. I don't even realize how much my leg is shaking until he mentions it.

"Are you nervous?" His eyes are on me as his head tilts to the side.

"I guess I am a little," I say. "It almost feels like a redo of a first date for some reason." Big lie. It feels like I am going to dinner with the enemy, that's what it feels like.

"I know what you mean, how about we take it as it comes, we go to get some dinner and you decide how you feel. If for any reason you want to leave, I'll take you straight home."

An enemy that is talking like the hero of the story. "Sounds perfect."

"How do you feel about fish?"

"I love fish."

"Wonderful."

We drive off and end up on the seashore of Bordighera, the city beside Vallecrosia. The little restaurant he picked is right on the beach, and we get seated at a table on the patio outside. The sea air is definitely helping with my upset stomach and I am very glad it is. My eyes close for a few seconds as I take a deep breath in, filling my lungs with the tingly aroma surrounding us.

"This will always be my favourite sight." Eros's words feel so distant as I start to count how many little white tables are outside on the patio. Nine.

His eyes are on me, his arms crossed on the table making him lean slightly towards me.

I pick up the menu in front of me and start reading. "I feel like having some spaghetti *alla pescatora*."

"Now that's a good idea, I might get that too. Should we get a bottle of white with that?"

Yes, alcohol, good idea. "White wine is perfect. Chardonnay."

His lips turn into a grin. "Chardonnay it is, pri—Anima."

Here it is. He stopped himself. Everything is totally fine. Keep it together Anima. It's a word. Just a word. Nothing more than that. Or is it? It's funny how something that is supposed to represent me ended up hurting me like it does. Criselda saying it? No problems there, but him? It feels wrong. The waitress comes by and after we order and she brings out the wine, Eros breaks the silence.

"Anima?"

"Yes?"

"What is it?"

"I'm sorry, it's nothing, I promise."

"Please, talk to me."

"It's—you stopped yourself and you have no idea how much I appreciate that you did."

"It's hard not calling you by your title. I'm sorry."

"No, you don't have to apologize. You stopped yourself, I'm the problem here."

Eros rests his hand on top of mine trying to make me stop shaking. "You are not the problem. He is."

"It's—hard."

"One day you will be able to keep your chin up high and feel proud of that word."

"Am I? I feel that word is a synonym of solitude."

"Where is this coming from?"

"The second born law."

His look is perplexed. "I told you already. You have nothing to worry about. I am not going anywhere. We made sure. The gods have no interest in me."

"H—how?"

He sighs. "I don't think you want to talk about this right now."

"Why wouldn't I?"

"Just know that I am not going to be requested."

And then it hits me. The brothers weren't going to leave me. Not both of them. Eros never said he was going anywhere, he always said he would be with me. Dionisio is the one that has been saying he will have to leave. "Oh." Nausea hits me in a rush. My throat dries, it feels like I can't get enough air. "There has to be something we can do," I start saying, almost begging.

"It's the law, Anima. There's nothing we can do."

His voice is firm, cold. He isn't even looking at me. He's looking at his plate as if we were having the most normal conversation in the world. As if we were talking about the weather and not about his brother giving himself up for him—for me. "Ok, but is it really that—bad? I mean we certainly can go and visit him, can't we?"

He chuckles, still keeping his eyes down. "We haven't seen any of the sacrifices after they've left, Anima."

My eyes widen as his words arrive to my ears. "But that means——" He could go towards his death.

"Yeah—probably exactly what you're thinking." How can he be so detached to this?

A whisper escapes my lips. "A crown and a corpse." The words of the prophecy come back to me.

"Uh, I didn't even think about that."

"We have to do something."

"And what do you suggest we do? You can't change your destiny."

"It's my destiny, I absolutely can."

"Your destiny is ruling Dusäiga with me. He wasn't even supposed to be here. Besides—"

"Besides what?"

"He kind of offered himself."

"And you didn't stop him? Your brother, flesh of your flesh, goes in front of the gods and offers himself in your place and you just stand there and let him do that?"

"There was nothi—"

"I need a minute." I stand up before he can finish his sentence.

"Anima—" His words fade as I enter the building. I quickly ask a waiter where the bathroom is, give a quick smile and make my way there. After I lock the door, my knees buckle and I crash to the floor. My hands feel numb as I look at them getting greyer and greyer. My vision blurs at the thought of Dionisio. How he looked at me when I was running in the Gardens the night before. How his arms felt around me, when his skin touched mine, and our breaths mixed.

Everything is ok, everything is ok, everything is ok. Breathe in, breathe out. I wash my hands and pat my forehead with cold water to try and release some of the built up tension that is causing my head to pound. Forcing myself back to the table, I see Eros standing facing the sea.

"Do you know the waiter?" He asks, keeping his eyes on the water that is smashing against the rocks. "He checked you out."

"Uh, really? Didn't notice," I say, before I sit down, I grab a glass of wine. "We went to the same school, relax."

"Whatever you say."

"Are you seriously playing the jealousy card with the waiter right now?"

He shakes his head. "Sorry about that. Are you—feeling a little better?"

"Honestly? No, I'm not. I am not feeling better at all, actually, I feel worse."

"You wanted communication. Honesty. I am trying to give you that."

"I just don't understand how you can be so—detached about it."

"Detached? Anima, I have to be ok with it. It was his choice. He did this for me. I can only honour his decision."

"That is bullshit. When you care about someone you don't let them give up their fucking life. I am part of this just as much as you are and I am not ok with it." I down the entire glass like a damn shot. "I'd like to leave now."

"Easy there." He chuckles as he sits back down. A balmy, spicy taste burns down my throat. It reminds me of cloves. Now this is a weird tasting Chardonnay.

Heat rushes straight to my cheeks as my head spins for a few seconds. Why am I being so aggressive towards the person that is supposed to be my entire world?

"I'm sorry, I totally overreacted. Let's just eat and have a great time." My hand reaches his on the table. Something is wrong, the little control I thought I had is now fading away, and I am not sure why I just said—those words. They came out of me almost—automatically.

"Much better." Now that's an odd response, isn't it? His words fly past me as he brings my hand to his lips and leaves a peck on it.

As the food arrives and we start eating, the conversation gets much lighter and I find myself laughing, and blushing and enjoying my time completely. All the worries I had earlier, all the anger and frustration are gone. It's just me and Eros now and my heart feels full.

Right when the bill comes, he takes out his card, stops and looks straight at me with a devilish smirk on his face. "Do you still want me to drive you home? Because I had something else plan—"

"Then let's go." I don't even give him the time to finish the sentence that I am up on my feet.

"Someone is excited. Hopefully, the surprise isn't disappointing."

"That's impossible." I smile at him.

He gets up and as soon as the words come out of my mouth, his lips are on mine and I am locked in his intoxicating citrusy embrace. "Now we can go," he whispers in my ear. My legs shake as his voice sends shivers down my spine. I feel like I am made of jello and he is doing this to me, all of a sudden. It doesn't matter, right now I am happy. Chasing a high I haven't felt possible to get with someone else—with him.

We get into his car and as we take off, the only thing I can focus on is Eros's eyes going back and forth from me and the road.

"Is everything ok, babe?"

I blush at the thought of me staring at him. "Sorry for staring, that's absolutely wei—"

"Remember what I've told you about apologizing? I do that too, a lot, it's hard not to look at you."

"I don't know if I would have been able to do what you had to do—for me."

"What do you mean?"

"I mean knowing who I am and trying very hard to keep it to yourself for my safety."

"Of course you would have been able to, you're much stronger than I am. Anima, you have no idea how many times I was this close to just saying 'fuck it' and telling you everything, it was my brother that helped me stay sane."

"I wish—I guess I wish I also had someone like that too. I do, with Svetlana, but you know what I mean…"

"I do." As those two simple words come out of his mouth, he pulls into a small parking lot back in Vallecrosia, on the inside of town, the sea isn't visible from here. "You have me now though, and you always will." His hand reaches my thigh and gives me a gentle squeeze that sends electrical shocks all over my body. A throb beats between my legs. The sudden warmth makes my position a little uncomfortable and I gently shift, crossing a leg on top of the other hoping to get some sort of friction to see if I could calm down the sudden excitement. I hear him chuckle under his breath. He definitely noticed how such a small gesture got me so worked up.

Eros keeps his hand on my thigh and as he gets closer to my ear, he whispers, "I thought I was supposed to surprise you, but look at you, it's going to be tough keeping my hands to myself." That low husky voice could honestly become my favorite drug.

"Then" I inhale. "Don't." And exhale.

His lips crush on mine and the taste of white wine and his citrus cologne mix together creating a tingly dry taste that I honestly could have at any time of the day. It feels so good, his soft lips caressing mine and his tongue asking for permission to deepen the kiss. I nibble at his lower lip letting him in and his hand ends on my cheek, pulling me closer to him. We break the kiss only when we get to a point where we both need to breathe.

"Ready for your surprise?" He smirks, keeping a hand under my chin forcing me to keep my eyes on his.

"So you're saying that pulling into an empty parking lot isn't the surprise?"

"You're funny."

"A true comedian," I reply before adding, "I am absolutely ready."

Eros rushes out of the car and comes to my side to open up the door for me, a gesture that I'd find a little over the top any other day, but right now? Right now it just adds to the thoughtfulness of everything he did tonight. Letting him show the care he wants to give me makes me rethink everything I was worrying about until this exact moment.

Our hands interlock and as we start to walk down a narrow pathway, I realize how empty the streets are in this part of town. We are in the historical centre of Vallecrosia. The houses are all made of stone, and they almost look like they are piled on top of eachother. They remind me of Dusäiga, and that thought makes the corner of my lips lift up.

"What are you smiling about?" He notices my change in expression right away.

"Everything." My answer makes his eyes crinkle.

We stop suddenly, and Eros turns my body towards the front door of a shop. A pink peony lies on each side of the entrance and as I peek inside, I notice the fluorescent lighting still on. Black and white photographs are covering the white walls but no one seems to be in sight. I try to turn the handle, but as I imagined, the door is locked.

"I think we got here too late. It's ok, this was sweet, but we can come back another day. I have never seen thi—"

"We are definitely not too late."

"Eros, I tried the door is lock—" I don't even have the time to finish my sentence when he jingles a set of keys in front of my eyes. My mouth falls open as my eyes widen.

A chuckle escapes his lips. "We are right on time." His hand ends on the small of my back as the other goes to unlock the door of the small shop.

"I don't even know what to say."

"You don't have to say anything, just enjoy the private exhibit."

I skip inside the big studio, like a child on Christmas

morning ready to run towards the tree and unwrap all the presents. "This is amazing, do you know who the photographer is?"

"I do."

"Are you going to tell me the name?"

"Take a look for yourself and then I'll tell you."

I nod in agreement and begin from the wall on the left, the first picture closest to the window. I start looking at them, little stone houses, narrow steep paths that intricate inside a town. I move on, taking in every single detail, every oak tree, every brick, every window with green shutters. I see a stone bridge and up in the distance slightly to the right, an agglomeration of those little houses and right at the top is a castle. The castle. These are pictures of Dusäiga. I turn with wide eyes towards Eros. He's behind me, a metre away from me, leaving me some space to take in every picture. I go back towards the black and white photographs and I stop right in front of the picture of a stone well. I can almost feel the cold rock against my palms. My shoulders drop, I feel like I am losing my balance as a tear travels down my cheek.

"This is…" My voice cracks. "Dusäiga," I finally say.

"It is." His arms wrap around my waist. His body pressed on my back, holding me up.

"I don't even know what to say."

"I thought this could be good for your memory but maybe it was a little too mu—"

"No, this is—perfect. Thank you for bringing me here."

"You're welcome."

I turn my body so that I am facing him, still in his embrace. Our eyes locked on each other.

"Who took these? They're beautiful."

"Her name was Bol—" A loud crash outside of the shop startles us both, putting us on high alert.

"What was that?" I grip at his shirt, trying not to lose balance after the jumpscare I just had.

"Stay behind me," he says, pushing me back and making sure I'm protected by his body. As we approach the front door cautiously, three Opacums are staring straight at us and waiting in a line, blocking the little road that would take us back to Eros' car. I look at their hands closed into fists. They're ready to fight. Three against two. Not a fair fight.

"What do we do?" I whisper.

"You do nothing, you stay here, where I know you're safe."

"Eros—" He's already outside, his stance firm. His legs slightly open and his arms down ready to attack. Electricity crackles out of his hands, a neon-like light bursts into beams hitting the ground. His shoulders tense as he seems to focus on his powers, and the sparks of energy turn wider, stronger, until out of his palms, come two spheres of pulsating light.

The movements that Eros makes are completely different from his brother's. Dionisio uses his entire body, it's all about contact and grip and technique. He is smooth, quick, and precise. Eros on the other hand, is combined completely with his powers. His movements are poetic and look like a dance as the streams of energy continue to come out of his palms ready to block any kind of movement these Opacums have on him. He is a waltz of power, of opportunity, of light and darkness.

I slowly walk towards them. Two of the Opacums seem to be passed out on the ground, and I realize the third Opacum is about to hit Eros. He's about to stab him from behind while Eros makes sure the other two are disarmed and out for good. A dagger appears in his hands and that's when I jump into action.

I look straight into the faceless entity, and adrenaline kicks in. Running as fast as I can I put myself in front of Eros, creating a barrier. The lesson with Ginevra comes back to mind. My powers are attached to my emotions and if I don't ensure that my breathing is normal and I panic, then I will be useless to Eros and anyone else. Breathing in, my arm rises up midway and I point my palm at the Opacum as to make him stop approaching. A devilish laugh comes out of the creepy being and as a slimy voice follows the laugh, a strong wind seems to be coming out of my hand. The Opacum that was compelled to stop just moments before, now flies towards the wall of a house behind him. The last thing I remember is the sound of his spine cracking as if I had a branch in my hands that needed to be broken in half. Falling to my knees, I pant trying to keep awake, my breathing is heavy and my vision blurry. The energy I projected out is taking a heavy toll on my body.

I turn to look at one of the other two Opacums, now awake and staring straight at me. It's eerie how their eyeless faces can still feel on you. "She looks ready to me—" the entity has no time to conclude what they wanted to say, because Eros gets back in front of me and finishes off what he started.

My eyes close as I feel the cold stone under my palms reminding me of the well from Court I touched just the night earlier in my dream with Dionisio.

"Anima, are you ok? We have to go, now." Hands grab my arms, pulling me up. I don't even know how I end up in Eros's car.

I find myself fidgeting with the gold band around my index finger. What did that Opacum mean when they said I looked ready?

The drive to my apartment is a blur. My feet move on their own as we cross my front door. I stumble on the couch and rest my hands on my knees. Silence follows us. Words seem to be trapped in my throat as if a web is there to catch them and keep them in. My eyes stare at the left leg of the coffee table and I gasp at the sound of water running as Eros gets a glass of water in the kitchen. He sits beside me remaining in silence, his hand caresses my hair. A frantic knock on the door makes me jump to my feet. Eros tries to stop me but I practically run towards the entrance as something in my gut knows who is on the other side.

As I turn the handle and swing the door open, I glance at who is standing in front of me, heavily breathing. Green eyes filled with concern lock with mine. My heart skips a beat feeling as if I am finally waking up from a dream. No, not a dream. A terrible nightmare.

Chapter 23

The joint rings are magical rings bathed by the power of the four elements. It is a way to make sure that the individuals that wear them are safe. In Dusäiga culture it is custom to gift said rings to a family member, a friend, or more commonly, to a lover.

Dionisio's eyes are staring right into mine. Then, they shift to something, someone behind me.

"Of course he's here." I turn towards Eros, who now has his hands closed into fists resting on his knees. His face emotionless, looking at me—us. As if on cue, Eros's lips lift up into a smirk, my heartbeat picks up as his eyes look into mine. If I was feeling some sort of attraction moments ago, now it's completely replaced by fear.

"What happened?" Dionisio asks me, forcing my attention back to him. His hand ends on my cheek and as his fingers touch my skin and his forest green eyes look at mine once again, my vision blurs for a few seconds. I start blinking fast trying to recoup focus and as I rub my eyes with my hands, I start remembering the anger I felt at dinner. It comes rushing all at once. My body finally feels back in unison with my brain. Dionisio's touch snapped me back into reality.

Tears feel my eyes as I snap, "What the fuck did you do to me, Eros?" My jaw tightens.

"Nothing. We were having a good night and then we circled by a couple of Opacums and you decided to come out when I specifically told you to stay put."

Anima, what's wrong? You're scaring me, I hear Dionisio say in my head.

"I—I feel as though I've just resumed breathing after a prolonged period of apnea."

Eros sighs. "We were at the gallery when—"

"When what, Eros?" Dionisio shouts, his hand brushing his hair back. This is the first time I see him with his hair loose, not in a bun. His dark wavy locks framing his face perfectly.

"We were attacked," I whisper, looking at the ground with my hands closed into fists. Dionisio finally walks into the apartment and closes the door behind him. "I didn't feel you, the ring—"

"You didn't feel her through the ring because she was not in danger, I was with her and…"

"And?" Dionisio's attention goes to his brother.

"She basically saved my life. You had to see how good she was!"

Dionisio lifts my chin up forcing me to look at him. "I felt you right after. I feel you right now. What's wrong?"

"I—" Words can't come out. Nothing comes out.

Anima, please. I can't hear anything from you. Your mind, it's completely blocked off. My brows come together as the knot in my throat still blocks the words.

"She's fine."

"I wasn't talking to you." Dionisio's voice is cold. Raspy. Firm. He's trying to keep distance from his brother. It's at that moment that I realize how tense his body is. The veins on his forearm are popping out, his nostrils flare and his expression is tight. My hand grips his arm as my vision blurs once again and I lose stability for a second.

Dionisio—He relaxes as he feels our skin touching once more and my voice reaches his mind. A little shock wave travels down my spine as his attention is back to me.

"I think I'm going to be sick." I oblige myself to look straight at Eros. "I don't know what you did to me, but I was ready to go home and then I didn't want to anymore."

"Yes, I asked you and you said you wanted to stay."

No, I didn't. I did but... I didn't. My eyes feel heavy at the thought of not being in control of my own body. I run to the kitchen sink as the nausea hits me once again.

"Zia Ginevra really did wonders this afternoon with her. She made an Opacum literally fly away with such force, I was speechless." Eros continues to explain, completely ignoring what I just said. The crack of the Opacum's spine still resonates in my ears. I feel goosebumps covering my entire body.

"You did something, at dinner." I accuse him. Dionisio on my side pats my back and hands me a glass of water.

"Yeah, I paid full price for a plate of half eaten spaghetti. Anima, you were all over me two seconds ago, don't turn this on me, you wanted to be there just as much as I did. We were having a great time until, well, the Opacums."

"Eros, what the fuck? Are you listening to yourself? Do you even know how to talk to a woman? Jesus Christ." Dionisio shakes his head. He takes my hand and leads me towards the couch where he sits me down.

"She had no problems with it until you showed up."

"Leave." A whisper comes out breaking from my lips.

"What? I was jok—" Eros tries to brush off.

"Leave," I repeat. My voice is rigid just like my clenched jaw.

"Anima, prin—"

"Eros, go home, I'll take over from here." Dionisio's voice is low and firm.

"Of course you will. Dionisio, always ready to pick up the pieces. What a good son you are. Daddy is going to be so proud, too bad she is *mine* and not yours."

"I'm no one's. I am not yours, not yesterday, not now, not ever. We are done."

Eros scoffs. "Yeah ok Anima, we can't be done. We belong together."

"There is not even one cell in my body that wants to be with you. Get. Out."

"I don't know what the hell you did to her, or what is happening to you, but if you don't leave right now, I don't give a shit that you are my brother, I will break your jaw and you know I will make it hurt." Dionisio's hands are now grabbing Eros's shirt, impelling him to look him in his eyes. They remain in silence, clenching their jaws for a minute or two.

D, please. As soon as my words reach his mind, his hands loosen.

"I'd like to see you try." Eros laughs, freeing himself from Dionisio's hold and walking towards the entrance. "Remember how good you felt, Anima. Remember how incredible you felt the moment you realized you were in control of your own powers. I did that, not him." As soon as the wooden door closes behind him, tears start streaming down my face.

Dionisio' stare is locked on the door as if he expects his brother to barge back in at any second. His shoulders are tense, like the rest of his body. He's trying really hard to stay in control, for me. He's forcing himself so firmly not to follow his anger.

"I know you're not doing well, but please tell me what happened, little ninja. That... That was not my brother, it can't be." He paces towards me, sitting down beside me, his hands resting on his thighs. His head stays low staring at the floor.

"He asked me to go out with him tonight and… I said yes, after the dream we had I convinced myself I should give it another try."

"I know about him asking you out. I need to know what happened during the—date."

"I was nervous, on the edge, I was thinking about—it doesn't matter, but then he almost called me princess and I got even more nervous." I sigh. "We talked about the second born law and—he finally told me why it doesn't apply to him… and I kind of lost it."

"You do hate that word said by a man."

"I do." My lips are in a thin line. "You're not going to say anything about that, are you?"

"Right now I only care about you and what happened tonight."

Dionisio—I beg through the bond.

Remember what I told you last night. Now let me make sure you're ok. His words sound soft in my mind.

I shake my head. "I know I told him right after the fight that I wanted to leave."

"But you stayed."

"I did but… I didn't want to stay… I said I wanted to go home."

"Did you see him do anything to you while you were eating, maybe?"

"No, nothing."

"Maybe you turned for a moment and then he touched your forehead or anything like that?"

"The bathroom! I went to the bathroom to freshen up and when I came back, I drank some wine and told him I wanted to leave."

There's no way. He can't have stooped that low.

"I'm telling you, I came back, drank the wine and then my

body was absolutely on autopilot and my attitude towards him completely changed."

He picks out his phone and dials a number.

"What are you doing?"

"If he did what I think he did, there's only one way I know to confirm it," he tells me while he waits for the person on the other line to pick up.

"Hey Soteria, sorry to bother you this late, how are you doing?" He smiles when the woman on the other side replies. "I'm good, thank you for asking." I feel a pit to my stomach as I see how he shifts his body while talking on the phone. His hand brushes my arm as my thoughts start to travel. "Listen, do you know if Eros picked up some powdered Opal in the last couple of days?" A few seconds pass by and then he thanks the person and ends the phone call.

"If he got something, it wasn't at Court."

"But I guess he probably has ways to get what he wants without being noticed," I say more to myself than him. His nostrils flare. I can see his veins popping up on his forearms with how tight his fists are. "I am going to fucking kill him." Dionisio stands and races towards the door.

"Who's Soteria?"

Dionisio turns with a curious look on his face. "Soteria is just your maid, Anima."

"What? I don't need a maid."

"She works at Court because she wants to, don't worry."

"Sure she does," I whisper to myself.

You need to rest, little ninja and I need to go and find out what he did to you.

"D, please." I reach him, grabbing his arm and pulling him towards me. He goes rigid, the sudden touch surprising him for a moment, but then he wraps his arms around me, his head resting on top of mine.

"I can't let him get away with it. If you feel he gave you something, then I can't just let him walk freely."

I'm afraid to ask even though I already know the answer. "He gave me a potion, didn't he?"

"I'm afraid so. He didn't take any Opal from the castle, but —"

"What does Opal have to do with anything?"

"It's the main ingredient for—" He can't finish the sentence.

"For?"

A love potion.

My eyes widen as I hear the words. Then, I try to get back into focus. "Well, we don't really know—Soteria could be on Eros's side."

"That girl literally has been dying to see you since she found out you were back, I doubt—"

"Yeah now I don't believe her even more."

"How can you even say that without knowing her?"

"It's how you spoke to her. How you shifted your body as soon as she asked you how you were doing. You like her, it's written all over your face."

"Are you jealous, little ninja?"

"I am not jealous, I just had this feeling—maybe it's the fact that Eros gave me something and I did things against my will, I don't know. How can we trust anyone right now if the one person we thought was on our side clearly isn't?"

"Yeah, well, this is why I am going to deal with it—with him."

"Dionisio, please, don't go. Not tonight. I don't think I can be alone right now."

"Let me call Svetlana, she can com—"

"I don't need Svetlana, I need you to stay here. I need you to be calm and not with your hands covered in blood."

"I'd wear gloves."

"You know that's not funny, not right now."

"It is a little."

"Don't go." My voice cracks as my arms tighten around him, hoping it will be enough to make him stay.

Dionisio's shoulders relax as soon as my head rests on his chest. "I'm not going anywhere," He says, his lips leaving a peck on top of my head.

"Thank you."

"Don't thank me yet, the night is long, I might change my mind."

"It felt really empowering making that Opacum move so fast." My hand cups the back of my neck. "It scares me. Having so much power."

"You apparently made him fly. I would have loved to see you in action like that."

"The Opacum said something when they saw my power."

"What did it say?"

"I'm not completely sure but I think something like *she seems ready to me.*"

"I'm sending Markus to keep an eye on him right now."

"Is that wise? What if he hurts him?"

"He'll keep his distance."

"Would it—would it be possible to ask Markus if he can check on Svetlana?"

"Do you feel something?"

"I don't know. I just think I'd feel better if I knew she was ok, like actually having someone trusted that could see her and tell me she's ok. I don't want to call her and worry her, not right now at least."

"So you trust Markus now, someone you haven't met yet?"

"You really trust him."

"I do."

"With my life and yours," I add to my previous statement.

"Exactly."

I nod. "Then I trust him too."

"I'll have him check on Svetlana right away. Now can I make a small request?"

"Depends on the request."

"Would you go to sleep in that comfy bed of yours while I stay right here, making sure everything is in order?"

"Only if you promise me not to leave this apartment and commit murder."

"I won't leave your sight, I promise you Anima. I am not leaving you anymore. You're going to get sick of me because I will be staying right here beside you until everything is back in order and then even after that."

"Can you really make that promise?"

"I shouldn't, but I will spend my life trying to keep it."

I move towards my bedroom door and stop right in front of it. "Will you wake me up when you get any updates?"

He pours himself a glass of water. "Of course."

Chapter 24

I toss and turn until the first light of morning sprinkles through the window. It's around 5:00 a.m. when I decide to slowly mince towards the kitchen to grab a glass of water.

"You should be asleep." Dionisio's voice from behind me makes me jump. He's laying down on my couch, one arm behind his head.

"I could say the same thing to you."

He shifts his position, making space on the couch for me to sit on. "Touchè."

I couldn't really close my eyes for long, I explain.

I know. Me too.

His eyes widen as he takes a good look at me. The weather is getting warmer and my bedroom gets the most amount of heat in the entire apartment. For that reason my sleeping attire tends to be —very tiny. I'm currently wearing a navy blue tank top with thin straps and matching shorts. Are my shorts too short? Too long? How can shorts be too long, what am I even thinking about? "Nice pjs," he says grinning under his breath. *Definitely the perfect length.*

I roll my eyes, pretending to be annoyed by the comment, but we both know I am not. "Did Markus call?" I ask, clearing my throat, trying to change the subject.

"No, but I have something better." He takes out his phone and hands it to me. There on the screen, I see a picture of Svetlana sleeping.

"Ok, creepy much? Is Markus into vampire novels? Because that would explain a lot."

A chuckle comes out of him. The sound of his laugh warms up my cheeks. *Feel better?* He asks through the bond.

Much. Thank you. Can you thank Markus for me?

Of course.

"What about—our other problem?"

"He's still there, keeping an eye on E—my brother. He's been sending updates regularly."

"Nothing suspicious?"

"On the contrary, he looks a little too normal." He crosses his arms on his chest. "He's probably trying to lay low because he knows me. He knows I would send someone to watch him." The small gesture suddenly becomes a big one when I start fixating on how thick his arms look in the t-shirt he's unfortunately wearing.

I find myself swallowing air trying to get back to the topic of discussion. "He did something, D. I know he did."

"He's been doing something for a little too long and I will never forgive myself for letting him get this close to you."

"You had no idea."

"That's no excuse. I promised to keep you safe, and I thought you would be with him. He's supposed to be the one person I don't have to worry about. For fuck sakes! I don't know how you can even look at me right now." His voice is cracking, sounding desperate.

"You literally were told for as long as you can remember that me and him were supposed to be endgame. That we are this duo that must be together and save Dusäiga."

"Something happened to him, that—how he talked, that's not him. That's not my brother."

"The way he has been acting... He reminds me a lot of Jeremy."

"He could have gotten to him."

"Could he be under a spell or something like that?"

"That's the only explanation I can come up with at the moment."

"I'm sorry." I sigh, crossing my arms to my chest and hug myself. Maybe if I stayed in Chicago I could have at least kept Eros and Dionisio safe. Everyone else would have been doomed, but *they* would be safe.

"Why are you sorry?"

"Because, Jeremy is a problem because of me."

Dionisio's jaw tightens as a low growl comes out of him. "Don't." His hand squeezes my thigh gently. "Do not ever feel like you are the reason for any of this."

"Aren't I? I am the one that went out with him and started all this."

"He's the one who manipulated you, and I am the one who will kill him."

"You've been saying that a lot in the past twelve hours."

"It's a promise, Anima. He won't get to you again."

The energy I used to fight off the Opacum on top of everything else I'm feeling makes standing up or really, any kind of maneuver, a huge task at the moment. I move towards the stove and put on a moka pot, coffee will fix everything.

"Can I ask something of you?" I say while moving around the kitchen.

"Anything. You can ask anything, always."

"Can you please not give me the silent treatment? Not after the other night."

His words come out after a few seconds of quietness. "The dream we shared—I needed to clear my thoughts. I'm sorry, it won't happen again."

"Good."

"Can I ask you something now?"

I nod. "Of course."

"Before the attack last night, did you—have fun? Aside from the huge mess and my asshole of a brother."

"You did it, didn't you?" I smile at him.

"What?"

The gallery.

"Did you like it?"

"I did, a lot."

"Good."

I suppose that's the reason you were nowhere to be found as well.

"One of the reasons, yes."

"I had a lot of fun, it could have been the perfect gesture. But —"

Dionisio finishes the sentence before I can. "But it got ruined, I know."

"No, I was going to say that it would have been perfect if— you were with me."

His steps towards me are slow and meticulous. "Anima—" He stops right in front of me. No touching, just our eyes locked onto each other.

"No more secrets, Dionisio, only the truth," I almost beg.

He sighs. "I would have loved being the one you shared that moment with."

His words cause me to lose control of my body. My hands land on his chest and my lips end up on his, no hesitation. I couldn't wait any longer, not after the moment we shared the other night. Not after last night. We are here now, together and this is the only thing I am certain of. Our breaths mix together. This is right. It takes him a moment to realize that what is happening is real and not a dream, but when he does, his arms wrap around me, bringing me closer to him. One of his hands ends up on my cheek. I feel his calloused fingers on my skin and the small gesture feels like an electric shock. I move my arms and lock my hands around his neck to make sure we get even closer to each other.

Here we are again, my braless body pressed against his firm chest. We fit perfectly, like this—together. His beard tickles my chin and a giggle escapes my mouth. He groans at the sound of my voice and as he picks me up, my legs wrap around his waist and we end up laying down on my couch. Cedarwood fills my nostrils and the intoxicating smell mixed with everything else happening makes the lower part of my body throb. He hardens on top of me and I can't stop myself when I raise my hips to try to feel him better. I moan at the friction being created. And then, he comes out for air. "We should not be doing this, Anima."

"That is bullshit and you know it," I reply, breathing heavily.

"God, you're so beautiful." His hand moves a chunk of hair from my face before he gets up when the sound of the moka pot alerts us that the coffee is ready.

I remain on the couch for a little longer, trying to get my normal heartbeat back. My legs feel like jello and I am not sure I can get up. As if on cue, Dionisio is back by my side extending his hand to help me up.

I stumble in his arms. My hand on his chest and my eyes

focus on his. Green is my new favourite colour. It has been for a while. I could take pictures of his eyes all day in every single light condition. He smiles before moving his head down. Is he going to kiss me again?

"We're training today. You can take all the pictures you want after though," He whispers in my ear. His husky voice makes me shiver all over. My entire body throbs as I think about his soft hungry lips on mine. God, self control is so hard to maintain around him.

I clear my throat when I ask, "Do you think that's wise?"

"Why wouldn't it be? We're going to work on your new power. I can't wait to see—"

I don't even let him finish his sentence. "D, no, I could hurt you, real bad." I shake my head. "I can still hear the bones cracking in my head. I absolutely will not do that to you."

"Good thing you made some healing potions the other day."

"That's not funny," I reply with my hands on my hips.

"It wasn't supposed to be funny." He pokes the point of my nose making me wiggle it.

"I'm not going to hurt you. Not even with healing potions close by," I repeat, hoping he would drop it.

"That's the right attitude, come on, let's get moving."

I sigh. "I can't, D."

"Anima, you won't hurt me" His hand caresses my cheek in apprehension.

"No, like I have a newborn session I have to do"

"Oh, work. True, that's a thing people do."

"Yes, and I need to keep my job, I like my job. The session is at nine."

"I know you do… Thing is, I promised I wouldn't let you out of my sight."

"Well then, be ready to handle a child, because you've just been promoted to photography assistant."

"Wait what? I have to hold the baby? Why would I be holding the baby?"

His sudden worried voice makes me chuckle. "I can ask Svet —"

"No no, I am not going anywhere. But if the child falls, it's on you."

"You'll be fine." I laugh at his concern. Then I reassess the photographs from the night prior and how much time he must have spent the day before getting the gallery ready—for me.

"Last night, before the attack Eros was about to tell me who took the photos…"

His eyes widen. "He didn't tell you?"

"He said the name was B something, I don't remember it right now."

The corner of his lips lift and as he takes my hands in his, he says, "Bolina."

"Bolina, such a different name, I like it. Is she in Dusäiga? Because her eye is absolutely incredible. I haven't felt so absurdly attached to images in a very long time. I felt as if I was in the picture, they were so beautiful."

His lips leave a peck on my hair and then his forehead gently touches mine. "Bolina Psiche."

Psiche. I've heard that last name before. It was—is mine. "But that means—"

"Yes." He's shaking when the words finally come out of his mouth. "Those pictures are your mother's."

CHAPTER 25

"My mother took photos—like I do."

"Yes." He nods. "Are you—ok?"

"I think so," I answer, as I sit down on my couch. He follows right after. "I just can't believe we had something in common even if we weren't—together." My eyes feel full of tears ready to burst at any second. "I wish we could have had time—more of it." My hand clenches on the key around my neck. "It's bittersweet, but it gives me something to hold on to." His thumb catches a tear traveling down my cheek. "Maybe we both would have spent hours and hours in a dark room, laughing and developing photographs together." A short laugh escapes my mouth as I try to control the tears.

"I've always wanted to learn how to develop film." His voice caresses my ear. "Maybe you can show me one day."

I turn my face towards his. "I'd like that." My lips beam at the thought of Dionisio and I in a dark room developing images.

You're so strong. His fingers brush my hand, and I tingle at the touch, at the closeness.

Sharing these gestures with Dionisio feels like breathing, like walking. They come naturally, and I don't think I can stop. "Thank you for letting me see this side of her."

"I'd love to take all the credit but my father helped quite a bit with this one."

Now I really wish I could have shared that moment with you. I sigh and with my head down low I stand up and mope towards the window in the living room.

"You did," he replies from behind me.

I stare at the street, people walking and driving by. So unaware of the things happening around them, they have a place they have to get to and they just go. I can see those photographs crystal clear in my head, my memory is soaked in them. As I open the window to let the air in, I close my eyes, breathe in the sea essence and I find myself running through the gardens of the castle. I hear myself laugh, I see the well getting closer and closer with every step that I take, and then, as I turn to look behind me, a child stands there, arms crossed on his chest, smiling back at me. I could recognize those green eyes anywhere.

"I—did."

"You made me relive it with the dream we shared, seeing you run like that again. And your laugh, god, I think that's my favourite sound, and maybe I shouldn't say it—"

"Don't ever stop. Please."

"Your laugh, Anima, that damn laugh." He looks up at the ceiling and shakes his head. "You don't understand the effect that you have on me, the effect that your happiness has on me."

"Di—" Every word that I would have wanted to get out now disappears as the sound of my ringtone infests the room.

"It's ok, get the call, I'll see if Markus has any news. Say hi to Svet for me."

I nod and walk towards my bedroom.

"So?" She asks as soon as I accept the call and bring the phone to my ear.

"Hello."

"Oh no, see this is why I shouldn't leave you an entire night on your own. I wanted to give you some privacy and look, now we are back at a simple 'hello', it's outrageous really."

"There is some news."

"Oh fuck, you're pregnant aren't you? It's ok, it's fine, I get it. It's a little sad because it came from a night of bad sex but look on the bright side, you always wanted a kid with strawberry hair!"

I chuckle and then cringe at the thought of procreating with Eros. "Definitely not pregnant."

"Oh, thank fuck. Ok, I am done with the sarcasm, spill it."

"I kissed Dionisio."

I hear her spitting something from the other side of the line. "Excuse me?" She asks, coughing her lungs out.

"He kissed me back, like a lot."

"Hold the fuck up, go back, rewind, I thought Dionisio was avoiding you."

And with that, I tell her everything that happened after she left my apartment last night. Eros taking me to dinner and us fighting. The possible potion he gave me, the pictures my mother took and how I ended up making an Opacum hit the wall and break his spine from the collision.

"Holy shit, remind me not to get on your bad side."

"Then we went home, Dionisio arrived and as soon as he did I guess I snapped out from the effect of the potion. I got upset obviously, and kicked Eros out."

"And Dionisio stayed."

"He did."

"And you fucked."

"Svet, no, we did not sleep together."

"I truly don't understand what you're waiting for… Do I have to remind you that he looks like a god?"

I scoff at the reminder. "No, trust me, I know he does. He feels like one as well, his chest is literally rock solid."

"Oh nice, now we're talking! Did you lick it?"

"No, I did not lick it… He had clothes on."

"Boo! Clothes are overrated," she whines. "You wanted to though, right?"

I sigh. "Yeah. Real bad."

"Ok so, get to the kissing part, you have a newborn session to get to."

"Right, ok so we began talking about everything, how something is clearly happening with Eros and then he said he won't leave my side and I just…went for it."

"And?"

"And he kissed me back."

"And?"

"And then he deepened the kiss."

"And?"

"And the kiss became a really hot steamy makeout session on my couch."

"And?"

"And that's it, we stopped."

"Well, I guess today is not the day I find out how big his dick is, cause girl, that is a big one and you deserve a nice big one."

"You are something else." I look over towards the door to make sure it's still closed.

"I have to lighten up the mood or I will think about Eros giving you something against your will and then I would have to stab him, which by the way, might actually happen."

"What is it with you and Dionisio wanting to murder people?"

"Stab stab. I'm sure you can find a spell to hide the evidence after. It will be quick and painless. For me at least. He will be crying like a little bitch."

"I love you Svet."

"I love you too, don't ever make me wait this long again, I'm glad Dionisio is there, you look good when he's around. He makes you smile, and I love seeing you smile."

"No stabbing though, I really think Jeremy is behind this."

"Your taste in men, until this morning, was terrible, let me tell you."

I check the time and see I'm running late. "Gotta go, I'll keep you posted if anything else happens, and maybe I'll see you later?"

"You bet."

I change into a pair of black leggings and a black tight t-shirt, and I go back into the living room where Dionisio is looking outside the window.

"You can tell Svetlana that it's massive, by the way."

"Shut up" I chuckle, my cheeks burning up.

"It's so big I have to pay property taxes on it."

"Sure it is."

"It's basically a third leg really, it gets pretty uncomfortable."

"No eavesdropping on girl talk."

"I didn't even have to, it's this special thing going on between us where you can't contain your filthy thoughts about me."

"Ok time to go shoot a kid." I clap my hands together before I widen my eyes and realize what I just said.

"Is that a new kind of birth control?" Dionisio chuckles.

"Photo shoot, I meant photoshoot." I restate. "Now I see why you and Svet get along so well." I shake my head trying to contain a laugh.

"So I wanted to check out something before we go out with the day as planned," he says scratching the back of his neck.

"What is it?"

"Markus said Eros is at Forestiero, acting a little strange, like he looks normal but almost like he's on autopilot?"

"Ok… then let's go."

As we leave my building and approach the entrance to the bookstore, a sense of restlessness rushes through me. Words can't come out of me as a knot of needles closes my throat.

You're so strong, little ninja. I feel Dionisio's hand brush my arm before stepping inside the shop as if nothing bad had happened in the last 24 hours. God, in the last three months, really.

I follow him inside and as soon as I look up towards the counter, I see Ginevra smiling at me.

"Good morning, beautiful, how wonderful to see you again so soon! Are you two off to the gym?" She asks with a warm look on her face.

"We are, right after a newborn session I have in about half hour, which we probably have to get to soon, D," I reply, turning to the man standing right beside me.

"Are you her assistant now?" Eros's voice catches us off guard and my eyes widen at the sound of it. I can tell he's right behind me just from the citrusy fragrance arriving right up to my nostrils. I thought it was inviting at first. Now, it feels violating.

"Eros, hi." My voice trembles as I turn to look at him, his eyes staring right back at me. What catches my attention is how his lips curl into a grin as soon as he sees me. His hand caresses my cheek and for a slight second, I glance at my peripherals and notice a sudden move from Dionisio.

"Be careful with her, brother," he says to Dionisio without taking his eyes off of me.

"Always," Dionisio's voice sounds as firm as his jaw is.

With that, Eros walks back to the small office and goes back to work.

What was that? I ask through the bond.

"Time to go, boss." His voice gruff, while he keeps an eye on his brother.

"Yes, let's go." My response comes out more like a whisper. "Nice to see you, Ginevra."

"Bye beautiful. Be safe you two."

"Bye, zia." Dionisio leaves a peck on his aunt's cheek.

As we make our way back towards my studio to grab my camera, we see Svetlana running towards us, and she reaches us right at the entrance of my place of work.

"Svet what's up?" I ask as soon as she reaches us.

"I think I know what's wrong."

"What are you talking about?" Dionisio questions.

"Ok, so while you were out last night I might have ended up on a couple of forums."

I raise an eyebrow at her. "A couple?"

"Ok, maybe more than a couple." She places her hands on her hips. "I think I know how Eros has been making you feel attracted to him."

"Svet—" I try to stop her.

"The carnations."

I unlock the door and as soon as we get inside, I lock it back up."What do you mean by that?"

"I might have left a question about the significance of flowers and specifically carnations in one of these forums I was on and I got a reply literally fifteen minutes ago."

"You asked the internet about witchcraft," I state, not a question.

Her eyes narrow at me. "Yes, I asked the internet about fucking magic, and the internet replied with valuable information."

Dionisio's laugh makes Svetlana's nostril flare, and with that, she slaps his arm. "Ok ok, no need for violence, it's just—a little funny."

"Funny? I am trying to help you here. I thought you of all the people would be more interested in my discovery. Carnations are used in potent love potions!"

Dionisio sighs. "Svetlana, I like you. You are clearly the most incredible friend Anima could ever ask for, and me as well now, but carnations aren't used in love potions."

"What did they say about the flower?" I ask disregarding Dionisio's statement.

Are you serious right now? I hear his voice in my head. I swiftly glare his way, my eyes informing him of my answer.

"Carnations are used to make the attraction spring. Passion and lust. They're given as a gift of fascination towards a person. Then, apparently the use of oranges is also used a lot in love potions and spells, it attracts the prey as they say on those sites."

My eyes widen. "O—ranges?" That can't be possible. That would mean that every single thing I have ever felt towards Eros —was a lie. He captured me just like Jeremy did. Like how a lion catches a gazelle.

"Yes, why, what's wrong?" Svetlana's eyes on me are filled with concern.

"Have you ever smelled Eros? He only uses a citrusy cologne. It smells like oranges."

"Anima, oranges are used in literally any men's cologne." Dionisio's voice is low as if he was trying to convince himself more than anyone else around him.

"Not in yours though." I tell him looking straight into his green eyes.

"I know you have to go, but I really think there's something here and maybe I can find more information about it in the Royal Textbook."

I look at the time on my phone. It's eight forty-five. The thought of Eros playing with me since day one makes me feel lightheaded and right now I have to stay in control of my emotions. "You would have had more luck with the Book of Souls." Dionisio's voice snaps me back into reality. My ears pop as his words reach me.

"The book is in my bedroom. Keep us posted."

"Of course." Svetlana's arms close into a hug. "We will figure this out, Anima."

"Are you sure that's wise?" Dionisio asks me right as we break the hug. "If what we're saying is true, Eros is dangerous and also has access to your apartment."

"Wouldn't it be stupid for him to hurt the person I care about the most?"

"He just lost his. I don't know what he's capable of. The person I knew as my brother isn't here anymore."

I turn to Svetlana. "Grab the book and bring it to your apartment. He's at the bookstore now. He won't know."

Dionisio sighs. "I don't like this at all. I'm calling Markus to watch over you."

I nod in his direction. "Yes, that's a good idea."

"Who's Markus?"

"My future Royal Bodyguard."

"What the fu—"

"Ok let's go, you know I hate being late."

Dionisio and I get to my photoshoot appointment just in time, and as I get to work, I notice how gentle he is with everything that is surrounding him right now. His steps are so meticulously slow and soft around the new entry of this family. His laugh is even softer, and I get lost at the sight of him holding the baby. His big arms wrapping this little cocoon, that almost gets lost on him. He's so focused on how the baby moves, even how his little mouth moves. I never thought of having a family, children of my own. It's one of those things that always seemed impossible and it never occurred to me that I would ever want—need them in my life. Now, seeing this newborn wrapping their little hand around Dionisio's pinky and holding on for dear life, makes my heart burn.

You'll have everything in life, Anima, I will make sure of it. His words come to me like a wave of cold water. I rub my eyes trying to contain the tears and get back to work.

You'll have everything as well, Dionisio. I promise.

Today's training is in an open field in the middle of nowhere. Dionisio thinks it's better for mixing the use of my new power, but I still think it's an unwise decision to try to repeat what happened to the Opacum.

"We've been trying for like an hour, can we just call it a day and strategize or something?"

"We're not leaving until you make me hit that tree, Anima." Then chuckles. "Or the ground. Just make me fall or hit something."

"Why do you want to get hurt? Is pain one of your kinks?"

Do you really want to know, little ninja? His amused grin makes my legs wobble. "Is this it? Is this why you're not concentrating? You are not going to hurt me."

"But what if—"

His hands grab mine and together he brings them to his lips. He leaves a small peck on each one. "You're never going to hurt me."

"Fine. But I really don't know how I did it, I think I was under pressure, maybe? I was scared Eros was going to get hurt? I know

Ginevra said I have to maintain control of my emotions, meditating with her helped a lot with that."

"Ok ok, so we can meditate or I can try to scare you. I can't really catch you by surprise, you can read my mind all the time which is unfortunate right now, but here's the thing." He continues to talk and talk, probably to distract me from his real intentions. As he goes on with his river of words that really starts to make zero sense, he throws a big branch at me. Instinctually, I raise my hand to cover my face and from it, a strong wind bursts out, making the branch fly away from me and towards Dionisio. The strength of the throw makes him fall flat on his back and I rush towards him, making sure he's ok.

"Oh my god, D, please tell me you're not unconscious," I ask, falling on my knees beside him.

A laugh escapes his mouth. "That was fucking outstanding," he says while chuckling.

"You are an idiot, I could have seriously hurt you!"

"But you didn't and now we know your magic reacts to fear and keeps you safe. This is good, Anima, amazing."

"Is it? I could literally get a jump scare watching a horror movie in a theatre and throw a child into a wall, in what sense is this amazing?"

"Well, look at it this way, no child should be watching a horror movie in a movie theatre so I'm sure you'll be fine."

"How are you so calm? This is insane!"

"Sweetheart, you're going to control this in no time, just like you've been doing with everything else."

Sweetheart. This is the second time he has called me that in the last 24 hours. His husky voice calling me the most ridiculous pet names makes me feel warm and fuzzy. I never liked being called anything aside from my name, but Dionisio could say anything and my cheeks would heat up, no questions asked. A feeling of emptiness arises. My pulse races as his hand reaches a chunk of hair that came out of my ponytail and pushes it back behind my ear.

"Anything I want, sweetheart?" he repeats as my eyes close, enjoying his fingers touching my skin.

"Do we want to talk about what happened earlier?" I manage to ask as the sense of him remains on me like an invisible tattoo.

"I don't know if I can, Anima." He sighs before adding, "you know exactly how I feel, it's hard for me to keep it to myself but I can't let that happen again, I don't think I could survive it if—"

"If you're not the person destined to be with me."

"Yes."

"Well, good thing I don't believe in soulmates."

"What are you trying to say?" He questions, his head tilting a little to the side.

"I am saying that I am not going to pretend this is nothing. I physically can't. You've come to know me so deeply in such a small amount of time. This bond we have—"

"I know what you mean."

"Even if it's not forever, I don't want to live the rest of my life regretting what we could have been. Even if it's just a day."

As the words come rushing out of my mouth, his lips crush onto mine with the force of a hurricane. Desperation fills the taste of this kiss as his arms wrap me into his embrace. He needs me close, as if he has to try to make himself understand that I won't go anywhere. This is how I should be feeling. This is how we have to be. The taste of my tears reach our lips and I don't want this to end. Hope is all I can think of as my hands land on his cheeks bringing him even closer to me. The relish of our present is found in our entangled tongues, promising each other that we will give this a try, despite everything else. As we deepen the connection, an image of us as children comes rushing back to me. This bond we share, it was our secret, even as kids, it was there. It has always been there. Our eyes widen in shock as we come out to breathe.

"What does this mean?" I ask him as I feel him panting on me, our chests following the same rhythm.

"I don't know. But we will find out—together." He promises, brushing his mouth on mine.

"Together." I repeat on his lips.

OUR HANDS ARE INTERLOCKED AS DIONISIO UNLOCKS THE DOOR to my apartment. He's taking me to Dusäiga, to his father and together we are finally going to fix everything. As we enter and turn on the lights, the hair on the back of my neck rises while Dionisio's body comes to a full stop. We are not alone. Eros is sitting on the loveseat with his feet propped up on the coffee table. A glass of wine in his hand.

"Well, well, will you look at that? Seems like not even presumed fate could keep you two apart. To be fair, I could have tried harder, but I really thought my supposed brother would respect the gods and let me have the woman who's destined to be mine."

"I am not yours, Eros, I don't know how yet, but the prophecy is wrong."

"You're saying that the gods told us a lie? Really?" He laughs.

"What I'm saying is that you lied to me. Since day one. You drugged me, Eros. There's not even one inch of my body that can forgive that. Ever."

"This is so very Psiche of you. Coming up with your own conclusions. Your father would be so proud. Both of them would if they were still alive of course. But they are not. I made sure of that."

"You—what did you do, Eros?" Dionisio shouts, rushing to him.

My heart stops as my hands and legs go numb. Then, my doorbell rings and my biggest fear comes like a stab in the chest. The hair behind my neck rises as I turn towards the door. Knowing exactly who is behind it.

Chapter 26

Carnations and oranges are potent aphrodisiacs used in lust potions. If the subject is surrounded by said items, they will be easily manipulated into thinking their feelings are real and lasting.

The tall, dark-haired man, I would have called handsome only a year and a half ago, stands in front of me. His piercing grey eyes were all I could think of at one point. I used to think they were dreamy, and now they are a synonym of a nightmare. I thought I'd lost all my emotional attachment to him and that without it, I could finally see how persistent and egocentric he really was—still is. It's this idea he portrayed of himself that once made him so special and unattainable, he forced me to put him on a pedestal. What a toxic cycle. But now I know that I have no attachment to the version of himself that I created—that he made me feel was real. Jeremy stands, smirking right here, at my doorstep and I am ready to confront him.

"I thought I heard the party was here. Look at you Anima, as gorgeous as usual. Royalty really does suit you, princess." His fingers try to touch my arm. The pet name sends shivers down my spine.

"Don't touch her." Dionisio is quick on his steps pushing me away from Jeremy's reach.

"Aw, that's cute." Jeremy blows me a kiss as he walks right past me, completely ignoring Dionisio in front of me. "Now there, I don't want this to turn ugly for anyone. Eros? Be nice and pour me a glass of wine."

"Of course, come in, sit down, let's have a chat."

"Your brother is so kind, so very hospitable," Jeremy says, never taking his eyes away from me. If turning into an ice sculpture was a feeling, this is it. The way his cold irises are looking into mine is intruding, possessive and absolutely terrifying. Dionisio's hand on me makes me realize how cold my body has turned.

"My brother is clearly not ok in the head." Dionisio's voice is low and firm. His grip on me is hard to the point of leaving a mark on my skin. As the thought comes to mind, he loosens his hold. *I'm sorry.* I hear his words through the bond.

A laugh comes out of Jeremy. "Not your brother. Hers." The man of my nightmares points in my direction.

"What?" My stomach grumbles like a washing machine. My chest feels heavy as if a boar is laying on it, putting an incredible amount of pressure on my ribcage. Breathing seems impossible as if the air in this space is so thick it just can't get into my lungs.

"Yes, Eros is not Dionisio's brother. He's yours."

"How's that possible?" My voice cracks as I ask, looking at my hands shaking.

"Your dad had some fun."

"You're lying." Dionisio steps in, his hands closed into fists.

My stomach carouses with the rest of my insides as a sudden tautness assails my belly. "That is impossible—if that was true it would mean—I am going to be sick." My vision begins to cloud and my knees start to buckle, if Dionisio wasn't standing by my side to catch my elbows, I would've crashed to the ground. But his firm hold keeps me steady.

"You loved every second of it, princess. It felt so right, didn't it?"

"You are disgusting." Covering my mouth with my hand I try to stop the nausea from taking over my entire being.

"Not what you said when you moaned my name while I had my face stuffed between your legs."

"How can you even talk like this? How could you work for him?" Tears come streaming down my face as I lock eyes with Eros.

As he grins he replies, "you should ask Jeremy that question, not me, princess."

I take a few steps back trying to put my mind around it. Understanding that the person that was behind everything has been right here the entire time.

"You belong to us, Anima, not him. He would never be able to give you the power you would have with us. The kind of compulsion you have? You can take over the world." Jeremy tries to reach for me.

"Don't you fucking dare touch her." An energy ball blooms on Dionisio's hand. It takes both of us by surprise as he throws it towards Jeremy. It bursts across his chest, slamming him down to the floor, temporarily immobilizing him. Dionisio doesn't have acting powers, everything he does with magic is made from the outside. This? This was coming from inside. His veins. His flesh. His heart. Dionisio's entire body was electric. Covered completely by lightning and rage. His jaw clenches down hard as he tries to normalize his erratic breathing. He is glowing. His entire body is glowing with blue and yellow lighting that covers every inch of his skin. If there was anything that he could have done to look more like a god, this was it.

"Didn't you tell her, Dionisio? How you left your supposed little brother in the hands of an Opacum?" Eros's words are what bring Dionisio back to his regular self. The blinding lights turn off as the toneless voice reaches his ears.

"I felt guilty my entire life for it. I sacrificed everything for you Eros, and for what? For you to turn against us—against her?"

"What is he saying, D?" I ask him, confused as my chest tightens. His green eyes wide open staring at me.

"The day your memories were wiped, Dionisio left me in the middle of the gardens while he was taking you to safety." Eros continues.

"The woman with no face." I whisper under my breath. "She wanted to play a game with us." My hand covers my mouth as if I just discovered one of the missing puzzle pieces of my memory. I can almost reach her curly hair with my hand as the images of that day fill my vision. Her voice sounded like a siren song. It was so pretty. So enchanting. Hypnotizing.

"Yes, and then Dionisio came running, ruining everything. We were supposed to be together from the start, and then he took you first, leaving me there."

"I was following orders, Eros, and you know it. You know exactly what happened. You know what I did trying to regain your trust. I gave up everything for you. I gave up my heart, and you just shattered it into pieces." Dionisio spits out grabbing my hand to make sure I'm within reach.

We need to leave, I need to take you to safety, now, he says through the bond.

"Dionisio the martyr, yeah yeah, we all know the story. She's still mine, my blood, my sister, my other half. Your little bond means nothing. It's just another lie."

"That—is totally illegal, isn't it?" I ask, trying not to think about the intimate moments we shared together. My eyes search for Dionisio's. The only thing I am sure of is the bond we share.

Always, little ninja. I hear his words in my head. His hand squeezing mine.

"Oh come on, royal bloodlines have done it since the beginning of time," Eros utters with a gruff voice.

A chuckle escapes my mouth. "Are you serious right now?" My hand is still interlocked with Dionisio's.

"We are destined to rule together, sister, to fulfill the prophecy in our own way but I know you won't feel the same attraction as I do now that you know what we are to each other. With time it will be back."

"With time it will be back? Eros, you lied to me from the start. Everything I've ever felt for you was a lie. The only real thing right now is the abhor I feel towards you. There's no affection, only deep loathing. You can't change that."

"I did it to protect you. Even Jeremy is around for that reason. All I want is for you to be where you belong. By my side."

"Protect me? You only fed me deception and pain, Eros. If this is your method of protection, then I sure as hell don't want it. Now if you'll excuse me, I am going to puke and then run far far away from you and all this."

"Of course you are, love, you enjoy playing the gazelle so much, don't you? I can't wait to catch you for the last time." Jeremy's words come rushing through me as Dionisio picks his limp body from the floor and throws it on the kitchen table. Glasses crash on the floor colouring it in crimson. A mix of wine and blood.

Eros is quick on his feet but as he tries to approach me, a voice inside of me makes him stop just a few inches aways from me.

Kneel.

Eros drops and an evil laugh comes out of him. "This is going to be so much fun." I don't even have the time to scream as an energy ball hits Dionisio's side as he throws himself in front me.

"Fuck, that hurts," he says as I try to get him up. Eros is still petrified on his knees and Jeremy is on the ground laughing as he sees his magic hit Dionisio just like he expected. He's covered in blood as well, my floor completely painted in red.

"Why did you do that, you knew I would have stopped it!" My voice breaks as I try to stop the bleeding of the open wound on his left side.

"I couldn't risk it." His hand presses on mine as his blood moistens my skin dripping down like a broken faucet. We finally get on our feet, Dionisio's back rests against the kitchen counter while I keep pressure on the wound. I reach for the cabinet where I know I have some healing potions. As I open it, my eyes widen realizing it's empty. Of course. Classic rookie movie, Anima.

I need to take you out of here, Dionisio states through the bond.

You're bleeding to death.

I'm fine. They won't be down for long.

Pacing towards the door to my apartment, we hear a chuckle from behind us.

"Run little gazelle," Jeremy says, "let me enjoy the hunt."

CHAPTER 27

"We need to get you to my father right away."

"D, you're bleeding way too much." I feel as if my left index finger is burning in the flames of hell. The sensation travels up on my hand and arm and goes straight to my heart. "Is this what you feel when I get hurt? Because holy shit." My hand closes into a fist as I bring the finger with the golden band to my mouth.

"Pretty much. Maybe this will make you stop getting concussions."

"That is not funny at all."

"Anima, sweetheart, look at me." I do as he asks. "I'm going to be just fine." His bright green eyes look with purpose searching for mine. He really does believe his words.

With that we start pacing towards the warehouse, but a sudden shiver on my back makes me stop. "We can't," I say looking straight ahead.

"Anima we gotta go."

"No, I—I feel like something is close by. Opacums. Multiple.

Too many for us to take on ourselves." The power that I thought was supposed to alert me when my soulmate was close by, turned to be my body warning me about danger. Every little detail starts to make more sense now that things are out in the open.

"Fuck, ok. Let's go to my car. I should have a healing potion lying around somewhere."

"Why didn't we go there right away? You are literally bleeding to death!"

"That's a little"—he inhales—"Overdramatic." Exhales.

"Sure, you're just ready to pass out on me like it's nothing."

"You're cute when you're worried." He smiles and pokes the point of my nose. The idiot now smiles at me as if his blood isn't drying on my hands.

"I would stab you if you weren't already terribly injured."

"Didn't think you'd be into knife play, but fuck, okay, I'm down."

"Shut up and walk faster."

"Do I have to remind you that I am currently bleeding to death? I might need a little bit of time to, you know, get there."

"You're infuriating even when you're about to die." I say through clenched teeth as it becomes more difficult getting to his car.

I feel the weight of his body getting heavier as he tries to keep on his feet and use me to keep his balance. I swallow some saliva as I try to keep a straight face, even if I'm on the verge of panicking. My palms get sweaty as I grip on his other side, making sure he won't fall on the ground. His legs seem to get more and more numb as he misses a step or two.

"I'm going to be fine, little ninja."

"I know, I am making sure of it." Determination fills my voice. In the distance I finally see the black car parked in the usual lot. As we get closer, the hair on the back of my neck rises up, once again. I turn for a second and notice an army of

Opacums marching towards us at a fast pace, too fast in comparison to the rate we are moving.

"Fuck fuck fuck," I swear under my breath.

"You're getting into that car, Anima, and you're going to let me deal with them."

"Are you insane? You can barely stand."

"I need you to take my phone, my keys and go far away from him—them."

"You know I would never do that."

As we continue to argue, the army of Opacums gets closer and my heart is throbbing to the point of burning in my chest. I turn towards the darkness that's about to hit us, the pain that we will be feeling if they get to us and the thought of seeing Dionisio not get a chance to survive all this makes a spark ignite inside of me. Under my skin, ready to come out. I take a deep breath in and as I turn to the countless faceless bodies in front of me, the voice that was waiting to come out from my chest emerges.

"Stop." A guttural sound emerges from my lips. An almost robotical sound that makes them pause. My hand stretches in front of me with the palm facing them. My eyes lock on them, with the fear of breaking the hypnosis I have them on. Unmovable. The voice that I have been feeling inside of me, that part of me that could compel a person, is now out in the open, commanding an entire army.

Dionisio's mouth opens, trying to mumble something but no words come out.

Unlock the car D, I say through the bond, keeping my eyes on the bodies in front of us.

"With pleasure." I hear him move, the sound of the car being unlocked comes a couple of seconds after.

As soon as I hear him close the passenger seat knowing that he is safe in the vehicle, I run to the driver's side and start the car. The Opacums snapping out of the incantation are now running towards us again, and it's at that point that I get out of the parking lot and start driving in the opposite direction.

Dionisio beside me breathes heavily. I see him pulling out his phone, dialing a number.

"Markus, keep Svetlana away and send someone to have the warehouse cleaned out, a swarm of Opacum is blocking the entrance." He then gives him a brief rundown of what happened.

"Thank you, Markus." He closes the phone call and as he makes a sudden move to put back the phone in his pocket, he swears under his breath from the sting of the wound.

"Can you please take this damn potion now?"

"Definitely will do that, just gonna have to make a quick batch while you drive."

"Excuse me, what?"

"Turns out I don't have a vial ready." He chuckles. "How ironic is that?"

"It isn't, like at all."

His ringtone starts playing. "Saved by the King," he says as he puts the call on speaker. "Hi dad, so we are in a bit of a pickle here."

"D, stop being sarcastic while you're bleeding in the passenger seat." I yell at him, completely ignoring the fact that the current King could hear everything.

"Did you know Eros was my brother?"

"Markus just filled me in. I—I don't know if that statement is true, Anima. You're only a month apart. I can't even wrap my head around it." The King's voice cracks before he clears his throat. "Go towards Triora and find Gregorio. He'll have some supplies ready for you. Camp out for the night while we take out the Opacums blocking the warehouse to have Anima arrive safe at court. Try to heal and rest."

"Sounds like a plan. Anima, take the next left." Dionisio instructs.

"What are we going to do with Eros and Jeremy?" I ask both of them.

"We'll deal with them together when you'll be here, at Court, where you belong." The king's voice sounds calm and reassuring. "It's so nice to hear your voice, Anima, so very nice."

"It's nice to hear you as well, King? Your highness? Majesty?"

He gives a light-hearted laugh. "Ares, for you I will always be *zio* Ares. You'll soon be the one with the crown, as it should be. See you soon, Princess Anima." The call drops, making me think of my title and how innocent it sounded said by the king, it feels right when it's used properly, it bothers me less and I am glad it does.

"Not a pet name, a title, your title, little ninja, that's all it is."

I nod. It is my title, and it sounded right from Ares's voice. "Can you get on with the potion making now?"

"Yes, absolutely." He opens the glove box and takes out a velvet bag. "Tell me the steps."

"What? D, I am already freaking out enough while driving us to safety, I think adding a little field test is unnecessary."

"What did I say about that word? Come on, tell me how to make a healing potion."

I make another turn and start driving up the hill. "You're unbelievable." I sigh. "We need ginger root, dried lavender, lemon and some water."

"Correct." He reaches the back of my seat and grabs a plastic container.

"No wait, no plastic, I don't know why but no plastic."

"Good catch. Then?" He reaches for a glass container of some sort that he has on the back seat. Who casually has a glass container lying around in their car—you know what? Nevermind. This is Dionisio we are talking about. I shouldn't really be surprised by anything at this point.

"You squeeze the lemon in the container first." I take a breath in and try to remember everything that Eros told me to do. "Then you slice an inch of ginger into thin coins."

"Can you keep pressure on the side while I cut the ginger?"

"Yes" I quickly change gear and press my hand on the wet cloth he's been using to keep the wound together. "Of course," I add as he continues with the potion.

"Then?"

"Do we really have to do all the steps?"

"Yes, then what do I do?"

"Water, you add water. A tablespoon." He grabs a water bottle that is sitting on the passenger door. I take another turn on the steep narrow road we are driving on.

"And now I add the dried lavend—"

"No wait, you light up the lavender and as you drop it you say something."

"Good, very good, what do I say?"

"Oh come on you know exactly what Latin phrase you have to say, I am already driving like a maniac, can't you just do it and make me stop worrying?"

"I'm afraid not."

"Please?"

You know exactly what I have to say. Come on, little ninja.

"It's virtus, something." I quickly take my hand off of his side, change the gear and start pressing the wound again. A small grin appears on his face as his fingers end on top of my bloody hand.

"Yes, virtus?"

Medendi.

"Good girl." The praise makes my cheeks heat up. Or maybe it's the panic.

"Now can you get it over with, please?"

"Yup." Opening the glove box again he takes out a lighter, as he lights up the lavender, he quickly opens up the window to let the smoke out of the car to make sure my vision is clear enough to drive. "Virtus Medendi" He chants as he drops the burning lavender into the mixture. As soon as the flower is in, the window opens ready for the small explosion. He doesn't even spend time pouring the mixture into a vial, he drinks straight from the source. And as I see his Adam's apple move, I finally exhale as if I have been keeping my breath until this exact moment.

His eyes close as he leans back on the seat, enjoying the instant relief that the potion is giving him. I slowly take the cloth off of his side, noticing the wound closing up. As the last bit of skin reattaches, I swipe gently on where the injury was to make sure it's indeed all healed.

"I told you I was going to be ok." His hand brushes mine. "Thanks to you. You saved me, Anima."

I park in the little square in the centre of Triora and turn off the engine. I turn to face him and grab his face in my hands crushing my lips on his. "Don't you dare do that again."

"I've got this knife here, if you wanna use it now that some of the potion is ready."

"Don't tempt me," I reply, resting my index finger on his lips.

"Ok, time to get some stuff and continue our drive." As he talks, a knock on the window makes me jump. "That's Gregorio with our supplies," Dionisio adds, reassuring me. He opens his door and walks on my side of the car greeting the older man. My door also gets opened and I slide out to help Dionisio put the stuff in the trunk.

"Anima, this is Gregorio."

"Pleasure to meet you, Gregorio."

"The pleasure is all mine, Princess Anima."

"Gregorio here was a citizen of Dusäiga, fell in love with a mortal and decided to come live in Triora." Dionisio's hand rests on Gregorio's shoulder giving it a gentle squeeze.

"That's so lovely."

"It is. It was definitely the right choice." Gregorio's lips lift up into a warm smile. His grey short hair and the sign of his face make me think he's in his seventies, his hands are the hands of a worker. Lived. Full of calluses.

Dionisio closes the trunk after putting in the tent and some other bags that Gregorio had prepared for us. "Time to get you to safety," he states as I pass him the keys.

"Thank you for everything, Gregorio," I nod towards the older man in front of me.

"Anything for Aiakos's daughter. You'll do great things, Princess."

Dionisio paces towards the passenger side door, opening it for me.

"After you."

"Sure you can drive?" I ask, raising the dirty t-shirt he's still wearing, making sure he is really healed, that it wasn't just a dream.

"I'm sure, sweetheart, I am better because of you, now let me make sure you're also safe." His hand caresses my cheek. His lips leave a small peck on my forehead and with that, I sit in the passenger seat and Dionisio is back in his spot. "Can you put some Taylor Swift on? I feel like singing. Actually, I made a playlist the other day that you are going to love. It's called 'If Taytay and Alex The Terrible were friends', absolutely immaculate."

"Oh boy, here we go." I chuckle as I press play on the ridiculous juxtaposition of songs that were on the list.

I don't realize I drifted to sleep until the car comes to a full stop.

"Hey sweetheart, we're here." A soft whisper caresses my ear.

My eyes open, and I am welcomed with a pair of green ones looking right back at me. Dionisio's nose pokes mine and I smile at the soft touch.

"I didn't realize I fell asleep."

"Just for a few minutes," he says, taking the keys out of the ignition. "You're exhausted, it makes sense. You were able to finally let your body relax."

"I'm fine."

"Anima."

"I'm—"

"You fell asleep with death metal blasting in your ears."

"It's relaxing."

"You just discovered you can compel an army of evil veneficus. An army. Not one at a time. A freaking army."

"Yeah that was intense."

"And there's also the other little detail—"

"Could that even be true?"

"I don't know. If it is, I don't think my father knew. Your dad and mine—they were like brothers." He sighs. "Ready for some camping?"

Looking around me, I realize we are literally in the middle of nowhere. The urban scenery has been replaced by grass, pine trees, and rocks. The surrounding mountains make me think we are close to the border with France. I used to hike a lot with my father around these forests. It all looks so different, but also the same. If we put a tent in the middle of the woods here, it will be very hard to find us. The perfect hiding spot. Reception is also not the best here, which is a plus, it leaves a very faint signal of where we might be. As I get out of the car and follow Dionisio to the trunk, I take a deep breath in and enjoy the new fragrance around us. No tingly sea air here, just a resinous aromatic scent probably coming from the pine trees. I hug myself as I admire the vertical imposing guards surrounding us, the mountains look like silhouettes of giants, there, in place, ready to keep us safe.

"Didn't take you for the camping type," I reply, trying to lighten up the mood. Dionisio quickly turns to me while opening the trunk of his car. He's smirking.

His green eyes locked on me."There are lots of things you don't know about me, sweetheart."

My lips end up on his, taking him by surprise. The bags he's holding drop on the floor as his arms wrap around my torso bringing me closer to him. This, how we fit right now, in each other's embrace, this is the only thing we were born to do. Everytime our mouths connect, every time we share breaths, it feels like a piece of myself comes back into my heart.

I break the kiss to look into his eyes. "Will you tell me all those things?"

"Anything you want to know." The sun hitting the green of his irises make the specks of gold rise up. Golden leaves filling the sea of grass that are his eyes . "Let me mount the tent first, though."

We grab the bags he dropped and start walking towards the woods. Hand in hand, two souls so different yet so impatient to mold together.

Our feet stop only when we find some lowland to set up the tent for the night. Dionisio looks at me with a raised eyebrow when he sees me opening up the bag knowing exactly what to do next.

"I didn't take you for the camping girl type," he says, smirking at me.

"There are a lot of things you don't know about me as well, sweetheart." I reply, winking at him.

A low grunt escapes his mouth. "What if I wanted to learn those things?"

"Here? Out in the open? Kinky," I say, winking at him.

"You did not just say that."

My hand caressing his chest. "Oh, but I did." Up and down, making him shiver all over.

"Get in the tent."

"So bossy."

"You know exactly what you're doing and I don't know if you're ready for what you're asking."

"Ok, cocky much?" I reply while unzipping the tent we just mounted. A fire inside of me is building and if he doesn't come into this tent with me right now, I don't know how I will cool myself down. I will probably have to find a lake and jump head first to clear my thoughts. My extremely inappropriate thoughts.

"God Anima, if you continue thinking like that, I don't think I'll be able to control myself."

"What if I want you to lose control?"

"Being around you, kissing you, hugging you is one thing. This? I don't know if I could survive leaving you after this."

"Don't you see it? Feel it? I want you, every day because what we have is way truer than what your—*my* brother has been feeding me for the entire time."

"Anima, you had me when we were kids, you have me now, and you'll have me in the future whatever it will be."

"Then please, stop trying to stay away from me, stop pushing me, stop pushing yourself in the wrong direction."

"I never wanted to push you away."

"We were fed lies from the start, Dionisio. This is our present now, you and me, here, together. I can't go on another day knowing what we could have been."

"Please, get in that tent. I will give us something to hold on to for the rest of our existence."

"I like a man that says please."

"Oh you are a little devil, aren't you."

We kiss. Hungrily. Feverishly. His hand lands on the back of my head protecting it while he slowly lowers me down, never breaking the seal of our lips. He settles on top of me like it's the only thing he can do to stay alive.

"Are you sure you want this, Anima?" He asks me again.

I flip us over. If this doesn't convince him, I don't know what will.

"Positive." I say taking my shirt off in one move.

"Fuck." He sighs. I feel his hands on my back, my shoulders, my neck, he doesn't know where to touch first. I feel the same eagerness as when his shirt comes off. As my eyes travel on his body, a small tattoo on his chest catches my attention. It's a black and grey flower. A small sprig of lavender. On his left pec. Right over his heart.

Lavender. I say through the bond. A tear trailing down my cheek.

His thumb brushes it away. *My heart, always.*

"Are there any other tattoos I am going to discover?" My eyes are on his and I smirk waiting for his response.

"There's another one, but the only thing I will say about it is that I lost a bet with Markus. Maybe one day he will tell you the story behind it."

"Well, you have me intrigued now." My lips lift up. "Is it where I think it is?"

He grins at my words. "Yup, it's right on my left ass cheek." As he says the words, I move quickly and grab his belt. His hands close around my wrists. "Patience, little ninja. You'll see it."

We lay side by side, our mouths entangled, our hands travelling across our bodies, learning every edge, every curve, every secret spot.

"Can I ask you something?" My words almost die on his lips. My palm rests on the tattoo on his firm pec.

"I told you, you can ask me anything," he whispers in my ear. The low husky voice makes me shiver and sends signals to that sensitive part between my legs. Every single word that comes out of him is a throb of excitement.

"Why did you even decide to come here, to Vallecrosia?"

"I told you, my father gave us specific orders."

"But you could have easily just sent Markus, and you didn't."

"No." He leaves a kiss on my temple. "I didn't." Then one on my cheek. His hand caressing my hip, up and down.

A small sound escapes my mouth. "Why?" I'm barely able to ask when his lips nibble my left ear.

"I wanted to live my last moments of freedom."

"And you call this, all this situation, freedom?"

"Being around you makes me feel free. Looking at the light in your eyes, admiring your skin and how it looks in the sun, turning almost golden. How your hair glows when the rays hit it a certain way and how it looks in the wind. It's the way you move, the way you walk, the way you laugh." He stops shaking his head. "God, I love your laugh." His lips leaving a trail of kisses down my neck, getting closer to my breasts. "It's the way you look at me and you see me, under the mask I put in front of everyone else. You are my freedom, Anima."

"Then enjoy your freedom, Dionisio." I unclutch my bra.

"You did not just make a pun out of that." His hands slowly pull it off of me.

"I absolutely did." Our lips connect again. "You're my freedom, Dionisio."

As the small piece of fabric hits the ground, his mouth ends on my nipple. And while I gasp at the sudden wetness that his lips are creating on one side, his other hand starts playing with the other.

"You're so beautiful, Anima, so damn beautiful." His low husky voice sends signals to every part of my body. The feel of him against my skin makes me arch, making my flesh brush against his now rock hard shaft.

"Please, I need you, now."

"This is just the beginning, little ninja, there's no way I'm rushing into this, I am going to take all the time we need."

God have mercy.

He grins at me before grabbing the edge of my leggings. "You won't need these for a while." I lift my hips in the air, letting him do exactly what he wants to. The only thing on my body now is a black cotton thong. "Can you do something for me, sweetheart?"

"Anything." It's all I'm able to say as his hand brushes on the inside of my thigh.

"Turn over for a second, I've been dying to do one thing."

I do as he asks and as soon as my back is exposed to him, I hear him sigh. "You ok?"

"God, no I am not ok, just looking at you is making me ready to spill right in my boxers." I don't even have the time to reply that I feel his mouth on my spine, making me gasp. He commences leaving a trail of kisses towards my ass. His hands on the hem of the thong, playing with it. And then, his lips are on my ass cheeks as he slowly takes that small piece of fabric off my flesh. That last barrier that was dividing my skin from his tongue. I can almost feel myself dripping from how wet I am already.

"Ok so we just established you're an ass guy," I manage to say between a kiss and a caress.

I hear him chuckle. "Not an ass guy." He squeezes a cheek. "I'm an Anima guy." He then kisses it. "I like every inch of you." He leaves another kiss a little lower on my thigh. "I love every inch of you." He continues on the inner thigh. "I *crave* every inch of you." He goes back on the ass cheek and gives it a nibble, making me gasp in surprise. "I want to lick every inch of you."

He proceeds to travel with his tongue closer and closer between my thighs.

The air in the tent is starting to become thick, and this is just the beginning. He lets me turn over again, giving him full access to my folds, right there in front of him. Dionisio's eyes darken, he looks ready to get a taste.

Not a taste, an entire meal, he says through the bond before lowering himself between my legs. He keeps me in place as he grips onto my thighs and goes in for a sample.

My back arches at the sudden touch, as I get warmer and warmer with every little thing Dionisio does to me. I try to make him come up to me but my hand ends in his hair, gripping it into place as his fingers gently brush my wet flesh.

"D, please, I need more," I beg him.

"Anything for you, anything you want, it's yours." His teeth play with my clit as his fingers circle my entrance. "I'm yours."

"Please." Another beg escapes my mouth as a finger goes inside.

"You're so strong, Anima," he says as he moves his finger in and out. In and out. His tongue back on my skin. "You're a fighter." Another finger goes in. "The most beautiful being walking this earth." He gives a gentle nibble on my clit. And as he continues pumping his fingers, I clench when a wave of pleasure hits me, my back arches as a reaction and I can't contain the moans that my mouth makes as I come on his lips. He doesn't just eat his meal. He devours it. Dionisio's fingers stay inside of me as my body continues to spasm every time he kisses me anywhere. I let his hair go as he slides out and comes up to my face, finding my lips. I can still taste myself on his mouth and the thought of it makes me get wet all over again.

"That was—" My words break. "Incredible."

"That was just the appetizer." He laughs on my lips. "And having you holding me in place? That was the hottest thing ever."

I reach for his pants, and this time he doesn't stop me. I unbutton his jeans and with quite the skill he slides them off with one hand keeping the other one flexed so that he can stay on top of me.

"My turn," I say as my hands reach his firm chest and push him away, guiding him down beside me.

"Anything you want, Anima." He lets me get between his legs. Now my hands are on the hem of his boxers and as I look at his pecs moving up and down, I notice how he tries to control his breathing. I slide them off unleashing his erect member out in the open. I gasp as I notice the size of it, the girth of it. Wondering how much he would stretch me open when I let him slide into me. My tongue circles my lips as my eyes are locked on his. I grab him in my hands, squeezing him a little before my mouth ends on his length.

"Fuck, Anima, if this is the effect you have on me just by grabbing my dick, I don't know what will happen when I shove it deep inside of you."

"I guess we will find out what happens very soon," I say before sliding him into my mouth as much as possible.

His body goes rigid as I start moving my head up and down, sucking him as much as possible. My hands follow the movements of my mouth. I spit on the head as I come up for some air and I hear him swear under his breath as I do so.

"Anima, fuck, if you want me to last a bit longer, you might want to stop this."

"So soon?" I grin at him before giving him another round with my mouth. I take him in so deep I almost feel the head hit the back of my throat. As I do, I feel his hands grab my head begging me to stop before it's too late.

"You are absolutely perfect," he says as our eyes lock. My hand still grips his cock.

"Can you do something for me? Actually, two things." My words are a soft breath on his shaft.

He swallows air before he says, "Yes, whatever you want me to do."

"Let me see the butt tattoo." I squeeze his cock making him gasp before a chuckle escapes his mouth.

He turns over, and with a wide smile I look down. There, on his left cheek a red heart with flames coming out of, is inked. A white banner strikes through the middle and the words 'it's fine art' are neatly calligraphed across. I laugh out loud as soon as I read it. "I mean your ass is definitely fine art," I manage to say before giving it a soft spank. His eyes darken as soon as my hand leaves his ass. He grabs my wrist and as I gasp in surprise.

"What's the second thing you want me to do?" The forest shade of green in his eyes is almost black now. Hunger pours out of his every pore. Cedarwood and mint impregnating my nostrils and skin. I feel as if I am bathing in his essence, and I wouldn't want anything else in life. This? This is the kind of drug I would never be able to say no to.

"Fuck me, Dionisio, let's take our freedom back." He doesn't need to be told twice. He reaches the pocket of his jeans for a little packet that he quickly brings to his mouth and rips open with his teeth. As soon as the condom is on, he settles between my legs. "Please, Dionisio, now, I need you now." He slides in one motion and I think I see stars for a second. He slowly comes out and goes back in, stretching me, letting my body learn about his.

"God, you feel so fucking good," he whispers in my ear before nibbling it. Then as the motion continues, his mouth settles on my neck, sucking and kissing and absolutely making me go insane for the taste of his lips on mine.

I feel his hand gently grab my neck as he thrusts in and out of me, picking up the perfect rhythm, hitting the perfect spot, reaching deeper every time. As I feel the build up of pleasure getting closer again, he tightens his grip on my neck a little more before his mouth settles on mine. "Come again, Anima, come for me." And I do as he asks. My body spasms once again as he thrusts in with more determination. "You're perfect, always."

"Dionisio." A louder moan escapes my mouth as I clench around his cock.

"Fuck if you say my name like that again, I won't be able to contain myself."

"Then don't."

"There's no way I'm letting you get away with only two, little ninja, you need to come at least once more."

The thought of reaching this state of ecstasy once more is all I need to start feeling the build up again.

"Then let me come while I am on top of you."

"Yeah, you're fucking perfect," It's all he says before flipping us over, letting me settle on top of him. As I sit on him, gently making him slide back in, I see his eyes roll back and close, clearly enjoying the feeling as much as I am. I start bouncing up and down, locking my eyes on his.

Dionisio's hand lands on my clit, circling it and making me moan even louder than before. The other one is on my nipple, pinching it hard and making me see stars while his cock is buried inside of me. It takes a very short amount of time for me to feel another orgasm arriving. This one is stronger than the previous ones.

"There you go, yes, good girl, come all over me." He says as I feel my body pulsing once again. He follows quickly after with his own orgasm. Our lips locked as we collapse together and reach a state of bliss that I don't think either of us has ever felt before.

Our bodies are still entangled together in an embrace as we try to regain our regular heartbeats.

"That was—" he starts.

"Perfect," I finish his sentence.

I look at him, his eyes narrowed on me. "You're glowing, Anima. Like literally glowing. You have a golden aura around you. I clearly am a sex god."

"Sure you are." I give him a soft slap on his arm playfully.

We fall asleep like this, in each other's arms. My head resting on his chest. Feeling full. Happy. Free.

Until I get shaken awake right in the middle of the night.

"Fuck, are you serious?" Dionisio's voice makes my eyes open up wide in shock.

"What's happening, are we under attack?"

"It's not Opacums," he tells me while getting up. The sudden emptiness on my side makes me feel cold. Not feeling his heartbeat in my ear feels wrong.

"What is it then?"

"Cows. There are fucking cows around the tent."

Chapter 28

THE CONNECTION WILL SNAP INTO PLACE WHEN THEY WILL REACH MATURITY, AND WHAT WAS FORGOTTEN WILL FLOURISH ONCE AGAIN. THE GOLDEN ENERGY WILL BE THE ANSWER TO THE EQUATION.

"Excuse me, what?"

"Cows. We've gotta move."

"They're harmless, go back to sleep, I was finally drifting off," I reply, annoyed that he woke me up for that.

"Harmless until they start walking on the tent."

"That sounds a little overdramatic. Come back to bed D, we both need it."

"I guess…" He lays down beside me and as soon as he does, I rest my head on his shoulder and my hand on the small tattoo on his left pec.

Not even five minutes later I feel like the tent is getting smaller and smaller. I instinctively jump on my feet to open up the zipper and as soon as I do, I come up face to face with a big ruminative mouth. I can feel the cow's breath on my face. My nose is basically brushing the animal's.

I turn towards Dionisio, who is now sitting with legs and arms crossed with the 'I told you so' look on his face. Even when he's annoyed he's impossible not to stare at. Especially now, I could literally spend hours tracing his chest, just admiring it really. Maybe take a picture or two. Maybe a thousand.

His annoyed look turns into a smirk as he listens to my thoughts. *You can take all the pictures you want, little ninja.*

"Ok, maybe you were right," I say, poking his arm trying to stop making a fool of myself. "Can't we just put a spell around the tent?"

"Not really, guarding spells don't work on regular animals."

"So… I guess we have to move."

Dionisio passes over my clothes before replying, "No kidding." He then opens the zipper and steps outside, turns towards me, grabs my hand and pulls me to him.

The night breeze cuts me like a knife and I fight the urge to shiver by clenching my jaw shut. I look at the big green field surrounding us and the cows, hundreds of them having their early morning snack.

"Look at them, pretending they've done nothing." I shake my head. "They're cute though."

He chuckles at my comment. "Yeah, they are kinda cute."

We start moving our things more into the woods, slowly preparing camp to try to rest for another couple of hours before we hear from Court. I inhale the fresh air. Damp moss, Pine trees mixed with sweet mountain flowers. The only way I can describe it is, ambrosial. Everything here smells—good.

As Dionisio finishes securing the tent on the new lot of land we picked, I listen to the sounds of the forest. Wind rustling trees, animals moving, and from a distance, the sound of water alerts me, creating a mixture of beautiful melodies. I start walking towards it, hoping to find a river.

I continuously walk and then, here it is, a stream of water is right there in front of me. The moon reflecting on it makes it look sparkly, like a pool of glitter.

Arms wrap around my body and I relax at the sudden touch knowing exactly who it is behind me.

"You're freezing." His hands rub on my arms trying to warm them up. My eyes close at the small quick relief my body gets from those couple of seconds of warmth.

"The sound of the water moving makes me feel at peace, that's why I love the sea so much, it's the movement of the waves. And the smell—I didn't think I could love the sensation of salt on my nose so much. Does that sound crazy?"

"Not crazy at all."

"What makes you feel at peace?"

He sighs. "Where do I even start?" His chin rests on the top of my head. "I find storms extremely relaxing, and—you. When I close my eyes, your face comes into focus and the world around me falls silent. You're my biggest internal hurricane, a rupturing torment—and I never thought I could love like this, a consuming foolish uproar." He takes a breath before adding, "I should call you Anima, my personal storm." I feel his smile caressing my temple.

Anima Psiche, the storm. What a way to call me. Psiche, this is the first time that I associate my last name to my name.

"Do I have to change my last name now?" Stupid question.

He chuckles on my hair, before leaving a peck. "You can be Anima Soleri in Vallecrosia, and Anima Psiche in Dusäiga. You don't have to change anything. Like I do."

"Wait, your last name isn't Forestiero?"

"Forestiero in Vallecrosia, Fobos in Dusäiga."

Fobos. Would that be the last name I'd have to pick if we would get married? Don't royals change last names? My eyes widen and my cheek flush from the embarrassment I am about to go through.

I would be the one taking your last name, Anima. You're the royal lineage. He explains through the bond.

Oh wow, really? Would you even be ok with that?

Anima, sweetheart, it would be all I would talk about. His lips end on mine.

Images of him protecting me from Eros and Jeremy come back to me and I rethink of Dionisio and how his anger turned into power. "You were glowing yesterday, D. Did you even see that? You looked like—"

"A god if I remember correctly."

I slap his arm. "Stop making fun of me. I've never seen you use active powers before."

"That's because I never was able to use any kind of active power before yesterday. I guess I really have to get pissed off."

"Your veins, they were lighting up."

"You were glowing all over not that long ago as well." He smirks at me. "Golden radiance all over you. I guess I have another active power as well."

"Modesty isn't one of your powers, that's for sure."

His laugh is so contagious. I look at him, his perfect teeth and how he feels relaxed here with me. How I feel at ease here with him. Tiptoeing, I brush my lips on his one more time. His forehead rests on mine. "This is all I want, D."

"This is what I will spend my life trying to give you, Anima. I promise we will figure this out. Everything. What mess our parents made and how to fix it. You deserve—*will* have everything." A promise I know he will do anything to keep. His nose brushes mine before he adds, "Can I ask you a weird question?"

"Depends. How weird?"

"What is your favourite way to eat Triora bread? Like what do you like on it?"

"Well, that is certainly a random question." I chuckle. "Olive oil, salt and—"

"Oregano," He finishes the sentence for me.

"Yes, how did you know?" My head tilts to the side.

"It has always been your favourite. I was curious to see if that changed," he starts before adding, "It's mine as well." That little detail makes me smile so big I have to hide my face in his chest.

We remain in silence, looking at the water moving in each other's embrace.

"D, why didn't you tell me about the lavender tat—"

My phone goes off. "Saved by the bell." As I look at the screen, my eyes widen. Eros is calling.

"Put it on speaker," Dionisio instructs.

I take a deep breath in and then exhale.

Click.

"Are you done running away from me, gazelle? I don't want to use Svetlana as bait, but you're not leaving me many options here. I'll see you at Forestiero." The call drops.

Do you know that feeling where you know you're about to pass out but you don't? You're hyper alert, you see dots tarnish your vision, your legs weaken but somehow you're still standing. My hands are rigid, cold. My vision is blurred. As my phone slips from my hands, Dionisio's arms catch me.

"We're going right away, little ninja." A hand lands under my chin, forcing me to look at him.

"She—she has to be ok."

"She is ok. Eros is just messing with us ok? She's with Markus."

"What if—"

"Anima, please, you've gotta stay with me." His hand brushes my face. "Let's pack up and go. We're going to think of what to do while we drive, ok? Eros is not that stupid, he won't touch her."

"You don't know that. We don't know what he's capable of anymore. Jeremy would."

His lips are thin. His eyes are on me, concerned about my state. Svetlana is the reason I am still alive. She's my voice of reason, my biggest supporter. My family. Without her I would be lost. It's funny how incredulous I was when I was told I had a soulmate. I have had one since I can remember. *She* is. Svetlana is my other half. I'm the moon to her sun.

Words become futile when there's so much at stake. Svetlana's life, Dionisio's, and mine. If accepting Eros' terms could save them, then so be it. Because if Svetlana is my other half, Dionisio might as well be my entire heart, my brain, my essence. And if I could make sure that they would be ok, then a life of misery would be worth it.

"Don't you even think about it."

"I'm going to save Dusäiga."

"Yes, and you're not losing me or Svetlana in the process, there's no fucking way I am leaving."

I sigh. "Let's go." My voice is soft, low, basically a whisper.

We put our bags into the trunk of the Lancer, and take off.

"The drive is long, I know it's hard, but you should try to sleep a little."

"You should sleep as well," I reply almost as a whisper.

He gives me a reassuring smile. "I'm fine, the cows woke me up for good."

My feet sink into the ground as I stride myself towards nothingness.

The floor is so cold beneath me. Where are my shoes?

I have—need to find him. Now I know. He is in danger—they all are and it's all my fault. I should have gotten here sooner.

I can't see a foot ahead, only a dark pitch around me as I keep my arms in front of me not to stumble against one of the huge bookshelves populating the space.

I take a deep breath in, and a hint of vanilla fills my nostrils.

Shivers run down my spine as an icy breeze follows me from the slightly open window on my left.

I have to be quick before he finds out what I'm doing.

Wax from the candle I'm holding falls on my hand, making it sting so methodically.

Here's the door, the dark wood separating me from him. I open it gently and there he is, Dionisio, laying on his side, sleeping.

My golden light. I have to tell him everything.

Just as I reach forward with my free hand, a drop of wax falls on his shoulder.

He quickly turns and as I start to speak, his eyes widen from something he sees behind me.

I turn my head towards the entrance and as I focus on the image in front of me, Jeremy stares back into my eyes with a grin on his face.

As I sprint for the door, I bump into something. Someone. My eyes stare at the perfect copy of mine. Eros?

"I told you already, princess. You could have kept him alive. I would have kept the throne, and in exchange to that, I would have let him breathe. Without you, he would have been fine. Accept the fact that you are destined to rule this world with me."

And then suddenly, Jeremy and Eros walk towards each other, standing face to face. A laugh comes out of them.

The two become one.

And the new essence wants to get to me.

I need to run. Fast. Now.

I GASP FOR AIR AND ALMOST JUMP AT THE EDGE OF THE PASSENGER seat.

"You ok?" Dionisio asks, trying to keep his attention to the road and not on my wide eyes.

"Jeremy and Eros. It was—holy shit."

"Anima, please take a deep breath and try to tell me what you saw."

"Eros and Jeremy turning into one being."

"What?"

"Is that even possible?"

"That's—really dark magic."

"Yeah well, if they become one, the new essence they will have—that's going to be really powerful."

"We're not going to let them do it," He states.

"No. We're not."

We pull into the parking lot in Via Roma and as we step out of the car our eyes meet. This is it. Things will change now. Now it's time to go save my lives. Dionisio and Svetlana. Now it's time to save Dusäiga.

Dionisio paces towards me, his hand ready to grab my cheeks. "It's us, Anima, you're not alone in this. I will always make sure you're safe." His lips brush mine. *Always*, he repeats.

No matter what? I ask.

No matter what, he promises.

Our feet start carrying us towards uncertainty. Hand in hand we approach Forestiero. Our fingers gripping tight on each other as to never let go, to make sure we are alive, here, together once again. As we reach the entrance, I glimpse at Eros. He's sitting on a chair, arms crossed, with a smirk on his face, ready to face us.

"Let me walk in first," Dionisio starts.

"There's no way." My hands grip his arm, trying to stop him.

"Anima, don't start now."

I sigh. "Fine, but I'm going to be right behind you."

"Good girl."

Dionisio walks in, and I follow.

Ginevra is sitting on the other side of the shop, tied up on a chair. Her eyes go wide as soon as she sees us. She mumbles something that we can't obviously hear because of the tape on her lips. I try to move towards her, but Dionisio grips my arm and keeps me at his side. He's staring motionless at something. As I turn towards where his eyes are focused, Eros chuckles, cracking his neck left and right.

"The fugitives are back. Hi fake brother. Hello princess. Did you have fun last night? Because that is the last moment you will have together," Eros commences before making Dionisio fall on the floor. The burning sensation on my index finger starts to appear once again. My jaw drops as I realize he's using compulsion on Dionisio.

"What... what did you do to him?" I ask, holding my palm at and keeping him away from Dionisio's body on the floor.

"Princess, I know you figured this out already, so let's get this all out in the open. You are the heir to a throne that I want. We are two sides of the same medal. We share the same blood, I might not have the same level of compulsion you have, but I definitely have enough to keep him on his knees." He chuckles at his own words while he looks down at Dionisio. "You and me. Together, we are more powerful than you can ever imagine. As soon as the transformation is complete and I am back into one soul, you won't be able to stop me. You want Dionisio to live? Rule with me, and I'll spare his life. I'll spare Svetlana's life too. Yes, baby girl, I know she knows. If you try to look for my brother even once, I will do everything in my power to revolt the citizens towards you, and take Dionisio's life." He raises an eyebrow at me, following it with a grin. "I know about the dreams. I know about the bond. I know everything, Anima. It's not the suspirium. That's only a myth. You and him, god, it's truly diabetic. He should have stayed in his place."

"I rule with you, and you let Dionisio and Svetlana live."

"Yes, as simple as that, and you and I will be the most powerful king and queen the hidden world has ever seen. We will become legends."

"I don't care about power," I say. My voice is firm. My hands close into fists.

"You will."

"It was you from the beginning wasn't it? Jeremy. He's part of you. How does it feel to get rejected twice?"

"How does it feel to lose control and let a guy decide what you do about your life?"

"Bastard." I spit, my body completely immobilized.

Eros walks towards me. We're face to face. My nostrils twitch. I turn to look at Dionisio, now back on his feet. He looks like he's paralyzed.

"Touch her, and I will kill you, brother or whatever the fuck you are." Dionisio's words make Eros laugh.

"But I already did touch her, and she liked it."

That's all Eros has to say before Dionisio jumps on him. This was a human fight. No magic. Dionisio wanted to spill his blood using his fists. His anger. Eros continues to laugh as he's being used as a punching bag. What a sadistic asshole.

As the fight gets more intense, I notice Eros looks at me with the same grin as before. He is going to use his magic. My body wants to stop me from jumping in. It has another idea completely. I remain there, breathing heavily. Watching the two getting more crimson out of their systems.

I close my eyes and see the two children with different eyes. Eros, and I. One with long, sandy blond hair, the other with auburn curls gently moved by the wind. One whose skin was amber and one whose rosy cheeks were the only color on otherwise blemish-free, fair skin. And in the distance here it was the boy with green eyes, the same green of moss, forest and nature—who was always ready to come to their rescue. My rescue. Dionisio.

We were running, playing, until the sky turned dark with an unforgiving gloominess.

The beginning of the end.

Before I could say a word, a figure appeared out of thin air only meters away, and slowly walked towards the two of us, petrified from fear. The long dark curly hair was the first thing that Eros and I noticed, then, the smoothness on her face. No eyes. Replacing them, there was a layer of skin. An Opacum.

Her voice was like a siren's chant.

And then, Dionisio ran towards me. A golden aura around him. Glowing.

"I will always protect you, Anima." His words have always been the same.

An unbreakable bond. The connection will snap into place when they will reach maturity, and what was forgotten will flourish once again. The golden energy will be the answer to the equation. The prophecy comes back to mind. An unbreakable bond. The connection that snaps into place. The golden energy around us. We are the answer to the equation. We always have been.

My eyes open up again and as I stare at Dionisio today, the same golden aura appears again.

I remember now, everything. And there's only one thing I can do.

"I, Anima Soleri Psiche, offer myself as a Royal candidate to the Ancient Trials."

Dionisio and Eros stop moving and turn to me with wide eyes.

"You don't know what you're requesting," Eros says, keeping a grip on Dionisio.

"I remember everything."

Anima—

The golden aura, I see it too, on you.

Dionisio's look softens for a quick second as he realizes what I have just said to him. He tries to walk towards me, to get to me, on my side. *The golden energy will be the answer to the equation.*

"Why do you have to make everything so damn difficult?" Eros shouts.

"You can't deny what she requested. It's her right. She is the heir to the throne, not you." Dionisio stops him.

My feet try to move towards the two. I turn to look at Ginevra, her tears coming down as I get stopped by something. Someone. Jeremy is behind me, keeping me in place. My eyes widen with surprise. His low chuckle makes my skin crawl. I try to look down at my arms, but it's impossible. I am completely petrified and the only thing I can hear is my heartbeat picking up speed. I can feel it throbbing in my ears. The spell he did on me turned me into a human statue, making it impossible for me to reach Dionisio.

And then I don't even have the time to predict what Eros is about to do next. A dagger appears out of thin air in his hands. "Let's make this interesting then." He jumps on Dionisio so fast I have no time to realize what is happening.

"No no no no no." I beg, screaming as my eyes stay focused on Eros's moving hand. Tears of sorrow follow the blade piercing Dionisio's body. It goes in too deep and as he looks at me with surprise, I see the blood starting to spill out of his skin, damping his shirt. My mouth drops open but no words come out. Dionisio's hand reaches the handle while he quickly looks down, realizing the dagger is still in. I feel as if my heart is getting ripped out of my body. My hands are numb as his green eyes stare at me with no essence in them.

"Why, Eros, just tell me why?" My voice cracks in despair.

"Power, princess. I am doing it for power." He lets Dionisio's body fall to the ground. "My mother, though." He chuckles. "She's doing it for revenge."

Suddenly I'm alone, no hold on me and I crash to my knees, the heartbreak too consuming to feel any other pain as I hold my soulmate's motionless body in my arms.

…TO BE CONTINUED

Dusäiga

THE CROWN'S SOUL PROPHECY
VOCABULARY

<u>Italian Terms:</u>

Zia: aunt, also used as an affectionate term for a close family friend

Zio: uncle, also used as an affectionate term for a close family friend

Nonna: grandmother

Forestiero: stranger, foreigner. Name of the bookstore and also the owner's lastname.

Tavoletta: Italian version of a charcuterie board. The term literally means small board.

Bar Cobalto: this is the fictional name for the coffee shop where Anima goes often. Bar in Italy is where you go and get coffee. Cobalto is the colour Cobalt.

Via Roma: name of the street where Anima lives. Via means street, road.

Via Aprosio: name of the street where Forestiero is.

Ristorante Corallo: fictional restaurant where Eros and Anima have their first date. Corallo means coral.

Psiche: Anima's real lastname. Psiche means psycho.

Spaghetti alla pescatora: spaghetti with seafood, typical dish served in coastal towns.

Latin Terms:

Clypeo protego te: I protect you with a shield
Loquere: speak
Ignis: Fire
Ventus: Wind
Humus: Soil
Fluvius: River
Suspirium: Whisper
Nemo: no one
Striga: witch
Veneficus: wizard
Veneficum: neutral term for wizard
Opacum: dark, obscure
Virtus medendi: the power of healing
Igneus: burning

Acknowledgments

How do I even begin this? I started thinking about this story a very long time ago. I wrote it and rewrote it so many times I can't even count them anymore. The Throne of Dusäiga duology is my love letter to my home country, to my region, Liguria. It's my love letter to the people that saw me grow up and stayed by my side when the times were good and when they were bad.

Now this is where I am going to be sappy because I obviously have specific people I would like to thank personally.

Mom and Samu, I dedicated this book to you because you are the reason I am the person I am today. Thank you for always being there ready to support me and letting me be my over the clouds self. Mamma, siamo arrivate a Capo Nord.

Mitch, let's be honest here, being around me while I poured myself into this new adventure was truly difficult, but you stayed by my side the entire time and supported me from day one. I could never ask for a better person to spend my days with. Thank you for being my personal version of the perfect book boyfriend.

Chiara, what am I even supposed to say here? You know it all. I truly hope everyone has the fortune to have a friend like you in their lives because I couldn't do it without you. You know exactly how this story sparked into my head and when I told you I was writing it down; you cheered me the entire time and helped me get through all of it. My real life Svet. My soul sister. My family.

Connie and Mell, the friends that when I told them I was attempting to write a book, just replied with a "it just makes sense." Thank you for listening to my rambling, for accepting my baffling mood swings and disappearances from the group chat because I was probably trying to fix something that just didn't want to be fixed.

To my wives: WH Lockwood, LH Blake, Rebecca Quinn and Letizia Lorini. What would I do without you? Probably just complain about not having you in my life. I am so fortunate to have met you through this journey and I am so happy to have you to rely on and talk to when struggles arise, of really any kind. We started as a writing group and now I feel you are my little safe place. Isn't it wild that some of my favourite authors are my friends? It's truly wild.

TJ Knight, you wonderful human being. I could go on and on at how quickly we became an inseparable duo. You're the best critique partner I could ever ask for and your perennial support absolutely means the world. Thank you for being there, ready to laugh and give me advice every single day. EVERY SINGLE DAY. Like I even would get annoyed with myself if I constantly blabbered to myself, not you though, you're always ready to reply and cheer me up when needed. I can't wait for the world to fall in love with your words and stories… and book boyfriends. Can't forget those… *Insert heart shaped eyes emoji here*.

Dionisio thanks you as well *wink wink*, cause he truly is a bit your as well.

To my beta readers, Taylor, Kaila, Jordan and Austin. Thank you doesn't even begin to cover it. Your enthusiasm and important feedback made the story take the shape I really wanted it to take.

Austin, your constant support through it all, made me feel from day one, part of this secret society that it is being an author.

Taylor, you helped me question things that needed to be answered, and made me feel seen, your snaps commenting the story, were what I listened to every night before bed, and I am so happy to have you in my life.

Jordan, your comments made me chuckle, question my choices and filled my days with happiness.

Kaila, in such a small period of time you became part of my everyday life and I can't believe we met through booktok. It feels as if it has been much longer and I am so glad to be able to call you my friend. One of the best really. My cancer twin. Dionisio is a Swifty thanks to you. One day we'll make a squishmellow out of that veneficus. Thank you, thank you, thank you.

And that's it…

Yeah, you truly thought I wouldn't close this sappy thank-you letter without thanking Letizia Lorini properly? Yeah no chance. She would get all pissy pissy at me.

Leti, let's face it, without you and our 8 hours video calls leaving our partners upset at us, our infinite numbers of voice messages, our calls from the car at random times, this book would still be a baffling rough draft. Just an idea. A shell of a story. Literally nothing.

Thank you for being my Letizia. Ah, yes, I just said that… wrote it down even. Your support and friendship is something I hope to cherish for a very long time. Forever I hope. I wouldn't want anyone else to have my same personality, interests, and name. So thank you, my soul twin.

And to conclude in style, thank you, yes you, the reader, the person who got to the end of this super long sappy letter, because let's be honest here, the fact that even just one person picked up my story is truly wild. Thank you, and I'll see you soon in Dusäiga… or should I say back in Dusäiga? I'm gonna go sniff some Lavender in the meantime.

About the Author

Letizia Firmani is the author of the Throne of Dusäiga duology. She has a weird obsession with Draco Malfoy (no seriously… she even has a body pillow with his face on it!) and anything fantasy related. Her current comfort movie is John Wick 2 just because Riccardo Scamarcio speaks English in it. Her first approach to writing was through music and she dreamed of becoming a songwriter for most of her life. Letizia spends most of her days daydreaming about fictional characters, adding hot sauce on everything she eats, and creating your next book boyfriend. She lives between Italy and Canada with her partner and way too many cats.

Want More?

A bonus chapter is on the way, but in the meantime you can keep up to date with Letizia's writing journey by following her on social media pages and website: www.letiziafirmani.com